R. 28/5/19

Prada
and
Prejudice

Available by
Katie Oliver

Dating Mr Darcy
PRADA AND PREJUDICE
LOVE AND LIABILITY
MANSFIELD LARK

Marrying Mr Darcy
AND THE BRIDE WORE PRADA
LOVE, LIES AND LOUBOUTINS
MANOLOS IN MANHATTAN

Prada and Prejudice

Katie Oliver

CARINA™

This edition is published by arrangement with Harlequin Books S.A. CARINA is a trademark of Harlequin Enterprises Limited, used under licence.

Published in Great Britain 2015
by CARINA, an imprint of Harlequin (UK) Limited,
Eton House, 18-24 Paradise Road,
Richmond, Surrey, TW9 1SR

© 2014 Katie Oliver

ISBN 978-0-263-91805-2

98-0915

Harlequin (UK) Limited's policy is to use papers that are natural, renewable and recyclable products and made from wood grown in sustainable forests. The logging and manufacturing processes conform to the legal environmental regulations of the country of origin.

Printed and bound by
CPI Group (UK) Ltd, Croydon, CR0 4YY

Katie Oliver loves romantic comedies, characters who 'meet cute', Richard Curtis films and prosecco (not necessarily in that order). She currently resides in northern Virginia with her husband and three parakeets, in a rambling old house with uneven floors and a dining room that leaks when it rains.

Katie has been writing since she was eight and has a box crammed with (mostly unfinished) novels to prove it. With her sons grown and gone, she decided to get serious and write more (and, hopefully, better) stories. She even finishes most of them.

So if you like a bit of comedy with your romance, please visit Katie's website, www.katieoliver.com, and have a look.

Here's to love and all its complications...

To my husband, Mark, who always knew I'd do it; to my family (you know who you are); to my good friends (and beta readers), Jane, Michael, Karen, Danielle, Margaret, Ian and Leigh; to Helen Williams and Lucy Gilmour at Carina UK/Harlequin for their editing expertise; and to my agent, Nikki Terpilowski…without your unswerving support, this book would never have happened.

CHAPTER 1

Honestly, Natalie Dashwood thought irritably as she folded a stack of knickers on the display table for the third time, if I hear 'The Holly and the Ivy' one more time, I'll put my head in the loo. And hold it there. Until I drown...

Five too many glasses of champagne at her sister Caroline's birthday party last night had left her head throbbing and her outlook decidedly un-festive. And the relentless blare of Christmas carols over the department store's tinny sound system did nothing to improve matters.

If grandfather hadn't been desperate – an outbreak of flu had left Dashwood and James' flagship department store seriously short-staffed – she wouldn't be here, working in the lingerie department a week before Christmas. Natalie hadn't worked in the family store since she was seventeen, nearly six years ago. But she couldn't possibly say no to Sir Richard.

Besides, if she refused, he might cut off her quarterly allowance. And that wouldn't do at all.

Her mobile phone vibrated. With a furtive glance round – mobile phones were strictly forbidden on the sales floor – she took it out and glanced at the screen.

"Grandfather! Good morning. I'm so glad you called. The new 'Poppy' handbag just arrived in Smart Accessories." She was breathless with excitement.

"What in God's name is a 'Poppy' handbag?"

Natalie opened her mouth to explain that Poppy and Penelope Simone were the two hottest 'It' girl sisters in London – correction, in the world – and that Poppy's new handbag was destined to become a classic, but she refrained.

Grandfather would never understand.

"It's a very coveted handbag," she said instead. "I know I shouldn't ask—" guilt stabbed her, but she ignored it "—but might I put it on my store account? Please?"

"How many handbags do you need?" Sir Richard asked reprovingly. "You have dozens already."

"If you let me put it on account," she pleaded, "I promise I'll never ask you for another thing."

They both knew this was utter bollocks, but Sir Richard refrained from comment. "You need to learn economy, Natalie. You know the stores are in serious financial trouble."

Natalie's gaze swept over the store's selling floor. Although the first floor was busy at the moment, she knew it was only because this was the last week before Christmas, and the smell of fake pine and desperation hung heavy in the air. In years past, shoppers thronged the aisles during the holidays. The line for Santa's Grotto wound twice around the third floor and required a special permit from the fire safety inspector.

She sighed. "I know. I'm sorry. That's horribly selfish of me, isn't it? Forget I asked."

"Excuse me."

Natalie looked up to see a man, late twenties, possibly thirty, dark blond-brown hair, standing before her. Under his jacket (Barbour) he wore a cashmere sweater (brand uncertain, but definitely expensive) and jeans; sunglasses hid his eyes.

He looked like a celebrity. But if he was a celebrity, he must be a B-lister, she decided dismissively, because no self-respecting A-lister would shop in Dashwood and James.

She indicated the phone at her ear. "I'll be with you in a moment."

He pressed his lips together but said nothing.

Sir Richard sighed. "Very well, get your handbag. I'll allow it this once. But no more," he warned her. "And you must promise me that you'll come to the board meeting on Monday morning. It's imperative that you attend."

"Oh? Why is that?" Natalie asked, her heart sinking. She usually avoided the board meetings; they were horribly dull, and – to her, at least – a complete waste of time.

"I've hired a new Operations Manager. I'm introducing him at the meeting, and I want you there."

"Excuse me, please. I need assistance." Barbour jacket was growing impatient.

"And I said I'll be with you in a moment," Natalie snapped. She'd forgotten what a pain in the arse customers could be.

She returned her attention to Sir Richard. "Sorry, grandfather. Of course I'll be there."

"Good. We start at nine o'clock, in the fourth floor conference room. Mind you're not late." And he rang off.

Blast. She flung her mobile aside and turned back to her customer – he looked more than a bit irate now, actually – and fixed a polite smile to her lips. "Sorry. How may I help you?"

"Ah, help at last! How very kind. I thought I might have to chew my own arm off or relieve myself on the carpet to get a bit of attention."

"I'm sure that won't be necessary," Natalie said, her words frosty. "Did you wish to buy a gift for someone?"

"That was my intention, but God knows, I don't wish to inconvenience you." He scowled. "I'm looking for something upscale, and suitable for a lady."

"Upscale?" She glanced doubtfully around the department, which hadn't changed since 1982. "I'd go to Agent Provocateur, then. You won't find much that's upscale here."

"But I'm here now, so let me see what you have, please." His mobile vibrated; he thrust a hand in his jacket pocket to retrieve it. "Yes, Tom," he said, an edge to his voice. "Sorry. I'm dealing with a store clerk at the moment."

She glared at him. He plainly equated store clerks with lower life forms... single-celled organisms incapable of thought or, God forbid, intelligence.

She turned away and strode across the carpeted floor to the glass display case where the better lingerie was located. There was no ring on his finger, so the gift must be for a girlfriend. As she bent down to unlock the case and pulled out some lacy, sexy underclothes, she tried (and failed) to ignore the jackhammer pounding of her head.

Back at the counter, she laid out a half-dozen bras and knickers for his inspection. "These are very nice," she informed him. "Notice the lace detailing."

He prodded at a pair of knickers with his free hand and, with a cursory glance, shoved them aside as if they were £1.99 cotton pants. "These won't do. Let me see your nightgowns."

She bent down with a put-upon sigh and withdrew several negligees from beneath the counter. "These ones are lovely—"

"I need those cost overrun estimates ASAP," he said into the phone, and dropped the mobile back into his Barbour. "Haven't you anything that doesn't look as if it came out of a stripper's closet? The lady's tastes are conservative."

"Well in that case," Natalie said with barely concealed irritation, "we have a nice assortment of flannel granny gowns."

He leaned forward, his expression combative. "Show me something else." It wasn't a request. It was a command.

As Natalie glared back, her mobile came to life, vibrating on the counter behind her. "Excuse me." Before he could object, she dove back under the counter to (1) look for the least sexy nightgown she could find and (2) take her call.

The moment she saw Dominic's name on the screen, Nat pressed 'Answer'. "Dom!" she hissed. "Where were you last night?" His side of the bed hadn't been slept in.

"Went back to mine," he said, and yawned. "I had a few pints with the boys, got pissed, passed out."

This, Natalie knew, was probably a lie. Not the 'went back to mine' part, but the 'passed out' part. He'd likely spent the night in bed with his latest slag du jour.

"Don't forget, Alastair's anniversary party is tomorrow night," she reminded him.

"Oh, shit," he groaned. "All right, just be ready when I pick you up." He paused and added ominously, "We need to talk."

She frowned. "Talk? About what?"

"I can't go into it on the phone, can I?" he snapped.

Natalie sighed. When Dom was in One of His Moods, a single cross word from her could easily escalate into a shouting match. She hadn't the energy – or time – to deal with him now.

He might be playing Glastonbury this summer, and he might rock a guitar, but on a day-to-day basis Dominic Heath was a nightmare. His temper was legendary. Last week he'd trashed a curry house in Soho because the vindaloo wasn't spicy enough.

Nor had two years of therapy cured his sex addiction; Natalie recently discovered he was shagging his sex therapist.

Good thing she planned to dump him at Alastair's party tomorrow night.

Her customer leaned over the counter. "What are you doing down there, having a chat with the bras and knickers?"

"I'm on the phone," Natalie retorted. "Do you mind?"

"Actually," he replied, his expression grim, "I do."

She glared up at him and returned to her call. "We'll talk later," she hissed, and rang off.

Natalie rummaged under the counter until she found a negligee and a matching dressing gown of apricot silk. She stood and tossed both on the counter. "I think the Queen herself would approve of these."

He studied the items with a frown. "Very well, ring them up. And hurry. I haven't got all day."

Wordlessly she complied. He paid the entire bill – just over £250 – in cash.

"Oh, and I want them gift-wrapped," he added as Natalie pulled out a carrier bag. "Can you manage that, do you think?"

"Sorry, but I haven't any boxes."

"You do," he retorted. "I see them, there—" he pointed to the shelf behind her "—and I see tissue paper, as well."

"Oh, fancy that! Right you are." Natalie grabbed up a couple of flat boxes and tissue, flung the items inside, and thrust the boxes in the bag. "Here you go. Happy Christmas."

"What about wrapping paper? Bows? Ribbons?"

"You have to go to the gifting counter for that." She glanced at the *Guardian* Mrs. Tuttle had left under the counter. "I could wrap it in yesterday's newspaper, if you like. Is the *Guardian* all right? Or do you prefer the *Telegraph*?"

"We're talking about an overpriced Christmas gift," he said, his jaw set in a tight line, "not yesterday's cod. And I haven't time to wait in another queue. Just give me the damned boxes so I can be on my bloody way."

Natalie held the carrier bag out. "Here you go. Have a lovely day," she gritted out. "Hope to see you again soon!"

"Oh, you will," he promised her grimly. "Count on it."

"I'll look forward to it," she muttered as he departed, carrier bag in hand. "Like the plague. Or my next gyno exam."

Thank God, Natalie consoled herself as she rang up a bra and a pair of Wolford tights for the next customer in the queue, I'll never, ever see him again.

CHAPTER 2

She probably shouldn't have had that third glass of Pinot.

Of course, Natalie reminded herself as she made her way unsteadily through the crowd, she hadn't actually drunk the wine; she'd hurled most of it at Dominic.

Too bad she'd missed.

Natalie paused in the drawing room doorway. Her gaze swept past the clusters of elegantly-dressed people clutching glasses of champagne, intent on finding the door. The exit had to be around here somewhere.

As she lifted her tissue – already soggy – and blew her nose, Natalie scowled.

Bloody Dominic.

This disaster of an evening was entirely his fault. After all, they'd come to Alastair's party together. She'd even bought a new dress for the occasion. But she never imagined Dominic would dump her halfway through the party to announce his engagement… to his ex-wife.

Natalie sniffed. She honestly didn't give a fig if Dom and Keeley got back together again; they deserved each other. No, it was the public humiliation factor that upset her.

She'd seen the furtive glances of surprise and pity cast her way when Dominic announced the engagement, not to mention Keeley's smug little smile as she lifted her hand to show off the ginormous diamond ring glinting on her finger.

Those glances of pity had stung. She didn't want to be the girl everyone felt sorry for, the girl everyone whispered about.

Not ever again.

As everyone lifted their glasses to toast Dominic and Keeley's happiness, Natalie's humiliation curdled into fury. She hadn't meant to fling her glass of Pinot Noir at that well-dressed bloke in the bespoke suit; she'd been aiming for Dom. But two glasses of wine drunk in quick succession had left her light-headed, furious… and her aim a bit off.

Where in *hell* was the door?

Ah, there it was. Lovely door, marvelous door! She'd leave here and… Natalie frowned. Well, with no money for a minicab, and no ride home forthcoming from Dominic, she'd figure that out when she left.

Her hand closed over the doorknob, and she flung it open. Rows of coats hanging on wooden hangers met her gaze. Oops… not the front door, then, but the coat closet. She could've *sworn*…

"Excuse me," a male voice behind her asked in mild concern, "are you all right?"

She whirled around – which, truthfully, didn't help her spinning head – and snapped, "Of course I am. I'm fine." She glared at him, and her heart sank. Those penetrating blue eyes… that expensive bespoke suit…

Crikey. It was the bloke she'd just doused with Pinot Noir.

"Your attempt to exit via the coat closet – not to mention the state of my shirt and tie—" he glanced down at the wine staining his front "—tells me that you're far from all right."

"I told you, I'm sorry about your shirt," she said stiffly. "I'll pay for the dry-cleaning bill."

"That's not necessary. Have you a ride home?"

"No," Natalie said. She narrowed her eyes as she glimpsed Dominic, holding court in the drawing room with his arm draped around his new fiancée's shoulders. "Not any more."

He plucked the empty wine glass from her hand and put it on a passing tray. "Look, I have to leave. I find I need a change of clothes," he added dryly. "I'll give you a lift home if you like."

For the first time, she studied him. He had dark blondish hair and blue eyes, coupled with a rugged build and a lived-in sort of face. Not classically handsome, perhaps, but compelling, in a Daniel Craig-ish sort of way.

Perhaps that's why he seemed vaguely familiar.

"I'd be happy to take you home, Natalie."

Ian Clarkson stood before her. Although married to her best friend Alexa, and darkly handsome, Ian always made her feel a tad uncomfortable. He'd made it clear he was interested in her, the cheating sod. He was definitely a wolf in posh clothing.

"I'm taking her home." Daniel Craig left no room for argument.

"But Natalie doesn't know you," Ian challenged him, "does she?"

Before hostilities could escalate further, Alastair James made his way towards them. "Natalie, darling, there you are! You're not leaving, I hope?"

"I'm afraid so." She kissed his cheek. "Grandfather wants me at the board meeting tomorrow morning, God knows why. Congratulations, by the way! How has Cherie put up with you for so long?"

He laughed. "I've no idea." Still handsome despite the grey that peppered his dark hair, Alastair put his arm around Nat's shoulders. "I'm glad you made it to our anniversary celebration. Ah, Mr. Gordon," he added, and thrust out his free hand. "I see you've met my goddaughter."

"Wait – you two know each other?" Natalie said in surprise.

"Only by reputation," Alastair said, and raised his brow. "And quite a formidable reputation it is, too."

"Oh. Well, he's offered to take me home." Natalie regarded Alastair quizzically. "Should I accept?"

His eyes met Gordon's. "I'm sure I can trust you to see Sir Richard's granddaughter safely home, Mr. Gordon?"

"Of course," he replied, and extended his hand to Alastair. "I'm a man of my word, if nothing else. Unlike some."

The smile he directed at Alastair, Natalie noticed, was chilly. Odd, that… but no one else seemed to pay any mind.

"Congratulations, by the way," Gordon added. "I apologise, but the state of my clothing prevents me from staying."

Alastair frowned. "Yes, Natalie, what happened? I'd no idea you and Dominic had parted ways."

"It was a… mutual decision." She refused to cry over spilt wine; Dominic *so* wasn't worth it. "I planned to break up with him after the party, but he dumped me first. I've apologised to Mr. Gordon for ruining his suit."

"No harm done. Are you ready?" Gordon asked her.

She nodded. "Yes, let me just get my coat."

He put a hand on her back and guided her out through the crush of people. As he stopped to collect their coats, Natalie glimpsed Dominic halfway across the reception room, and he glanced over at them with narrowed eyes. She resisted the urge to flip him the bird.

After all, one of them needed to be an adult. It might as well be her.

Outside, Mr. Gordon gave the valet his keys and helped Natalie on with her coat. "How are you feeling?"

"A bit dizzy," she admitted.

Five minutes later, the valet roared up on a gleaming Triumph Thunderbird motorcycle and brought it to a stop before them. Natalie's eyes widened. "Is that yours? You can't expect me to ride on the back of that... in this!" She looked down at her short coat, shorter dress, and six-inch heels.

"I'm afraid you've no choice, if you want a ride home." He produced two helmets from the saddlebag and handed her one.

Natalie eyed the gleaming silver-and-black motorbike doubtfully. "I'm really not dressed for it—"

He gave her legs and her strappy shoes a critical once-over. "If you weren't wearing those bloody stripper heels—"

"They're not stripper heels!" she protested. "They're Louboutins, and very expensive."

"Well, you and your very expensive shoes will have to sit sideways. Put on the helmet. And button up, it's cold." He swung one leg over the motorcycle and waited.

"Bloody hell but you're bossy." Natalie did up her buttons and sat sideways behind him, shivering in the unseasonably cold night air, and wrapped her arms around his waist. "I won't fall off, will I?" she called out anxiously over the growl of the engine.

"Not if you hold tight. Where do you live?"

"Ladbroke Grove." She gave him the address and rested her helmeted cheek against his back in mingled trepidation and anticipation. Her head spun, but in a good way. *Sod Dominic, and Keeley, and her ginormous engagement ring*, she decided. She was ready to have some fun.

He revved the engine, and with a satisfying, throaty roar, they were off. Natalie tightened her hold on him as they turned off Holland Park Avenue onto the A40. It was already unseasonably cold, but with the wind in her face, it felt about three degrees.

As they roared through Notting Hill, Natalie nestled closer, glad of his warm, broad back. He smelt of soap and leather, and also, rather strongly, of Pinot. Strange, she thought as he skillfully wove in and out of the evening traffic and onto her street, since Dominic had dumped her, she ought to feel gutted. But she was having too much fun to care.

The Triumph growled to a stop in front of her building. Natalie slid from the seat, stood up unsteadily, and removed her helmet. "My hair must look a sight."

He took her helmet and removed his as well, then hung them both on the handlebars. "A bit. But it suits you."

"Thanks." She looked up at him with wide grey eyes and murmured, "You know, actually, you're quite sexy."

"And you're quite drunk." He held out his hand. "Come on, let's get you inside. It's cold out here."

"No, wait." Natalie pressed herself against him and slid her arms up around his neck. She giggled as she stumbled and his arms came around to steady her. "I've never said this to anyone before," she breathed as her eyes locked with his, "but I really, really want to have sex with you."

He removed her arms gently but firmly from around his neck. "No, you don't. You don't even know me."

"That's the whole point, isn't it? To…" she hiccupped "… get to know you."

"Miss Dashwood—"

"Why don't you want to have sex, then?" she demanded.

"Because you're drunk," he said again, his words patient but firm. "And because you're mad at that boyfriend of yours—"

"—ex-boyfriend," she interrupted.

"—and I won't be your revenge sex."

Natalie sniffed. "He's been engaged to Keeley for two weeks! I still can't believe it." A tear trickled down her cheek. "It's not that I *care*, mind you. It's just that I – I couldn't bear the way everyone at the party was looking at me, as if they felt *sorry* for me."

"I think it was curiosity, that's all," he said. "They wondered how you'd react." He lifted his brow upwards. "Is Pinot Noir your usual weapon of choice?"

"No. Prosecco." She giggled and wound her arms round his neck again. He smelled of some deliciously expensive aftershave and, very faintly, of Pinot. "Come upstairs," she murmured. "I haven't a flat mate. And I don't—" she hiccupped again "—I don't want to be alone tonight."

He swore under his breath. Her fingers were caressing his hair, and it was getting harder, in more ways than one, to refuse.

"You're a lovely girl, Miss Dashwood, and your offer's very tempting; but I have to decline."

"Decline? But... why?" she asked, bewildered. "Don't you want to have sex with me? Doesn't *anyone* want to have sex with me?" she wailed.

He met Natalie's wide grey eyes. "Believe me, I'd like nothing better," he murmured. "But," he added firmly as he untangled her arms once again from his neck, "that's the last thing you need tonight. Trust me."

"Never trust a man who says 'trust me'," she mumbled. "Grandfather taught me that."

"Your grandfather's a very wise man. Come on, inside with you. Let's go."

"Won't you at least kiss me goodnight?" she asked forlornly, her words softly slurred.

"No." He put his hands on her arms. "You need a good night's sleep. You'll thank me in the morning. Now come along, put your arm around my waist, there's a good girl."

And with that, he helped her up the stairs to her flat – really, Natalie thought, the bloody stairs had a mind of their own tonight – unlocked her door, bade her a polite good night, and turned to leave.

Suddenly her sister's dog shot out the door, a tiny white ball of lightning intent on escape, and made for the stairway.

"Nigella!" she cried, and lurched after her. "My sister Caro's dog," she explained breathlessly. "I'm dog-sitting."

"Got her," Gordon said, and bent down to grab the teacup-sized ball of fluff as she darted past. She sank her tiny teeth into the fleshy bit between his thumb and forefinger. "Shit!" He dropped her, and she promptly took a wee on his shoe.

Nat gasped, horrified, and picked her up. "Nigella!"

"Have you a towel?" he asked evenly as he eyed his dripping shoe.

"Of course." She led him inside the flat and returned a moment later with a rumpled, coffee-stained tea towel.

He wiped his shoe and returned the towel. "Thanks. Now I really must go, before you – or your sister's dog – destroy another article of my clothing."

"I'm terribly sorry," she said again, her eyes luminous and wide as she met his gaze, "I really am—"

"Forget it." He turned away, his expression unreadable. "It's been… memorable, Miss Dashwood. Goodnight."

Dazed, Natalie blinked at the empty doorway. Crikey, but she felt awful. First his shirt, then his shoe... yet he'd been quite decent about it all. She brightened. She'd ask grandfather to send a cheque to cover the damages. Except... she didn't know Mr. Gordon's proper name, much less his address.

"Wait!" she cried again, and dashed into the hall to run after him. She paused unsteadily at the top of the stairs. "Mr. Gordon – wait! I don't even know your first name!"

But the roar of his motorbike engine, fading rapidly away into the night, told her that he was already gone.

CHAPTER 3

The blare of the alarm clock woke Natalie from a deep sleep on Monday morning. She opened her eyes – ugh, felt like they were glued shut – and rolled over to turn off the alarm. It was 8:15 a.m.

Bloody hell.

The Dashwood and James board meeting grandfather wanted her to attend started at nine. She had less than forty-five minutes to shower, dress, and make her way to Knightsbridge from Ladbroke Grove in London rush-hour traffic.

Bloody, *bloody* hell…

She picked up her phone and called a minicab. In twenty minutes flat she showered, dressed, flung some dog kibble into a dish for Nigella, and thrust her feet in a pair of Prada pumps.

"Where to, love?" the driver asked as she rushed down the steps of the mansion flat and flung the door open. Despite his best efforts, they didn't reach Sloane Street until nearly an hour later.

"Thanks." Natalie flung a twenty-pound note at him, slammed the door, and ran up the steps into Dashwood and James' flagship store. She glanced at her wristwatch. Between traffic and roadwork delays, she was twenty-seven minutes late.

"Good morning, Miss Natalie," Henry the lift operator greeted her as he slid back the private car's door. "Fourth floor?"

"Yes, thanks, Henry. Is everyone here for the meeting?"

"Oh, yes, everyone, including the new chap. The one," Henry added darkly, "what's supposed to save D&J's bacon."

"What's he like?" Natalie asked him curiously.

He drew his bushy silver brows together. "He didn't say much. Kept himself to himself, if you know what I mean."

On the fourth floor, which was given over to offices and conference rooms, Henry slid back the elaborate turn-of-the-century lift door for her and touched the tip of his cap. "Here we are, Miss Natalie. Best of luck to you."

"Thanks, Henry. I've a feeling I'll need it."

As she approached the closed conference room door and eased it open, Natalie was desperate for an aspirin. Her head was pounding. But she hadn't anything but a petrified cough drop.

"Sorry I'm late," she apologised as the door swung open. "I didn't hear the alarm—"

When she caught sight of the man standing at the head of the conference table, Natalie's voice trailed away. Her eyes widened in mingled dismay and horror.

Oh, blimey, no. It couldn't be.

He had darkish blond hair and blue eyes. He wore a Thomas Pink shirt, obviously a different one today, because this one was striped, without a wine stain. And he most definitely didn't reek of second-hand Pinot Noir or dog wee.

Natalie cringed inwardly. To think that only last night she'd twined her arms around his neck, pressed herself shamelessly against him, and begged him to have sex with her.

"Natalie," Sir Richard said, "allow me to introduce our new Operations Manager, Rhys Gordon."

Mortification swept over her as their eyes met. Rhys Gordon rescued companies from the brink of financial ruin and turned them back into the black. He was famously good at what he did. Photos and articles about him appeared regularly in the business pages of newspapers and magazines, and occasionally in the tabloids as well.

Natalie bit back a groan. She'd thrown herself at Mr. Gordon, grandfather's newly hired Operations Manager, like a cheap slapper.

Just let me die now...

Gordon's expression gave nothing away. "You're late." He levelled a dark blue gaze on her. "The meeting started half an hour ago."

"Sorry." She wasn't, not really. She hated meetings and hated apologising, but needs must. Natalie glanced at him, noting distractedly that his eyes were a deep and penetrating blue, and shrugged. "I overslept. I had a—" she flushed "—a bit of a late night last night."

The men at the conference table – Ian Clarkson, Alexa's husband, actually *winked* at her, the cheeky bastard pushed back their chairs and rose as Natalie rounded the table and kissed her grandfather, Sir Richard Dashwood, on his papery cheek.

"Next time, Miss Dashwood," Rhys said sharply, "you'll get here on time. Or you can bloody well stay home."

Natalie bristled. So, the media stories about Mr. Gordon were true. He had a reputation for being abrasive, arrogant, and impatient... and those were his good qualities. Nor did his expertise come cheap. But he was said to be worth every penny.

If you didn't stab him with the nearest letter-opener first, she reflected grimly.

"My granddaughter usually gives these board meetings a wide berth, Mr. Gordon," Sir Richard informed him. He gave Natalie a look of mild reproof. "You're lucky she showed up at all."

"It's no matter to me if she shows up or not," Rhys responded. His gaze locked with Natalie's. "But if she cares anything about saving the family business, I'd suggest she take a more active interest going forward."

"This store is my birthright, Mr. Gordon," she retorted. "It's been in the Dashwood family for 150 years. Whilst you," she added tartly, "are merely an employee."

His eyes narrowed, but he turned away and said, "We've a lot of ground to cover, gentlemen. Sit down, Miss Dashwood, so we can get back to the matter at hand."

Alastair James gestured Natalie into a seat. "Rhys was just about to discuss his findings as a mystery shopper."

"Mystery shopper?" Natalie echoed. With a sense of impending doom, she sank down next to Alastair. "Do you mean to say Mr. Gordon pretended to be a store customer?"

"That's exactly what he means." Rhys looked at her the way the devil must eye a new arrival to Hell. "I've visited all of the store's departments recently to assess our customer relations. You're just in time for my report."

Her heart sank into her Prada pumps. She remembered she'd been particularly rude to that bloke in the Barbour jacket on Saturday. She only hoped he hadn't lodged a complaint. But even if he had, perhaps – she cast a sidewise glance at Rhys Gordon – perhaps the new Operations Manager wouldn't mention it.

"First," Gordon began, "I want to address the issues I encountered in the lingerie department. My treatment was abysmal," he said as his hard blue gaze met Natalie's, "in every respect."

"*Your* treatment?" she squeaked. She sat up straighter as she realised with dawning horror that *he* was the customer she'd waited on. She hadn't recognised him, dressed in his Barbour jacket and jeans. No wonder he'd worn those sunglasses! Her eyes widened and her lips parted, but no sound emerged.

"Not only was my sales clerk rude and unhelpful," he went on, "she encouraged me to shop elsewhere; carried on a personal conversation on her mobile, which, by the way, is forbidden on the sales floor, refused to wrap my purchase, and—" he paused for the maximum effect "—when I left, told me she looked forward to my next visit, like the plague… or her next gyno exam."

Several gasps went round the table, the loudest one being Natalie's own.

"Who was this cheeky little madam?" Sir Richard demanded, outraged. "I shall have her sacked at once!"

"Oh, you don't want to sack anyone, grandfather," Natalie said hastily, before Rhys could respond. "It's the holidays, after all! You know, good will to men. And women. And perhaps," she added as she glared at the new OM, "the sales clerk was having a bad day. She might even have been a bit hung over."

"If customers in this store are treated the way I was, Miss Dashwood," Gordon retorted, "then it's no wonder that Dashwood and James is losing its arse. And if nothing is done to remedy the situation, it bloody well *deserves* to lose its arse."

CHAPTER 4

Sir Richard slapped his age-spotted hand on the conference table and leaned forward to glare at Rhys, seated at the opposite end of the table.

"We're all agreed that something must be done," Sir Richard snapped. "But what, precisely? Can you tell us that?"

Rhys eyed him. "Not to put too fine a point on it, Sir Richard, but financially, your stores are in the crapper. Unless you take cost-cutting measures at once, doors will have to close. Jobs will be lost. Is that what you want?"

"Certainly not," Alastair interjected. "That's why we hired you."

Sir Richard's scowl deepened as he flipped through the pages of Rhys's business plan. "You want to get rid of the children's wear department."

"Sell children's clothing online," Rhys said. "You'll save on operating costs and better utilise your floor space."

The assorted executives and board members ranged around the table gave cautious nods; a few of them shifted uneasily in their seats. Sir Richard was notoriously resistant to change. Would he listen to reason from the new OM?

Not bloody likely.

"We've got to increase the advertising budget," Rhys went on. "Dashwood and James need more visibility on television and radio, and in the print media as well."

"Bah!" Sir Richard snorted. "Waste of money."

"At the very least," Rhys continued as if he hadn't spoken, "you'll need to refurbish the flagship store and increase publicity… or you'll never climb out of the red."

"And where is all this money to come from?" Sir Richard demanded.

"From better use of the money you have." Rhys threw his pen down. "Make maximum use of your retail floor space, offer a wider range of merchandise, make the departments more inviting, and dwell time will increase."

Natalie frowned. "'Dwell time?'" she echoed.

"The time a customer spends on the selling floor. Currently, it's barely twenty minutes. That's abysmal."

Sir Richard gave a derisive snort. "What is it you want us to do, Mr. Gordon? Cut, or spend?"

"Both." Rhys stood and swept a challenging glance around the table. "The flagship store needs an update." Cautious nods all around. "To do so won't come cheap. We'll cut expenses elsewhere—" he lifted a folder filled with a thick sheaf of papers "—for example, shut down that antiquated lift—"

"What? You can't do that!" Natalie gasped, horrified. "Henry's operated that lift for fifty years!"

"Indeed?" Rhys said, and raised his brow. "Then that's twenty years too long, Miss Dashwood. The man is nearing eighty. He should be retired."

"And you plan to decide that *for* him, do you?" she shot back.

"There's a perfectly good, modern lift in the middle of the store." His words were steely. "Using the original is expensive, probably unsafe – and pointless, as well."

At the thought of Henry – so proud of his uniform and cap – being made redundant, Natalie stood up. "I won't allow it!"

"Sit down, Miss Dashwood," Rhys snapped. "We'll discuss this offline, after the meeting."

She glared at him. "You can be sure we will, Mr. Gordon." She sat back down, quivering with outrage.

He returned his attention to the men ranged around the table. "Now, gentlemen, as to the store's return policy—"

"What's wrong with the return policy?" Sir Richard barked. "It's worked perfectly well for all these years."

"It's too generous," Rhys retorted. He threw the folder down before him like a gauntlet. "Any return is accepted, no matter how long since its purchase, even without a receipt. That's madness. The company's haemorrhaging money it can't afford to lose."

"Nonsense—"

"I recommend that after thirty days' time, or if the customer has no receipt, we no longer accept returns or exchanges."

A hush fell over the conference table. Only the muted sounds of London traffic four storeys below broke the silence. Implementing a change of this magnitude to the generous and longstanding Dashwood and James return policy was blasphemy.

Sir Richard leaned forward, his face flushed. "What's to make our stores stand out if we do away with our return policy?"

"Quality," Rhys responded. "Excellent customer service, and good value for money." His gaze swept the table. "The fact is, Dashwood and James have become irrelevant. We can't hope to compete with Selfridges or Marks and Spencer unless we update the store and, more importantly, update its image. If you aren't willing to do that, gentlemen—" he reached out to take up his folder, his face set "—then I'll leave you to it."

Silence greeted his words.

"Gordon's right." Alastair eyed the men ranged round the table. "We can't move forward if we cling to the past. Sir Richard, if you're in accord, I suggest we take a vote on the matter."

Ten minutes later, it was settled.

"The 'ayes' have it," Alastair announced. "George, please note that there was one 'nay'."

Everyone looked at Natalie. She pressed her lips together and tilted her chin up in defiance.

"Thank you, gentlemen," Gordon said. "You've made the right decision."

Natalie snorted.

"Have you anything to add, Miss Dashwood?" Rhys crossed his arms against his chest and met her eyes. "The floor is yours."

She glared, but shook her head. What was the point?

He turned back to the other board members. "We've a lot of work ahead. I'll want your input. I need viable suggestions for improvement when we re-convene tomorrow morning."

The men rose. One by one they filed out and murmured their goodbyes to Natalie. She smiled, despite the renewed throbbing in her head, and waited until no one was left.

No one, that was, except Rhys Gordon.

Fury swept over her anew, and she stood up and launched into him. "Henry will be devastated if he loses his job, Mr. Gordon. Everyone adores him. He's a fixture here at Dashwood and James, and so is that bloody lift!"

"I see. Are you quite finished?" he asked evenly.

Natalie blinked. "Well… yes, I suppose I am." She frowned. "Is that all you have to say?"

"No." He tossed the folder he held onto the table. "Henry often takes customers to the wrong floor; he can barely see. We've had complaints, and they'll only increase if something isn't done. If he retires, he'll receive a generous pension. If he stays, we'll find him a job in the office. I'll let Henry decide." He folded his arms against his chest. "Does that meet with your approval, madam?"

"I suppose," she said, grudgingly. Her eyes narrowed. "You knew who I was when you bought that nightgown from me on Saturday, didn't you? And you knew last night."

He didn't look up as he began thrusting papers into another folder. "Yes, on both counts." He glanced up. "I saw the wine in your hand and the murderous look in your eye when Dominic made his announcement. So I did the only thing I could, and put myself in front of you."

"You stepped in front of Dominic on *purpose*? Why, in sod's name? I ruined your suit!"

"Because, my dear, clueless girl, there was a photographer from the *Mirror* behind you, and one from *Hello!* on the side, waiting to snap publicity shots of Dominic and Keeley. How would it have looked if you'd doused them both with Pinot?"

Natalie flushed. "Not good," she said in a small voice.

"I don't want Dashwood and James immersed in a lawsuit. Bad press is the last thing we need right now."

Natalie sank into one of the high-backed chairs. Her head pounded like the drums at Salamanca. "I don't know why I didn't recognise you at the party," she murmured. "I should've done."

"You might have, if you weren't so trolleyed... or if you ever read the business section of a newspaper."

Natalie bit her lip. "Do you suppose we could just... forget about last night?"

"If that's what you want." He gathered up his things, his face unreadable.

Natalie studied him through her lashes. The tabloids said he was a womaniser who could turn on the charm whenever he chose. Not that she'd seen any evidence of *that* so far...

"Tell me – are things at Dashwood and James really so bad?"

"Honestly? They're worse. There's a long, uphill climb ahead if we have any hope of re-establishing profitability."

Her eyes widened. "That sounds serious, indeed."

"It is. Sir Richard wouldn't have brought me on, otherwise."

"Do you really think," she asked, scepticism plain on her face, "that you can drag Dashwood and James, kicking and screaming, into the 21st century?"

As his gaze met Natalie's, Rhys couldn't help but notice her wide grey eyes, liberally fringed with thick dark lashes.

"I do. And I will." He forced his attention back on the remaining papers scattered on the table before him. "It won't happen overnight, of course, and it won't be easy. But it *can* be done."

"And you're just the man to do it, are you?"

"I am." He regarded her with one brow lifted. "Whether you believe that or not is strictly up to you."

"I don't believe things are as bad as you say."

"Profits are down by sixty-one per cent, Miss Dashwood. I can show you the figures. And as I stated in the meeting, the average dwell time in the stores is less than twenty minutes."

"How much should it be?" she asked, curious.

Rhys slid a folder into his briefcase. "Ideally, forty-five minutes to an hour. That's why Sir Richard needs me."

"Quite sure of yourself, are you?" The challenge in her gaze was unmistakable.

"I know what needs to be done." Rhys snapped his briefcase shut. "And I'll do it… with the board's approval, of course."

There was a knock on the conference room door, and Gemma, Rhys's newly assigned personal assistant, strode in. "Mr. Gordon, I have the tabloids you wanted." She flicked a glance at Natalie. "Miss Dashwood."

"Gemma." Wearing a black sheath dress, her dark auburn hair pulled back in a sleek ponytail, Gemma Astley was attractive, well-groomed, and terrifyingly efficient.

As Gemma handed Rhys a neatly fanned-out assortment of tabloids, Natalie felt a sudden flicker of unease. She remembered the white glare of flashbulbs last night when Dominic had announced his engagement to Keeley.

Her unease increased. Surely they hadn't got any photos of *her* last night? As Gemma left, Natalie came around the table beside Rhys and peered over his shoulder…

…and wished for the second time that day that she could die. Or disappear into the floor – whichever came first.

She and Rhys were splashed on the front pages of the red-tops – the *Daily Mirror,* the *Sun*, and the *Star* among them. Natalie's photographs, thank God, looked OK. No melting mascara, no wildly smeared lipstick.

The headlines, however, were another story.

She let out a sharp breath as Rhys flicked through the *Sun*. 'Rhys Gordon's Latest Takeover' read one headline, above a photo of Rhys with his face close to hers. Another image, this one featuring Natalie tossing her wine at Rhys's shirt, was captioned, 'Ex Marks the Spot!'

But worst was the photo of Rhys, his hand resting low on Natalie's back as they left the party, headlined, 'Gordon and Dashwood – Spreadsheets, or Bed Sheets?'

Natalie squealed in outrage, then grabbed the *Daily Mail* from Rhys and began to read aloud. "Rhys Gordon, hired to rescue the troubled Dashwood and James department stores, attended a Holland Park soirée Friday evening, along with Sir Richard Dashwood's granddaughter, Natalie.

"Dominic Heath, Ms. Dashwood's pop star ex-boyfriend, announced his engagement to Keeley, ex-wife and former lead singer for The Tarts. Unfortunately, 'Ex' did not mark the spot for Natalie…

"Gordon stepped between the pair and got a chest full of Pinot Noir for his trouble. Sorry, Ms. Dashwood, but Gordon prefers his wine, like his women, of a more mature vintage…"

She flung the paper down. "This is a bloody nightmare! Everyone'll think we're having an affair!"

Rhys shrugged, unperturbed. "The publicity will generate interest, not just in us, but in Dashwood and James. And that's what we want."

"It's not what *I* want! And there *is* no us! This is awful!"

"Lesson number one," Rhys said. "There's good publicity, and bad. You want to get as much of the first as you can and as little of the second as possible."

"But I don't want Dominic – and all of London – thinking we're an item!"

"Why? Are you worried that Dominic will believe it's true? He dumped you, if you recall, in a very public way."

She glared at him. "Thanks for reminding me. And no, I don't care what Dom thinks. It's just... I hope grandfather doesn't see this. He'll think that I... that we..." her words trailed off.

"Your grandfather may be old, but he's shrewd, Miss Dashwood. He'll see this for what it is – media speculation, nothing more." Rhys smiled slightly. "Don't forget lesson number one – good publicity is always preferable to bad."

She resisted the urge to clutch at her hammering head. "And what's lesson number two?"

He eyed her pale face. "That the best cure for a hangover is a good fry-up. Unless I miss my guess, you're hung over."

"I don't have a drink problem, if that's what you're thinking," she said, defensively.

"I think you've had a lousy couple of days." He took her arm. "It's nearly noon, so you'll have to make do with lunch instead. Come on. You and I have a lot to talk about."

CHAPTER 5

Rhys took Natalie to an Italian restaurant around the corner. "Two house salads and two orders of lasagna," Rhys told the waiter when they were seated. He glanced at Natalie enquiringly. "What will you have to drink?"

"Do I have a choice?" she asked, irritated. "Why don't you order that for me, as well?"

"Sorry, it's a bad habit of mine." He leaned forward, completely unrepentant, and added, "The lasagna's very good, but get whatever you like."

"I'll have the lasagna," she told the waiter, ignoring Rhys's smirk as she handed back her menu, "and water with lemon, please."

"Tell me about yourself," he prompted, and fixed that intense blue gaze on her. "Where did you go to school, what sort of jobs have you had?"

She raised her hand to stop the flow of questions. "Blimey! Is this an interview? I thought you wanted to talk about the store."

"I do. But I want to understand why you're not more involved. Sir Richard tells me you have a dual degree in business and marketing. Why not use it?"

Natalie shrugged. "The store was always grandfather's thing. I worked there when I was a teenager, on holidays and during the summer."

"What did you do?"

"What didn't I do? I worked the perfume counter, and ladies' shoes. I manned the till, or answered phones and filed paperwork when grandfather's secretary was out, and I unpacked and shelved merchandise in the stockroom."

"Did you plan any events for Dashwood and James?"

She shook her head. "Grandfather says store events are costly, and a waste of time."

"He's wrong. Dashwood and James are in dire need of some public relations magic right now."

The waiter brought their salads, heaped with shaved Parmesan and fragrant with basil and oregano. Rhys speared a forkful of greens. "What are you doing now? When you're not attending soirées in Holland Park, that is."

"Oh, the usual," she replied airily. "Christening ships, cutting ribbons – just another day in the exciting life of a department store heiress." She unfolded her napkin and laid it across her lap.

He smiled slightly. "Fair enough, I suppose I deserved that."

"You did." She took a bite of salad. "I took a gap year after uni to travel. I do some charity work, and I help mum with the odd church boot sale…" Her voice trailed away. "But I don't… work… at the moment." As she said the words aloud, Natalie felt, suddenly, a bit ashamed. Defensively she added, "I'm not really the nine-to-five type."

The truth was, she didn't do anything useful, or clever. She couldn't knit, or do decoupage, or balance spreadsheets, or play the guitar. Ever since she'd met Dominic, she'd drifted along in his wake. Her gap year had stretched into two. And now, she began to realise what a waste most of it had been.

But she'd never, ever admit as much to Rhys.

"I see. So how do you fill your time?" he inquired.

"Well... I weekend with friends in the country, and I go on tour with Dominic – not now, obviously – and I shop—"

"Ah, yes." He leaned back in his seat and eyed her, his gaze inscrutable. "Judging from the bills pouring in from every boutique and department store in London, shopping is an art form you've mastered admirably well."

"What's that supposed to mean?" Natalie demanded.

"It means your spending is out of control. It'll have to stop. And as for Dominic—"He paused. "It's a good job that he dumped you. He's destructive and irresponsible."

"He's an artist," she said in his defense. "He's temperamental—"

"Temperamental?" Rhys echoed, incredulous. "He's a bloody nightmare! And he treats you like crap, yet you defend him."

"Dominic can be incredibly sweet."

"So can ethylene glycol," Rhys retorted, "but it'll kill you, just the same." He paused as the waiter delivered their entrees. He lifted a forkful of lasagna to her lips. "Here, try this."

Startled, she tasted it. "Oh," she admitted, and wiped a bit of sauce from her mouth, "that's really good."

"You won't find better anywhere in London. As to Dominic," he added, "I suggest you avoid him. And watch your behaviour when you're in public."

She bristled. "My behaviour? Why, for heaven's sake? I'm not a member of the Royal Family!"

"No." He leaned forward. "But you're in the public eye. You never know when a photographer might be around, or someone with a camera phone. You need to behave with the utmost decorum, especially now. After all, stories about our alleged affair are already all over the tabloids."

"Crikey," Natalie exclaimed as she flung down her napkin, "that's hardly *my* fault, is it? Am I doing anything *right*? You've done nothing but criticise me! My behaviour, my spending habits, my relationships—"

"You're a smart girl who's been sheltered from your family's financial problems – and life in general – for far too long. That's probably not your fault."

"Well, thank you for *that*—" she sputtered.

"—but it's time you learned what we're dealing with. Things can't go on as they have." He studied her. "I'm here to help your family, Natalie. I'm not the enemy."

"Yes, you were brought on to help Dashwood and James," Natalie agreed, stung by his criticism, "so I suggest you stick to your hire agreement, and do your job. But my behaviour – and my relationship with Dom – is none of your bloody business!"

Rhys threw down his own napkin. "I don't give a shit about your relationship with that guitar-smashing fuckwit," he snapped. "It's your life; throw it away however – and with whomever – you wish. But I'd appreciate it if you'd refrain from making yourself the next four-colour photo op in the *Daily Mail*... for the store's sake, if not your own."

She blinked, outraged. "How dare you! You have no right—"

"I haven't time to waste discussing your messy personal life, Miss Dashwood. I've better things to do, like trying to keep your grandfather's stores solvent. Because the truth is," he added coldly, "some of us actually *do* have to work for a living."

Natalie blinked, too astonished to speak. The diners nearest to them had gone quiet; even the clink of silverware had ceased. Mortification washed over her as she realised they'd heard every outrageous word Rhys said to her.

"You can run grandfather's company however you like, Mr. Gordon," Natalie said, her voice unsteady as she pushed her chair back. "But you won't run me. I'm not one of your projects, and I don't need advice on how to conduct *my* messy life – particularly not from a rude, arrogant prat like you. So you can just – fuck right off!" She let out a single, hiccupping sob and fled.

CHAPTER 6

As she emerged on the street, fury catapulted her forward. She scrabbled in her handbag for her sunglasses and thrust them on. Her head was pounding and her thoughts were in turmoil.

She pondered various ways to kill Rhys Gordon. Which would be more satisfying – a slow, torturous death, or something quick and violent? Tough call, that…

"Natalie!" someone shouted behind her. "Is it true you're having an affair with Rhys Gordon?"

Suddenly she was surrounded by paparazzi, jostling one another as they thrust microphones and cameras in her face. "How long have you two been seeing each other?"

"Will Rhys turn the company round, or is Dashwood and James past redemption?"

"Tell us, Natalie – is Gordon as hard-driving in bed as he is in the boardroom?"

"No comment," she managed, flustered. She began to tremble. Thank God she had sunglasses on; if they saw her tears, they'd probably say she'd had a lovers' spat with Rhys!

"What does Dominic Heath think of your new boyfriend?"

"Rhys Gordon is *not* my new boyfriend!" Natalie sputtered. "He's not my boyfriend at all!"

Suddenly Rhys appeared, thrusting his way through the crowd of reporters, and took possession of her arm.

"Is it true, Rhys?" a female reporter for the *Mirror* called out. "Are you and Natalie an item, or not?"

"What does Miss Dashwood say?" he countered, unperturbed.

"She says you're not."

He glanced at Natalie, his expression unreadable. "Then we're not." He turned back to the reporters. "Now bugger off, the lot of you."

Shaken, she let Rhys draw her away. "Thanks," she murmured, and cast a hunted look over her shoulder as the media hounds dispersed to return to their cars and news vans to sniff out a story elsewhere. "They came out of nowhere. Even after two years with Dom, I still hate it."

Reporters had often waited outside Dom's townhouse in Primrose Hill, hoping for a quote or a photograph. It was a nuisance; but it went with the territory when you dated a pop star.

No, far worse was the débâcle with her father when she was a child. Journalists had loitered at the gates to her family's Warwickshire home for days, bristling with microphones and cameras, and shouted rapid-fire questions at the car as mum drove past, questions ten-year-old Natalie hadn't understood.

But at least mum had shielded her and her sister Caro from the worst of it…

Natalie realised that Mr. Gordon had spoken. She looked up at him with a guilty start. "I'm sorry, what?"

He raised a brow. "You were a million miles away. Are you all right?"

She nodded. "A bit shaken, that's all. I'm fine."

"You never really get used to it," he observed, and walked beside her as they headed back to Sloane Street. "The media, that is. You learn to handle them," Rhys said, "and you learn to be firm. That's the only thing they understand."

She gave him a sidewise glance. "Spoken like someone who's been there."

"I have, more than once." A shadow passed over his face, gone as quickly as it came. "I'm sorry if I was a bit hard on you in the restaurant."

"It's all right." She added, "It won't be easy to turn Dashwood and James around, you know."

"Believe me, I know." His words were grim. "The store's finances are a bloody mess, and I've a lot of work ahead to get things sorted. But I shouldn't take my frustration out on you. I apologise."

"Sorry I told you to fuck off."

Rhys smiled briefly. "Forget it. If you've time when we get back, Miss Dashwood, I'll show you a couple of spreadsheets to demonstrate how bad things really are."

Natalie groaned. "I despise spreadsheets, truly. But I suppose I could fit it in. I haven't any ships to christen at the moment."

As they rounded the corner onto Sloane Street, Natalie was conscious of his hand at her back. She realised that her headache was gone.

"Shit." Rhys slowed his pace. Several reporters waited outside the store. "Normally I'd deal with them, but I haven't time today. Come on, we'll slip in the back entrance."

But they'd been spotted. With a couple of shouts, the journos abandoned the front steps and pelted after them.

Natalie, her hand gripped tightly in Rhys's, ran with him around the corner and gasped, "This is crazy!"

As they ducked into the store's service lift, Rhys glanced back at her. "You're not upset?"

"Why would I be upset?"

"Well, we're being chased by the paparazzi... your famous ex-boyfriend is engaged to his ex-wife... and you and I are the featured story in every red-top in London."

Nat shrugged. "Oh, well – being papped goes with the territory when you date a celebrity. And Keeley and Dominic? They deserve each other. He never got over her, you know." She smirked. "Or losing access to the masses of money she makes."

As they stepped off the service lift to the fourth floor, Natalie checked her mobile. There were four messages from her mum, one from her sister Caro, and one from... Ian Clarkson? How did *he* get her number? "I've got to check my messages," she told Rhys with a frown. "You go ahead. I'll be right there."

"Don't be long," he cautioned. "My meeting's in twenty minutes."

She nodded, already listening to her messages.

Bleep. "It's mum. Why don't you come for dinner tonight? I've hardly seen you lately."

Bleep. "I don't know what's going on," her mother began ominously, "but reporters are outside, armed with cameras and microphones. I can't leave the house! Please call me."

Bleep. "Sarah Hadley called to say you and Rhys Gordon are all over the tabloids! You're not sleeping with that man...? I don't care what you're doing, Natalie, call me at once!"

Bleep. "I'm turning the hose on those reporters. This is insufferable! The answer machine is clogged with messages from every tabloid in London." Natalie heard the hissing sound of spraying water, and a chorus of muffled shouts, then her mum cried triumphantly, "Take that, you lot!"

Natalie groaned. Poor mum. There was no time to call and explain now; she'd call back after the meeting with Rhys. Bleep. "I'm on my way to fetch Nigella," Caro chirped. "Thanks, Natty! Love you."

Finally, she scrolled to the last message. Ian Clarkson.

Bleep. "Natalie, Ian here." He paused. "Call me. I need to speak with you. It's important."

Ian was married, his wife Alexa expecting their first child, yet each time he saw Natalie, he asked her, in that suggestive, smarmy way of his, to lunch or drinks. She always turned him down. She had no doubt that his message was more of the same. Without hesitation, she deleted it.

Ian was trouble she didn't need. Or want.

She hurried back to Rhys's office. Just outside his door, she paused. He was talking to someone on the phone.

"—the tabloids? No, there's no affair, just media speculation. Not that I'm complaining, mind. It's great publicity for Dashwood and James."

Natalie blinked. Every tabloid in Britain was running the story of her 'affair' with Rhys; reporters had badgered her, and brought up bad memories, and besieged her mum's house; and Rhys Gordon thought it made for 'great publicity?' Her fingers tightened on her mobile.

"The stores need every ounce of attention they can get," Rhys went on. "What better way to grab the headlines than an 'affair' with Sir Richard's granddaughter, Natalie?"

Fury swept over her. How dare Rhys use her like this, like some kind of − of media catnip? Why, the opportunistic, manipulative little *prat*—

"Attractive?" Rhys said into the phone. "Yes, very. But she's not my type," he added dismissively. "As to what she's like... well, you'd have to ask the boyfriend, Dominic." He let out a throaty chuckle. "Probably a hellcat in bed, not that you'll ever find out, mate..."

Her cheeks flaming with mortification, Natalie stood rooted to the spot.

When she'd flung the wine at Dominic, Rhys Gordon had stepped in to save the day − not to avoid publicity, but to guarantee it.

It all made perfect sense. She remembered how he'd offered to take her home, how he'd leaned his head close to hers when they spoke, and put his hand on her back when he walked her outside. He'd demonstrated such concern for her...

....all for the benefit of the bloody photographers.

Natalie turned to go. She left, glad Gemma wasn't at her desk, and blinked back tears of anger and humiliation.

"Natalie?" Gemma called out behind her. "Were you looking for me?"

She paused to collect herself before she turned around. "Yes. Would you tell Mr. Gordon that I can't stay? I had a call... my mother... something's come up."

"Is everything all right?" Gemma asked as she came closer, her face etched with concern. "You look upset."

"I'm fine. Thanks." And before her tears could give proof to the lie, she fled.

CHAPTER 7

When Natalie came downstairs, she saw reporters loitering outside the front doors. They were as persistent – and irritating – as midges. Thrusting her sunglasses on, she detoured once again to the back service entrance and peered cautiously out. No one was in sight.

Halfway down the alley to her car, Natalie heard a shout behind her.

"Natalie! Where's Rhys? Is it true you're seeing each other?"

"How do you feel about Dominic and Keeley's engagement? Give us a quote, love!"

She flung herself inside the car and slammed the door, then gunned the engine. Her heart pounded as she threw the Peugeot in gear and screeched out onto Sloane Street, narrowly missing a taxicab in the process. She looked in the rear-view mirror. Thankfully, no one followed her.

Natalie found a parking spot on a side street and let out a ragged breath. Bloody media! What she needed was someone to talk to. Someone calm and sensible…

She grabbed her mobile and scrolled to Sir Richard's private number. "I need to see you, grandfather," she said without preamble when he answered. "Right now." Her voice wobbled. "Thanks. I'll be there in ten minutes."

Cherie James peeled the last potato, ready to add it to the others arranged around the roast, when the phone rang. "Yes?"

"Hullo, darling, it's me."

"Alastair," Cherie said as she eyed the roast, "don't tell me you're working late again. You promised to be home in time for dinner tonight—"

"I know, and I'm sorry. But Gordon wants ideas to improve our bottom line, and he wants them by tomorrow morning. I don't know when I'll get home. Don't wait up."

"Don't worry," Cherie said tightly as she put the roast in the Aga and slammed the oven door, "I won't." The meat would taste like a boot by the time Alastair finally sat down to eat.

"I'll make it up to you," he promised. "We'll go to that new French restaurant you've wanted to try. I'll make reservations for Saturday night when I hang up."

Despite her anger, she relented. "All right," she said finally. "It's not your fault. It's just that you're always staying late. I'm bloody sick of my own company."

"I know, and I'm sorry. But at least Hannah's there."

"Another year and she'll be off to university." Then what would she do? Cherie wondered, and fought back the sudden rise of despair. "I miss you," she added softly. "I miss us."

"As do I, darling." He paused. "Look, if I push it, I might finish up by ten o'clock. Wait for me?"

"Of course. I'll see you then."

She rang off and wondered, not for the first time, if Alastair was having an affair. But as quickly as the idea occurred, she discarded it. He wasn't that sort of man. Besides, if anyone was entitled to have an affair, Cherie reflected irritably, she was. Putting up with Alastair's late hours, worrying about their daughters, what with Holly living on her own in London, and Hannah, off to uni next year—

Oh, stop, she scolded herself. *You've a good husband and two lovely daughters who've never given you a moment's trouble. You've nothing to worry about.*

She took out the flour and sugar and decided to make a treacle tart for dessert.

Affairs were for other people, after all. Not for people like Alastair and her.

Miraculously, there were no reporters outside Sir Richard's townhouse when Natalie arrived. Nevertheless, she parked around the corner and made her way cautiously to the front door.

She'd barely raised her hand to knock when the door swung open. "Come in, miss, your grandfather's expecting you."

"Thank you, Lyons." She smiled at Sir Richard's butler. "Is he in the drawing room?"

"He's in his study, miss. Would you like a drink?"

She'd like more than a drink, she'd like an entire bottle, thank you, and no need for a glass. But, "No thanks," she said, and walked quickly to the end of the hall. Sir Richard stood before the window, his hands clasped behind his back.

"Grandfather," she said in a rush as she tossed her handbag aside, "I'm so glad you're here. You'll never believe what that awful Rhys Gordon's done now!"

He turned away from the window and fixed a rheumy eye on her. From his desk, he picked up a copy of the *Daily Mail*, held it up, and asked, "Has it anything to do with this?"

A photograph was prominently featured on the cover. It was a long shot, and grainy, but it unmistakably showed Natalie standing on the pavement in front of her flat, pressed against Rhys with her arms looped around his neck. It was headlined, 'Exclusive Photos! D&J Heiress Gives Gordon the Business'.

She grabbed it from him, shocked. "What?!"

"I read the papers every morning, and occasionally, I read the tabloids. Although today, I wish I hadn't. You can imagine my dismay to see my granddaughter prominently displayed on the cover of this—" his lip curled in distaste "—publication."

Natalie hurled the tabloid aside. "This is all Rhys's fault! He engineered all of this for publicity!"

"Well, then," Sir Richard said, "it seems he's succeeded."

"Is that all you can say?" she demanded. "He's using this fake affair nonsense to get Dashwood and James in the headlines! He's using *me* as tabloid fodder! At the party, he pretended to help me, after I… when I…" She faltered, and bit her lip.

"After you got drunk and threw your drink at him?" he said, his expression forbidding. "An action meant, if these stories are true, for that twit of a boyfriend of yours."

"Ex-boyfriend," she murmured.

"Natalie, sit down," he commanded. "It's time we talked."

Grandfather rarely issued commands, most especially not to her. This was serious, indeed. She sank without a word into one of the wing chairs facing his desk.

"First of all, I know it was you Rhys referred to in the board meeting this morning," he informed her. "It was you who treated him so shabbily. I know, because I asked you to cover for Mrs. Tuttle in the lingerie department last Saturday."

"I was hung over—" she began.

"It doesn't matter, Natalie," he cut in sharply. "There's no excuse for treating a customer – *any* customer – so poorly. I won't have it."

"But he was insufferably rude—"

"He was testing you. He wanted to see how you'd handle the situation. You failed miserably, by the way."

"It was sneaky, what he did!"

"I may not care for his tactics, but his instincts are spot on. Nor does he avoid unpleasantness. Unlike you, Natalie, who's avoided unpleasantness – and work – for two years."

"That's not fair," Natalie protested. "I worked. I did! Well, for a bit… but I wanted to be with Dominic instead."

"Ah, yes. *Dominic*." Distaste was plain upon his face.

"I thought… I was sure I was in love with him."

"Yes. So you followed him on tour, putting your own life on hold, and let him treat you like – pardon my vulgarity – shit." He held up a hand as she protested. "Ever since you met him, you've drifted along like an unmoored ship. I allowed it, because I thought eventually you'd settle down… to something, or someone. But you haven't. And now, this."

"I can explain—"

"Can you indeed? Can you explain how Rhys Gordon 'engineered' this photo of you, pressing yourself against him with your arms round his neck?"

Natalie blushed. "I was drunk, and furious at Dominic. But nothing happened. Rhys took me home, and left."

"Then you're very lucky. I'm not so far past it that I don't remember what young men can be like, especially when it comes to taking advantage of a situation.

How fortunate for you that Mr. Gordon behaved like a gentleman."

Natalie hung her head.

"Your mother called me earlier. Reporters and photographers are camped out in front of her house, ringing her telephone—"

"I know. She left me four messages."

"Did it never occur to you to call her back?"

"I couldn't! I had a lunch meeting with Rhys and couldn't check my messages until this afternoon."

Sir Richard regarded her, his expression unreadable. "I hate to say it, Natalie, but things can't continue on as they are. You must either find employment, or settle down with a more suitable young man. I won't allow you to throw your life away in this irresponsible manner any longer."

She looked at him in alarm. "What do you mean?"

"You must learn to make your own way. You've been provided with an excellent education and every privilege a young woman could want. Natalie, I love you dearly. But I will not tolerate – or finance – your bohemian lifestyle any longer."

"But… how will I pay the rent on my flat without my quarterly allowance? Or put petrol in my car?"

"You'll find a job, I expect, like the rest of the world." He paused. "You might even find that you like being useful."

Stiffly, Natalie stood and retrieved her handbag. It was unbearable to hear grandfather echoing Rhys's own words. "I came here because I thought you'd understand. Instead, you're telling me you're cutting me off unless I find a job, or a husband. Have I got the gist of it?"

"I dislike having to say these things as much as you dislike hearing them. But they must be said."

"I feel completely blindsided," Natalie whispered, and her throat tightened. "Dominic's dumped me, Caro's getting married... everyone's getting on with their lives, doing things, building careers. Moving on... and leaving me b-behind."

Sir Richard drew her into his arms and stroked her hair as she wept. "None of that, now. You have a lot to offer, Natalie, and it's only yourself that's holding you back. I know your father's suicide gutted you. It was a terrible thing. He was my only son, you know." He patted her back as she hiccupped out a sob. "But life – and business, unfortunately – continues. We must soldier on."

Natalie forced a watery smile and lifted her head. "You sound like the Queen."

"Dashwood and James are in serious trouble. We owe money – taxes, a great deal of them – and I need help to straighten out the mess. Rhys is right to implement his changes. I don't like them any more than you do." He sighed, and he suddenly looked like what he was, a tired old man. "But he's our only hope."

Then we're in serious trouble, she thought grimly, but didn't say it. "He asked for my help today."

"Did he? Good. I'll speak to him about hiring you on and putting you in that small office next to his." He picked up the telephone. "Now, I'm ending this tabloid nonsense. I won't have you or your mother bothered by reporters."

Natalie kissed his papery cheek. "Thanks, grandfather. I love you masses."

"I love you too, you cheeky girl. Run along, now."

She paused at the study door. "I'll need new clothes if I'm to look like a proper businesswoman, won't I?"

He regarded her sternly. "Natalie, I've already allowed you to get your 'Peony' handbag—"

"Poppy," she corrected him. "It's a 'Poppy' handbag."

"—but I must reiterate that we cannot afford these sorts of expenditures any longer. I'm sure you can find something suitable to wear from within your own overstuffed closet."

She sighed. "Oh, very well. I suppose I might unearth something, even if it's last season… It's just so dreary, practising all this economy. I'm not used to it."

"I know it's difficult. But if we do our part, and live more frugally, and if Rhys Gordon makes good on his promise to turn things around, things will improve."

"I hope you're right." Scepticism coloured her voice. "But you have far more faith in Mr. Gordon than I do." She smiled and waggled her fingers. "Goodnight, grandfather."

"Goodnight, my dear. Don't forget your mother's birthday luncheon in the tearoom on Monday. Eleven o'clock sharp. And don't be late!" he called out after her.

When she'd gone, Sir Richard took a pill out of his pillbox, his hand trembling slightly, and swallowed it with a grimace. Blood pressure pills… angina pills… pills to help him sleep and pills to keep him alert. It was a dreadful thing, to have to take so many damned pills.

But as he pressed the box closed, a smile curved his lips. He would sleep well tonight, with or without his pills.

Natalie would be sorted, at last. That was one worry he could cross off his list.

CHAPTER 8

"Keeley," Dominic ventured as he tossed the last carrier bag from the day's shopping on her sofa, "how about loaning me some cash? To tide me over until the tour starts."

"How much?"

He flung himself on the sofa. "Oh, I dunno. A couple of hundred?"

"Two hundred quid?" She shrugged and reached for her handbag. "OK."

Dominic let out a snort. "Two hundred quid? You must be joking." He thrust a cigarette in his mouth. "No, I meant two hundred thousand. Although I suppose," he mused thoughtfully as he reached in his pocket for a lighter, "I could just about manage on a hundred."

"You're the one who must be joking!" Keeley snapped. "And put that bloody cigarette out! I told you, no smoking in here."

With a muttered apology, he took the cigarette out, unlit, and tossed it aside. He looked at her, one brow raised expectantly. "So, what do you say?"

"Dominic, we've been engaged for three weeks and you want me to hand over two hundred thousand pounds, just like that?"

"Well, Porsches and '57 Strats are expensive," he said defensively. "And it's not like you can't spare it."

"That's not the point, is it? I'm your fiancée, not your banker!"

"We'll be married soon," he pointed out. "So what's yours is mine, and what's mine is—" he waved his hand "—whatever."

She snorted. "Bit of a bad deal, that, since all you have are debts. You go through money like a coke addict through blow. Look, Dominic, just be more frugal. Sell one of your Porsches, and you've got the cash you need. Problem sorted."

Dominic scowled. Plainly there was to be no financial aid forthcoming from the Keeley front. Fucking hell.

Late that afternoon, Cherie James heard the front door open and slam shut. She looked up from the courgette she was slicing for dinner and called out, "Hannah? Come here, please."

There was an aggrieved sigh from the front hallway. "I've got masses of homework, mum—"

"Mr. Compton called," Cherie said when Hannah appeared in the kitchen doorway. "You were late to class this morning, and yesterday as well."

"So? I'm acing his bloody assignments— "

"Why were you late, Hannah? You left with your father in plenty of time this morning."

"I stopped to talk to someone before class, that's all. It's not a big deal—"

"It *is* a big deal. Mr. Compton said you've been hanging around with Chloe Robinson."

"What of it?"

Cherie felt her patience begin to slip. "Hannah, Chloe's been in and out of trouble since school began. Last year she was expelled! She's not the ideal person to spend time with."

"Oh, so now you're choosing my friends for me?" Hannah demanded. "You don't even know Chloe—"

"I know she cuts class. Your attitude since you've been seeing her speaks for itself." Cherie pressed her lips together. "If you're late to class again, you'll be grounded until school ends."

"That's so unfair!" Hannah erupted. "You treat me like a child! All of you – dad, Mr. Compton – even Duncan!"

"You and Duncan aren't fighting, are you?"

"No, mum, we're not fighting. We broke up! He dumped me. Are you happy now?" Hannah turned and stormed away up the stairs, and slammed the bedroom door behind her.

Cherie sighed and picked up her knife, and cut the courgette into matchsticks. Life would be easier, she reflected grimly, if Alastair were home more often. He coped with Hannah's dramas much better than she did. Hannah was so prickly these days…

The phone rang. Probably Alastair, calling to say he'd be late again. "Hello," she said shortly.

"Cherie? Is it a bad time?" Duncan's father asked.

"Neil! No, of course not. I was just… brooding."

"I hope nothing's wrong."

"No, just feeling a bit sorry for myself." She paused and added, "It's too bad about the divorce, by the way. How are you and Sarah managing?"

"Taking it day by day," he replied. "I've let a flat in Fulham. Duncan's adjusted to the changes without too much drama. I see as much of him as I can."

"It's difficult, I imagine. Living with a teenager isn't easy under the best of circumstances." Cherie sighed. "I've just had a row with Hannah. She and Duncan have broken it off."

"Yes, that's why I'm calling, actually."

"I see." She laid her knife aside. "What's happened?"

"Nothing serious, just something I thought you ought to know." He hesitated. "Sunday night, while you and Alastair were celebrating your anniversary, Hannah had Duncan over."

Cherie sighed. "I don't like the sound of this already."

"Nothing happened. You know Duncan's keen on his music career, so when things began to go a bit too far, he told Hannah they should wait. She was upset, and asked him to leave."

"I see." And suddenly, she did see. Hannah had offered herself, probably for the first time ever, and been – however tactfully – rejected. She sighed. "I'm very glad Duncan didn't take advantage. Most boys would have done."

"Yes, it's usually the other way round, isn't it?"

"You're lucky, you know. Girls are much harder than boys to deal with at this age. I'm sure Duncan's never given you or Sarah a moment's trouble."

"Oh, he has his moments. But he's always been focused on his music, from the time he was small. It's kept him out of trouble for the most part."

"Hannah can't seem to stay out of trouble, lately."

"She's a teenager. You'll get through it."

The front door opened and Alastair called out, "I'm home! Where is everyone?"

Cherie cradled the phone against her ear and picked up her knife once again. "Thanks for calling, Neil. And thanks for the advice. I'm sure you're right." She rang off just as her husband entered the kitchen.

"Here you are." He kissed her. "What advice was that?"

"Oh, nothing," she said lightly. "Perhaps we should let Hannah work at the store this summer. What do you think?"

"I don't see why not. Is she in trouble?"

"She's been late to class, twice. Ever since she broke up with Duncan, she's been impossible."

"I didn't realise they'd broken up." Alastair lifted his brow. "Shame, he's a nice young man. If you like, I'll speak to Sir Richard tomorrow and arrange something."

"Yes, please do. Dinner's almost ready. Go wash up, and tell Hannah to come down."

As he disappeared upstairs, Cherie rinsed her hands and wondered why she hadn't told Alastair about Hannah's failed attempt to lose her virginity, or Neil's phone call.

Surely there was no need to trouble her husband with a litany of Hannah's misdeeds. He had enough on his plate with the company's finances in turmoil; he didn't need to fret over his daughter's budding sexuality as well.

And there was no reason for her to feel guilty for having a chat with Duncan's father, she told herself firmly.

No reason at all.

"Why didn't you return my messages?" Natalie's mother reproved her at dinner that evening.

"I couldn't, I was at lunch with Rhys Gordon. He wanted to discuss the store and the problems we're facing."

Celia Dashwood's eyes narrowed. "You're not having sex with that man, are you?"

Natalie nearly choked on her water. "Mum, honestly! No, I'm not. We don't even like each other."

"It looks as though you like each other well enough, judging from those photos in the tabloids."

Natalie nudged at a bit of chicken with her fork. "It's only publicity. And those pictures… they were taken out of context. They were innocent."

"Innocent?" her mother echoed, and raised her brow. "Is that what you call it? You were pressed against that man in full view of the world, twined round him like a garden hose!"

Natalie dropped her fork to her plate with a clatter. "Mum, please! I can't bear any more. It's mortifying."

"Oh, very well. Tell me about Rhys Gordon," her mother said, her face alight with curiosity as she took a sip of wine. "Is he as difficult as they say?"

Natalie felt a renewed wave of humiliation as she remembered his comments to the man on the phone. "He's worse." She could still hear Rhys's words, could see him leaning back in his high-backed chair, could hear his throaty chuckle as he discussed her with his friend.

Probably quite a hellcat in bed, not that you'll ever find out, mate...

"He's ruthless and crude and sneaky," she went on. "I despise him."

"My word, you make him sound dreadful, like Machiavelli," Lady Dashwood said mildly.

"Picture Machiavelli on a motorbike, and you're there."

"I'm sorry I missed the board meeting, I wanted to meet him." She glanced out the window. "At least those reporters are gone." She stood up. "I'll go and fetch our pudding."

Natalie stood. "I'll get it." She'd do anything to escape her mother's questions about Rhys.

As she entered the pantry and grabbed a serving spoon from the drawer, her mobile rang. She frowned. She didn't recognise the number. She hoped it wasn't a reporter... "Hullo?"

"Natalie? It's Rhys."

She froze, spoon in hand. "What do you want?"

He paused. "I called to see if everything's all right. You never came back. Gemma said you were upset."

"I'm fine," she said, her words chilly. "You needn't worry."

"Why did you leave so suddenly?"

"Something came up. Sorry, I have to go." She pressed 'end call' and set it to vibrate.

Almost immediately it began to buzz like an angry bee. Rhys again! Stubborn, pushy, awful man... Furious, Natalie tossed the mobile on one of the pantry shelves.

...there's no affair, just media speculation. Not that I'm complaining, mind. It's great publicity for Dashwood and James...

"Natalie," her mother called out, "are you bringing the trifle?"

"Yes, sorry." She picked up the bowl and hurried back into the dining room.

As they settled down to dessert, Natalie fumed. Rhys must've got her mobile number from Gemma, the interfering cow. She scowled and pushed the trifle around on her plate, creating aimless chocolate swirls on the china.

"Darling," her mother said in exasperation as she laid her fork aside, "what's wrong? You barely touched your dinner; now you're playing with your trifle! Don't you like it?"

She smiled wanly. "I love it. I just... had a difficult day." She pushed her plate away. "I think I'll go home and turn in early—"

The throaty roar of a motorcycle engine pulling up outside interrupted her.

Before Natalie could do more than exchange a startled glance with her mother, the doorbell rang. Then someone pounded on the door.

"Who in heaven's name is that, and at this hour?" Celia Dashwood harrumphed. "If it's another reporter—"

"I'll get it," Natalie said, her words grim. She rose and tossed her napkin down. "It's probably Machiavelli."

"What—?"

Nat strode to the door and flung it open. Rhys Gordon, his hand raised to knock again, stood on the doorstep. Anger suffused his face.

"I'm not leaving this doorstep," Rhys told her with grim determination, "until you tell me what the hell's going on."

CHAPTER 9

Natalie glared at him. "What do you mean?" She remained in the doorway but drew the door shut behind her. "And how'd you know I was here?"

"Gemma told me. Never mind that – what the hell's going on?" Rhys snapped. "And don't say 'nothing'," he warned, "because something's obviously wrong."

"There's nothing wrong! And Gemma's an interfering cow."

"Something happened after lunch today," he said grimly. "And whatever it was, it got your knickers in a twist."

"Ah, yes, my knickers… that's a subject that really fascinates you, isn't it?" Natalie flung back. Her fists were clenched at her sides.

He stared at her. "What?"

"I heard you myself," she accused him, "when I came back to your office. You were talking about me on the phone."

He frowned. "I talked to my brother for a few minutes. And we didn't talk about you… or your knickers." He cast his mind back over their chat – football scores, Jamie's promotion to sous chef… and Alastair James's party. "We didn't talk about anything objectionable. And you shouldn't have been eavesdropping," he added pointedly.

"I could hardly help but overhear you, could I? You were speculating about how good I'd be in bed! You don't consider *that* objectionable?"

"You're mistaken."

"I know what I heard," Natalie insisted, her voice undercut with fury. "Don't add lying to your sins. You were so kind after Dominic dumped me at the party, you even offered to take me home. But you had an ulterior motive. You were making the most of the publicity, and you used me to do it!"

"It wasn't like that—"

"No? How was it, then?" she demanded. "And don't tell me it doesn't boost your male ego, seeing photos of us in the tabloids, adding another affair to your long, sordid list—"

"It's preferable to seeing photos of you tossing wine on Dominic Heath."

Her lip trembled. "You used me. You knew I was drunk, and you took advantage—"

"Used you? Really?" he asked, incredulous. "Because unless you were too inebriated to remember, you asked me to have sex with you, not once, but several times."

She squeaked in outraged mortification.

"I could've given you what you wanted," Rhys went on, fuelled by his rising anger. "I could've shagged you in your flat, or on the Triumph, or on the pavement, for that matter—"

Natalie paled. "You're the crudest, most disgusting man—"

"But I didn't! I fucking well didn't, precisely because—" he stepped closer and lowered his voice "—I didn't want to take advantage of you. I know Dominic humiliated you at Alastair's party." He scowled. "And I know you think I'm a

heartless bastard with no redeeming qualities. Maybe I am.
But I did *not* take advantage of you."

Natalie sniffed, only partially mollified. "You made it
look like we were having an affair—"

"I used the situation, Natalie. Not you." He looked
at her, his eyes intense. "It was damage control. I turned
what might've been a bad situation to advantage. I did it to
protect Dashwood and James from a lawsuit, and to protect
you. I won't apologise for that. I'd do it again."

"You told your brother I wasn't your type." She dropped
her gaze from his and fiddled with her wristwatch. "And
when he asked if I were any good in bed, you said he ought
to ask Dominic. And that you imagined I was probably a...
hellcat."

To her utter amazement, he began to laugh.

"It isn't funny!" she sputtered.

"Oh, but it is." He shook his head. "You've got the
wrong end of the stick. That's what happens when you
eavesdrop."

"I didn't eavesdrop!" she protested. "I couldn't help but
overhear your crude comments. Don't deny it – I *heard*
you."

He held up a hand in surrender. "I did say those things,
it's true. And they weren't very gentlemanly, I suppose."
He paused. "But I wasn't talking about you."

She gazed at him with mingled distrust and confusion.
"You... weren't? Who were you talking about, then?"

"Keeley."

"Keeley," Natalie repeated.

He nodded. "When I told Jamie that Dominic had
dumped you for his ex-wife, Keeley whatsit—"

"Oh, it's just 'Keeley'," Natalie supplied. "No last name.
Like Madonna. Or Posh."

"—he was over the moon with excitement that I'd seen her at the party. According to Jamie, she's the hottest pop singer in Britain. He's had a crush on her since he was twelve."

She regarded him with scepticism. "You must've lived in a cave for the last ten years if you've never heard of Keeley."

He shrugged. "I left home at seventeen. I was working, going to school at night, so I didn't keep up with that sort of thing. I didn't have time."

"So... you weren't talking about me," Natalie said in a small voice.

"No." He shoved a hand through his hair. "I shouldn't have said those things about Keeley, about anyone. But I was talking to my brother, bloke to bloke." He eyed her accusingly. "And I didn't know *you* were listening."

"Is everything all right?" Natalie's mother inquired suspiciously as she opened the door.

"Fine," Natalie said quickly, and turned to her mother. "Mum, this is Rhys Gordon. We were just discussing... a problem."

Rhys leaned forward and thrust out his hand. "It's lovely to meet you, Lady Dashwood."

"Mr. Gordon." She took his hand in her best queenly manner and cast Natalie a keen glance. "I've heard a lot about you."

"None of it good, I'm sure," he said equably.

"Very little," she agreed. "But I prefer to make up my own mind. I'm sorry I missed the board meeting. Please, come in. I've just made coffee."

He shook his head. "Thank you, I can't stay. I'm working tomorrow."

"But tomorrow's Saturday!" Natalie objected.

"Yes, and the offices are closed. But I've a lot to tackle and I get more done when no one's there." He gave Nat's mum a warm smile. "It was a pleasure to meet you, Lady Dashwood."

She smiled and toyed with the pearls at her throat. "Celia, please. I enjoyed meeting you as well, Mr. Gordon. I must say... you're not at all what I expected."

Natalie eyed her mother in amazement. If she didn't know better, she'd almost think mum was flirting with Rhys.

"Can I give you a lift?" Rhys asked Natalie as he turned to leave.

"Thanks, I drove." She grabbed her handbag and keys and turned to kiss her mother goodbye. "Goodnight, mum."

"Goodnight, darling."

As Lady Dashwood returned to the drawing room to gather up the cups and saucers, she heard a buzzing sound coming from the pantry. Mystified, she set the plates down and pushed open the pantry door. "What on earth—?"

Natalie's mobile lay on a shelf, buzzing madly away.

"Oh, dear." She snatched the phone up and hurried back to the front door, but Natalie and Rhys were gone.

She looked at the caller's name. *Rhys Gordon*. Should she answer? She didn't like to think of Natalie driving home at this hour without her mobile. Suppose her car broke down?

"Mr. Gordon? Yes, it's Celia Dashwood. No, she left her mobile in the pantry." She paused. "Would you mind? Silly of me, but it's late, and she's without it. Thank you so much. Yes, call and let me know she got home safely. Goodnight."

"I can't believe it." Natalie thumped her fist on the steering wheel in frustration. Halfway home, the car just...

stopped. She eased the Peugeot off the road, and stared at the gauges to assess the situation.

Oh. Crikey. She was out of petrol.

She groaned. The petrol gauge's needle was in the red, pointed firmly at 'empty'.

"My mobile," Natalie muttered, and grabbed her purse. She'd call mum. *Where is it?* she wondered as she scrabbled through her handbag, *I know it's in here somewhere—*

Suddenly she remembered. Rhys and his infuriating, persistent calls... she'd thrown her mobile on a shelf in the pantry. She closed her eyes. Bloody hell! Would this endless, endless day never end?

She couldn't stay here. It wasn't that late, and she was more than half way home, but it was too far to walk. She eyed the dark street uneasily. There was a petrol station nearby, wasn't there?

Natalie bit her lip. She'd lock up her car and walk. Even if the station was closed, they'd have a phone box, and she could ring mum to come and fetch her. She couldn't stay here.

Resolutely, she got out and locked the door. She gripped her handbag and began to walk quickly down the street. She heard the echo of her high-heeled footsteps, and the distant swish of cars on the A4.

Somewhere behind her, growing closer, a motorcycle approached. She walked a bit faster. The low growl of the engine grew louder, and she glanced over her shoulder to see the motorbike slowing down, until it drew up alongside her.

Natalie looked back nervously but kept walking. She couldn't see the rider's face; a visored helmet obscured it.

Her legs turned to jelly. Should she run? Scream? Dial 999? No, scratch that, she couldn't call for help – she didn't have her bloody mobile. *Stupid, stupid—*

"Natalie?"

She came to a stop, her heart beating wildly. "Rh-Rhys?"

He lifted the visor. "I saw your car abandoned back there," he said, concerned. "What happened?"

Relief washed over her. "I can't believe I'm saying this, but I'm really glad to see you!" she said fervently. "I ran out of petrol... I didn't have my mobile—"

"So I heard," he said, his words grim. "Get on, I'll take you home. You can tell me about it on the way."

Sheepishly she took the helmet he held out. "This is getting to be a habit, you rescuing me. How did you know to come looking?"

"After I left, I rang to see that you got back safely. Imagine my surprise when your mum answered." He glared at her. "She found your phone in the pantry."

She dropped her gaze, embarrassed. "Well, I didn't want to talk to you earlier, did I?" She knew what was coming next – the bloody lecture.

And the thing was, she reflected, this time she absolutely deserved it.

He opened his mouth to ask her what the hell she'd been thinking, putting herself in such danger, did she know what might have happened? But he caught sight of her face, pale and exhausted, and let out a short breath.

"Never mind. I'm just glad you're all right. Now put on that helmet, and let's get you home."

CHAPTER 10

The sound of the door buzzer echoed through the flat the next morning. Natalie lifted one side of her eye mask to see sunshine streaming in through her bedroom curtains.

"Coming," she croaked as she rolled out of bed and stumbled to the bathroom. She peered into the mirror. Crikey could definitely be better.

She splashed water on her face and tugged at the wrinkled Blondie T-shirt she'd slept in – second night in a row, must do laundry – and went to the door. The buzzer sounded again.

"Hold on!" she muttered, annoyed. Tarquin was impatient. And *early*. Natalie already regretted asking him to go clothes shopping with her. Much nicer to have a nice lie-in, then a late lunch, perhaps pop in to Chanel for a look around...

She pressed the speaker button. "Come up." She barely had time to drag a comb through her hair and brush her teeth when Tarquin knocked on the door.

"You won't believe it, Tark," Natalie said as she swung the flat door open, "but I forgot about going shopping today— "

"You, forget about shopping? Impossible."

It took a moment to process the fact that it wasn't Tark who stood in her doorway, but Rhys Gordon.

Rhys *bloody* Gordon! He looked at her as if he'd never seen a girl in a T-shirt and… well, to be honest… not much else.

She crossed her arms self-consciously against her braless chest. "Rhys! What are you doing here?"

"I've had your car filled with petrol and brought round. I tried to call," he added, "but your mobile's turned off and your telephone's been disconnected."

Although he didn't say it, she knew he longed to criticise her for these latest infractions.

But all he said was, "Sorry if I woke you. I know it's a bit early, but I'm on my way in to work."

She leaned against the doorjamb. "I really appreciate your help last night," she said, and meant it. "I don't know what I'd have done if you hadn't come along."

"Check your petrol gauge now and then. And don't hide your phone in the bloody pantry. I'm just glad I was able to help."

She opened the door a bit wider and stood aside. "At least come in and let me give you a cup of tea – or coffee? – before you go. I owe you that much."

He nodded. "I wouldn't say no to a coffee. Thanks."

"Let me grab a pair of jeans first. I'll be right back."

"I can't stay long," he called out after her. "The bloke from the petrol station followed me in your car; I've got to take him back."

"Is he perched on the back of your motorbike?"

"No, I've got the Jag."

Natalie emerged from the bedroom five minutes later wearing jeans and a T-shirt, with her hair sorted and a slick of lipstick on her mouth. "I'll get that coffee. Won't take me a second, it's only instant."

She switched the kettle on and spooned Nescafé into two mismatched mugs. "Sorry I don't have real coffee. I need to do a shop but I haven't had time."

"Oh, you cook?"

"You needn't sound so surprised," she said, indignant. "Yes, I cook. I make a great spaghetti Bolognese. And my Victoria sponge is better than mum's."

The kettle whistled. She poured hot water into their cups and handed one to Rhys.

"Thanks. Stop by my office later and we'll go over those numbers."

"I can't. I'm going shopping with Tark this morning." At his puzzled look she added, "Tarquin Magnus Campbell. He's heir to the fourth earl of Draemar and he's my dearest friend. He and Wren are getting married in Scotland next month, so of course I need a dress… and a wedding gift."

Rhys narrowed his eyes. "I don't like the sound of that."

"What do you mean?" she demanded.

"If you need clothes, it means you plan to spend money. That's never a good thing."

"Ha bloody ha. Perhaps I might stop by your office after lunch? You could show me the figures then."

He nodded. "I'll see you later, then."

The buzzer sounded again. "That's Tarquin," Natalie announced. She walked over and pressed the button. "Come up."

"I should go," Rhys said. "Thanks for the coffee." He added pointedly, "Try to buy something on sale. And if your car ever breaks down again, promise me you'll lock the doors and stay put."

Natalie's gaze collided with his. He really did have the most penetrating blue eyes. "You know," she blurted, "you're almost nice when you want to be."

He raised his brow. "Only almost? I'll have to work on that."

Several rapid-fire knocks sounded on the door.

Natalie let out an exasperated breath. "It's like Waterloo Station in here this morning! Excuse me."

She left Rhys in the kitchen and hurried down the hallway to open the door, then froze. "Dominic!" She pulled the door shut behind her and stepped into the hall. "What the hell are *you* doing here?" she hissed.

Dominic leaned one shoulder against the doorjamb. He reeked of stale Gitanes and whiskey. "We need to talk, Nat."

"You're drunk, Dom. And we've nothing to talk about. You're with Keeley now."

"I'm not, not really! It's all for publicity. There's no reason we can't still see each other. I miss you, Nat." He leaned forward unsteadily to kiss her.

Natalie backed away in disgust. "You want me as your bit on the side, you mean."

"Come on, Nat, it's not like that. Besides," he pointed out, "the tabs all say you and Gordon are having a go—"

The door swung open. "Is everything all right?" Rhys asked. He fixed his piercing gaze on Dominic.

Dominic turned back to Natalie with an accusatory glare. "What's 'e doing here?"

Natalie glanced at Rhys. "I ran out of petrol last night, and Rhys—"

"—I brought her home, mate," Rhys finished, and lifted his coffee mug to Dominic in mock salute.

Nat leaned forward, playing along, and stood on her toes to kiss Rhys on the cheek. He smelled enticingly of soap and aftershave. "You were a star last night. Thanks again."

He handed her his half-empty mug. "You're welcome. Now I've got to go. I'll see you this afternoon?"

Natalie nodded. "I'll be there."

Rhys left, and Dominic's scowl deepened. He looked like he was about to spontaneously combust. He swayed slightly on his feet and demanded, "What's going on? I've seen the tabloids. You're not shagging that plonker, are you?"

A distracted smile curved Natalie's lips. "Not yet." Her smile vanished as she added crossly, "What do you care, anyway? You broke up with me, or have you forgotten?"

"Look, Nat," he protested, "he's 28, practically old enough to be your... your uncle! Besides, I still love you—"

"Oh, piss off, Dominic. Go sleep it off. And then go... smash a guitar, or something." She left him in the hall, scowling, and shut the door smartly in his face.

Dominic didn't take Natalie's advice. Instead he found himself, two hours and a half a bottle of Chivas Regal later, slumped next to Keeley in the front row of Klaus von Richter's spring preview fashion show.

How in bloody hell had that happened?

He crossed his arms against his chest and slouched back in the folding metal chair. He'd refused to go. But Keeley glared at him and hissed, "Remind me again why I agreed to this engagement, Dominic. Perhaps I should call it off."

So here he was, crammed in with a gazillion fashionistas, all crossing their stiletto-heeled legs and shouting into their mobiles in rapid-fire French, English, and Italian.

"Why am I here?" he grumbled to Keeley as his right eye was nearly taken out by the wildly gesticulating editor of Italian *Vogue* sitting next to him.

"Because I need clothes for our honeymoon," she snapped, "and because Maison Laroche's show is the

absolute best. People would *kill* for front row seats. Klaus'
clothes are genius."

Dominic snorted. "Don't know why any of this lot
bothers going to fashion shows. All they wear is black."

But as the lights dimmed and the show began, Dominic
leaned forward, intrigued despite himself. Clouds of fog,
pulsing techno music, and long-legged models striding out
on the catwalk combined to create a throbbing spectacle
of light, sound, and beauty. The clothes were all right, he
supposed...

...but the models were bloody amazing.

Keeley poked him sharply in the ribs. "You can roll your
tongue back in your mouth anytime," she hissed in his ear.

When the show ended – all too soon, in Dominic's
opinion – Keeley grabbed him by the arm and dragged him
backstage to meet the iconic fashion designer. Klaus von
Richter was bald, and he wore black, from the cashmere
scarf flung around his neck to his black-booted feet. What
was it with fashion people and black? Dominic wondered.

"Klaus!" Keeley gushed. "The show was fantastic." She
air-kissed him on both cheeks.

He took her hand in his black fingerless gloves and lifted
it to his lips. "*Merci*, my dear," he said in German-accented
English. "What can I possibly create that is beautiful
enough for you to wear, eh?"

Keeley smiled. "Everything you create is beautiful,
Klaus. I love the black velvet strapless dress – stunning..."

Although Klaus nodded distractedly, his eyes lasered in
on Dominic. "You," he purred, "you are Keeley's fiancé,
non?"

"Yeah," Dominic muttered. The way this German bloke
stared at him – like a half-starved alley cat eyeing up

a dish of Devonshire cream – made him more than a bit uncomfortable.

Klaus reached out and grabbed Dominic's jaw in his hand, tilted his head this way and that, and pronounced, "You haf excellent bone structure. You haf modelled before?"

Dominic scowled and jerked his head free. "No! I'm a rock singer, not a bloody model."

"You will model for me, for Maison Laroche," Klaus announced. It wasn't a question; it was a command.

"I don't do that modelling shit."

"But you will, for me. You're perfect." Klaus narrowed his eyes and walked slowly around Dominic, one hand on his chin. "You haf exactly the look I want. However, your clothes—" he eyed Dominic's faded Levis and Motörhead T-shirt "—must go. We will dress you in von Richter, no?"

"No!" Dominic snapped.

Klaus snapped his fingers at one of his assistants. "Bring the sample suit to my dressing room. *Jetzt!*" He turned back to Keeley and Dominic. "Come back with me, and we will talk."

"Come *on*," Keeley hissed, tugging on Dominic's arm as he balked. "Are you mental? Do you know what an honour this is?"

"Honour, my arse," Dominic hissed back. "He's a nut job!"

The designer came straight to the point once they were seated in his dressing room. "I haf created my first men's fragrance. I want Dominic to be the face of *Dissolute*. He has exactly the look I want – insolent, aristocratic, a touch dissipated. Perfect for the print ads… like a modern-day Dorian Gray, no?"

Dominic had no idea what the old queen was banging on about. "I don't know shit about modelling, and I don't know Dorian Gray, neither. I can't do it, anyway. I'm starting a new tour next month. Then I'll be in the studio. Sorry, mate."

"We'll work around your schedule." Klaus flipped open an enamelled case and withdrew a tiny pinch of snuff, then thrust it delicately up first one nostril, then the other. "You will pose for print ads in the fashion magazines, and film a television commercial. Nothing more will be required of you."

"Nah, sorry, can't do it," Dominic said firmly. "My fans would say I'd sold out." He paused as one of the models came in to get a cigarette and blatantly eyed him up. He smiled. Hm... perhaps he should reconsider. How bad could it be, if doing this gig for Klaus meant he could hang out with girls like that?

Klaus saw the mingled lust and indecision in Dominic's eyes, and moved in for the kill. "You'll be well paid." He leaned forward almost coquettishly, and whispered a sum in Dominic's ear.

"Blimey." Dominic blinked. With the amount of dosh Klaus had offered him, he could pay off his debts, buy that new Maserati Ghibli he'd had his eye on, and still have enough left over to buy a '57 Strat...

"So?" Klaus said finally, with a touch of impatience. "What do you say? You will sign with Maison Laroche to be the new face of *Dissolute*?"

Keeley looked over at Dominic, her eyes shining, and nodded imperceptibly.

Dominic let out a short breath. He hated to sell out. But he really needed the dosh that von Richter was offering him.

Sod selling out. Sod his fans. Filthy lucre won the day.

"OK," Dominic said finally, and stood. "Send me the contract and I'll have my lawyer take a look."

"Excellent." Klaus clasped him firmly on the shoulder. "We haf a deal. You've made a very wise decision."

Dominic made no reply. Why did he suddenly feel as if he'd made a deal, all right...

...a deal with the devil?

CHAPTER 11

"I can't decide between the Missoni or the Cavalli," Natalie said with a frown as she emerged from the dressing room with two dresses draped over her arm. "They're both gorgeous."

"Well, at least you've narrowed it down to two," Tarquin said with resignation. He'd spent the past hour slumped in a chair as Natalie tried on dress after dress.

"I have to find the perfect outfit for your wedding."

"What about this?" Tarquin suggested hopefully. He plucked a dress from a nearby rack that cost much less than either of Natalie's choices.

"I'm not buying off the rack for your wedding, Tark. I need something worthy of the occasion."

"The newspapers say that Dashwood and James aren't doing well, Nat," he said, choosing his words carefully. "Perhaps you should be a bit more – erm, frugal."

"Frugal?" Natalie echoed. "I know you Scots are famous for thrift, but I refuse to scrimp when it comes to your wedding!"

"Perhaps you should get them both," Tarquin said finally, defeated.

She beamed. "Brilliant!" She dropped an impulsive kiss on the top of Tark's head on her way back to the dressing room. "I'm almost done."

As she changed back into her clothes, Natalie considered possible wedding gifts. She wanted to give Wren and Tark something special – Waterford crystal, perhaps, or one of those hideous metal sculptures Tark fancied – something suitable for his Scottish castle…

…something to show how much his friendship meant to her.

"I have to get you a wedding gift," Natalie told him a few minutes later when she emerged from the dressing room. "We'll shop once I pay for this lot."

Alarmed, Tarquin rose and followed her to the front desk. "I don't need a present, Nat! Besides, Dashwood and James are in real financial trouble," he added in a low voice. "Rhys Gordon's only called in if things are very bad."

"How did you know grandfather hired Rhys?"

"It's in all the business pages." Tarquin reddened slightly and added, "I hate to bring it up, but the tabloids are also saying that you and Mr. Gordon are – erm…"

"—having an affair?" Natalie pressed her lips together. She refused to be embarrassed. Why should she be? She'd done nothing wrong. "We're not. It's only for publicity."

"Well, that's a relief! He's bloody awful, isn't he?"

"Oh, he's not so bad," Natalie said airily. "At any rate," she added as she handed her credit card to the sales clerk, "Dashwood and James have been around since 1854. We'll pull through this little slump. There's nothing to worry about."

As they left, Tarquin came to a stop. "Nat, about the wedding gift," he said. "You've already spent a small fortune on clothing—"

"You sound like an accountant, Tark. Or worse, like Rhys," she added darkly. "I'm getting you a wedding gift, and there's an end to it." She smiled. "And I know just the thing."

Laden with carrier bags, Natalie strode along the crowded pavement as Tarquin trailed behind, her earlier promise to meet with Rhys Gordon completely forgotten.

"Hannah!" Cherie called out from her dressing table on Saturday evening. "Your father and I are going to dinner tonight. We won't be too late, should be home by eleven or so."

No reply from Hannah's room.

"I've left you a casserole in the warming oven. I'll take it out before we leave." Cherie applied lipstick and blotted her lips on a tissue.

There was still no reply.

Cherie sighed. She'd survived Holly's mood swings and teen angst; now it was Hannah's turn. Overnight, her normally sunny child had turned into a moody, disaffected stranger.

Their house had become a war zone of slammed doors and meals that ended in shouting and recriminations. Cherie knew Hannah's moods had everything to do with Duncan Hadley.

The phone rang. "Hello," Cherie said, and cradled the receiver against her ear as she picked up her pearl earring.

"Hello, darling."

"Alastair! Are you on your way? Or shall I meet you at the restaurant?"

There was an ominous pause. "Neither, I'm afraid. I just got out of a late meeting with Rhys, and he wants me to rework the markdown budget. I'll probably be working most of the day tomorrow as well."

Cherie focused on the eardrop dangling between her fingers. "Can't you work on it tomorrow? Surely it can wait."

"I'm sorry, darling, but it can't. Everything has to be reconciled for our finance meeting on Monday. I'm just as disappointed as you."

"I doubt that," Cherie said acidly.

"Look, why don't you go, and take Hannah," Alastair suggested. "Don't let the reservation go to waste."

"Hannah wants nothing to do with me at the moment." She laid the earring aside. "Which you'd know, if you were ever here. And the whole point of this evening was to have dinner with my husband. Not my daughter."

"I know. I've let you down. Again." He sounded tired, and defeated. "Rhys is letting Henry go, did I tell you? Poor old chap."

"Henry? How awful," Cherie echoed, her disappointment forgotten. "He must be devastated. Mr. Gordon is heartless."

"He's only doing what Sir Richard and I should have done already. Henry should've retired years ago. It's madness right now, with Rhys making so many changes. It won't always be this way."

"No." Cherie sighed. "I suppose not. Well, there's no point letting the reservation go. I'll ring Sarah and ask her."

"Duncan's mum? Good idea," Alastair agreed. "I'm sure she'd welcome a night out. Going through a divorce isn't easy."

"No. I'll talk to you later, then. Goodnight."

Cherie rang off and called Sarah. She hesitated when Neil answered. "Hullo," she said. "Cherie here."

"Cherie! How are you?"

"Fine," she said. "Alastair's just backed out of our dinner reservation. I thought Sarah might like to go instead."

He paused. "I'm sure she would… but she's gone to Bath for the weekend. I'm staying with Duncan until she returns next week. So Alastair backed out tonight, did he?"

"Yes, he's working late again. Things are chaotic at the store at the moment." She glanced at the clock. "If I'm to keep our reservation, I need to go. I won't keep you."

"You're not keeping me from anything but an evening in front of the TV. Where are you off to?"

"Chez Rouge, a new French restaurant in Soho." She paused and added, "Have you had dinner yet?"

"No. On the menu tonight at Chez Hadley is leftover roast and frozen Yorkshire pudding."

"Why don't you come along?" she said impulsively. "I've never liked sitting alone in a restaurant. I feel as though everyone's staring at me, wondering who that sad woman is."

"Oh, I doubt that. I'm sure they find you intriguing… a woman of mystery." He paused. "Of course you know that if we dine together, tomorrow it'll be all over Cavendish Avenue that we're an item. Sure you want to risk it?"

Cherie didn't hesitate. "I'm quite sure," she said, and added, "Shall I meet you there?"

"No need. I'll pick you up in fifteen minutes."

"OK. See you then." With a smile, Cherie hung up the phone and retrieved the pearl eardrop once again.

Perhaps this evening wouldn't be a total waste after all.

The bill arrived on Wednesday, innocuously enough, in a thick cream envelope. Gemma Astley slit the flap, ready to add it to the pile of invoices for Rhys's approval. As she scanned the page, her eyes widened. She hurried in to Rhys's office.

He didn't look up from his ledgers and spreadsheets. Gemma noticed that the black-framed eyeglasses he wore, hideous on anyone else, looked downright sexy. "Yes, Gemma, what is it?"

"You'd better have a look at this."

He glanced briefly at the invoice she held out to him. "Yes, it's a bill. Add it to the pile and send it to accounts payable."

"Look at the amount."

He frowned and looked at it more closely. The invoice listed one Missoni tank dress, £919.27; one Roberto Cavalli sheath dress, £372.32; and one Waterford Regency crystal chandelier, shipped to Draemar Castle, County Clare, Scotland, net cost—

Rhys paused, and dropped his pen. "Good God. Eleven thousand pounds... for a *chandelier*?" He closed his eyes.

Natalie. This had to be her doing. No wonder she hadn't shown up on Saturday afternoon to look at the store's financial spreadsheets; she'd been too busy shopping for designer dresses and overpriced chandeliers.

"Gemma," he called out grimly, "get me Sir Richard on the phone. I need to speak with him straight away."

CHAPTER 12

Who would've thought London had so many bridal salons?

Caroline Dashwood stopped to slip off her shoe and rub her foot. She'd tried on and rejected a dozen wedding dresses. She was hungry and discouraged, and her feet hurt. "I'll just elope," she grumbled. "It's so much easier that way."

"Don't give up yet," Natalie scolded her older sister. "After all, it's only our first day shopping. We'll find something."

"Right now, I'd settle for a white dress from Oxfam and a glass of Chardonnay."

"Vera Wang," Natalie said suddenly. "Something simple but elegant, in cream satin—"

"We can't afford designer things any longer, Natalie," Caro reminded her. "We need to practise economy."

Natalie ignored this totally unwelcome (but unfortunately true) assessment of the family finances. "I've just had the most fabulous idea!" she exclaimed. "*I'll* buy your gown. It'll be my wedding gift to you."

"Nat, it's Saturday, and your new job doesn't start until next week, so you won't get paid until the end of the month. You can't afford a knock-off from Marks and Sparks right now, much less a designer gown."

"No, but with this—" Natalie held up a credit card "—I can afford anything. Besides, I want to do something for you. You've done lots for me, over the years."

And it was true. When thirteen-year-old Nat snuck off to Glastonbury with a friend and nearly got arrested, Caro brought her home, and didn't tell mum. She'd given Nat lifts, turned a blind eye when Nat borrowed her Barbour (until Nat ripped the lining and Caro slapped her, hard), and offered advice (most of it rubbish) and a shoulder to cry on.

Her sister deserved to have the wedding of her dreams, just as Tarquin and Wren deserved a truly fabulous wedding gift. And so Natalie would buy Caro the perfect dress.

She found it, as she'd hoped, at the Vera Wang atelier. A slim column of cream silk with a low, draped back, the dress was simple but stunning.

"Oh, Caro, it's beautiful!" Natalie breathed. She turned to the bridal assistant. "We'll take it."

Doubtfully her sister demurred. "It's far too expensive," she murmured. "I can get a perfectly nice dress off the rack."

Natalie shrugged. "It's pricey, but you only get married once." She smirked. "Well – let's hope so, anyway."

As Caro tried on the dress and a fitter made adjustments, Natalie followed the bridal assistant to the front desk and handed over her card. A minute later the assistant returned, her face looking like the back end of a horse.

"I'm sorry, Miss Dashwood, but your purchase was not approved. Your credit has been declined."

Rhys wiped his face with a towel and draped it around his neck. "I win again. Better luck next time, mate."

Ben Harris thrust his squash racket into its case and tossed Rhys a bottle of water. "Not bad for an old guy," he conceded.

"This old guy just kicked your arse." Rhys drank his water down in one go and wiped his mouth with the back of his hand. "Are we on for a re-match next Saturday?"

Ben followed him off the squash court and into the changing room. "Can't. Sophie needs help choosing wedding napkins."

"Wedding napkins?" Rhys raised his brow. "A napkin's a napkin, or so I thought. You wipe your mouth with it."

"They're to have our initials. And she wants them folded into flower shapes."

"Origami napkins... bloody hell." Rhys stripped off his sweat-drenched T-shirt and shorts and stepped into the shower. "Better you than me, mate."

Ben towelled himself off. "What can I say? It makes Sophie happy. You're coming to the wedding, aren't you?" he called out over the rush of water.

"Of course... sorry I couldn't be your best man. I just can't fit it in right now."

"Yeah, saving Dashwood and James's arse must keep you busy. How's that going, by the way?"

Rhys emerged from the shower. "With the exception of Sir Richard's granddaughter, Natalie – who thinks it's her mission in life to bankrupt the company – it's going OK, I suppose. No one likes change."

"Least of all you," Ben observed dryly. He glanced at Rhys. "Sorry it didn't work out with you and Cat."

Rhys threw his locker door open and began to get dressed. "I was a fucking idiot for ever getting involved with her." Rhys slammed his locker shut. "Have time for a coffee before I go to work?"

"Sure." Ben dropped the subject of Caterina. He and Rhys had known each other a long time, but even best mates didn't talk much about their relationships. They shared a drunken regret or two over a pint, and never spoke of it again.

As they left the squash courts and emerged onto the street, they passed a newsstand. Photos of Rhys and Natalie Dashwood featured prominently on most of them.

"Well, you and Natalie Dashwood are certainly popular with the paparazzi these days," Ben remarked, and smirked. "Sorry, but I have to ask. Are you two really—"

"Sleeping together?" Rhys finished tersely. "No." He thought of Natalie, wearing a T-shirt that barely covered her bum, and shoved the image resolutely aside. "Sir Richard and Natalie are clients. And I don't mix business with pleasure."

Ben grinned. "Maybe you should. You know what they say… all work and no play—"

"—makes Ben a dead man, if he doesn't shut the hell up," Rhys retorted.

Ben followed Rhys into the coffee shop. "Are you bringing a plus one to the wedding?" he asked as they took their cups and sat down.

"No."

"Why not bring Natalie?"

"And give the tabloids more fodder for speculation?" Rhys said, and sipped his espresso. "No, thanks."

"Isn't that what you want? It's more publicity for the store. Besides, you like her, I know you do—"

"Miss Dashwood is spoilt and selfish and has no concept of what it's like to do without. I'm sure she thinks 'austerity' is a clothing label. And even if I were – hypothetically speaking – attracted to her, a relationship between us simply can't happen. Natalie works for me, or will do soon, and Sir Richard – her grandfather – is a client."

"So? Plenty of girls marry their bosses."

"Fuck me! Who said anything about marriage?" Rhys glared at him. "Drop it, Ben, or I won't come to your bloody wedding at all."

"Just think about it," Ben said, unfazed by Rhys's outburst. "That's all. You're only inviting her to a wedding, not proposing. Now – more importantly," he added, and leaned forward, "when can we schedule a rematch? Because I'm wiping the floor with your arse next time."

Natalie plunked her bag on the counter and frowned. "Declined? That's impossible. Run it through again. Must be some sort of a-a credit glitch thingy."

The clerk handed her card back. "There's no mistake, madam. Your credit has not only been declined, the account's closed out."

"Closed *out*?" Natalie knew she sounded like a demented parrot, but what was going on? "That's impossible! I'm Natalie Dashwood. My family own Dashwood and James department stores."

"I'm sorry," the clerk said firmly. "Now if you'll excuse me—" she reached out to take the cocktail dress Natalie held, ready to whisk it behind the counter "—I'll return this to the floor."

Natalie clutched the hanger more tightly. She'd searched everywhere for the perfect dress to wear to Caro's wedding; the violet silk dress was divine, and she wasn't about to let it go. "Wait! Here—" she reached in her purse and scrabbled until she found another card "—try this one."

The clerk took it, her patience rapidly diminishing, and swiped it through the machine. She looked at Natalie with a chilly smile and handed the card back. "Declined. And closed. Sorry." She snatched the dress.

Natalie knew she wasn't sorry, not one bit. *The rude cow.*

Caroline reappeared next to her, a look of concern etched on her face. "Is there a problem, Nat?"

"My cards have all been declined!"

"Is your credit maxed out?"

"No!" Natalie fumed. "At least... I don't think so. Well, perhaps," she admitted, remembering the designer dresses she'd bought for Tark's wedding. Not to mention that Waterford chandelier... "But that's not the problem – the accounts have been closed! On all of my cards."

The ladies behind them in line edged away from Natalie as though she had a rare – and highly contagious – retail disease.

"Oh, Caro – this means I can't buy your gown!" Natalie's eyes welled with tears. "Your beautiful, perfect wedding gown—"

Caroline slipped an arm around her shoulders. "It's OK, Natty, it's only a dress," she soothed. "I'll find something off the rack, don't worry." She glared at the clerk. "Probably cost much less, too."

"I'm such a numpty," Natalie mumbled, and turned away to hide the tears spilling down her cheeks. "Everything I do turns into a disaster."

"Nat, that's not true!" Caroline looked at her in surprise and pulled her aside. "What makes you say such a thing?"

"It *is* true! Look at my relationship with Dominic – he cheated on me with his ex-wife, and he's marrying her again – today! Not that I give a toss, honestly – but I *hate* being the object of everyone's pity. My credit's a disaster. I have no career, I can't remember to put petrol in my car, and it's all over the tabloids that I'm having an affair with R-Rhys Gordon—"

"Yes, I saw the article in the *Daily Mail*."

"Even grandfather had a go at me," Natalie went on. "He ordered me to find a job, and a 'more suitable young man.' Of course he meant I should get married, to some doddering old viscount, no doubt. He disapproves of my 'bohemian lifestyle'."

"Well, Nat, he has a point. You haven't done much of anything since you took up with Dominic. Why is that?"

"I thought we'd get married, eventually," Natalie said defensively. "And I liked touring with him and the boys. It was a lark! I couldn't have done that if I'd had a job."

"Right, so you put your life on hold for two years for that half-baked rocker," Caro said, disapproval plain in her voice. "Oh, well, Dominic is about to become Keeley's problem now, till death do them part."

"I wasn't invited to the wedding."

Caroline took her arm and drew her out of the shop. "Why would you even want to go? You're well shed of him, Natty."

"I know that. And I don't *want* to go. It just hurts a bit to be excluded, that's all. We were together for longer than two years, you know."

It was true. They'd practically grown up together in Warwickshire. But of course, Dom was a different person then…

…a very different person.

Natalie followed her sister out the door. "I start work at Dashwood and James on Monday. I'll be assisting Rhys."

"Doesn't he have a PA? That terrifying redheaded girl?"

"Yes, her name is Gemma. I'll be helping with marketing, and things." She bit her lip. "I'll probably make a mess of it, like I do everything else."

"None of that, now," Caroline said firmly, and grabbed her hand. "What you need is an ice cream. Come on."

When they were settled at a marble-topped table with dishes of ice cream, Natalie dug her spoon in. "Dad used to bring us here, remember?"

Caro nodded. "I was always planning my wedding. I was determined to get married in Windsor Castle, on a pink pony."

"No, I'm sure it was a pink unicorn." Natalie smiled. As she thought of the gown they'd just left behind at Vera Wang, her smile faded. "I'm sorry I couldn't get your dress, Caro."

Caroline squeezed her hand. "Wanting to get that dress was the nicest thing anyone's ever done for me... even if you couldn't actually buy it."

The sting of having her credit declined filled Natalie with renewed anger. She'd never been so embarrassed in all her life. Well, except for the humiliation she'd endured when Dominic announced his engagement to Keeley.

Nat scowled. She knew how Cinderella must've felt when her gown changed back into rags and nothing waited to take her home but a useless old pumpkin.

And she'd bet her granny's knickers that Rhys Gordon was to blame.

Her mobile rang. She dug it out and glanced at the screen with a frown. Why was Rhys's personal assistant calling her, and on a Saturday? She pressed the answer button. "Gemma?"

"Natalie? Good morning. Rhys would like a word with you in his office, right away."

"But I'm shopping. And it's *Saturday*." Natalie paused, listening. "Indeed? Well, we'll just see about that." She tossed her mobile in her handbag and stood up. "Sorry, I've got to run. His lordship, Rhys Gordon, has summoned me to his office."

"But we're still shopping!" Caro protested. "Besides, he can't just snap his fingers and expect you to drop everything—"

"You obviously don't know Rhys." Nat pressed her lips together. "I've no doubt he's the one who's closed out my accounts, the backstabbing, number-crunching prat. I can't believe it, especially after we practically spent last Friday night together!" she finished, indignant.

Caro regarded her in alarm. "Oh, Natalie – you aren't sleeping with him, are you? I saw those photos in the *Mail*—"

"No! We're not sleeping together! Why does everyone keep asking me that?" Exasperated, Natalie grabbed up her bag, waved goodbye, and stormed off.

CHAPTER 13

Rhys pressed the intercom and scowled at his laptop screen. Losses for the past quarter were worse than he'd anticipated. Drastic measures were needed – reduced operating hours, pay freezes... and job cuts, something he'd wished to avoid.

And the fact that Natalie Dashwood was spending for England didn't help matters.

"Gemma, send Alastair in." He sat back in his chair and waited, tapping his pen impatiently against his thigh. When Mr. James arrived five minutes later, Rhys said without preamble, "The markdown budget figures are worse than you originally forecast. Come and look, please."

Wordlessly Alastair came around his desk to peer at the computer screen.

"We're losing money at a higher rate than projected. If the numbers you give me aren't good, Mr. James," Rhys said tightly as he tossed his pen down, "how can my decisions based on those numbers be of any bloody use?"

"It appears the planning budget was underestimated," Alastair agreed, his heart heavy. He knew what this meant – more hours lost to number crunching, another round of apologies to Cherie, more tension between them.

"You need to update the budget, Mr. James."

"I'll get on it immediately." Alastair added, "However, I've made plans to spend tomorrow with my wife."

"Well, you'll just have to cancel them, won't you?"

Alastair's expression hardened. "I'm afraid I can't do that, Mr. Gordon. What's really going on here?"

"I beg your pardon?"

"You seem determined to take issue with me."

"I take issue with a good company going in the crapper. You and Sir Richard haven't done a proper job keeping costs down and revenues up. I can't do this alone."

"I understand." Alastair's gaze was steely. "But responsibility for the state of the company's finances doesn't rest solely with me. This tension between us is personal on your part, Mr. Gordon."

"Yes, it's personal, because this is *your* bloody company. While you may not be the only one responsible for the years of mismanagement, you're accountable all the same – just as I'm accountable for somehow turning this fucking mess around."

"Let me remind you, I managed accounts worth millions of pounds when you were still in nappies, Mr. Gordon," Alastair said icily. "I'm also a partner. As such, I demand respect. Remember – Sir Richard and I hired you. Not the other way round."

Rhys leaned forward. "You hired me, yes. And in order to do my job, Mr. James, you bloody well need to do *yours.*"

"And so I shall," Alastair returned, and tightened his jaw, "on Monday morning. Now, if you'll excuse me—" he gave Rhys a curt nod "—I'm leaving for the day. I'll see you on Monday."

Before Rhys could form a reply, Alastair turned on his heel and left.

Rhys became aware of a disturbance just outside his office. He glanced up with a scowl to see Gemma blocking the door. No one got past her. "Just a moment, Miss Dashwood," she protested, "you can't just barge in—"

There was a minor tussle at the door. Natalie shoved past and stormed into his office, Gemma on her heels, both of them quivering with righteous indignation.

"I'm sorry, Rhys," Gemma apologised. "I tried to stop her—"

He thrust his chair back and stood up. "It's all right. Close the door on your way out, please."

"Of course." Gemma shot Natalie a scalding glare and left, shutting the door smartly behind her.

Natalie advanced on him. "How... dare... you." She threw her handbag on his desk. Spreadsheets and marketing reports flew up and fluttered down to the carpet.

"How dare *I*?" Rhys demanded. "You dare to take an attitude with me, after running up bills the size of the national debt and using company credit to do it?"

"You closed my personal credit lines," she fired back. "All of them. You can't do that!"

"I can. I did." Rhys leaned forward and planted his hands flat on the desk. His face was inches from hers. "It's my job to cut costs and turn this sinking ship around. And the first step is to stop unnecessary spending. Yours, in particular. It stops here, and it stops now."

"I've always had a line of company credit, and so have mum and Caro! You can't take it away just to save a few pounds."

"We're talking more than a few pounds. And Lady Dashwood's line of credit remains open, as does your sister's. They manage their finances with restraint. You, however, do not."

"Grandfather will hear about this!" Natalie snatched up her handbag from between Rhys's outspread hands. "You'll find yourself out of a job before the day is over, Mr. Gordon."

"Go ahead." He eyed her with contempt. "Run to Sir Richard, because you know he has a soft spot for you, and you take full advantage of it."

She gasped, outraged. "That's not true—"

"But this time, it won't work. Because your grandfather not only agreed to cut off your credit—" Rhys bent down to retrieve a wayward spreadsheet from the carpet and threw it back on his desk "—it was his idea. Now, if you'll excuse me—" he came around the desk, took her firmly by the arm, and propelled her towards the door "—I've work to do. Why don't you run along and christen a ship?"

Natalie jerked her arm free and turned to face him. "Don't you dare to patronise me! This isn't over!"

"No, it isn't." His jaw tightened. "You're on a budget, effective immediately. You can't buy a box of Weetabix without my approval."

"What? You can't put me on a budget!" Natalie sputtered. "You're not my bloody husband!"

"And thank God for that," he said acidly.

"I won't be treated like an empty-headed adolescent—"

"Then stop acting like one," Rhys retorted, and returned to his desk.

"What about you?" she snapped. "Staying at the Connaught at the company's expense, swanning all over town in your Jaguar, making a bloody fortune to come in here and boss me round, turning everything upside down—"

"I worked my arse off to get here." His face was dark with anger. "I've worked since I was seventeen, going to school at night and working during the day, and it wasn't easy. But it taught me responsibility, and it taught me the value of a pound. Two things you've yet to learn." He scowled. "I make no apologies for who I am or how successful I've become, Miss Dashwood, because it's all down to one thing. Hard fucking work."

He snatched up a sheet of paper from the blotter and thrust it at her.

She flinched. "What's this?"

"That," he informed her, "is what's known as an invoice. It lists money owed for something which one has purchased."

"You needn't talk down to me! I can see it's an invoice—"

"Good. Excellent! We've made progress." He strode, scowling, from his desk to the window. "Now look at the figure owed. Here's a hint – it's on the bottom of the page."

Natalie looked more closely at the invoice. "Well... there's one Missoni tank dress, one Cavalli sheath, and one Waterford chandelier, shipped to Scotland..." her voice dwindled and trailed away. "Oh. Eleven thousand pounds... that's rather a lot, isn't it?"

"Rather a lot, yes."

She bit her lip. Guilt was plain upon her face. "I bought it for Tark and Wren. It's a wedding gift."

Rhys turned away from the window, his hands clasped tightly behind his back, and faced her. "Did it never occur to you to send them a nice set of wine glasses instead?"

"Wine glasses would still be pricey," she informed him. "The castle dining hall seats two hundred."

"Then why," Rhys went on, gathering steam like an angry locomotive, "if you were determined to be extravagant, didn't you purchase the chandelier from Dashwood and James? We carry Waterford, you know.

You'd get a ten percent discount. And free bloody shipping!"

"That would've been immensely tacky," she said indignantly. "The chandelier would've arrived at the castle in a big D&J packing box, and Tark would've known straightaway that I used my family discount to buy his present."

"Thank God your reputation for generosity with the rich and titled remains unblemished," Rhys snapped. "Do you realise that this store – the source of what little income remains to you and your family – is on the verge of total fucking collapse?"

Natalie fixed him with a glare. "I don't believe things are so bad. You make everything look worse than it is, so you can swoop in and save the day. All hail Saint Rhys."

"Let me make this as simple as I can, Miss Dashwood." He returned to his desk and leaned towards her, his hands pressed down on the spreadsheet-covered blotter. "The store's become a vast money pit, with more outgoing than incoming. That's not good. It can't continue any longer."

"You're mistaken," Natalie said stubbornly. "D&J still make a profit. I stand to inherit a fortune—"

"A fortune?" he echoed, incredulous. "The stores haven't made a profit in months. Sir Richard has an outstanding debt of nearly a million pounds. Once that debt is paid off, *if* it's ever paid off—" Rhys sat down, punched a few keys on his laptop, and pointed to a spreadsheet with a much tinier figure than Natalie could ever have imagined "—you might inherit enough to open a chip shop in Bermondsey."

Natalie was too shocked to speak.

"Unless things change drastically, and soon," Rhys informed her icily, "Dashwood and James will close its doors... forever."

As the opening strains of Pachelbel's 'Canon in D Major' heralded the beginning of the afternoon wedding service at St. Anselm's cathedral, the bride was in a panic.

"Where's Dominic?" Keeley demanded, fraught with nerves. "It's nearly time!" The church was packed with reporters, celebrities, and well over two hundred of their closest friends; even Klaus von Richter had condescended to come.

"I'm sure he's just nipped out for a fag," her mum reassured her. "He seemed a bit edgy." *Drunk as a sailor on payday, more like*, she almost added; but there was no point in upsetting Keeley any more than she already was.

"I'll kill him if he messes this up," Keeley fumed. It'd be just like Dominic to do a runner and embarrass her in front of everyone. She gathered up her voluminous Balenciaga skirts and sailed out of the dressing room to hunt him down.

But Dominic was nowhere to be found.

Furious, Keeley stopped near the broom closet to calm her shattered nerves and decide what to do next, when she heard a strange sound. It was rhythmic and steady, punctuated with whispery giggles and the odd moan. She stared at the closed closet door in dawning horror. Surely not even Dominic would be so bold, so brazen, and on their wedding day—?

Grimly, Keeley flung the closet door open. At the sight that met her eyes, she screamed.

Dominic stood, mid-bonk with one of her bridesmaids, whose legs were wrapped round his waist. He looked over his shoulder at Keeley and blanched. "Sorry, love," he mumbled to the girl as he pulled away and fumbled with his fly. "Gotta go. The bride's just arrived."

"Oh, don't stop on my account," Keeley said icily. "By all means, continue. Finish shagging the bridesmaid. Take all the time you need, because we're not getting married, you skeevy bastard. Not today, not ever!" She turned and stalked away.

As the other bridesmaids emerged from the church and hurried towards her, clucking like outraged hens, Dominic finished doing up his trousers and staggered out into the vestibule. "Keels, wait!"

She cast a scalding glare over her shoulder. "Piss off, Dominic! It's over between us!"

"Yeah, OK, it's over, I get that." He swayed unsteadily on his feet. "Um… the thing is, what about the honeymoon, then?"

She came to a stop and turned slowly around. "What?"

"I mean, since it's paid for and all, I thought I'd take—" he paused and looked back over his shoulder at the bridesmaid, smoothing down her skirts in the closet "—er, Victoria, right? Take Vicks with me to the Maldives instead. I mean, no sense in lettin' the trip go to waste, is there—"

He never finished the sentence, because Keeley flew at him, shrieking like a demented banshee, and it took all five of the wedding party's efforts to pull her off.

Alerted by the commotion, the tabloid reporters in attendance spilled out into the vestibule, and flashbulbs began popping. Blood was in the air. The story of Keeley and Dominic's disastrous celebrity non-wedding, accompanied by lurid four-colour photos, would be the biggest, juiciest scandal to hit the UK since… well, since ever.

"I hate you, Dominic!" Keeley screamed. "I'll make you pay for this, you bastard!"

Dominic staggered back towards the broom closet, momentarily blinded by flashbulbs. *Shouldn't have drunk that entire bottle of Chivas... probably not my best idea, upon reflection...*

Too bad no one had any drugs on offer, he thought. He could really do with a bit of oblivion right about now.

Then he passed out.

CHAPTER 14

Natalie sank into one of the chairs arranged in front of Rhys's desk. "I can't believe it," she murmured, stricken. "How did things get so bad?"

He leaned back in his chair. "A lot of reasons... overspending being only one of them." He glanced pointedly at Natalie, and she flushed. "But mainly because Sir Richard wants things done as they've always been done."

"He's stubborn," Natalie admitted. "I'm sure it's hard for him, keeping pace with technology. His grandfather started D&J as a market stall in Portobello, did you know that?"

"Yes. And I know Dashwood and James received the Royal Warrant from Queen Elizabeth in 1956, which it still carries today." He drew his brows together. "That's something to be proud of. That's why it's imperative we keep these doors open."

"Grandfather despises change."

"Sir Richard is old, and tired," Rhys said. He laced his hands behind his head. "Like Henry, he should have retired long ago. But with your father gone, there's no one to take over. Of course..." He eyed her. "There's you."

"Me?"

"God knows why, but Sir Richard trusts you implicitly. You might be the answer to D&J's troubles."

Natalie stared at him in astonishment. "But I don't know the first thing about the stores, or how they're run."

"Of course you do. You told me yourself you worked here every summer, in every department." Rhys picked up his pen and toyed with it. "You can start with your grandfather. Show him some department store websites, and explain how D&J would benefit from a more robust presence on the internet. See if Dominic will do a television advert for the store, as a favour to you. I've no doubt he would."

After slamming her door in Dominic's face and telling him in no uncertain terms to piss off, Natalie wasn't so sure. "Well," she said slowly, "I know a few people. Poppy Simone, Keeley..."

"Poppy Simone... the supermodel?" Rhys was suitably impressed. "Good. We need to attract younger customers."

"Maybe she'll model a few outfits."

"That's an excellent idea. Of course we can't afford to pay anything at this stage."

"Oh, she'll do it for me," Natalie assured him. "I've known her and Pen for yonks."

"Pen?"

"Her sister, Penelope. Pen's very arty; she designs her own jewellery. Poppy's the goofy one. Perhaps I can persuade Pen to design a few pieces for the store." She beamed at him. "I never knew work could be so much fun!"

"It can be, if you're motivated. Are you free for dinner tonight?"

The unexpectedness of the question left Natalie blinking. "I... erm, yes, I am."

She imagined sitting across from him in a posh restaurant, sharing smouldering glances across a candlelit

table as he fed her prawns and ripe, juicy strawberries...
and then she imagined him leaning forward to kiss her,
murmuring, 'Miss Dashwood, you bewitching creature,
you taste enticingly of strawberries...'

"I'll have Gemma order takeaway," Rhys announced.
"Chinese, or Indian if you prefer. We can discuss our plans
in the conference room."

Her visions of candlelight and chateaubriand in a
romantic French bistro vanished abruptly, replaced with
takeaway cartons, plastic cutlery, and grease-spotted
bags. A *business* dinner... why on earth had she expected
anything more?

"I don't like Indian takeaway." She crossed her arms
over her chest, feeling suddenly like a petulant child.

"Then Chinese it is." Rhys leaned forward and pressed
his intercom. "Gemma, order in some shrimp lo mein for
me, and—" he paused to glance enquiringly at Natalie.

"Garlic broccoli," she murmured sulkily.

"—garlic broccoli for Miss Dashwood, please. And
spring rolls. You can leave once it arrives. Thanks."

"Are you quite sure we can afford it?" Nat snapped.

"I think we can just about manage." He lifted his
eyebrow. "I see you get cranky when you're hungry."

"Blimey." Natalie sat back, and despite her irritation,
regarded him with grudging admiration. "How do you do
it?"

He thrust on his glasses and begun tapping at his laptop.
"Do what?" he asked.

"Well, you... you make things happen. I came in here
ready to throttle you; instead, we're about to plan D&J's
future together over spring rolls and plum sauce."

He shrugged. "I just get on with it."

The food arrived, and once the cartons and spring rolls and packets of soy sauce and mustard were sorted, they went to work.

"Gemma said you went shopping with your sister this morning," Rhys said as he expertly wielded his chopsticks. "Did she find a wedding gown?"

Natalie squeezed Chinese mustard liberally on her spring roll. Gemma had a big bloody mouth. "She found the perfect dress at Vera Wang. I was going to buy it for her. But unfortunately—" she glared at him "—my credit was declined."

"That must've been inconvenient… and embarrassing."

"It was. I was furious, had a bit of a meltdown. Caro said the dress was too expensive anyway."

"I'm glad at least one of you is sensible." He caught the packet of plum sauce she flung at him. "Why not ask your designer friend – Pen, is it? – to recommend an up-and-coming designer to make your sister's wedding dress?" he suggested. "A bespoke gown from a rising fashion star—"

"Yes! We could feature the dress in store ads, and offer a limited number for sale," Natalie mused. "Women love limited editions. And not just wedding gowns! We could feature a new designer line each season."

"Available only at Dashwood and James," Rhys agreed.

"We could sponsor a yearly event," Natalie went on, her excitement growing, "and offer makeup consultations and makeovers, and accessories – handbags, shoes – to go with the outfits. We could have a fashion show!" She looked expectantly at Rhys, her eyes shining. "Well, what do you think?"

"I like it… dependent upon the cost, of course. Draft me up a business plan."

"Oh, it shouldn't cost much; we'd only need to put up a marquee outside, provide light refreshment, hire a couple of DJs. We'd give a real boost to a fledgling designer's career if we featured their clothing line in-store." Excitement overtook her. She was actually enjoying this! "I'll do up a marketing plan."

Rhys frowned, which meant he was deep in thought, and probably not listening to a word she'd said.

Natalie bit into her spring roll. "Tell me a bit about your brother, the one who fancies Keeley. Is he a workaholic, like you?"

"Jamie? He's a sous chef with a 60-hour work week and a girlfriend he rarely sees." He paused. "So yes, I suppose you could say he's a workaholic. But he's more likeable than me."

Natalie raised her brow. "I should hope so. You're not likeable at all."

He chucked a packet of Chinese mustard at her and said it was time they got back to work.

Hannah James flicked through the racks of new spring clothing with a satisfied sigh. A Saturday afternoon spent browsing in Topshop and H&M always cheered her up.

"Let's go somewhere else," she told her best friend, Jo. "I don't see anything I like."

As they emerged onto the pavement, Jo glanced at Hannah. "We could go to D&J…"

"No way. The clothes are vile. Even mum says they're only fit for old ladies."

"True." They passed a music store, and Jo grabbed Hannah's arm. "Han, look, isn't that… it is! It's Duncan!"

"Where?" Hannah froze and glanced through the window, past the guitars and amps and racks of sheet music, and she saw him.

He stood with a slender blonde girl, the two of them looking at a sheet of music Duncan held, oblivious to anyone around them.

"Who's she?" Hannah demanded. "I've seen her before, somewhere—" she broke off as she saw Jo's guilty expression. "You know who she is! Tell me."

Jo sighed. "Her name's Theodora, she's a new sixth-former. Her friends call her Theo."

"Come on," Hannah decided, "let's go. I don't want to see Duncan... or *Theo*," she added.

They were turning away when Duncan glanced up and saw them through the window.

"Oh God, he's seen us," Jo muttered. She waved. "Shit! They're coming out. Sorry."

"Jo, I swear, I'll kill you for this!" Hannah hissed.

The door opened, and Duncan and Theodora joined them. "Hullo, Jo, Hannah," he said, his expression unreadable. "What are you doing here?"

"Shopping," Hannah retorted. "What else?"

"This is Theo," he said. "She's a new music student. Theo, this is Jo and Hannah."

Theo's hair was looped and clipped into a messy up-do. She looked like one of those annoying French girls – chic, without even trying. She wore dangly eardrops and hardly any makeup. She didn't need it; her skin was flawless.

Hannah was consumed with jealousy.

"We're looking for sheet music," Theo said, and smiled at Hannah. "I'm singing a solo for a vocal competition, so Duncan's helping me find the proper music."

"How nice." Hannah cast Duncan a pointed glance and turned to Jo. "Let's go. We've got shopping yet to do."

Duncan glanced at her empty hands. "No luck yet?"

"Not yet," she said breezily, "but something'll turn up. It always does."

"You know," Jo confided later as they boarded the bus to go home, "Theo seemed pretty cool."

"How can you say that?" Hannah snapped. "She stole my boyfriend, Jo!"

"But you broke up! And they're not dating, they're just friends. Duncan's tutoring her—"

"Oh, I just bet he is." Hannah flung herself on a seat in the back of the bus as it lurched forward. She clutched her carrier bags on her lap and stared, unseeing, out the window. He'd probably already had sex with Theodora. She was probably on birth control—

"Well, I thought she was nice," Jo said stubbornly. "You're overreacting."

"You don't know anything about it."

"Why? Because I don't have a boyfriend?" Jo asked her sharply. "Well, neither do you, now."

"Oh, do shut up, Jo. Just leave me alone."

"No problem." Jo stood, gathered up her bags, and found a seat near the front of the bus.

When Hannah got home it was nearly seven. She closed the front door, hoping no one heard her come in. She didn't want to talk, or answer a dozen questions.

But the rustle of the carrier bags gave her away.

Her father appeared in the kitchen doorway and smiled as he saw her bags. "Bought out the store, Hannah Banana?"

"Don't call me that!" she snapped. "I'm not your Hannah Banana any more, dad, am I? I'm not six years old."

Alastair, taken aback by her outburst, frowned. "Sorry, pet, I didn't realise it bothered you so much."

"I'm sick of everyone treating me like a child."

"Well, then," Alastair told her evenly, "perhaps it's time you stopped behaving like one."

Hannah glared at him. Wordlessly she grabbed up her bags and stormed past him, up the stairs to her room.

As Cherie came into the hallway, Alastair looked at her in consternation. "I can't seem to put a foot right where Hannah's concerned these days."

She leaned forward and kissed him on the cheek. "Welcome to my world, darling," she said dryly.

Rhys took off his glasses and rubbed the bridge of his nose. "It's nearly nine, Miss Dashwood. It's time you went home." He reached for the phone. "I'll call a taxi."

"No need, I drove. I even topped up the petrol in the Peugeot before I left this morning." She got to her feet. "Besides," she added primly, "taxis are a needless expense."

"You're learning," he said, and smiled in approval. "Go home. And no more £11,000 chandelier purchases, mind."

"Don't worry," she said, and gave him a cheeky smile in return. "I've no other weddings on the immediate horizon."

He leaned back in his chair. "Unfortunately, I can't say the same. My best mate's getting married soon, poor sod." He hesitated. "Would you like to come along?"

Natalie gazed at him in mild surprise. He'd actually asked her out. She'd come in to Rhys's office, ready to thrust a nice, sharp Sabatier between his shoulder blades; now she was contemplating an invitation to go to his best friend's wedding.

How had *that* happened?

He added quickly, "I'll understand if you're busy—"

"No! I'd love to go," Natalie said, equally quickly.

"Good." He cleared his throat. "It's next Saturday afternoon. I'll fetch you at two o'clock, if that suits?"

"Perfect."

"I'll see you here on Monday, then, nine a.m. sharp. Don't be late."

"I won't. Goodnight, Mr. Gordon."

"Goodnight, Miss Dashwood."

After Natalie left, Rhys tapped a few more keys on his laptop, his thoughts elsewhere. On a pair of wide, grey-blue eyes, to be precise, and a pert little bottom encased in nicely-fitted jeans...

He closed his laptop with a snap. *Don't go there, mate*, he warned himself grimly.

He'd gone and asked Natalie to Ben's wedding. What in *fuck* was he thinking? Now he'd have to introduce her to Ben, and Sophie. At this rate, he'd be taking her round to meet his mum, and then *he'd* be the next poor sod to walk down the aisle...

Perhaps Ben was right. What he needed was a pint and a pretty distraction. A girl who looked nothing like Cat...

...or Natalie Dashwood.

He punched in Ben's number. "You'll be pleased to know I've asked Natalie along to your blasted wedding," he said without preamble. "Let's go grab a pint."

"OK." Amusement coloured Ben's voice. "Are we celebrating something?"

"The only thing I'm celebrating," Rhys said as he gathered up his briefcase and gym bag, "is the end of another work week in this financial hellhole. Hurry your arse up. I'll meet you at the Bull and Feathers in twenty. And if you're late," he added as he left the office, "you're buying the first round."

CHAPTER 15

"I'll put a pair of armchairs there," Natalie said on Monday morning, pointing to one corner of her new office, "and a desk – Sheraton – here. As for the carpet—" Natalie eyed the beige Berber with distaste "—it's got to go."

Rhys appeared in the doorway. "Good morning, ladies. What's going on in here?"

"Miss Dashwood has decided to redecorate," Gemma informed him. She lifted one perfectly arched brow. "She wants an antique desk in her office... and new carpet."

Natalie held a swatch of toile fabric against her smart new Armani jacket for Rhys's consideration. "What do you think of this for the armchairs?"

"I think, Miss Dashwood," he said shortly, "that you'll make do with the same desk and chair that everyone else has."

Her gaze swept over the grey metal desk with its sticking drawer and the lopsided wheeled chair in dismay. "But you said I might make the space my own."

"And you certainly may." He regarded her levelly. "With a plant, or a picture. Right now, I suggest you get whatever supplies you need from Gemma and get settled. Let's meet in my office in twenty minutes. We've a lot of ground to cover." And he turned on his heel and left.

"Well, that's you, off to a great start," Gemma said to Natalie with a smirk. "Come on, let's get you sorted with pens and pads and things, so I can get on with my own work."

"Thanks." Uncertainly Natalie asked, "Where does one get a latte around here?"

"Coffee's in the kitchenette. It tastes like burnt cork. If you want a latte, you have to go to the coffee shop."

Natalie followed the PA out. "I'll need a cup before I meet with Mr. Gordon." She went into the tiny kitchen and took a Styrofoam cup from the stack and poured herself some coffee. It smelled like wet dog. There was a glass jar labelled 'Coffee Fund' half-filled with pound coins.

Guiltily, Natalie eyed the jar. She hadn't any cash; but she was in desperate need of caffeine. She promised herself she'd stick in a couple of pounds the next time she came in.

Cautiously she took a sip of the brew, and nearly spat it out. Gemma was right — it was awful.

"Well, hello there."

She gave a violent start and turned around.

Ian Clarkson stood in the doorway, one shoulder resting against the doorjamb. "First day at your new job, is it?"

"Oh! Yes. Sorry, you startled me." She indicated the carafe. "I tried the coffee just now, but it's noxious."

"There ought to be a hazardous warning sticker on the pot. We can skip out and get a cup round the corner, if you like."

"Oh, no thanks," she said hastily. "I've got to get back. I'm meeting with Rhys. Gordon," she added unnecessarily.

"I mustn't keep you, then. You don't want to be late for a meeting with Mr. Gordon on your first day. And I won't tell him you didn't put a pound in the coffee jar." He winked as he lifted his coffee mug to her. "Well, I'll see you around, shall I?"

She nodded and brushed past him, uncomfortably aware of his smirking presence in the doorway, and fled.

With pencils, pens, and steno pads in hand, Natalie returned from the supply closet to her office and dumped everything on her desk. She frowned. There was something about Mr. Clarkson that unnerved her.

Her stomach rumbled. Thank goodness she had a packet of HobNobs in her desk drawer. What with getting up early and racing around to get dressed, she'd had no time for breakfast. She tore open the packet and withdrew a cookie.

The intercom on her phone buzzed, startling her, and she dropped the HobNob. It rolled under her desk. "Mr. Gordon will see you now," Gemma said crisply.

Natalie eyed the intercom with dislike and the cookie with regret, gathered up her pad and pen, and hurried through to Rhys Gordon's office.

"Let's get started. First of all," Rhys began as she sat down, "set me up a meeting with IT for next week. Monday's the best day—" he consulted his schedule "—in the early afternoon, if possible. I want to discuss our website options."

Natalie nodded and scribbled furiously.

"Next, convince Sir Richard to increase our advertising funds. We'll need to rob Peter to pay Paul in order to make it happen, but that's to be expected." He frowned. "As to that, I'd suggest we eliminate… needless expense…"

As she wrote down his instructions, Natalie's hand began to cramp. Crikey, she was ready for a break already! It felt like she'd been writing for hours. She snuck a glance at her wristwatch. It was barely nine-thirty.

She'd taken notes for all of twenty minutes. She bit back a groan. It looked to be a long, long day…

"…and don't forget to talk to Penelope about that jewellery line, and Poppy, and Dominic about the advert. We need them all on board so we can get started. I want everything ready in time for the re-launch."

"Re-launch?" she echoed, and looked up.

"Yes. Once I've implemented my changes, and the new ad campaign's in place, we're re-launching Dashwood and James in a big way, with a stellar event here at the flagship store." He leaned forward. "You'll handle the planning, start to finish. Draft me up a business plan with the details."

Natalie tapped her pen irritably against the steno pad. "Was there anything else?" *Shall I run ten thousand double-sided copies of the employee handbook? Organise the supply closet alphabetically? Clean the lav with a toothbrush?*

"Yes. After we're done here, go to the coffee shop and get me a tall espresso macchiato."

Natalie surged to her feet. "This is ridiculous!" she snapped. "You promised to treat me like anyone else, but you're treating me far *worse*! You've loaded me up with work, and it's not fair. I'm not fetching you a bloody espresso, macchiato or otherwise. I've half a mind to—"

His blue gaze collided with hers. "To what, Miss Dashwood?" he asked evenly. "Go to your grandfather?"

She glared at him. Blimey, sometimes she despised him, the smug arsehole! "No," she said through gritted teeth. "I only meant I've got to get started on your bloody *list*."

"Good. Oh, and I like my espresso strong," he called out after her as she left. "No sugar."

Natalie stiffened in the doorway, but made no reply as she stalked out of his office.

She stopped at Gemma's desk. "Mr. Gordon wants to meet with IT Monday, in the early afternoon if possible—"

Gemma didn't look up as her fingers flew over the keyboard. "Call IT yourself. I'm Mr. Gordon's PA, not yours."

"Oh. Yes. Right, I'll… do that." Natalie slunk back to her office with as much dignity as she could muster and picked up the phone. *Rude cow.* She scanned the phone list. Where was IT on the list? What exactly *was* IT, anyway? Something to do with computers, she knew that much—

"Miss Dashwood?" Rhys called out from his office. "Did you get that espresso yet?"

"On my way," she called back. *Out the bloody door, past Gemma's desk, never to return again*, she thought darkly. "I'll be right back."

By the end of the day, Natalie was exhausted. She'd telephoned, consulted, copied, fetched, and faxed until her head spun. Rhys wanted a working lunch and, since Gemma was gone for the day, Natalie picked up sandwiches from Prêt. Over tomato-and-cheese ciabattas, Rhys outlined his plans for the re-launch as Natalie scribbled madly to keep up with his thoughts.

At the end of the week Rhys approved her draft business plan for the re-launch. "Good job. I made a few changes."

"Thanks," she said, pleased. "I'll make the changes and run you a copy."

He nodded, his attention already focused elsewhere. "Make copies for the board members, too. We'll need their approval."

When Rhys's changes were made, Natalie headed to the copier. "Gemma," she called out as she passed the PA's desk, "I'll need these copies GBC bound when you get a chance."

Gemma fixed her with a withering look. "I told you before, I support Mr. Gordon, not you—"

"Mr. Gordon's orders," Natalie replied crisply. "Speak with him if you take issue. Oh, and I need them by the end of the day. Thanks!"

Natalie strode down the hallway to the copier, leaving an outraged Gemma behind. *Please let the bloody copier not jam*, Nat prayed as she entered the copier room and stacked the business plan's pages into the collator. *Now, how many board members were there—?*

"Hullo, Natalie."

She glanced up, and her heart sank. "Oh. Mr. Clarkson."

"Ian, please. No need to be so formal." He paused. "I left you a message on Saturday, by the way. Did you get it?"

Oh, crap. "Yes, I did. Sorry, I'm afraid I forgot, I've had a lot of… stuff, going on." Twelve copies, she decided, that should do it.

"Ah, yes. I've seen the tabloid stories about you and Mr. Gordon. That must be rather embarrassing."

She shrugged. "Well, it's not true, so it doesn't matter."

"So you're not?" he asked, amused. "Having an affair with Rhys Gordon, I mean."

"No," Natalie retorted, "I'm not." She pressed the start button. "Look, I don't mean to be rude, but I've a lot to do."

"Yes, I can see that." He thrust his hands into his pockets. "Are you free for lunch? There's something I'd like to discuss with you."

"How's Alexa?" Natalie asked pointedly. "She's due in a couple of months, isn't she?"

"Yes," he said. His smile remained in place. "And yes, I take your point – I'm married. Still, there's no reason we can't have lunch together, is there?"

"There's every reason!" Natalie exclaimed. She lowered her voice as someone walked past. "Alexa's my friend, Ian, and I won't do that to her. So please stop hitting on me. I'm not interested."

"You've made that very clear." He took a step closer. "But we really do need to talk. It's important. We can do it privately, or we can do it right here—"

Just then Gemma stuck her head around the doorway. "Ian, there you are. Would you be a lamb and carry some supplies to the closet for me? The boxes are quite heavy."

"Yes, of course." He gave Gemma a thinly-veiled glance of irritation and turned back to Natalie. "We'll talk another time, Miss Dashwood."

Not if I can help it, you smarmy jerk, she thought as she watched him leave.

A few minutes later Gemma returned. "Are those copies ready?" she asked crisply. "I have a few minutes to spare." Before Natalie could answer, she added in a low voice, "I heard Ian asking you to lunch."

"He makes my skin crawl." Natalie shuddered as she gathered up the copies and handed them to Gemma. "And did you notice? He doesn't wear his wedding ring, the cheating worm."

"You want to watch him. He's hit on every woman in the office under thirty – including me."

"How did you get him to stop?"

Gemma smiled. "The direct method. I kicked him in the balls."

Natalie gasped, and giggled. "You didn't."

"He couldn't walk properly for a week. It was a month before he spoke to me. But he never bothered me again."

Gemma turned on the GBC machine and together they worked in companionable silence to assemble the covers and spines for Natalie's business plan.

Dashwood and James's tearoom was festooned with birthday banners and balloons as Lady Dashwood blew out the candles on her birthday cake. "This is lovely! Thank you all so much."

Natalie's gaze swept over the faces gathered to celebrate her mum's birthday. She'd arranged for the cake to be brought out on a trolley after lunch. Although her mother complained about the calories, she tucked into her slice with relish.

Natalie took her paper plate and sat next to Sir Richard. "Did you look at my business plan for the re-launch?"

"Yes. Alastair and I were quite impressed. Rhys says you've already had some good ideas."

"Did he? I'm surprised he had anything good to say about me." She took a bite of her cake, resisting the urge to lick the frosting from her fork.

Sir Richard stirred his tea. "He finds your spending habits deplorable, Natalie, as do I."

"Oh, grandfather, don't start!" she groaned. "Let me enjoy my cake without another lecture about fiscal responsibility. I've had enough of that from Rhys." Her mobile rang, and she took it from her purse. "Excuse me."

"Natalie? Rhys. I need you at the IT meeting in ten minutes. They'll want suggestions on how to improve the Dashwood and James website; I want your input."

She bit her lip. Ian designed the company website; he'd certainly be at the meeting. The thought of spending an entire afternoon in a conference room with Ian, a knowing smirk on his face whenever he looked at her, made Natalie's stomach clench.

I really do need to talk to you. It's important. We can do it privately, or we can do it right here...

"But I'm just having cake!" Natalie stalled. "I'm at mum's birthday luncheon."

His voice warmed a degree. "Tell her I wish her a very happy birthday. Sorry I couldn't be there."

Natalie relayed the message; her mother beamed.

"This meeting may drag on," Rhys warned her. "I have a lot of recommendations. Ian and his staff will be very busy."

"Actually," she hedged, anxious to avoid the meeting, "I doubt I'll make it in time." She turned away from Sir Richard and added in a low voice, "The tearoom at D&J was booked, so we had to go to... Croydon."

"No, you didn't. You're upstairs; I saw the reservation on the schedule." He paused. "Natalie, if you don't get your arse down here in ten minutes," he added curtly, "your career will be over before it's begun." He rang off.

Outraged, she glared at her mobile before thrusting it in her bag. "Prat," she muttered.

"What's wrong, darling?" Celia Dashwood asked.

Natalie stood. "I've a meeting in ten minutes. I have to run." She bent down to kiss her mother. "Happy birthday, mum."

"Thank you, dear. I'll call you soon."

Sir Richard smiled as she leaned down and kissed his cheek. "He's not cutting you any slack, is he?" he murmured.

"No," Natalie said grimly. "None."

His eyes twinkled. "Well, we wouldn't want him to be accused of favoritism, would we?"

"No. We wouldn't want that." Natalie waved goodbye and dashed towards the lift.

CHAPTER 16

An hour later, the IT meeting ended, and Rhys stood.

"All right, Clarkson, I've seen enough." Rhys gathered up his notes. "Make the changes we discussed, and we'll meet again next week. Thanks." He clapped Ian briefly on the shoulder, glanced at his watch, and left.

Natalie moved to follow him. Relief that the meeting had lasted only an hour washed over her. And Ian hadn't given her a glance, not with Rhys's dizzying list of changes to implement—

"What did *you* think of the website?"

As if her thoughts had summoned him, Natalie looked up to see Ian standing before her. "Well, like anything, it could do with improvement," she hedged. She realised with sudden unease that they were alone in the conference room.

"How very diplomatic. Your boss hated it."

"Rhys can be a bit blunt."

"A bit blunt?" Ian echoed. "He ripped it to shreds. We'll be working late for a week straight."

"It's not personal." She gathered up her notepad and pen and prepared to leave. "That's just Rhys's way. Now, if you'll excuse me, I've got to get back—"

"Don't rush off!" he chided, and blocked her way. "I thought we might have a drink after work. Have that talk."

"Talk about what?" she asked, and cast him a wary glance. "We have nothing to say."

"Oh, I have a lot to say. It concerns your father."

Before she could reply to this cryptic comment, Rhys returned and told Natalie, "I need you to fax a release form to Dominic's publicist straight away. I have another meeting in five minutes, and Gemma's not available."

"OK." Relieved, Natalie brushed past Ian and followed Rhys to the door. "Sorry, I've got to go."

His smile didn't reach his eyes. "No problem. I'll see you around... in the kitchen, or at the copier. You never know. But I've no doubt we'll talk again."

"Natalie," Rhys said on Friday morning, "I'm meeting with Klaus von Richter at ten o'clock. I want you there."

She paused, her skinny mocha halfway to her lips. "But... he's the creative director of Maison Laroche!"

"Yes. Dashwood and James don't carry much in the way of haute couture clothing. I think it's time that changed."

Promptly at ten o'clock, Klaus arrived and Gemma showed him into Rhys's office. He wore black jodhpurs, a grey shirt, and black riding boots. Grey tinted aviators concealed his eyes.

He bent over her hand and resumed his ramrod straight posture. "I am charmed, Miss Dashwood."

"Thank you," Natalie murmured. She half expected him to click his heels together. "Would you like tea, or a coffee?"

"*Nein*," he sniffed. "I want to know what this is about."

"I'll come straight to the point, then," Rhys said when they were seated. "We'd like to carry a selection from your couture line in our flagship store."

Klaus narrowed his eyes but said nothing.

"We'll carry a selection of pieces from the clothing line," Rhys continued, "and accessories as well – handbags, shoes—"

"I am not interested." Klaus's words were flat.

"But... why not?" Natalie asked, surprised by his refusal.

Klaus's smile was chilly. "Maison Laroche is haute couture, Miss Dashwood, not ready-to-wear *Scheisse*." He made a moue of distaste. "My items are bespoke, and definitely not made for women who shop in second-rate department stores."

Natalie bridled. "Second rate? Dashwood and James is one of the oldest and most highly-regarded department stores in London—"

"Once, perhaps," von Richter said dismissively. "Not now." He lifted a brow. "Your store, my dear, is a has-been. It is dull and pedestrian. Rather like the English cuisine."

Natalie glared at him. She longed to tell him to stuff his attitude up his condescending German arse, but instead said airily, "No worries. Lots of designers want to be showcased in our store. And truthfully, we're after a younger, fresher vibe. Because let's face it, Herr von Richter, Maison Laroche of late has become a bit... predictable."

Rhys glanced at her sharply, but said nothing.

"And who exactly are these designers clamouring to be carried in your stores, eh?" Klaus sneered. It was plain that he didn't buy Natalie's story for a minute.

She bit her lip. "Well, um..." Suddenly she had a brilliant idea. "I can't disclose details until we reach an agreement. But we're in talks with Phillip Pryce." She saw Rhys's frown deepen into a scowl at her fib, but she ignored him and forged ahead. "Poppy and Penelope are already wearing some of his pieces. He studied at Central Saint Martins—"

"I know who Phillip is," Klaus said icily. "He interned at Maison Laroche, after all. I taught him everything he knows."

"Oh, I'm sure you did," she assured him. "But with all due respect, Phillip is an innovator, a fashion trailblazer… not a follower." Natalie couldn't resist adding, "Poppy Simone is modelling his clothes at our re-launch. And Dominic and the Destroyers are performing."

"Poppy? That is indeed a coup, Miss Dashwood. But as for Dominic…" he shrugged. "I'm afraid he won't be performing at your re-launch. He's signed on with Maison Laroche to represent my new men's fragrance."

Natalie blinked. "*Dominic* is your new male model?" After the Wedding-gate disaster, how had Dominic Heath landed a contract to model for Maison Laroche's men's fragrance campaign? Modelling *so* wasn't his thing.

But money was. Her eyes narrowed. Klaus must have offered him shedloads of cash. And with Keeley threatening to sue Dominic for mental anguish, he'd need every penny.

Klaus's smile was smug. "Dominic is the face of *Dissolute*. The advertising campaign launches next week."

"But he's already signed a contract to perform at our re-launch," she protested.

"Well," Klaus said with a shrug, "it's up to the lawyers, no? But there is a clause in his contract which strictly forbids him from working for another fashion house, label, or—" he paused smugly "—department store."

"But he's headlining Glastonbury next month! You don't mean he's cancelling his concert, as well?"

"No. His concert and recording schedule is a different matter altogether."

Natalie felt panic rising, and struggled to keep her words calm. "But Dominic sells tickets, and he'll pack people in at the re-launch. We had him first, and we mean to keep him."

Rhys studied Klaus. "I'm sure we can work something out, Herr von Richter." His words were polite but steely.

"Perhaps. As to the rest, I wish you luck. Phillip Pryce is talented, but untried. I hope you don't regret your decision to feature him in favour of more established talent. You are taking a great risk."

"Yes," Natalie agreed coolly, "but fashion *is* risk, isn't it? Today's unknown might be tomorrow's Next Big Thing." She sighed in mock sympathy. "But I understand your hesitation. After all, Maison Laroche quit taking risks long ago."

He stood, quivering with outrage. "You haf wasted enough of my time. Good day to you both." And he stormed out.

Rhys looked at Natalie, his brow hiked. "That went well."

"It did, actually," she said defensively. "Well, except for Dominic not being allowed to do the re-launch. We'll have to find a way around that. But at least I gave him something to think about. Phillip Pryce is younger and edgier; and Klaus is quite vain. He won't want to be outdone by his own pupil."

"I hope you're right," Rhys said, and crossed his arms against his chest. "There's just one flaw in your plan. You haven't talked to Phillip yet, have you? Or Poppy Simone."

"Well... no." She paused. "I haven't actually asked Dominic yet, either. But I will do. Today."

Rhys let out an exasperated breath. "See that you do. I'll find out what our options are if Maison Laroche holds

Dominic to his new contract." He scribbled a note on his blotter. "We'll go with your idea to use new, young designers," he added as he tossed his pen down.

She looked at him, eyes wide with surprise. "We will?"

"Yes. Screw the haute couture houses. Dashwood and James will showcase new talent instead, one or two designers each season. We'll all get plenty of publicity into the bargain." He stood up. "Do you fancy lunch? I know a great little Italian place around the corner."

"Only if you let me order for myself this time," Natalie said warily. "And promise not to criticise me over dessert."

"I promise." Rhys came around the desk and headed for the door. "I want to discuss your idea in more detail." He paused at the door, looked over his shoulder at her, and frowned. "Well, get a move on, Miss Dashwood. We haven't got all day."

CHAPTER 17

As Rhys and Natalie arrived at the restaurant, Natalie's mobile rang. She paused on the steps and glanced at the screen. *Dominic.*

"Sorry, I have to take this," she told Rhys. "Go ahead in, I won't be a minute."

"Dominic!" she hissed into her mobile as Rhys went inside. "Where are you? You're all over the tabloids—"

"Never mind that," he interrupted tersely. "I'm standing by the post box."

"What—?" Puzzled, Natalie glanced around. "I only see a dodgy-looking bloke in a cap and sunglasses—"

"That's me! I don't want to be recognised, do I?"

Doubtfully she approached him. "Dominic—?"

"Shh!" He grabbed her arm and pulled her around the corner. He slid his sunglasses down his nose. "I've really fucked things up this time, Nat."

"Oh, Dominic," Natalie said in exasperation, "why do you always do this?"

"Do what?"

"Self destruct! If something's good, you always screw it up. I mean, look at us – we were happy once, weren't we?"

He nodded.

"But you trashed it all, with your cheating and your constant lies. Now you've gone and trashed things with Keeley, too. Why?"

"Oh, well – what can I say? I fancied Victoria. And she wanted it as much as I did."

Natalie rolled her eyes. "The point is, Dominic, you don't do those sorts of things if you love someone."

"I don't love Keeley," he snorted. "We used each other for publicity." Dominic scowled. "Only now her music career's skyrocketed, and mine's gone straight into the crapper."

"You must've known you'd get caught in that broom closet, especially so close to the start of the ceremony."

"I was drunk, Nat! I only wanted a quick shag before I got myself shackled for life to Keeley."

"She's furious, you know. She's saying all manner of nasty things about you to the press." Nat smirked. "She told the *Sun* that you need sat nav and both hands to find your willy."

"Bitch." But there wasn't any venom behind it; Dominic was too gutted to muster any real anger. He sighed. "I know I humiliated her, and I don't blame her for retaliating. I don't even blame her for suing me. I deserve it."

Natalie raised her brow. "Do you think?"

"All I've got left is the ad campaign for Klaus... and he's not best pleased with me now, either."

"You're all over the media, isn't that what he wants?"

"Yeah, but it's not exactly the kind of publicity he wants for *Dissolute*."

"Look, I'm sorry for your problems, Dom, but I've got to go. Rhys is waiting."

"Don't want to keep Rhys waiting, do we?" Dominic snapped.

She thrust her mobile back in her handbag. "Look, Dominic, I don't know what to tell you, except to ride it out and hope it goes away eventually." She smirked. "Rather like your bridesmaid, Victoria." She started to walk away.

"Nat – wait." He grabbed her hand. "You're not really serious about Gordon, are you?"

She turned back and stared at him in surprise. "*Rhys?* No, of course not! We work together. That's all."

"I know when a bloke's interested in someone, Nat. And he's definitely interested in you."

"That's ridiculous," she scoffed, even as she blushed. "It's none of your business, anyway. Why do you even care?"

"I'll always care about you, Nat," he said staunchly. "We go back a long way, you and me. We were mates before we ever… well, you know. I just don't want to see you get hurt by that Scottish plonker, that's all."

"Rhys is all right, Dom. Really." Her indignation faded. "So you needn't worry." She turned to go, then paused. "By the way, I've a favour to ask. A huge favour."

"Sure. Whatever you need. Unless it involves Gordon," he added with a scowl. "Then all bets are off."

Briefly Nat explained about the re-launch and their need for a few big names to draw customers in. "And no one's more famous than you," she pointed out. "Except, perhaps, Keeley."

"What is it you want me to, exactly? Put on a show in the middle of the menswear department?"

"No, of course not! We'll film a commercial, with you kitted out in clothing from the store, and we'll do a print ad. There's to be a fashion show, and a concert – starring you."

Just then, Rhys appeared on the restaurant's steps. He cast Dominic a glacial glare. "Are you coming, Natalie?"

"I'll be right there." She turned back to Dominic. "So, are you in, Dom? Will you do it?"

Dominic cast a dark look in Rhys' direction. "I'll do it," he said, and added more loudly, "for you, Nat. Not for him."

She squealed and threw her arms around him. "Thanks so much, Dom – you're a star! Truly, you won't be sorry. It'll be great publicity for you *and* for the stores."

"Yeah, right, whatever. Just text me the date and I'll clear it with Max."

Max, Natalie knew, was his long-suffering agent. "I'll send you the details tomorrow," she promised.

"Natalie?" Rhys snapped. "If you don't come in soon, they'll be serving bloody breakfast."

"Sorry." She gave Dominic an apologetic smile and turned to go. "Thanks again, Dom," she said over her shoulder.

"Yeah, no problem. Just don't say I didn't warn you," he called after her ominously, and jerked his head in Gordon's direction.

As she went up the stairs into the restaurant, Natalie couldn't help wondering if Dominic was, perhaps, right. Did Rhys fancy her? And more to the point – how would she feel about it if he did?

Patrons crowded the bar at the Bull and Feather on Friday night as Natalie arrived at the pub after work. She went in search of a table, narrowly avoiding a baptism in stout from an over-friendly drunk.

"Are you OK? That was close."

Natalie looked up to see Holly James, Alastair's eldest daughter, standing at a nearby table. "Holly! I'm fine, no thanks to that great ginger-haired lout over there." She glared at the man who'd nearly ruined her new 'Poppy' handbag. "What are you doing here?"

"I came with a mate from work. She's here somewhere. Want to join us? There's plenty of room."

"If you don't mind hanging with us old folk," Natalie joked as she slid into a seat. "Thanks."

"What do you lot want?" Holly James called out as Nat's sister Caro, trailed by Tarquin and Wren, arrived.

"A pint. And crisps! I'm starving." Natalie hadn't eaten since her lunch with Rhys, and she'd only nibbled at a salad.

"Same for me," Tarquin said.

"Water with lemon for me," Wren, Tarquin's fiancée, said. "I'm on detox this week. No alcohol."

As they sat down, Tarquin asked, "How's your new job, Nat?"

"I've been insanely busy. Rhys runs me off my feet."

"What's he like?" Caro asked. "According to the newpapers, he's more exacting than Gordon Ramsay."

But Natalie didn't answer. She'd just spotted Rhys, leaning against the bar talking to a long-legged brunette. A dove-grey coat was draped over her arm, and a black sheath emphasised her curves; but her towering Perspex heels cheapened the look. She laughed at something Rhys said.

Nat's eyes narrowed. What was Rhys doing here, chatting up that half-baked Carla Bruni wannabe? She was plainly out of place in the Bull. The girls here wore high-street clothes, not Céline or Chanel… and they didn't wear Perspex heels.

She was probably a call girl, Natalie decided, meeting her client – Rhys – to make arrangements for a night of hot monkey sex together—

"Earth to Nat," Caro prodded as Natalie sank down into a chair. "I said, what's your new boss like?"

Natalie couldn't take her eyes away from the bar. "Rhys? He's full of… surprises." She stood up as not-Carla laid her slim, no-wedding-ring hand on Rhys's sleeve. "Excuse me."

As she wove her way through the crowd and arrived at the bar, Natalie feigned surprise. "Rhys! I didn't expect to see you here."

"Natalie." He didn't look particularly pleased. "I didn't expect to see you, either."

"Obviously." She cast a pointed glance at the brunette and waited for Rhys to introduce them. He didn't.

"Nina," she said in a soft French accent as she offered Natalie her hand. "We were just discussing business."

Right, then, even worse. She was a *French* call girl!

"Business," Natalie echoed, plainly unconvinced. "Are you a lawyer, then," she prodded the girl, "or an advertising executive?" Surely there was a reasonable explanation.

"Nina isn't a lawyer, or an advertising executive," Rhys said, and popped a crisp in his mouth. "She's a stripper."

Natalie's eyes widened. *That explained the tacky shoes, then*. She couldn't seem to formulate a proper response. *Was* there a proper response?

"I've just hired her for my best mate's stag party next Friday night," Rhys told her. "We're hammering out the details." At her look of outrage, he added, "You *did* ask."

"Yes," Natalie said tightly, "and I wish I hadn't."

Rhys smiled. "Remember what I said about making assumptions?" he murmured in her ear. Aloud he said, "Nina does a striptease act. Very tasteful, so I'm told."

"I didn't realise a striptease act could *be* tasteful," Natalie said with as much dignity as she could muster. "Well, I'd best get back to my friends. Nina," she added with a frosty nod of her head, and stalked away.

"What was that about?" her sister asked when she returned.

"Nothing. I saw Rhys, and I stopped to say hello." Desperate to change the subject, she added, "He and I met with Klaus von Richter yesterday."

Wren leaned forward, intrigued. "Klaus von Richter, the fashion designer? How did that go?"

"Not well." Natalie paused as Holly returned with drinks and packets of crisps. "Rhys asked him if we might carry his clothing line in the flagship store. He turned us down flat."

"The nerve!" Caro exclaimed. "Why?"

"He said Dashwood and James is second rate." Natalie took a long sip of her pint. "He couldn't be arsed to even *consider* letting us carry his precious couture line."

"Klaus is a prat," Holly agreed as she sat down next to Natalie. "Thinks he's Yves St. Laurent and Karl Lagerfeld rolled into one."

"Well, I shut him down," Natalie said smugly. "I told him we wanted a younger, edgier vibe, and that we were in talks with Phillip Pryce. Of course we're not – not yet, anyway – but Klaus didn't know that. He was livid."

"Who's Phillip Pryce?" Wren asked, curious.

"He's the Next Big Thing, according to Sasha Davis." Holly took a crisp from the bag. "Sasha's my boss – the psychotic bitch – and editor-in-chief of *BritTEEN*. She's right about one thing, though – Phillip's very talented. He's having a moment. There's a party at his place tonight—"

Natalie grabbed her arm. "You *know* him?" she demanded.

"He did a shoot last month for the magazine. We featured his envelope clutch." Holly sighed. "It's brilliant."

Natalie squealed in excitement. "I need to set up a meeting with him. Do you have his mobile number?"

"Hang on." Holly picked up her mobile and scrolled to a number. "Phillip!" she said brightly after a moment. "Hi, it's Holly James. Yes, the intern from *BritTEEN*. You remembered!" She beamed. "I'm sitting here with Natalie Dashwood. What? Yes, *that* Natalie Dashwood!" She covered the phone. "He knows who you are, from the tabloids."

"Oh, my God," Natalie groaned. "Tell him I'm NOT having an affair with Rhys!"

Holly obligingly relayed the info to Phillip. She giggled. "Phillip says if you're not interested, he is. He says Rhys's quite the gay icon... What? Well, Natalie wants to discuss a possible business partnership with you—"

They all heard an ear-splitting shriek of excitement emanate from Holly's mobile.

"Great Portland Street? Okay, see you soon – and thanks!" Holly said goodbye and disconnected. "The party's at his atelier, it's on right now, and we're all invited."

"Oh, Hols, thanks!" Natalie leaned over and kissed her. "You're brilliant. You've just solved my problem. Well, one of them, anyway. Now I just have to convince Phillip to partner with Dashwood and James on his first clothing line."

"It won't take much convincing. Phillip's desperate to get his own line started, but he doesn't have financial backing yet. You'll be the answer to his prayers."

They finished their drinks and stood up to leave, and Natalie's gaze flickered to the bar. Nina and Rhys were gone.

She didn't know whether she was disappointed or relieved.

They arrived at Phillip's warehouse on Great Portland Street twenty minutes later. They heard the party before they found it; thumping bass emanated from the ground floor of the three-story building. Phillip wore black leather trousers and a jacket with skinny lapels, and his trademark Louboutin trainers.

"Lovely to meet you!" he shouted at Natalie as Holly introduced her. "Come upstairs, it's quieter there."

"I've followed you in the tabloids, Natalie," Phillip said as they trooped after him up the narrow stairs to his top-floor workroom. He beamed at her over his shoulder. "I'm inspired by you. You're even on a couple of my mood boards."

She blinked. "Inspired by... me?" Blimey.

"Oh, yes. Your style – it's refreshing, very Audrey-Hepburn-meets-Charlotte Gainsbourg."

"Thanks," she managed lamely. "I do my best."

The truth was, mixing off-the-rack pieces with designer ones was a financial necessity. She had Gemma Astley – and several afternoons spent in High Street shops – to thank for her eclectic new look. Although their shopping expeditions began out of necessity – Rhys ordered Gemma to show Nat how to shop more frugally – by the time they'd hit Zara and Topshop and H&M, their frosty relationship thawed into a cautious friendship.

Phillip grabbed a bottle of champagne as his partner, Jacques, brought glasses and poured them all drinks. "Von Richter's a genius, no question. When it comes to fashion, he's not only brilliant; he's an icon." Phillip paused. "But he's also a vindictive prick. And he hates me."

"Why?" Natalie asked, surprised. "He was your mentor, after all. You interned with him at Maison Laroche, didn't you?"

Phillip nodded. "Klaus designs haute couture pieces that cost thousands of pounds. The workmanship is superb and the materials are exquisite, and there's a tiny group of women who can afford his clothing. But my fashion philosophy is quite different to his."

"I see. And what's yours?" Natalie asked, intrigued.

"I believe everyone should have access to beautiful, wearable clothes, not just the ladies-who-lunch set. There's no reason clothing can't be well made without costing the earth. Don't get me wrong, I won't put my name on a watered-down collection, and I don't like cheap clothing or knock-offs, either. If you were to sum up my philosophy, I suppose you could say I'm a fashion egalitarian."

"*Liberté*, *égalité*, Rodarte," Jacques said dryly.

"Ooh, I like that!" Phillip exclaimed. He held up his glass in a mock salute. "*Liberté*, *égalité*, Versace!"

"What Phillip hasn't told you," Jacques added, "aside from the fact that he's had a bit too much to drink, is that he dumped the old German queen to set up shop – and house – with me. So neither of us is at the top of Klaus's hit parade."

Natalie winced. "Oh. No wonder he looked like a thundercloud about to rupture when I mentioned Phillip's name."

"Don't worry, chickpea." Phillip clinked his glass of champagne against hers. "You and I will make beautiful clothes together… with or without Klaus von Arsehole's approval."

After concluding his business with Nina, Rhys accompanied her outside and flagged down a taxi. "Where to?" he asked her as he held the door open.

"My hotel room," she said, and slid inside the cab. She eyed him expectantly. The invitation was plain.

"St. Giles Hotel, Heathrow," he instructed the driver, and leaned back down. "Sorry, love. I'm... involved with someone. I'll see you on Friday." He shut the door.

"Are you sure you won't reconsider?" she pouted.

He nodded. "I'm sure. Goodnight."

"*Bonne nuit.*" With a sigh of regret, she rolled the window up, and the taxi pulled away.

As he re-entered the Bull and Feathers for a nightcap before he returned to his hotel room, Rhys's glance skimmed over the crowded interior.

He squeezed in at the bar and his glance strayed to the back corner table. A rowdy group of young men and women had replaced Natalie and her friends.

As he signalled the publican for his bill, Rhys couldn't decide if he was disappointed or relieved that she was gone.

Relieved, he told himself as he paid his tab. He could've had Nina in his bed tonight; that was plain enough. She was young, certainly, and lovely, and undeniably willing; but there was one thing she wasn't.

She wasn't Natalie.

CHAPTER 18

"Are you free on Sunday?" Rhys asked as Natalie gathered up her things to leave the following Friday.

She picked up her sunglasses. "I might be," she said cautiously. "I can't work, if that's what you're asking— "

"I never work on Sunday. It's my ironclad rule. No, I wondered if perhaps you'd go shopping with me."

Her eyes widened in surprise. "You're asking me to go shopping? You're always on at me for overspending!"

"It's my money we'll be spending, not yours."

"Well in that case, OK. Why are we shopping, anyway? And what are we shopping for?"

"I've bought a flat in Covent Garden. I'm tired of living out of a hotel room." He thrust his hands in his pockets. "I'm staying at the Connaught as part of my hire agreement; but it's costing the company money it can't afford. I thought about what you said." He raised a brow. "I won't be accused of 'swanning about' at the company's expense."

Natalie dropped her gaze and fiddled with her sunglasses. "I shouldn't have said that—"

"No, you're right. I can't help Dashwood and James if I'm contributing to the problem. Besides, I need a base of operations in London, and the flat's a good investment." He scowled. "It ought to be, it's costing enough. But to answer your question—" he paused "—I'll need furniture, and lamps, and cookware. And I haven't a clue where to begin."

"OK," she agreed. On impulse she added, "What are you doing next Friday night? If you fancy dinner at mine, I'll make you my famous spaghetti Bolognese."

"I wish I could. But I've got something on next Friday – it's the stag night for my mate, Ben. His wedding's on Saturday. You said you'd go," he reminded her.

"Oh yes, the stag night," Natalie said, her heart sinking. "Of course you can't miss that... or Nina's *tasteful* striptease act." She sniffed. "At any rate, I've better things to do than make dinner for someone who'd rather eat peanuts and swill beer while he watches some tart wriggle out of her knickers."

Rhys stepped closer, and his dark blue gaze lingered on her upturned face. "If I were really the oversexed Neanderthal you seem to think I am," he murmured, "I'd say I'd much rather see you wriggle out of your knickers. But I'm not... and it wouldn't be proper. So I won't say it." He grinned and turned to go. "I'll see you Sunday, Miss Dashwood. Wear your best knickers."

On Saturday morning, the promise of coffee lured Cherie James off the rainy street and into her favourite bookstore.

She closed her umbrella and tucked it in her handbag, deciding to treat herself to a book first, then coffee. She needed a nice, soapy novel with lots of sex... something with a plot about a neglected wife and her workaholic husband...

Cherie couldn't bear the thought of spending another Saturday alone, with Alastair working, and Hannah at her gran's.

She was just reaching out for the latest Katie Fforde when she heard her name. "Neil!" she exclaimed, surprise mingled with pleasure as she turned around. "What are you doing here?"

He smiled. "The same as you, I expect."

"Ah. Feeling sorry for yourself and looking for a good, trashy novel, then?"

Neil laughed. "No. I'm with Duncan. He's looking for a Chopin biography for a revision paper."

"You mean he came here willingly?" she said, and raised her brow. "I have to drag Hannah in, kicking and screaming. I, on the other hand, can't resist a good book."

"Nothing wrong with that." He smiled, and his eyes crinkled at the corners. "Thanks again for inviting me to join you for dinner. I enjoyed it."

"I did, too. The food was lovely."

"It was certainly a vast improvement on leftover roast and frozen Yorkshire pudding."

Cherie went to the magazine shelves, where she studied the tabloids on offer. "I imagine you're glad to be back home, now that Sarah's returned."

"Oh, she's still in Bath. Her mum had complications after the surgery, so I'm staying on with Duncan a bit longer. Tonight we're going out to dinner. You're welcome to join us."

"That sounds lovely. But I've already taken out lamb chops." She took her items to the till and turned back to Neil. "I'm headed upstairs for a coffee if you'd like to join me."

"I would. A cup of coffee sounds perfect."

"As long as you don't mind if I peruse the tabloids while we have our coffees," she warned him.

"Not at all." He smiled. "Reading the tabs is my second-favourite guilty pleasure."

She raised her brow. "Oh? And what's the first?"

"I'll never tell." He tucked her arm inside his, and together they went upstairs to the café.

Alastair James glanced at his wristwatch as he entered the bookstore. He had just enough time to buy a gardening book for Celia Dashwood's birthday – a few days late, unfortunately – and get a coffee and croissant to go before he returned to work.

He bought the most expensive gardening book on offer and headed upstairs. What a pity that Dashwood and James had such vile coffee in the employee lounge; sad that one had to go to Starbucks or Costa just to get a decent cup—

He saw the two of them as soon as he entered the café. They shared a table, each with a coffee and Cherie with a croissant. They laughed about something; then Cherie reached out and touched Neil Hadley's arm.

Alastair felt a knife-twist of jealousy.

"Excuse me, please," a woman behind him said politely.

With a start, Alastair murmured an apology and moved aside.

He turned away before they saw him, his heart heavy and his appetite gone, and returned to his office, and the pile of work waiting on his desk.

That evening, Cherie settled herself in bed next to Alastair and opened her new book. The dishes were put away and the kitchen restored to order, and Alastair had even managed to come home on time for dinner.

Poor man, Cherie reflected as she glanced at him, propped against the pillows with his glasses perched on his nose as he read the *Guardian. He's tired. He works six days a week, after all—*

As if he sensed her gaze, Alastair looked up. "I went to the bookstore this afternoon to get a book for Celia Dashwood's birthday." He put the paper aside. "I saw you there."

Cherie slanted him a quick look. "Oh? You should have said. I ran into Duncan's father while I was there. We had a nice chat… and a cup of coffee."

"I'm surprised you didn't think to mention it to me."

She stiffened. "Why on earth would I? I don't tell you when I run into Emily Morley at Waitrose—"

"Emily Morley isn't an attractive divorced man, is she?" he asked tightly.

"Oh, Alastair, you can't be serious!"

"When I couldn't take you to dinner a few weeks ago, you said you'd ask Sarah." He took his glasses off and laid them aside. "You went with Neil instead. I know, because Hannah told me that he came to pick you up."

"Only because Sarah was gone, and Neil was at a loose end. You bailed on me! You can't think there's anything going on between the two of us—?"

"I wonder that you didn't mention it to me before, that's all," Alastair said. "Should I be concerned?"

Cherie shut her book with a crack. "I can't believe we're having this conversation! Neil and I are friends, nothing more. If you don't believe me—" she reached over and snapped off the bedside lamp "—there's really nothing more to say, is there?"

She rolled over without waiting for an answer, and lay awake for some time before she fell into a troubled sleep.

Early Sunday afternoon, Rhys picked Natalie up in his XJ9 and headed for Knightsbridge.

"This is much nicer than the motorbike," Nat observed as she settled back in the Jaguar's soft leather seat. "What sort of furnishings do you like, anyway? Modern? Traditional?"

"Modern, but nothing too bizarre. And no chintz."

"And what's your budget?"

He shrugged. "I don't have one. The sky's the limit… but I draw the line at £7,000 sofas or £50 cheese graters."

"OK, then. First," Natalie decided, "let's go to Conran. They have very reasonably priced cheese graters."

They found a sofa at Habitat that they agreed was perfect – a chocolate brown sectional with lime green toss pillows. Rhys bought a pair of lamps as well, and a coffee table of burled walnut. Then it was on to Peter Jones for cookware and glasses, and an overpriced gastro pub for lunch.

"Tell me," Natalie ventured as they returned to the car, laden with carrier bags, "what goes on at a stag party? I've always wondered."

Rhys shrugged. "The usual, I suppose." He opened the boot and tossed the bags in.

"And what's that? Does a girl jump out of a cake? Cavort naked on the table? Grab your tie and pull you into a back room?"

He held the door open for her. "Not at any of the stag do's I ever went to. Perhaps I'm going to the wrong ones."

"You can't tell me there aren't girls," she persisted as Rhys settled himself behind the wheel and started the engine.

"Of course there are," he conceded, "but they usually have surgical enhancement and two inches of slap on their faces. Not my thing at all. Mostly, we get drunk and tell dirty jokes, then reel home to sleep it off. And pay the price the next day with a whacking great hangover."

"That's bloody stupid."

"It *is* bloody stupid. About as stupid as the typical hen night, I imagine."

Nat smiled wryly. "Touché. So – when do I get to see this flat of yours?"

"No time like the present."

In Covent Garden, he turned onto Endell Street and came to a stop in front of a row of buildings. "Mine's that one," he said, and pointed to a white-fronted, three-storey house in the middle. "Three bedrooms, three levels, a private terrace, and..." he lifted one brow "...two reception rooms."

"Oh, Rhys," Natalie breathed as they entered the first-floor reception room, "it's gorgeous!" Two floor-to-ceiling windows faced the street. A black marble fireplace was the focal point at one end, built-in bookcases at the other.

The kitchen consisted of gleaming black marble counters and stainless steel appliances, with a breakfast bar and room for a table in the window nook. And the private terrace needed only a wrought iron table and chairs and a few potted plants to make it perfect.

"And fairy lights," Natalie added as she surveyed the terrace. "You've got to have fairy lights."

"I'll add them to the list." Rhys studied her, amused. She was as excited as a child on Christmas morning. He realised with a start that his attraction to Natalie had grown from appreciation of her physical beauty, to something more.

He liked the way she widened her eyes whenever she was surprised or indignant. He liked her quirky personality, and – despite the fact that she frustrated the hell out of him at times – he liked the challenge she presented.

Rhys allowed himself to imagine sharing this flat with her, imagined her walking around in that T-shirt he liked, and nothing else. With a sigh, he shoved the thought aside.

Natalie Dashwood was Sir Richard's granddaughter, and off limits. He'd invited her along to Ben's wedding; that was enough. Further involvement would only lead to trouble. They made a good working team. He didn't want to complicate things with a relationship.

Hadn't he learnt his lesson with Cat?

"I should go," Natalie said finally. Shadows stretched across the terrace as she made her way back to the French doors. "Tomorrow's Monday, after all."

"At least let me buy you dinner," Rhys said. "I owe you that much, after you helped me furnish my entire flat." He paused. "Not to mention, you found me a reasonably priced cheese grater."

She smiled. "OK. I'm starving, anyway. I'm ready to eat my shoe."

"I think," Rhys said as he took her arm and led her downstairs, "that we can do a bit better than that."

CHAPTER 19

As they lingered over a delicious dinner of chilled courgette soup and butterflied mackerel at The Harwood Arms on Fulham Road, Natalie let out a sigh of contentment.

"That's the best meal I've ever had," she told Rhys.

"I'm glad you liked it." He reached for the bottle of Pouilly-Fuissé and topped up her glass. "I always try to come here when I'm in London."

"Where else have you lived?" she asked. "Besides Edinburgh."

He shrugged. "I worked in New York for a couple of years. Then Amsterdam, Brussels, Verona…"

She pouted. "That's not fair! I've lived here all my life, and I've only ever been to Scotland, to visit Tark."

"Ah, yes. Owner of the Scottish castle and the £11,000 chandelier." Rhys leaned back. "What was it like for you, growing up?"

Natalie shrugged. "Fine, I suppose. We lived in Warwickshire, and the house always needed roof repairs or a plumber. There was always damp, and limescale on the taps and toilets. The water came out brown and smelt like rotted eggs."

Rhys raised a brow. "Sounds disgusting."

"It was. Dad once hung out a sign on the gate: 'Limescale Peeling'. Her smile faded. "It was his little joke." She paused. "He killed himself. When I was ten."

"Yes, I remember it was in all of the papers. I'm sorry."

"Mum found him. He'd taken an overdose of sleeping tablets. Halcion. Half the bottle was gone." She toyed with the stem of her wine glass. "People think it's an easy way to die, but it's not. It's... horrible."

Rhys was silent.

Natalie lifted her glass and took a long sip. "The hell of it was," she said finally, "we never knew why he did it."

"There were no business problems? No signs of depression?"

She was silent, remembering.

"Why do those men from the newspapers take pictures of us, mummy?" she'd asked, when a firestorm of flashbulbs erupted as their car emerged through the gates and turned onto the road one morning.

Her mother, attention focused on the road ahead and her mouth set in a grim line, replied, "It's nothing to worry about, darling. Your father owns a very famous department store."

"But other people own famous department stores," Natalie persisted, *"and they don't have their picture in the newspaper. And they're taking pictures of us, not daddy—"*

"Never mind," Lady Dashwood said sharply. "Do sit back and be quiet, Natalie, or you and your sister will be late for school."

"Natalie?" Rhys prodded gently.

She shook her head. "No. My father seemed fine, if a bit preoccupied sometimes. He worked long hours. The stores were doing really well then. So well, in fact, that after the repairs were made to the house, he let Caro have a horse.

He got her a black mare, Sheba." She smiled briefly. "I was insanely jealous."

"Crazy for horses, were you?"

"Like most ten-year-old girls." Natalie hesitated. "The day before he died, he and I had a falling out. He said I couldn't have a horse until I was older. I was furious, told him I hated him, that he was the worst father in England. In the world." Her throat tightened.

"Natalie," Rhys said, his face creased in concern, "please, don't upset yourself—"

"I told him I wished he were dead." She raised her eyes to his. "And the next day, he was. My words – those horrible, childish, awful words – God, you can't imagine how many times I've wished I could take them back. But of course, I can't."

He covered her hand in his. "You were a child," he said softly. "You can't possibly blame yourself."

"But I did. For the longest time, I thought he'd killed himself because of me. Of course he didn't; but I still wonder, sometimes, if what I said to him wasn't the tipping point."

"It wasn't your fault." His voice was low but firm. He leaned forward. "You may never know why he killed himself. But whatever it was, it had nothing to do with you."

She gave him a tremulous smile. "I think you missed your calling. You should've been a psychotherapist."

"In that case," he said as he signalled for the waiter, "I prescribe a crème brûlée, or perhaps cake. A good pudding can set anything right."

When they emerged from the restaurant an hour – and one shared slice of chocolate torte – later, a gaggle of reporters and the unwelcome flash of cameras greeted them.

"Bloody hell," Rhys muttered. He took Natalie's arm and drew her closer. "Someone must've seen us and tipped the press off. Let's talk to them for a moment."

"Can't we just make a dash to the car and ignore them?" she whispered as she surveyed the handful of reporters.

"Lesson number three," he murmured. "Always make nice with the press when you can. Chin up, darling. We're on."

Rhys skillfully deflected half a dozen rapid-fire questions, making jokes and answering queries without revealing anything of consequence. He told them that he and Natalie were working together to re-launch the Dashwood and James department stores, and promised the British public would love the results.

"Natalie, you stated that you and Dominic Heath are finished. How do you feel about that?" a female reporter asked.

"Relieved," Natalie replied, and they all laughed. "Of course, I wish Dominic the best of luck. But I've moved on."

Rhys held up his hand to stop the flow of questions. "Thank you all. Goodnight."

"Rhys," Natalie said in admiration as they drove away, "you were brilliant. They loved you."

He snorted. "Trust me, the press is fickle. We'll see in the morning, when the story hits the tabloids."

CHAPTER 20

The next morning, after stopping to buy a copy of the *Mail* and the *Mirror* on her way to work, Natalie returned to her car and threw the tabloids on the passenger seat. She'd read them once she got to work.

She was halfway down Pont Street when her car died.

As she gripped the steering wheel in disbelief, the Peugeot shuddered, let out a rattle, and ghosted to a stop. The car behind her let out an impatient – and very loud – honk. Natalie stared at the instrument gauges in consternation. The car's lights were still on; the bloody petrol tank was *full*.

But the engine refused to turn over.

She tried to start it again, but nothing happened, only a horrible sort of grinding noise that didn't augur well.

Another couple of horns joined the one behind her. A man got out of the car behind and strode up to the driver's window.

Cautiously she lowered the window.

"Are you out of petrol?" he asked.

She shook her head. "No. My car just… stopped."

"Then we'd best get you out of the road."

As she remained at the wheel to steer, he pushed the little car out of harm's way and called a towing service.

"They'll be along shortly," he informed her. "It's probably your fuel pump."

Natalie thanked him and offered to pay for his trouble, but he waved her thanks off and returned to his car.

Good thing he'd declined, because thanks to Rhys' ridiculous budget, she had no cash. She'd just spent her last five quid at the newsagents.

Ten minutes later, a tow truck arrived and the ginger-haired driver jumped down and hitched the Peugeot's bumper to a winch. "Where're we takin' 'er, then?" he asked.

"Dashwood and James department store," she replied, "on Sloane Street. There's a car park nearby."

He opened the tow truck door for her. "Right. In you go."

Fifteen minutes later the Peugeot was unhitched and deposited in a parking spot. "That'll be fifty quid," Ginger-Hair announced as he wrote up the bill and handed it over.

Natalie blinked. Fifty quid! "I haven't any cash on me," she apologised as she scrabbled in her handbag for her wallet, "but you take credit cards, don't you?"

He nodded. "All the majors."

As she withdrew her wallet and flicked through dozens of plastic-encased credit cards, Natalie suddenly remembered that Rhys had closed all of her accounts. Every. Single. One.

Oh, crikey. She had no way to pay the tow-truck driver.

"Erm, you see, the thing is," she told him with a nervous smile as she dropped the wallet back into her handbag, "I haven't any cash on me, and my credit's been cancelled."

As his genial face darkened into a scowl, she added quickly, "But I have money upstairs, in my – in my desk." Of course she didn't. She'd just have to borrow fifty quid from the petty cash box and pay it back later. "If you wait here, I'll be right back—"

"Oh, no." He eyed her grimly. "I'll just go wif you."

Wordlessly she nodded, and together they went inside and took the lift to the fourth floor.

"Wait here," Natalie told him as she left him in the conference room. "I'll just be a moment."

"Awright. But if you're not back in five minutes—" he drew his bushy red brows together "—I'll come and find you."

Her heart thrumming, Natalie assured him that wouldn't be necessary and hurried off to her desk. At least it was early; no one else was in yet. She jerked open the bottom left drawer with trembling hands and took out the petty cash box.

She lifted the lid. A neatly stacked pile of notes was rubber-banded together. Her fingers were unsteady as she counted out fifty quid and laid it on the desk. She'd borrow the money from mum or grandfather and put it back later, just as soon as she paid off that nasty ginger-haired bloke—

"You're in early this morning, Natalie."

With a start, she looked up to see Ian Clarkson standing beside her desk. "Ian! You scared me to death. What are you doing here?"

"I came in early to work on the website. I might ask you the same question." He eyed the cash box inquiringly but said nothing.

"I had... things to do." Her glance strayed involuntarily to the tabloids and the packet of licorice allsorts she'd tossed on the blotter.

Ian reached down and picked up the *Daily Mail*. "'Rhys Gordon and Natalie Dashwood share an intimate dinner at the Harwood Arms. Full story and photos on page two'," he read aloud. He looked at her and smiled. "Well, well. You and Gordon are getting quite cosy, aren't you?"

Natalie put the cash box back and slammed the drawer shut. "It was a business dinner, Ian, nothing more. Now if you'll excuse me—" she pushed back her chair and stood "—I've things to be doing, and a tradesman waiting to be paid."

But he didn't move. He glanced at the fifty quid in her hand and said softly, "It looks to me as though you're stealing from petty cash. Is that what you're doing, Natalie?"

She stared at him, her eyes wide with unease, and opened her mouth to say no, of course not. But nothing came out. The words froze in her throat.

"Don't worry." His voice was a gentle caress. "Your secret's safe with me."

And as his eyes met hers, dark with amusement, she felt dread settle itself in her stomach.

"You don't know what you're talking about," she retorted. "Of course I'll put the money back. Not that it's any of your concern," she added as she picked up the money and moved to brush past him.

"You're right, it's not." He caught her arm. "But Rhys wouldn't approve of you nicking money from the cash box. Sir Richard would be shocked. His own granddaughter, a thief…"

Natalie stared him down. "Let go of me."

But his hand only tightened on her arm. "I could have you charged with theft." His lips curved upwards. "I caught you in the act, you naughty girl."

Real fear twisted inside her. "Are you threatening me?"

Ian dropped his hand from her arm. "Oh, nothing so dramatic. Don't worry, Miss Dashwood. Our little secret."

"'Scuse me," came the belligerent voice of the tow-truck driver from the doorway, "but I want me money."

"I'll leave you to it," Clarkson murmured. "Your tradesman is getting impatient," and with a wink, he turned away and strode back to his office.

After she paid the driver and made herself a cup of tea, Natalie returned to her desk and sank down in the chair. Her hand shook slightly as she lifted the mug of tea to her lips. Ian Clarkson was a nasty piece of work under any circumstances; but now that he'd caught her taking money from the cash box, he had something – no matter how trivial – to hold over her.

She glanced at her watch and saw it was already half eight. Gemma and Rhys would be in soon; she hadn't much time. She reached for one of the tabloids lying on her desk to have a quick look, and nearly choked on her tea.

Over a photo of herself looking up adoringly at Rhys, the headline trumpeted, "'I've Moved On," Natalie Says.' She let out an indignant gasp. They'd made it look as if she'd moved on, all right... straight into Rhys Gordon's arms!

"Crikey!" she said out loud. "So much for being nice to the press."

"You've seen the tabloids." Rhys, briefcase in hand, stood in the doorway.

She looked up, startled. "Yes. You're in early."

"I've a lot on today. So, you didn't like the stories?"

"No! They took an innocent comment and twisted it round to mean something entirely different," she fumed.

"Welcome to the British media," he said dryly.

Natalie frowned and held out a copy of the *Guardian*. "Oh – have you seen this? Klaus has made a deal with H&M to do a one-off line of clothing." She looked at Rhys in outrage. "After he turned us down flat!"

Rhys took the paper from her and scanned the article. "Did you notice the date his collection debuts?" Grimly he tossed the paper aside. "It's the Saturday of our re-launch."

Nat regarded him in dismay. "He wants to steal our thunder!"

"Not to worry. We won't let him." He turned to go. "Oh, before I forget… I've scheduled a ten o'clock with Phillip Pryce. I want you there. He's keen to talk to us about a possible joint partnership."

Natalie pushed the tabloids aside. "Good, I told him to contact you. He's amazing. He's not very well known yet, but all the fashion magazines say he's the next Olivier Theyskens."

Rhys looked at her blankly. "Who?"

Natalie sighed and turned on her laptop. "Never mind." She typed 'mechanics, London SW1' into the search engine. "Do you know anything about cars?" she asked as he disappeared into his office.

"A bit. Why?"

"Mine died on the way in. And no, I wasn't out of petrol."

"It just quit? Were the lights and radio working?"

"Yes, but the engine wouldn't turn over."

"Then it's not the battery. It sounds like the fuel pump needs replacing."

Natalie's heart sank. "How much will that cost?"

"You'll have to call a mechanic."

A mechanic meant more money, money she hadn't got. She felt a headache brewing…

"Here." Rhys returned to her desk and handed her a credit card and five quid. "Use this. You can pay me back later." He glared at her. "And you're not to charge anything else."

Her eyes widened. "Thanks. I won't. And I *will* pay you back. What's the cash for?"

"Fetch me a coffee when you get sorted," Rhys called out from his office, "a tall espresso macchiato—"

"—strong, no sugar," she finished, and grimaced. "How you can drink it without sugar is beyond me." Natalie stood and grabbed the five pounds and thrust the memory of her unpleasant run-in with Ian Clarkson firmly aside.

It was only fifty quid, after all. She'd borrow the missing money from mum and return it to the cash box this afternoon...

...just as soon as she'd been to the coffee shop to fetch Rhys his bloody espresso macchiato.

CHAPTER 21

The meeting with Phillip Pryce began in the conference room promptly at ten a.m.

"The British public love Natalie," Phillip enthused to Rhys, Alastair, and Sir Richard. "They can't get enough of her, or of her—" he cleared his throat "—affair with Rhys Gordon." He winked at Natalie.

"Ah, yes," Rhys said inscrutably, "that." His glance flickered to Natalie, who was blushing furiously, and back to Phillip. "Complete bollocks, of course. Good thing Dominic's Wedding-gate has eclipsed us in the tabloids for the moment."

Natalie forced a smile as laughter erupted at his words, but inside she was indignant, and a tiny bit hurt. How quickly Rhys dismissed their time together yesterday! Had it meant so little to him?

After all, she'd never told anyone about her guilt over her father's death, only Rhys. She pressed her lips tightly together and forced her attention back to the discussion.

"I've designed my line around Natalie," Phillip was saying. "It's targeted at young, on-trend women, available exclusively at Dashwood and James." He looked expectantly from Rhys to Sir Richard and Alastair. "If you gentlemen concur, that is."

Rhys leaned forward. "What price point are we talking about? Your pieces are normally rather expensive."

"About half the cost of my regular line... but still consisting of quality construction. The average secretary or bank teller can afford my clothing, even on a budget. And," he added after a dramatic pause, "I want Natalie Dashwood to represent the new line. She'll model in all of the print ads."

Natalie blinked. "But... I've never modelled in my life."

Phillip waved his hands in dismissal. "No matter, you're a natural! Slim, gorgeous, photogenic – and everyone adores you. They'll flock into D&J to buy my clothes, I assure you."

Sir Richard drew his brows together. "We need to see some examples of your work before we reach a decision, young man."

"Yes," Alastair, who until then had been silent, agreed. As he toyed with his pen, his gaze strayed to Rhys. It struck him, not for the first time, that Gordon reminded him of someone... but the thought, elusive and quicksilver, evaporated as quickly as it formed. "Let's see your ideas, Mr. Pryce."

"Of course. Jacques, please," Phillip called out. His assistant strode to the easel with a portfolio under his arm.

The sketches he displayed were exciting – a striped bateau top paired with a flounced skirt of floral and plaid; a vest with a crested pocket worn over a full-sleeved poet's shirt. Each sketch was more original and appealing than the one before.

"Have you a manufacturer in place?" Rhys asked.

Pryce nodded. "Everything will be produced in Nepal at half the expense of my regular line. What do you think?"

Rhys tapped a finger to his chin. "I like it. Sir Richard, Mr. James? Natalie? Are you all agreed?"

They voiced their shared enthusiasm for the idea.

"Have you any samples made up?" Natalie asked.

"Yes." Jacques disappeared and returned with a rack of clothing. Phillip passed the garments around for inspection. Natalie examined the flounced skirt. The seams were finished, and the plaid repeats matched perfectly. There wasn't a fault to be found in the quality or construction of any of the pieces.

"All right, Mr. Pryce," Rhys said, "it looks like we have a deal. We can't pay much up front – after all, you're new, and we're taking a risk – but you'll get a generous share in the profits, provided the collection sells well." He glanced at Natalie. "And I have it on very good authority that it will."

Natalie returned to her desk and realised with surprise that it was nearly noon. "Gemma," she called out, "where're you going for lunch?"

"I'm not," Gemma called back crossly. "I have a gazillion copies to run for Rhys. They have to be ready by the time he gets back, and the bloody machine keeps jamming."

"Oh. Well in that case, I'll eat what I brought, then. Unless you want me to go out and get you something...?"

"Thanks, no. I started a new diet today – all the green tea, kale, and cabbage soup I want. Unfortunately, it's turned my pee chartreuse."

Natalie left her desk and went into the kitchen. As she bent over to retrieve her lunch from the fridge, she heard someone come in. *Oh, sod's law, please let it not be Ian—*

"Hello, Natalie." Amusement coloured his voice. "You're looking very well."

She straightened abruptly and turned to see Clarkson lounging in the doorway. "Sorry, I haven't time to chat." She clutched her lunch bag. "I'm working through lunch."

"Well, I won't keep you, then. When can we talk?"

"We've nothing to talk about," Natalie snapped, and moved to brush past him.

His hand shot out to grip her arm. "You need to be a bit nicer to me, Natalie."

She didn't like the subtle threat in his voice. Her heart beat as rapidly as a hummingbird's wings in her chest. "What's that supposed to mean?"

"It means," he said as he glanced down the hall and drew her back into the kitchen, "that you and I are having lunch at that new bistro round the corner. My treat."

She yanked her arm free. "I've just told you, I haven't time for lunch, and I *don't* go out with married men, especially not when they're married to my best friend—"

"You'll make an exception. Or I'll go to Rhys and tell him you nicked fifty pounds from petty cash this morning."

"I'll tell him myself," she retorted, "right now. And I'll tell him why I did it. My car broke down, and I hadn't any cash or credit cards on me to pay the tow-truck driver. I'll return the money this afternoon."

"But you haven't returned it yet, have you?"

Natalie met the dark amusement contained in his eyes. "I won't be threatened, Ian. In fact," she added, "Rhys might find more fault with *you* for attempting to blackmail me. It might even be enough to get you sacked." She brushed past him.

He gripped her elbow and said in a low voice, "I have information about your father, Miss Dashwood. He committed suicide when you were ten, didn't he? Shame, that."

Natalie paled. "Yes, it's common knowledge that he killed himself. Why would you even bring that up?"

"Is it common knowledge that he embezzled money from Dashwood and James to support his mistress?"

She stared at him. "What? I don't know what you mean! My father would never do something like that—"

"Oh, but he did. And I have proof." He smiled, gratified to see the uncertainty and fear flicker across Natalie's face.

"What sort of proof?"

"I see I've got your attention at last. We'll discuss it further tonight, at the Connaught, since you can't make it for lunch. Shall we say, eight o'clock, in the Coburg bar?" His smile faded. "We'll have a drink, and finish our conversation."

Natalie took a deep, shuddering breath. "What do you want? Why are you doing this? You bastard—"

"That's not very nice, Natalie. You have a lot to learn about how this all works."

And he released her arm, turned on his heel, and left.

CHAPTER 22

When Natalie returned to her desk, Gemma was still at the copier. Rhys, back from his meeting and immersed in a phone call at his desk, didn't look up as she passed his office door. Her hand shook slightly as she sat down and picked up the phone to ring her sister.

"Caro, hi, it's me. Yes, I'm fine." She paused. "I can't make it for dinner at yours tonight, sorry. Work stuff, and my car's died. I'll call tomorrow. Yes, I promise. Love you."

As she hung up the phone, Natalie knew she'd be unable to concentrate on work. Ian and his threat hung over her like a poisoned cloud, unseen and noxious. She closed her eyes and considered her options.

She could tell someone... but who? Certainly not grandfather; his health was fragile at best, and the news that she was being blackmailed might provoke a heart attack. She loved him too much to take that chance. And mum – did she even know about this mess of her father's creation? Did she know he'd had a mistress?

Somehow, Natalie doubted it.

Her fingers tightened on the paper clip she held. She needed to calm her racing thoughts and think this through. Ian hadn't provided any proof of his allegations. Perhaps there *was* no proof, and he only wanted to get back at her, because she'd turned him down one time too many.

But even as the thought occurred, she discarded it. Ian was too sure of himself. He had something, something damaging. But what? The thought of sitting at a table, sharing a drink with him, made her skin crawl. Tonight, all he wanted was a drink with her, and to trot out his terms and conditions.

But next time... what then? How far might Ian take this? And more importantly – what did he want?

With sudden resolve, Natalie stood up. She'd march into Rhys Gordon's office right now, and she'd come clean about borrowing fifty quid from petty cash to pay the driver. He'd understand. And after all, she reasoned, it was Rhys's fault she had no money, what with his bloody unreasonable budget, and freezing all her credit cards.

Besides, the guilt was making her miserable. She made her way to Rhys's office and knocked on his doorframe. "Do you have a moment?"

He glanced up. A pair of black-framed glasses perched on the end of his nose; he took them off and tossed them aside. "Of course, come in. Good job on snagging Phillip Pryce and his collection. You were right – he's good. I'm no fashion expert, but even I was impressed."

Natalie blinked, surprised. Praise, coming from Rhys Gordon? Was the sky about to fall? "Thank you."

"You put in a lot of effort to get him." He leaned back in his chair. "Your contacts – Poppy and Penelope Simone, Phillip, even that manky little sod, Dominic – have proven invaluable. Are they all on board for the re-launch?"

She nodded. "All except Poppy – I haven't talked to her yet. But I know that she'll do it."

Rhys frowned. "You'd best ask her soon. I'm sure she's busy." He eyed her quizzically. "What was it you needed, Miss Dashwood? Did you get your car seen to?"

She stared at him, her thoughts churning. *Tell him the truth, tell him...* But when she opened her mouth to speak, nothing came out.

"Natalie?" A trace of impatience entered his voice.

"You were right, it was the fuel pump. It's in the shop. I-I wondered if I might leave a bit early today."

"Not feeling well?"

"I've a headache." It wasn't a lie; she really did have a headache, thanks to her car, the tow-truck driver, and Ian. "I can't seem to concentrate."

"No problem. There's nothing that can't wait until tomorrow."

"Thanks." She turned to go.

"Natalie," Rhys said, and waited as she turned back around, "you've worked hard these last few weeks. Well done."

"I've enjoyed it," she said, and realised she meant it. She liked the challenge, the teamwork... the satisfaction of knowing she'd contributed to helping remake Dashwood and James into a coveted place to shop once again. "I'm learning a lot. And I'm far too busy to buy anything."

"That's a good thing," he said dryly. "Perhaps—" he stopped. He'd been about to ask her out again. She was refreshing, like a Pimm's Cup on a hot summer's day. But she was Sir Richard's granddaughter, after all. And Rhys was her boss. Bad enough that the tabloids were already abuzz with their so-called affair...

He had no desire to make the bloody tabloids right.

"Never mind," he said abruptly. "I'll see you tomorrow, then, Miss Dashwood."

Natalie pushed through the store's revolving doors a short time later and emerged on the front steps. Thank goodness Rhys had let her go early; she felt better already, with the sun warming her face, and throngs of people laden with carrier bags, hurrying past on the crowded Knightsbridge pavement—

"Leaving early, Nat?"

Startled, Natalie looked up to see Alexa Clarkson, Ian's very pregnant wife, coming towards her. "Alexa, hi! Yes, I'm skiving off this afternoon. Are you here to see Ian?"

She nodded and held up a plastic bag, redolent of curry. "He's working late tonight, lots of changes to the website. He's quite put out. So I've brought him a late lunch. Or an early dinner, depending upon your perspective."

Guilt stabbed Natalie. *Working late, my arse*, she thought darkly. "Yes, he's got a lot to do, after his meeting with Mr. Gordon," she said.

"And how is the infamous Mr. Gordon to work with?" she asked with avid curiosity. "I've read all about you two in the *Mail*, you know."

Natalie blushed. "Oh, crikey, Alexa, there's nothing going on. It's publicity, for the store."

"Wouldn't mind a bit of publicity like that for myself," Alexa confided. "I'd shag Rhys Gordon in a minute."

Natalie laughed. "God, I've missed you. Things have been so manic lately. We really need to get together before the baby comes." She raised her brow. "I suppose a wine bar's out, though."

"Afraid so," Alex agreed ruefully as she glanced down at her stomach. "This little bugger's very particular about his likes and dislikes. Even though I'm allowed a bit of wine now and then, it gives me terrible indigestion."

"'His'?" Nat queried. "Are you having a boy, then?"

"Don't know. Don't want to know, I want to be surprised. But I've a feeling it's a boy. He kicks like a punter for West Ham."

"Seriously, though, you look beautiful. Pregnancy suits you."

Alexa snorted. "I look like a right cow, but thanks for the compliment. I'll take any I can get, these days." She moved the bag to her other hand. "Is Ian in, then?"

Natalie's smile faded. "Yes."

"I'd best get this curry upstairs before it goes cold. I'll call you next week," she promised. "We'll meet up for lunch, or something."

"I'd love that. Let's do it."

They hugged, and Natalie watched, smiling, as Alexa made her way up the steps and pushed her way through the revolving doors.

Her smile faded. Alexa was her oldest, dearest friend. They'd been through so much together – the loneliness they'd shared their first year at boarding school, boyfriend trouble, Nat's father's suicide – that saying nothing to Alexa while Ian played out this strange little game made her feel conflicted, ashamed – and guilty as hell.

She hated Ian for doing this, not just to her, but to Alexa. *You need to be nicer to me, Natalie.*

Abruptly she shook her misgivings aside and made her way to the Underground station. The hell with Ian Clarkson, she decided. This was probably all just a tempest in a coffee carafe, or whatever that old saying was.

Nevertheless, as she touched her Oyster card to the reader and sat on a bench to wait for the next train, her thoughts remained troubled.

CHAPTER 23

The Connaught hotel was quiet when Natalie arrived that evening. She'd tried on and discarded a dozen outfits, determined to dress as primly as possible, before settling on a knee-length skirt and a black, high-necked cashmere sweater. She gripped her Chanel clutch tightly and walked into the bar.

She paused in the doorway. The walls were panelled in soft green, and low armchairs upholstered in jewel-toned velvets were grouped around tables throughout the room. A fireplace burned invitingly at one end. Ian, seated at a corner table nearest the fire, stood as she approached.

"Natalie! Please, sit down." He indicated a chair upholstered in ruby velvet.

"Do I have a choice?" she bit off as she tossed her clutch on the table and sat down.

"You always have a choice. You've obviously made yours."

A waiter materialised at her elbow. "May I bring you a drink, madam?"

"Sparkling water, please," Natalie told him. She was keeping a clear head. "Thanks."

"I'll have another martini." Ian nudged the bowl of olives towards her. "I like it here. It's very intimate." His gaze drifted over her. "You look lovely tonight."

"I saw Alexa earlier." Natalie met his eyes. "She brought you lunch. Chicken curry, she said. How was it?"

He smiled, unperturbed. "It was good, but a bit cold."

They were silent as the waiter brought their drinks. When he left, Natalie took a sip of her Perrier and met Ian's gaze. "Let's cut the crap, Ian. What is it you want?"

"You do get straight to the point, don't you?" He smiled and thrust an olive in his mouth. "I like that. First, I'll give you a bit of history. My stepfather was the senior accountant at Dashwood and James." His words were measured. "He was blackmailing your father. It's one of the reasons why the company began its unfortunate tailspin into the red... and why your father eventually killed himself."

"And you know this how, exactly? You were just a child then, like me."

"I didn't know then, obviously. I overheard a conversation my father had. It made no sense at the time, but I remember that afterwards, I got a new bike. And we no longer went for a week's holiday in Blackpool. Instead, we went to Belize, or Ibiza – much nicer than spending a week on a rocky Cornwall beach."

Natalie pressed her lips together but said nothing.

He smiled briefly and moved his whiskey glass, leaving a damp ring on the table. "I was going through some boxes in storage, and I found a stack of my stepfather's old Dashwood and James account books... books that implicated your father in an embezzlement scheme. It cost a lot to keep a mistress, even then. The affair was all over the press, mostly gossip and innuendo, and a couple of photographs of your father and his mystery woman – but it stirred up a hornet's nest of trouble for him, and for the store. Shame, to dredge it all up again."

Natalie recalled her classmates' whispers, the neighbours' curious glances, the unexpected and frightening pop of flashbulbs that plagued their family outings when she was nine.

Now, she understood. Her father's affair must have become public knowledge. Poor mum.

She met Ian's eyes. "I'll go straight to the police and tell them you're blackmailing me—"

"And I'll go to the tabloids." His smile was cold. "Your father's name will be smeared like shit all over the media." He sighed in regret. "And with the store's re-launch just around the corner, it's not the ideal time for a scandal. Is it?"

Natalie felt as if the ground were dissolving beneath her feet. He'd planned this all, right from the start.

She raised her eyes to his. "What is it you want?" she asked finally, her voice a thread. "Money? A new car?"

"God, no. How pedestrian." He leaned forward. "I want something else altogether, Natalie." He paused. "I want you."

She let out a sharp, slow breath. "You're married, your wife is *pregnant*, for God's sake—"She stopped. He was plainly unmoved by her moral outrage.

He shrugged. "We're not close, Alexa and I. We go through the motions. I married her for financial rather than romantic reasons. It was all rather calculated on my part, I suppose."

"And does Alexa know that you don't love her? She's expecting your first child, Ian!"

His expression darkened. "I never wanted children. That was her doing, getting pregnant to trap me into staying with her. But it doesn't matter." He leaned forward. "I'm divorcing her, Natalie, and I want to start over, with you. We can get married." He glanced up. "And then you can recommend me for a partnership in Dashwood and James."

As the muted sounds of conversation and clinking ice cubes went on around them, Natalie stared at him. "Ian, that's absurd! If you divorce Alexa – your very *pregnant* wife   to take up with me – Sir Richard's granddaughter – he'd never give you a partnership, nor would Alastair! Surely you must see that we'd both be social outcasts."

"I don't care what people think. I'm used to their contempt."

Your mum's gone, Ian. He still remembered the landlord's wife, with her East End accent. *She's scarpered, and left the rent unpaid. Looks like it's a foster home for you, poor mite… but I reckon it's for the best. Your mum was a whore and no mistake. Taking in men at all hours… while you slept in the next room… not right, it weren't.*

His early life had been a succession of foster homes, each one more abusive and loveless than the last, until he'd been adopted at thirteen by his stepfather, and things had improved.

But love? Love was still a foreign concept. Although he understood it in the abstract, it meant nothing to him.

"I understand Dashwood and James in a way no one – especially not Rhys Gordon – ever will," Ian went on, his words measured. "I know what needs doing, and I'm not afraid to do it. I'll start by sacking the nonperformers and re-staffing. I'll insist that your grandfather retire. He's past it, you know. He's not capable of keeping up with technology or making the changes that need to be made."

"That's not true," Natalie protested, her face flushed with anger. "Grandfather's as sharp as a carpet tack. He looks on his employees at the store as family."

"Family," Ian said, and let out a mirthless laugh. "Business is business, Natalie, and sentiment only clouds the bottom line. I can make Dashwood and James something to be proud of again, given half a chance. And you're going to help make it happen."

"No." Natalie's voice was low but firm. "Rhys is already turning the store around. I'm not going to *marry* you, Ian! Alexa's pregnant, and she's my dearest friend."

"I'm sorry, but 'no' isn't an option, Natalie," he said. "Not if you want me to keep your father's past quiet."

He reached out to touch her face, and she flinched. "At the moment, I only want you to be a bit more... accommodating. That's not so much to ask, surely?" He leaned forward and laid his hand over hers on the table, and she moved to pull it away.

"Natalie," he murmured as he tightened his grip on her wrist, "listen to me. When I ask you to lunch, or out for a drink, I expect you to smile nicely and say 'yes.'" He let go of her hand and sat back. "I've given you a lot to think about. I'll let you mull it over." He drained the rest of his whiskey and stood up. "We'll talk again soon."

He withdrew several notes from his wallet and threw them on the table. "Goodnight, Miss Dashwood. I'll be in touch."

Rhys Gordon was tired. It had been a long, mind-numbing day filled with one meeting after another. As he headed back to the Connaught, he decided to duck into the bar for a drink.

"Whiskey, please," he told the barman. "Neat." He turned around to survey the room as he waited. His gaze drifted to a corner table near the fireplace and skidded to a stop.

Natalie Dashwood and Ian Clarkson sat at the table, talking in low voices over drinks. Rhys frowned. Natalie had her back to him, but he recognised her at once. He knew that Chanel clutch she always carried, tossed on the table between them.

What was she doing here, having drinks with Clarkson?

"Your whiskey, sir," the barman said.

"Thanks." Rhys turned back to pick up his drink from the bar and took a slow, measured sip. Then he returned his attention to the corner table.

Were they having an affair? He discarded the thought as soon as it occurred. To his knowledge Natalie had never encouraged Clarkson. On the contrary, she went out of her way to avoid him.

Why, then, was she having a drink with him in a quiet corner of the bar? Rhys took another sip of whiskey and watched as Clarkson reached out to touch her face. Natalie flinched.

Rhys's fingers tightened around his glass. He wanted to fly off the barstool and throttle Ian, but steeled himself to remain seated. Ian stood and tossed money on the table, and strode towards the door. Rhys turned back to the bar and waited until Clarkson passed. Then he glanced back over his shoulder at Natalie.

She sat alone at the table, staring down at her drink with a blank look.

Rhys set his glass down on the bar and stood up. Screw staying out of it. He'd get to bottom of this, and find out what that slimy bastard had said to Natalie...

His mobile rang. He glanced down at the screen. Phillip Pryce. *Bloody hell.* He had to take the call, it was important. "Phillip. Did you talk to the manufacturers? When can they start production?"

When Rhys finished his call a couple of minutes later, he turned back to the table in the corner.

Natalie was gone.

CHAPTER 24

"Don't forget, Alastair," Cherie warned him as she picked up the bedside phone that evening, "I've made reservations at Le Caprice next Friday. It's Hannah's sixteenth birthday."

"Yes, of course," he said, frowning distractedly as he scanned the latest overhead figures. It wasn't a pretty picture. "I'll add it to my calendar."

A week later, Friday night arrived. The phone rang. Cherie, dressed and ready to go to dinner, picked up.

"Neil!" Pleasure warmed her voice. "You're still coming tonight, I hope?"

"Yes. What time?"

"Seven-thirty. Alastair's running late. He'll meet us at Le Caprice."

"In that case, why don't Duncan and I pick you up?"

And so it was arranged. The pique Cherie felt towards Alastair remained, increasing exponentially when he phoned midway through the starters to say he'd be there soon.

"If I don't make it by dessert," Alastair told her, "go ahead and give my present to Hannah."

His present – a heart pendant with a tiny diamond suspended in its centre – was tucked in the jeweller's box in her handbag.

The mains arrived, and then dessert, but Alastair did not.

Cherie was tight-lipped with fury. It was one thing for him to cancel dinner with her; but to miss his daughter's sixteenth birthday celebration, after she'd reminded him several times – well, it was unforgiveable.

"Don't blame Alastair," Neil said later, as he stood in the foyer of her house. "He has a lot on his plate. I'm sure he's under a great deal of pressure—"

"Don't make excuses for him," she said tightly. "He missed Hannah's birthday dinner completely."

"Hannah doesn't seem to mind." She and Duncan had gone upstairs to see her new laptop. Neil followed Cherie into the kitchen and watched from the doorway as she made coffee, slamming drawers and cabinet doors in the process.

"Hannah," Cherie informed him shortly, "is far more forgiving than me."

Neil reached in the fridge for the milk. "Why don't you go with me to my book club meeting on Monday? I need an ally. The hostess is quite formidable."

"I'm surprised you have time for a book club," she said as she took down cups.

"I work from home two days a week. It's been a boon since the divorce; with Sarah in Bath, I get to spend the time with Duncan."

She poured the coffee. Hannah would leave soon, too, and the thought filled her with indescribable sadness. "Is Duncan ready for university?" she asked as she handed Neil his coffee.

He looked at her as he took the cup, and saw the telltale brightness of her eyes. "Cherie," he murmured, his face etched with concern as he set the cup aside and reached out to touch the tear that slid down her cheek, "don't cry," and then he was holding her, kissing her, and she was kissing him back...

Cherie heard Hannah and Duncan coming downstairs, and pulled abruptly away. "That shouldn't have happened. I'm sorry."

His eyes met hers. "I'm not."

Hannah and Duncan entered the kitchen, and Neil told his son it was time to go, just as Alastair arrived home.

"Thanks, Neil," Cherie told him, struggling to keep her composure as she walked him to the door. "For everything."

"Yes, thanks for bringing my girls home," Alastair added, and clapped Neil – a bit too hard? – on the shoulder. "Sorry I missed the festivities."

Neil avoided looking at Cherie. "It was my pleasure."

Alastair shut the door after them and turned to Cherie. "Darling," he began, his expression contrite, "I'm so very sorry—"

"Don't apologise to me," she said coldly. "Apologise to Hannah."

"I will, of course. I've made lunch reservations for the three of us at The Wisteria tomorrow. I finished everything up tonight so I'd have tomorrow cleared for my favourite girls."

The Wisteria, still a trendy West End dining spot, was crowded when Alastair and Cherie arrived for Hannah's birthday lunch the next day. She glanced at the other diners, mostly tourists and WAGs and Eurotrash, and saw a black-leather-clad young man in one corner, deep in conversation with the German fashion designer, Klaus von Richter.

"Look, mum, it's Dominic Heath!" Hannah whispered excitedly.

"Oh, yes." She gazed at the pop star with narrowed eyes. Although she was sorry he'd dumped Natalie Dashwood so publicly, Cherie was glad they'd split up. Her goddaughter deserved much better than that dreadful, hedonistic rock singer with his spiky black hair and tattooed arms. She shuddered.

As they were seated, Cherie felt a vague sense of disappointment. Of course, her negativity reflected her anger at Alastair more than any deficiency on the part of the restaurant. Still, her gaze was disapproving as she studied their surroundings. The gold fleur-de-lis wallpaper and rococo Victorian fittings, while perfectly suited to a bordello, looked tired and in need of refurbishment, Cherie decided.

Rather like her marriage.

"Why are we here?" Dominic demanded. "This place is naff."

"Shut up," Klaus snapped. "You're a spoilt rock star who normally dines on... what? Yellow M&Ms and Jack Daniels?"

"Krug and sushi," Dominic said indignantly. "Give me *some* credit." He waved aside the menu the waiter held out and said, "Just a lager, mate. Thanks." He glanced at Klaus. "What did you want to talk to me about, then?"

"I'm pleased with your work so far," Klaus said after he'd ordered a glass of Pinot. "Despite the wedding contretemps with Keeley—" he grimaced " —everything is going well. The commercial airs on television starting tomorrow."

"Yeah? Good, great," Dominic said dispiritedly.

"What's wrong? You should be happy."

He shrugged. The truth was, he was surprised to find that he missed Natalie. Yet he'd screwed things up so badly, there was no way she'd take him back. Not even his brand new Mascrati could make up for that...

…but it went a fair way towards easing the pain.

Klaus paused as their drinks arrived. After a moment and another sip of his Pinot Gris, he said, "I have a confession to make."

"Oh, yeah? What's that?"

He eyed Dominic. "I know who you are."

"Of course you know who I am," he retorted. "I'm Dominic fucking Heath, rock star."

Klaus shook his head and took another sip of wine. He leaned forward. "You misunderstand me. I mean that I know who you *really* are." His lips unfurled into an unpleasant smile. "You're Rupert Locksley, heir to the sixth Earl of Earnsley."

Dominic paled and nearly choked on his lager. "I don't know what you're on about, mate. I was born on a council estate in Swindon. My old man's a retired accountant—"

"You were born in Exeter," Klaus went on, as if Dominic hadn't spoken, "to Lord and Lady Locksley. You attended Eton. You speak fluent French and passable Latin."

Dominic snorted. "You've got a good imagination, mate. The only French I know is *pommes frites* and Dom Perignon, and I went to the local comp until I did a runner at sixteen."

"You're very convincing, but I know better," Klaus said. "I pay my staff well to unearth these facts. Of course, no one need know about your aristocratic background but us. Our little secret."

Dominic eyed him warily. "What do you mean?"

"I like to have insurance, Mr. Heath. Or should I say, Rupert?"

"Don't call me that," Dominic snapped. "It's not my name."

"Ah, but it *is* your name. I have proof. And since I know your secret, I suggest you do as I ask. Because if you don't,

I'll make sure your fans find out. They'll be outraged to learn you're one of the very aristos they so despise. You might have trouble filling seats at your next concert." He smiled unpleasantly. "So I suggest you humour me."

"Humour you how, exactly?" Dominic leaned forward and lowered his voice. "If it's me you're after, I don't swing that way, mate. I like the girls, myself."

Klaus waved his hand dismissively. "I have no interest in you. I want..." he leaned forward "...Phillip Pryce. Find out all you can about his new collection for Dashwood and James."

"Phillip Pryce? Who's he?"

"He's a fashion designer, you idiot!" Klaus hissed. He set his glass down with a crack, and Dominic flinched. "Talk to your ex-girlfriend, Natalie. Tell her you want to get back together, tell her you want to marry her – I don't care. Do whatever it takes to get information about Phillip from her."

"I *do* want to get back with her," Dominic said morosely, "but that's over with, now."

"Trust me, Dominic," von Richter said, his expression hard. "If you want something badly enough, no matter what it is, you find a way to get it."

"Are you having fun?" Sophie Harris asked Natalie the following Saturday. The wedding ceremony was over and the reception at Somerset House was in full swing as Sophie adjusted the bodice of her wedding gown in the ladies' lounge.

"I am." And she *was* enjoying herself. Ben and Sophie were lovely people, and obviously very much in love. "I can see why Rhys and Ben are best mates. Ben's a great guy."

"So is Rhys," Sophie said. She hesitated. "I know we only just met, and perhaps I shouldn't say this... but I'm

glad you and Rhys are together. You're just what he needs."
She looked quizzically at Natalie in the bathroom mirror.
"You *are* together, aren't you?"

"I'm not sure," Nat admitted. "I don't think so."

"Well, if Rhys likes you enough to introduce you to his
best mate," Sophie said with a smile, "then it's safe to say
you'll probably be meeting his mum next."

Natalie blushed. "Oh, I doubt that! I'm just his plus one,
that's all. Tell me, is Rhys... involved with anyone?"

"Not that I know of," Sophie answered. "He was in a
relationship for a couple of years. But it ended badly."

"What happened? If you don't mind my asking," Nat
added.

"Of course not. He met Caterina in Italy, in Verona. She
was married to a business associate. Which suited Rhys
perfectly," Sophie added as she reapplied her lipstick,
"until Cat made the mistake of falling in love." She
dropped the lipstick back in her clutch. "When he broke
things off, she threatened to kill herself."

"Good heavens," Nat murmured. "What did he do?"

"He tried to reason with her... but she wanted her cake –
Rhys – and her husband Paolo, too."

"So what happened?" Natalie asked her, curious.

"Rhys ended things, and she swore she'd kill herself. He
said he wouldn't be held hostage to her dramas any longer,
and quit his post in Verona to return to England. Cat slit her
wrists... and nearly died. Her husband found out about the
affair and blamed Rhys. It was very public, and very ugly."

Two of the bridesmaids came in just then, and Natalie
focused her attention on the mirror. She topped up her
lipstick, lost in thought. Poor Caterina...

...and how harsh of Rhys, to treat her so cavalierly.

Nat followed Sophie back to the reception and joined Ben and Rhys at the bar.

"So," Sophie teased Rhys as he handed her and Natalie each a champagne cocktail, "when can we expect an invitation to *your* wedding?"

"When I sprout wings out of my arse," he retorted.

"You can't let a couple of bad relationships turn you into a bachelor forever," Sophie chided him. "Right, Natalie?"

"If Rhys wants to die alone in his flat with nothing but a big-screen TV and a shelf full of Bang and Olufsen to keep him company," she said tightly, "then let him."

"Don't forget lots of beautiful women," Rhys added, his eyes gleaming, "to share my lonely, high-tech flat."

"Let me know if you need a flatmate," Ben joked. He held up his hands as Sophie glared at him. "Just kidding, love."

"Oh, Rhys has plenty of women at his disposal," Natalie informed them, "including a French stripper." She fixed him with a frosty stare. "Why stop at a chocolate bar when he can have the entire candy shop?"

"There are plenty of beautiful women in the world, Natalie," Rhys responded evenly. "Don't use them as a yardstick to measure yourself by. Because there'll always be someone more beautiful."

Her grey eyes flashed. "You arrogant prat, how dare you—"

"Just as there are plenty of better-looking men than me," he added, "as hard as that is to believe." He pulled Natalie, resisting, into his arms. "The only woman in this room I'm remotely interested in is you." He leaned forward and brushed her lips with his. "Would you like to dance, Miss Dashwood?"

Natalie, responding despite herself to the warm persuasion of Rhys's lips, felt her resolve disappear along with her anger.

It was usually awkward, kissing a man for the first time. You bumped noses, or made do with a hurried brush of lips, as if to get the 'first kiss' officially over and done with.

But it wasn't like that with Rhys. It wasn't like that at all.

The moment his lips touched hers, so firm and self-assured, Natalie's irritation melted away and turned into... need. She needed more of his mouth on hers, more of his arms around her. Her hands slid up and over his shoulders, revelling in his strength and his scent and his annoying, captivating, head-spinning... Rhys-ness.

"We're not dancing," Natalie breathed against his lips, and blushed.

His arms tightened around her. "Oh," he murmured, and raised a quizzical brow, "are we meant to be dancing?"

She knew she ought to slap that self-confident smirk from his face and walk away. And she would do, she promised herself as he lowered his mouth to hers once again...

...just as soon as this kiss – and this dance-that-wasn't-a-dance – ended.

"Get Rhys," Ben murmured to Sophie in grudging admiration as he watched him kissing Natalie on the dance floor. "Good save."

"You'd best devise a save of your own," Sophie informed him tartly, "because if you don't ask me to dance again soon, you're spending your wedding night alone on the hotel sofa."

CHAPTER 25

Phillip Pryce flung Natalie's dressing room doors open and surveyed the contents with approval. "Impressive! *Vogue's* fashion closet has nothing on yours, chickpea."

Natalie sat on her bed with a sigh. "I can barely afford Oxfam, now. Not since Rhys put me on a budget."

"Well, we'll have pots of money after the ad comes out and my clothing line hits the stores." Phillip riffled through her clothes rack. "With all this designer stuff, we won't need a stylist for the shoot," he declared. "We can do it ourselves."

Jacques brought in some carrier bags stuffed with accessories and set them down on the floor. He sniffed. "We can't afford a stylist with our tiny budget, anyway. Here's the giveaway stuff from *Marie Claire*."

Phillip waved a hand impatiently. "We won't need it, now."

"Wait!" Natalie cried, and sprang up as Jacques moved to take the bags away. She peered inside one and began pulling things out — a Ferragamo belt, a Marc Jacobs handbag — and said incredulously, "Who's Marie Claire, and why is she giving all this fabulous stuff away?"

Phillip rolled his eyes. "*Marie Claire* the magazine, silly girl. When the accessories closet gets cleared out, the goodies get thrown on the giveaway table. I have connections." He winked at her. "I'd planned to bring this stuff to the shoot tomorrow, but with your closet, we won't need it." He waved a dismissive hand at the carrier bags. "Keep the lot."

Natalie squealed and clutched the bags to her chest.

"These metallic flats are perfect for the flounced skirt," Jacques announced from within Natalie's closet, and set them aside. "And this wide leather belt goes perfectly with the poet's shirt."

"I've never done a fashion shoot," Natalie said, and chewed at her fingernail. She jumped as Phillip swatted her hand away.

"No nail biting," he scolded. "Early to bed tonight, and no alcohol. We start at eight a.m. tomorrow. And don't be late. Time is money on a photo shoot."

"Especially this one, when there *is* no money," Jacques added.

"Should I do my own makeup and hair?" Natalie asked.

"No," Phillip said. "My friend's a makeup artist, and very good. This is Tamara's first proper job, so she's doing it gratis. If things work out I'll throw more work her way. Jacques and I are styling the outfits ourselves."

"I'm terribly nervous," she admitted. "There's so much riding on this. I can't screw it up."

"You won't screw it up, chickpea." Phillip looked at her with steely resolve. "We won't let you."

"Ever worked in a stockroom before?"

Hannah James glanced up. Today was her first day of work at the store. A tallish boy with streaked blond hair – "Jago," he'd told her – eyed her sceptically. His eyebrow was pierced.

"No."

He took down one of the boxes stacked on the shelf. "Watch and learn, princess. Take a box off the pallet, scan it—" he demonstrated with a scan gun "—and throw it in that bin." He grinned. "Think you can handle it?"

"Don't be ridiculous." She snatched up a box. "A wombat could do this." She frowned as she struggled to operate the scan gun. "It doesn't seem to be working."

Jago grabbed the gun, scanned the box, and threw it in the bin. "Easy."

Hannah snatched the gun back, determined to get the hang of it. "I just need a bit of practice, that's all."

"Oh, but a wombat could do it," he reminded her. "Too bad *you* can't."

"It's my first day," she snapped, and glared at him. "At any rate, I don't plan to work here very long."

"Too right," he agreed, "'cause you'll be sacked before the week's up."

Hannah reached for another box. "We'll see about that."

"Reckon we will, Posh." He chucked an empty box into the waste bin.

"My name is Hannah. Hannah James," she added pointedly.

"I know who you are, Hannah *James*." He shrugged. "You're Mr. J's daughter. And you're just as much of a pillock as I expected you'd be."

Hannah glared at him, but he turned away to grab another box.

"So – you got a boyfriend?" he asked.

"No." She glanced at him, then away again. "Not that it's any of your business, but we broke up."

"What happened? Did he dump you?"

"No! We decided to see other people. He's going to university in the autumn."

"Ah." Jago nodded as he scanned a stack of shirts. "He dumped you."

"Shut *up*." Hannah eyed him. "What about you? Don't tell me *you* have a girlfriend…?"

"No. I go to school at night, don't have time."

"Oh? What are you studying?"

Jago hesitated. "Cookery. I want to be a chef."

"You need restaurant experience to be a chef."

"I work Saturdays in my uncle's chip shop, washing up and clearing tables." He grinned. "I'm a dab hand at frying fish."

Hannah glanced at him. "You work full time, go to school at night, and work Saturdays? When do you just hang out?"

"Sundays. Why, do you fancy hanging out with me?"

"Oh, absolutely," she retorted. "Can't think of anything I'd rather do."

"I'm game if you are. I'll even spot you lunch at me uncle's chippy."

Hannah rolled her eyes. "I can hardly wait."

He grinned. "It might not be dinner at the Savoy, but they're the best chips you'll ever have, Posh. I guarantee it."

At the studio in north London early the next morning, Natalie choked down some toast and a sip of tea at the craft services table to calm her nerves. She saw the art director, the photographer and his assistants, a hair stylist, makeup artist, and – most unnerving of all – Rhys Gordon.

"Phillip, what's Rhys doing here?" Natalie hissed.

"He's the client, chickpea. Your grandfather sent him along to represent the store." Rhys had his back to the activity around him, his ear pressed to his mobile.

"Natalie, over here, please." The photographer, an American in a Yankees baseball cap, waved her over. He pointed to a spot in the centre of a white backdrop. "Stay on that mark while I shoot. Your light's here—" he pointed to a cluster of umbrella lights "—and I want you loose, playful, relaxed. OK?"

Natalie nodded uncertainly. "Loose, playful, relaxed. Right." She felt about as playful and relaxed as a frozen cod.

Rhys wandered over, mobile clapped to his ear. "How are you feeling?"

Natalie bit her lip. "Like a virgin on her wedding night. With twelve people standing round the bed, watching and taking notes."

He grinned. "It'll all be over soon."

"So will my career as a model," Natalie said, and turned away to find the loo before the shoot started.

When she emerged, Phillip grabbed her hand and led her to the dressing area. "It's time to get changed. Jacques has everything ready."

When she was dressed and done with hair and makeup, Jacques handed her a yellow umbrella. Natalie frowned. "What's this?"

"It's your prop for the first few shots. Pretend it's raining."

"I feel ridiculous, but OK." She sighed and, affixing a playful, relaxed expression to her face, took her place in the middle of the backdrop, unfurled the umbrella, and waited.

Wasn't it bad luck to open an umbrella inside?

"Ready, Natalie?" the photographer asked, camera slung around his neck.

"Ready." She managed a smile. "Let's have a go."

She stepped on her mark and took a deep breath. She twirled the umbrella playfully on one shoulder; she held it over her head and looked pensively up at pretend clouds. She tilted the umbrella down, up, and sideways, until she was bloody sick of the sight of it.

Modelling was nothing like she'd thought. Each shot took time; the photographer adjusted her arms or legs just so, instructing her to turn slightly or tilt her face to the left, all while she kept to her mark. The hair stylist ran out to fluff her hair a few times, and music blared in the background.

"Beautiful, Natalie," the photographer said hours later, as she threw her head back and her arms out and pretended to laugh. "Perfect. And… that's a wrap. We're done!"

There was a smattering of applause.

"Well done, you!" Rhys said. "You were a natural."

"The pictures look great," the photographer told Natalie. "Poppy Simone couldn't have done a better job herself."

Natalie beamed. "Thanks." As she turned away to pick up her mobile, her smile faded. Crikey – she'd forgotten to contact Poppy about the re-launch. "I need to make a call."

"Go ahead. Come and see the shots when you're done."

She nodded distractedly and scrolled to Poppy's number. She'd completely forgotten to ask if her friend could appear at the re-launch. She only hoped it wasn't too late…

"Hi, Poppy," Natalie said. "Good, how're you? How's Pen? Super. Listen, I've a huge favour to ask, it's for the store—"

Five minutes later, she clicked off, her smile gone and her mind racing. She'd left it too late. Poppy was booked for a shoot in Sri Lanka and wouldn't return to London until the day of the re-launch. She promised to come if she got back in time.

Natalie closed her eyes. Rhys would be furious. She'd pitched Poppy in the business plan as the re-launch's biggest draw, second only to Dominic and the Destroyers, of course. Now the famous supermodel wouldn't be there.

Her heart sank. How would she tell him?

"Natalie, there you are." As if her thoughts had summoned him, Rhys appeared. "I wanted to talk to you, but we've both been so busy I've not had a chance."

"If it's about Poppy Simone, she can't do it," Natalie blurted out in a guilty rush. "She has another commitment."

He frowned. "Can't do what — the re-launch? Why?"

Natalie bit her lip. "She'll be in Sri Lanka."

He narrowed his eyes. "You said there was no question Poppy Simone would star in the re-launch fashion show. You hung your entire business plan on it."

"I know. But I... well, I left it a bit too late to ask," she admitted. "I forgot. I only just called her now."

"What?" Rhys snapped. "Natalie, we discussed this well over a *month* ago! You assured me you'd taken care of it!"

"I meant to, but with everything going on, I forgot."

Anger suffused his face. "We can't afford a mistake like this. We need a big name to bring people in, and now all we have is Dominic – that's *if* Klaus's lawyers let us use him."

Natalie blinked back tears. "I really am sorry—"

"Sorry doesn't cut it. Fix it. I don't know how, and I don't give a shit. But you'll get someone else, and straight away. Otherwise," he finished grimly, "the re-launch will be a failure, and your family can kiss Dashwood and James goodbye. And it'll be on your arse if it fails. Not mine."

He turned and strode angrily away, his intention to ask Natalie about her drink at the Connaught with Ian Clarkson completely forgotten.

CHAPTER 26

The print ad featuring Natalie in Phillip's exclusive new clothing line appeared simultaneously in *Elle*, *Bazaar*, *Marie Claire*, *Vogue*, and *Glamour* magazines, as well as in the London tube trains and stations.

If the tabloids hadn't already invaded her privacy enough, now it was impossible to go anywhere without someone shouting her name, or taking her photo, or asking if she'd sign her autograph on a bit of paper.

"It's insane!" Natalie complained to her sister at week's end. "I just want to make it stop."

"Oh, stop whingeing. You're Britain's 'It' girl, you're all anyone's talking about! I wish I had your problems," Caroline said irritably.

"No, you don't," Nat said, and felt the beginnings of a headache. "You have *no* idea what I'm dealing with."

Her sister set two cups of tea and a plate of chocolate biscuits on the kitchen table and sat down with a sigh. "All right, then, tell me what's wrong."

"I promised Rhys that Poppy Simone would appear at the re-launch. But I left it too late, and she's booked for a shoot in Sri Lanka, and now we haven't a single big name, other than –possibly – Dom's, for the fashion show. Rhys is livid. I've never seen him so angry."

"Oh, Natty," Caro sighed, "you've gone and made a mess of things, haven't you?"

"Yes, and I don't know how to fix it. Who can I get to appear at the re-launch on such short notice? I'm not exactly friends with Giselle or Heidi."

Caro stirred sugar into her cup. "You must know someone. Someone famous, I mean."

"Not really, not unless you count Phillip."

"Phillip? Isn't he the designer who's doing the clothing line for the store?"

Nat nodded. "His clothes are flying off the shelves."

"I'm not surprised, they're great. Everyone loves the ads, too." Caro set her cup down. "Natalie, I just had a thought."

"What? Ask Dominic to take me back? Not a bad idea, I suppose, since Rhys is sure to sack me. Maybe Keeley needs another backup singer—"

"No. Besides, you can't sing." Caro leaned forward. "There's a model who's the muse for a hot new fashion designer. She's very popular with the British public right now."

Natalie sniffed. "And who is this wondrous creature? Chloe Sevigny? Katy Perry? Do I know her?"

"You know her very well." Caro grinned. "I'm talking about you, you berk!"

"Me?!" Natalie scoffed. "You can't be serious."

Caro leaned forward. "Nat, the tabloids can't get enough of you and Rhys. A photo of you on the cover guarantees a sell-out. Mr. Banks owns the newsagents round the corner, and he told me so," she added. "And you said yourself that Phillip's clothes are flying out of the stores."

Natalie shrugged. "So?"

"So," Caro said with rising excitement, "*you* can do the appearance at the re-launch! You're every bit as popular as Poppy right now. You can model the clothes, sign autographs and pose for pictures. And perhaps Phillip could design something new, just for the re-launch."

"I don't know," Natalie said doubtfully. "I'm not a celebrity, or a supermodel."

"No," Caro declared, "you're not. Even better – you're *you*! You're real, and relatable. And you're the best chance we have to save Dashwood and James from closing its doors forever. Maybe," she added ominously, "our *only* chance…"

Early Sunday morning Natalie left her sister's house and returned to London. She'd heard nothing from Ian, thank God. On the other hand, Rhys was furious at her, and rightly so. Her promise to get Poppy Simone for the re-launch had fizzled. She'd let him – and Dashwood and James – down.

She parked across from the Connaught hotel. She intended to march up to Rhys's room and tell him her plan… and hope that he didn't laugh in her face or throw her out on her arse.

But the front desk clerk informed her that Rhys Gordon had checked out that morning.

Disappointed, Natalie thanked him and turned away to leave. Rhys must have moved to his new flat, then. He hadn't said a word to her, nor asked for her help. Hurt washed over her.

He hadn't spoken to her, other than saying necessary things like "get me the Dawes file" or "I'll be out of the office for two hours." The temperature in the office dropped to Siberian levels whenever one of them was near the other.

It was awful.

She missed their banter, the easy camaraderie they shared. Rhys's anger was like a wall of ice between them. It had to stop. And it was up to her to fix things.

Well, if the mountain wouldn't come to Mohammed... then Mohammed would bloody well go to Covent Garden. Natalie started the engine, and with a clash of gears, drove as fast as she dared to Endell Street.

"All right, bruv, where's this go?" Jamie Gordon asked Rhys, his arms full of boxes.

Rhys glanced up from the kitchen table he was assembling. "The top floor."

Jamie groaned. "I knew you'd say that." He turned away and trod up the stairs to the third floor.

Rhys picked up the assembly instructions and returned to the task at hand. *Insert screw A into cross-brace.* He scowled as he dumped a bag of nuts and bolts onto the floor. "Why is it always bloody screw A that goes missing—"

He broke off as the doorbell rang. Who could that be? He wasn't even moved in yet, for fuck's sake... "Jamie!" he shouted. "Get the door, will you?"

There was no answer. Bloody hell, he was probably on the phone with his girlfriend yet again. He should've asked Ben to help. Rhys tossed the instructions aside and went downstairs.

He swung the door open. "Yes?" he growled.

Natalie blinked. Rhys stood, in all his disheveled glory, in the doorway. He wore a faded pair of jeans and a Manchester United T-shirt, and his feet were bare.

She thrust out a box of Chelsea buns and a bottle of wine. "I came to say sorry... and to give you these."

His scowl thawed to a frown as he took the box and the wine. "Thanks. But it wasn't necessary."

"Well, you've moved house, so I owe you a housewarming gift." Natalie bit her lip. "We need to talk, and we can't do it at work since we're always busy. And I don't want to do it on your doorstep. If you'll listen, I may have a solution to the Poppy Simone problem."

Rhys lifted his brow but made no comment as he swung the door wide. He turned and led the way up the stairs to the kitchen, where he put the box and bottle on the counter.

"So what's your solution?" Rhys asked. He crossed his arms loosely against his chest. "Have you got someone else?"

"Yes." Natalie hesitated. "I know she'll do it, and for free. She's even available on the day."

"Are you sure about that?"

"Quite sure," she replied, "because—" her heart constricted in her chest "—it's me I'm talking about. I'll be the star attraction at the re-launch fashion show."

"You," Rhys repeated. His face was expressionless.

Natalie nodded. "Since the ads came out, I'm constantly asked for my picture, or autograph. The newsagents say the tabloids with my photo sell out. And—" the clincher "—Phillip Pryce has agreed to design some new pieces for the store. I'll debut them at the re-launch fashion show."

Before Rhys could respond, they heard a crash, followed by a string of expletives. He brushed by her and shouted, "If you broke anything, you git, I'll have your balls for breakfast!"

Natalie followed Rhys to the sitting room. A young man in jeans and a blue jersey looked doubtfully at an enormous box. "It isn't broken... I don't think. What is it, anyway?"

"It's the coffee table," Natalie said. She held out her hand. "We've not been introduced. I'm Natalie Dashwood."

"Sorry." He wiped his forehead with a rag and thrust it in his pocket. "I'm Jamie, Rhys's brother." He took her hand and grinned. "I'm younger and better looking than he is."

"Nicer, too," Natalie agreed.

"Thanks. You're famous, you know. My girlfriend bought that skirt and stripy top in the advert, and mum follows all the tabloid stories about you and Rhys and the affair…"

Jamie's voice trailed away as he caught sight of Rhys's murderous expression. "I'll go start on the boxes downstairs. You might've marked them," he added with a meaningful glance at Rhys, "but I'll sort it out."

"Help yourself to a Chelsea bun," Natalie offered.

"Don't mind if I do." Jamie lifted the lid on the bakery box, grabbed two buns, and thundered down the stairs, whistling.

"If I'm to get anything done today, I need to put this bloody table together," Rhys grumbled. He handed Natalie an instruction sheet and sat on the floor. "Read me the bit after 'insert screw A into cross-brace'."

She sat down across from him. "About my idea—" she began.

"Let's go with it. I think it's brilliant." He smiled briefly at her and picked up a packet of screws. "Now help me find this bloody screw A before the day's done, will you?"

Just before noon on Sunday, a horn blew twice outside the James residence.

"What the devil–?" Alastair muttered as he put aside his newspaper. He rose and went to the study window to investigate.

"Jago's here!" Hannah announced as she charged down the stairs. "Be back in time for dinner. Bye!"

Before Alastair could respond, the front door opened and slammed, and she was gone. "Cherie!" he called out irritably.

She appeared in the doorway a moment later. "What is it?"

"Hannah's going out with Jago Sullivan. I don't want him dating my daughter. And why didn't he come to the door?"

"Oh, Alastair... it's not a proper date – they're 'hanging out', according to Hannah."

"Whatever it's called, I don't like it. He's a stock boy, for God's sake, with a bloody ring in his eyebrow."

"If you make a fuss, she'll only be more determined to see him."

He sighed. "You're right, of course. I'm getting too old for this."

"She'll be gone soon, and you'll miss all this fuss."

"That's where you're wrong," Alastair grumbled, and resumed his seat. "I could do very nicely without it."

CHAPTER 27

Late Sunday afternoon, Natalie pushed away her bowl of spaghetti. "Jamie, that was amazing! Will you show me how to make the sauce?"

"Sure. It's dead easy." He held up the half-empty bottle of Barolo. "Another glass?"

"Careful," Rhys warned Jamie as he topped up their glasses, "the last time Natalie had wine, she ended up in every tabloid in London. *And* she ruined my suit."

"You got in the way. That wine was aimed at Dominic, not you," she pointed out.

"I'd love to stay and listen to you two argue," Jamie said as he stood, "but I promised mum I'd get her some sweets." He clapped a baseball cap on his head. "What can I say, I'm a good son."

"Bye, Jamie," Rhys said as he pushed back his chair and stood up, "Don't hurry back."

"OK, I can take a hint. Laters." He kissed Natalie's cheek, thundered down the stairs, and left.

Natalie stood as well and eyed the dishes. "I like your brother. He's much nicer than you."

Rhys came to stand in front of her. "I'm nice, too, sometimes. When I want to be."

"Really?" She tilted her head back to study him. "I haven't seen that side of you, sorry."

He reached out and wiped a bit of passata sauce from the corner of her mouth with his thumb. "Do you know the first thing that I realised about you?"

"What's that?" she asked, her voice husky.

"That your aim with a wineglass is terrible."

She caught her lip between her teeth. "Well, as it happens, I have talents in other areas..."

"Saving money isn't one of them," Rhys observed in a low voice as he brushed a strand of hair from her cheek.

"No." Electricity tingled through her at his touch.

"And you don't maintain your car," he added as his eyes met hers.

"No," she admitted, her voice barely a whisper. "But I *did* get the fuel pump replaced."

"And you've a bad habit of leaving things till the last minute," he murmured, and bracketed her face gently with his hands, "important things."

"Important things?" she echoed, her eyes wide. "Like what?"

"Like this."

His arms came around her and his mouth covered hers, and all thoughts of shirts and stains and fuel pumps fled. Desire thrummed through her with a sudden intensity that left her legs trembly and her thoughts scattered.

Rhys pressed her closer as he deepened the kiss.

Natalie clutched at his shirt, grabbing a handful of the soft cotton as desire, raw and sweet and powerful, overtook her.

She'd been kissed before, of course she had. But this? This was entirely different.

Every inch of her skin tingled and responded to his touch. The heat of his jeans-clad thighs against hers, the muscled length of his arms around her, his tongue seeking hers as they kissed – it set her thoughts whirling out of control. There was only his mouth on hers.

"Natalie," he breathed against her lips, lowering his hands to cup the curves of her bottom, "I've wanted you ever since that night at Alastair's party."

"Have you?" She closed her eyes as his lips moved away from hers and sought out the sensitive skin behind her ear. "I thought you despised me. I thought... ooh, that's nice..." She melted as he nibbled her earlobe.

"I thought you were incredibly spoilt—" his hands slid up her waist "—but also incredibly attractive."

"I don't know how you resisted me, then."

"I had a very long, very cold shower when I got home," he growled, and pressed her hard against the wall and kissed her again, more insistently.

Natalie was helpless to resist the onslaught of his tongue and hands and the hard, heated length of his body against hers. She wanted him with a strength that left her breathless with need.

As Rhys tore his mouth away and began impatiently to unbutton her blouse, Natalie's mobile shrilled from her jeans pocket. She groaned as he kissed and licked his way down her neck. "Ignore it," she gasped, "it'll stop in a second."

The ringing continued, insistent.

"Shit!" Natalie exclaimed, exasperated, and pulled away. "I forgot to forward it to voicemail, it'll just keep ringing. Let me just turn it off—"

Rhys grunted something unintelligible and continued to leave heated kisses along her neck.

She pushed him reluctantly away and pulled out her mobile to shut it off. When she saw the call screen, she froze.

Ian Clarkson.

"I've got to take this," she told Rhys, "it's important," and she clapped the mobile to her ear. "Hello?" Her voice was unsteady, her stomach a knot of dread.

"Natalie. I didn't think you were going to answer."

She gave Rhys an apologetic smile and murmured, "It's only Caro. Sorry, won't be a minute."

He kissed the side of her mouth. "See that you're not. And tell your sister I'm very put out with her right now." He padded off to the sitting room to give her privacy.

"What is it?" she demanded in a low voice when Rhys left.

"You're with Gordon, aren't you?"

"No," she lied. She glanced at the sitting room door. "What do you want?"

"You're a crap liar, Natalie. Meet me for lunch tomorrow. I've reserved a table at Carrafini."

"But someone might see us there! It's just down the street. Besides, I'm meeting with Phillip at eleven, I can't possibly—"

"Cancel it. Don't put me off, Natalie. You didn't return that fifty quid to the cash box yet, did you?"

She closed her eyes. She'd forgotten completely about the damned money she'd taken.

"I thought so. I'll see you tomorrow, eleven-thirty. Don't keep me waiting." He rang off.

With shaking hands Natalie slipped the mobile back in her pocket. Oh God, oh God... what to do?

"Finished your call?" Rhys asked as he came back in.

She nodded. "Caro needed help with her new DVR player."

He came behind her and took her in his arms. His breath was warm as he nuzzled her neck. "Stay tonight, Natalie."

She closed her eyes as she imagined sharing Rhys's bed. She felt safe in his arms, all her worries about Ian forgotten. She longed to spend tonight with him, God, yes… but Ian Clarkson had ruined the moment with his call.

"I can't," she said, and pulled away regretfully. "Nor can you. Tomorrow's Monday, after all. Work."

"Ah, yes, work." He kissed her again, his mouth lingering on hers. "We've a lot to do tomorrow." Rhys frowned. "Which reminds me… I meant to ask you something."

She looked at him inquiringly. "Oh?"

His eyes met hers. "I had a drink in the Connaught the other night. I saw you at a table with Ian Clarkson. You had your heads together, looked very serious."

Her thoughts raced. "We were discussing the website. He was put out that you tore it apart," she added lightly.

"Indeed." Rhys's eyes narrowed. "Odd that he wanted to discuss it with you, and over drinks, don't you think?"

"He… wanted an outside opinion. And he didn't want any interruptions."

"Natalie, you're a crap liar. Why were you with Clarkson? He's a slimy bastard. And he's married to your best friend."

"I told you, we were talking about the website—"

"That's bollocks and we both know it," he cut in. "I saw him touch you, I saw you flinch. What's going on? What's he got on you? Tell me."

Her legs were unsteady as she walked across the kitchen to the hallway. "Got on me? Nothing! You're imagining things."

"Natalie, I want to help you, but I can't unless you tell me the truth—"

"There's nothing to tell! Tell Jamie thanks for dinner. It was really good, and I-I'll see you tomorrow."

She grabbed her handbag and hurried down the stairs as Rhys stormed after her.

"That was him just now, wasn't it?" he demanded as she reached the front door. "It was Ian."

"Rhys, please, let it go," Natalie begged. "I can't... it's not—" She stopped, overwhelmed with conflicting emotions. "I have to go." And she flung the door open and fled.

CHAPTER 28

As she returned to her car, Nat's thoughts were in turmoil.

She hated being at Ian Clarkson's mercy. And she hated lying to Rhys even more. She had to *do* something. But what?

First things first, she decided as she unlocked the Peugeot. She had to put that fifty quid back in the cash box before someone noticed it was missing…

"Natalie! Wait up."

She looked up to see Jamie Gordon coming towards her. "Jamie! I didn't expect to see you lurking around out here."

"I didn't expect to see you, either. I thought you'd be spending the night with Rhys."

She was glad the darkness hid her blush. "Well, you needn't worry, I'm not staying over."

"Oh. Sorry. But not as sorry as Rhys, I imagine." He raised an eyebrow. "Fancy a pint before last call? We didn't get much of a chance to talk, before."

"Well… OK. Sure. Orange squash for me, though," she said as she re-locked the car. "I'm driving home."

"If you don't mind my asking, why *aren't* you staying?" Jamie ventured when they'd seated themselves and he returned with their drinks. "I know it's none of my business—"

"It's OK." She hesitated. "We had a row. There's something I need to tell him, but... I can't. I don't know how he might react. His temper—"

"Yeah, he *does* have a temper," Jamie admitted, and sipped his lager. "Our dad drank, a lot. Some people drink and get happy. But whiskey only made the old man mean. He was hit head-on by a lorry one night, walking home from the pub. For some reason, he was walking in the road. The lorry driver didn't see him until it was too late. Killed dad instantly."

Natalie looked at him in mingled shock and dismay. "How awful! I'm sorry."

Jamie shrugged. "Trust me, it was the best thing that could've happened. He couldn't beat our mam any longer."

Her eyes widened. "Did he ever hit you or Rhys?"

"He had a go at Rhys once. Rhys knocked him down and pummeled him until mum and one of the neighbours dragged him off. That's how his nose got broken." He glanced at her. "Told you it was an old football injury, did he?"

Natalie nodded slowly. That was exactly what he'd said.

"Rhys lets off steam on the squash court. And he has a right temper. But there's no one I'd rather have in my corner."

"He said he left home at seventeen."

"Yeah, after dad died, he got a job in Hoxton. He busted his ass to support us; dad was always skint. Mum and me wouldn't have made it without the money Rhys sent home. He put me through culinary school." Jamie drained his beer. "He's an arsehole sometimes. But he's always had my back."

"He doesn't talk much about himself."

"He won't. He doesn't like to remember those days."
He leaned forward. "Rhys is no saint. But he's not bad, as
brothers go. You could do a lot worse."

"I'm sure he'd say the same about you."

"I doubt it," Jamie said, and grinned as he stood up. "It's
getting late, you'd best head home. And Natalie?"

"Yes?"

"Whatever it is that's on your mind, tell him," he
advised. "I know he'll do whatever he can to help you."

Natalie had her doubts, but she nodded. "I will. I just
need to find the right time."

"Don't leave it too long." He leaned forward and kissed
her cheek. "It was great to meet you."

"You, too. Thanks for the drink and the advice."

They said goodnight and Natalie returned to her car and
drove home. As she inserted her key and swung the door
open twenty minutes later, wondering if mum might loan
her fifty quid, she froze. Wreaths of cigarette smoke drifted
towards her from the sitting room, and the TV blared.

Her hand tightened on the doorknob. Ian smoked. She'd
seen him before, having a quick, furtive cigarette standing
at the back entrance to the store.

Oh, God – what if he'd got in her flat somehow?

No, that was ludicrous…

"Nat!" Dominic's voice bellowed out from the lounge.
"Is that you?"

Her relief quickly turned to fury as she dropped her
handbag on a chair and rounded on him. "You scared the
crap out of me, Dom! What are you doing here? And give
me back your key!"

"All right, shit. Here." He rummaged in his pockets and
extracted the spare key from his wallet and handed it to her.

"I don't suppose you could loan me fifty quid?" Nat asked him. "I'll pay you back." *Just as soon as I borrow it from mum, that is...*

"Yeah, sure." He pulled a wad of cash out and peeled off three fifty-pound notes.

Natalie stared at him. "Dom, that's a hundred and fifty quid! I only need fifty."

He shrugged and handed it to her. "Keep it. I've plenty of dosh. I just got my first cheque from Maison Laroche. By the way," he added as he put his wallet away, "where've you been? I thought you'd never get back."

"Thanks," she said as she tucked the money in her pocket. "Never mind me, what are *you* doing here?" She narrowed her eyes. "That better not be a spliff—"

"It's not." Dominic squashed out the cigarette. "He knows, Nat," he said in a rush as he perched at one end of the sofa. "Klaus knows who I am."

Natalie blinked. "What? But... no one knows who you are but me! And your family," she amended. "How did he find out?"

"He's got someone on retainer to dig stuff up. Insurance, he calls it," Dominic said bitterly. "He knows everything, Nat – my real name, where I was born, all of it. He says he'll go to the tabs if I don't cooperate."

"For heaven's sake, Dom, being the son of an earl is nothing to be ashamed of—"

"It is when your fans think you're a working-class kid from a council estate in Swindon," he said flatly.

"True," she admitted. She sank down on the sofa next to him. "What about your father? Does he know?"

Dominic shook his head. "If this comes out, he'll disown me. He has nothing but contempt for my music career." He scowled. "Not that I give a toss about inheriting the title. I don't. I just…" He looked at her, his expression subdued. "I just wish he approved of me, at least a bit. You know?"

"Oh, Dominic," Natalie said softly, "I'm sure he does. You're his son, after all! He's just… disappointed you didn't follow his example."

"Right." Dominic let out a mirthless laugh. "Can you see me as lord of the manor, a glass of sherry in one hand and a dead pheasant in the other? I can't do it, Nat. That's my father's thing. And me? I'm his biggest disappointment."

Natalie patted his knee. "I'm sure you're wrong."

"I'm not." He leaned forward and took her hand. "God, I miss you, Nat. We were good together, weren't we?"

"No! We were a disaster." She yanked her hand away. "You treated me like crap, and you cheated on me—"

"I was a berk," he admitted. He grinned. "But you have to admit, the make-up sex was pretty spectacular."

"Tea," Natalie said hastily, and stood. "We need tea."

In the kitchen she plugged in the kettle and plunked tea bags into two cups – Dominic's with two sugars, lemon, no milk — and returned to the lounge.

"Now," Natalie said as she handed him a mug, "tell me exactly what Klaus wants."

Dominic sipped his tea and grimaced. "This could do with a shot of whiskey… He wants to know about a clothing line some bloke named Phillip's designing for D&J."

"What?" Natalie sputtered, outraged. "Klaus wants you to *spy* on Phillip Pryce?"

"Yeah. He wants to see his sketches, hear about any problems he's having, stuff like that." He frowned. "What'll I tell him, Nat? If I don't give him something, he'll go to the tabloids with my secret, and my career is over."

"Well, that's easy enough," Natalie said slowly. "We'll give Klaus the information he wants – we'll just make sure it's the *wrong* information."

It was after midnight when Dominic left. Too keyed up to sleep, Natalie made another cup of tea – chamomile this time – and curled up on the sofa. She remembered her first year at boarding school, when an older girl had bullied her. Alison took her pencil case one day, a packet of HobNobs the next. Natalie said nothing; she was too afraid.

The third time it happened, a prefect saw Alison yank Natalie's amethyst pendant, a present from her father, from her neck and shove her hard in the back. She fell on the gravel and skinned her knees. Between sobs, Natalie told her story to the head, who expelled Alison and called Natalie's father to inform him of the incident.

"Always face up to a bully, Nat," he'd told her quietly but firmly. "If you give in, you give them power, and they'll never stop bullying you." Was he thinking of his own situation, his blackmail at the hands of Ian's stepfather?

She bit her lip. In the end, her father hadn't taken his own advice. The threats and the pressure from Ian's stepfather must have overwhelmed him, until, unable to cope, he'd taken his life with an overdose of sleeping tablets.

Natalie set her cup of tea, gone cold, aside. She pressed her lips together in sudden determination. She refused to let Ian call the shots. Unlike her father, she intended to fight back.

She grabbed her mobile and scrolled until she found Ian's number.

CHAPTER 29

Alexa Clarkson was half asleep when Ian's mobile buzzed late on Sunday night. She raised herself on one elbow and peered at the bedside clock. It was half past midnight. She listened, straining to hear, but there was nothing. Ian must've let the call go to voicemail.

Curious, she waited until she heard the shower come on. As soon as he shut the bathroom door, she got out of bed – made awkward by her last weeks of pregnancy – and crept into the sitting room. She rubbed the swell of her stomach and frowned.

When had she and Ian last made love? She couldn't remember. Ages… She couldn't blame him, really. Who'd want to make love to a woman as big around as Brixton?

Not for the first time, she wondered if he was having an affair.

His mobile lay on the hall table. She picked it up, one ear cocked to make sure the shower still ran, and scrolled down the list of recent calls to the last one.

Natalie Dashwood.

Alexa's frown deepened. Why would Natalie call Ian so late on a Sunday night? Surely it could wait until morning, at work. And why hadn't he answered?

The shower stopped. She tossed the mobile back on the table and returned to their bedroom, sliding under the covers just as the door opened. Light spilled into the room.

"Alexa? I thought you were asleep." Ian, a towel wrapped round his hips, regarded her from the doorway.

"I was. Your mobile woke me, so I got up to take a wee. Who was it?" she asked, keeping her voice casual.

"Oh, it was just a message from Gordon." He dropped the towel to the floor and rummaged in his dresser for a pair of boxers. "We've a meeting at four and he warned me it'll most likely run long."

What an accomplished liar he is, Alexa realised suddenly. *What else has he lied about?* "Is it the website again?" she managed to ask, hoping her voice didn't betray her thoughts.

He nodded. "Final review and then hopefully we're done with the damned thing."

"I hope so. You've worked late, a lot." She stretched. "Well, bed for me. Maybe this time I'll actually sleep."

"Goodnight." He turned away. "I'll be in soon. I need to check my emails."

"Goodnight." Although she was tired, as she turned off the bedside lamp, Alexa couldn't stop thinking about Natalie's phone call. Why had she called Ian? Were they having an affair? How long had it been going on?

And just what, exactly, *was* going on?

There was no possible way that Nat and her husband were involved. The very idea was ludicrous. She and Natalie had known each other for yonks; they'd bonded over Enid Blyton and gobstoppers, and later over music and boys and clothes. Nat would never do something like this to her, or to their long-standing friendship.

Yet why else would she call Ian so late on a Sunday night?

Exhaustion finally caught up to her, and Alexa fell into a restless, troubled sleep.

Cherie found the photo albums in a basket on a bottom shelf of the sitting room bookcase. She knelt to pick one up and flipped idly through the pages.

She studied pictures of Hannah and Holly, their faces alight with excitement as they sat in front of the Christmas tree; Alastair, holding newborn Hannah with a look of equal parts adoration and terror on his face; Holly balancing unsteadily on her first two-wheeled bicycle.

She took an armful of albums and sat on the sofa, flipping the pages until she found photos of her wedding day. Her throat tightened. She and Alastair had been madly, crazily in love.

They had two lovely daughters and a pleasant, privileged life. Yet they'd become two strangers sharing the same house.

When had things gone so wrong between them?

"Hello, darling," Alastair said as he arrived with two cups of tea. He handed her one and sat down beside her. "Looking at wedding photos?"

Cherie nodded. "You were so handsome in your morning suit. I couldn't wait to get you out of it."

Alastair lifted his brow. "And here I thought you were so innocent."

"Oh, I was. But I wanted to sleep with you from the moment we met at that garden party at St. Anselm's."

"It seems I married quite a hussy," he murmured, and leaned forward to kiss her.

The album slipped from her fingers as Cherie kissed him back, and a photo came loose and fell to the floor. She bent down to pick it up.

She studied the picture of an attractive young woman seated at a desk. One perfectly groomed brow was lifted, her lips curved in a slight, knowing smile. Her dark blonde hair was twisted into a chignon at the nape of her neck.

"Who is she?" Cherie asked, curious. "She looks familiar."

Alastair took the photo and studied it. "Oh, yes, of course. That was Fiona, my secretary. You remember, darling – she quit just after you and I got married."

Cherie cast him a curious glance. "Why? Were you two an item?"

"Yes… but not for long. I remember she quit on a Friday, left her notice on my desk while I was at lunch, and never came back. No idea why she left. Hard to believe it was almost thirty years ago."

"You must've upset her when you married me." Cherie smiled, only half joking. "She couldn't bear it, so she flew the coop to nurse her broken heart."

He stared at the half-forgotten face of his secretary. She'd had eyes of such a deep and penetrating blue.

Something about those eyes niggled at him. What, exactly, he couldn't say. It lurked now at the back of his mind, but he couldn't put a finger precisely on what 'it' was.

Whatever it was, Alastair decided, there was something about Fiona Walsh that gnawed at his memory.

"What's wrong?" Cherie asked him. "You've got an odd look on your face."

"Nothing." Alastair put the photo aside. "Feeling my age, I suppose. It was a long time ago. Let's look at some more of those wedding pictures."

They spent a pleasant hour flipping the pages and passing the albums back and forth. As he enjoyed the rarity of relaxing at home with Cherie, Alastair's glance strayed once again to the photo of his secretary, tossed aside on the coffee table.

Although he didn't mention her again, Fiona Walsh remained in his thoughts for the rest of the evening.

Rhys arrived at work at eight a.m. on Monday morning. He'd slept restlessly – no thanks to Natalie's abrupt departure after the phone call she'd got – but at least he knew how to handle Ian Clarkson.

"Natalie's running late," Gemma said as he stopped at her desk. "She'll be in soon. Oh – and the breakfast has just been delivered for Sir Richard's meeting with the buyers. Shall I pay the boy out of petty cash? I'm skint at the moment, or I'd take care of it myself and expense it later."

With a nod and a brief stop to pick up his messages, Rhys went into his office and picked up the phone.

"Clarkson, Gordon here. I want to see you in my office, please. Immediately."

Rhys sat down behind his desk to wait. Ian was blackmailing Natalie; he was sure of it. He'd seen the fear in her eyes after last night's phone call. His expression hardened. He couldn't confront Ian directly with his suspicions; but there were other ways...

Gemma reappeared in his doorway a moment later, a puzzled look on her face.

"Yes? What is it?" he asked with a trace of irritation.

"I barely had enough money to pay for the delivery out of petty cash."

Rhys lifted his brow. "Sir Richard's secretary must have ordered one hell of a breakfast spread for his meeting."

"That's just it. She ordered the usual things – a dozen scones and croissants, and orange juice. But there's money missing from the cash box. Fifty quid, to be exact."

He rubbed the space between his eyes. "Natalie probably took the money out and forgot to deduct it from the tracking spreadsheet. Bloody hell! Can't she even manage petty cash without screwing it up?"

"Mr. Gordon?" Ian stood in the doorway.

"Come in. Shut the door, Gemma, please. We'll talk later."

"Sounds serious," Ian remarked as Gordon's PA nodded and closed the door. He took a seat in front of Rhys's desk. "Is Miss Dashwood in some sort of trouble?" he enquired guilelessly.

"No, but you are," Rhys replied. "Mr. Clarkson, are you aware of the store's policy regarding employee harassment?"

He raised his brow but said nothing, waiting.

"Let me refresh your memory. Harassment of a colleague – verbal or sexual – will not be tolerated. It's come to my attention that you've made a pest of yourself with the ladies."

Ian stiffened. "A bit of flirting hardly counts as harassment."

"Oh, is that what you call it – a bit of flirting?" Rhys leaned back in his chair. "Any woman made to feel uncomfortable in your presence is a victim of harassment, Mr. Clarkson. I've had complaints from my own PA about you."

"This is absurd." Ian stood up abruptly. "You don't like me, Gordon, and you never have. And the feeling is mutual. But you have no cause to accuse me of harassment."

Rhys stood as well, his blue eyes snapping. "I'm warning you, Clarkson. Stay away from the women in this office, and stay away from Natalie Dashwood. Because if you don't, I'll have your balls for breakfast."

"That's what this is all about," Ian said softly, "isn't it? You fancy Natalie yourself!" His smile was cold. "You speak to me of bylaws, and harassment. But I wonder what the bylaws say about a superior shagging a subordinate? Particularly when the subordinate is Sir Richard's own granddaughter—"

Rhys lunged forward and grabbed Ian by the collar. "That's enough, you nasty-minded little prick," he snapped. "Natalie's off limits, got it? If you so much as breathe the same air as her again—" his eyes glittered "—I'll fucking kill you myself."

Ian jerked free, his face flushed with anger. "I could have you arrested for assault, Gordon. Lay a finger on me again, and I promise you'll find yourself behind bars faster than you can say 'quid pro quo'." He turned away, flung open the door, and left.

Gemma looked up from her laptop as Clarkson stormed past her desk, his face like a thundercloud.

She went into Rhys's office. "What on earth did you say to Ian?" she asked. "He came out of your office just now like a juggernaut. I've never seen him looking so furious."

"I gave him a refresher course on store policy. I've had a number of complaints about him." He tossed down his pen. "He won't be bothering you – or anyone else – again."

Gemma crossed her arms against her chest. "It's not me he's after, it's Natalie. He corners her at the copier or in the kitchen at least once a week. He's a nasty piece of work."

"How long has this been going on?"

"Oh, since her first week here."

"And why do you suppose he's singled Natalie out in particular?"

Gemma shrugged. "I'm sure he fancies her, but I get the feeling there's something else going on." She glanced at him with a frown. "It's almost as though she's afraid of him."

"Like he's got something on her, you mean?"

"Yes. Although I can't imagine what; Natalie doesn't have any dark secrets, she's an open book."

Rhys leaned forward. "Unless the secret she's keeping isn't hers, but someone else's."

CHAPTER 30

"We can save substantially if we allow more vendors to provide merchandising services," Rhys stated at Monday morning's financial meeting.

"Then why don't we?" Sir Richard asked.

"To do so would necessitate redundancies. It's been my intent to create jobs, not eliminate them."

Alastair frowned. "Of course we don't want anyone to lose their job, but at the same time, costs must be cut. We're all agreed on that."

"What do you suggest?" Rhys asked.

"Well, since we've cut our stock, I recommend we cut the stockroom staff as well, at least until the autumn/winter season begins," Alastair said, and laid his pen aside. "If business improves, we'll re-hire." He glanced at Rhys. "Jago Sullivan and Frank Bamber are the two most recent hires."

Rhys made a note. "Very well. I'll consider your suggestion." He glanced at Natalie, who was running the slide show presentation. "Let's see the next slide, please, Miss Dashwood."

As she nodded and clicked the mouse, his thoughts wandered back to the first, incendiary kiss they'd shared. He'd kissed his share of women over the years, no question; but Natalie Dashwood was different... distractingly, tantalisingly different.

Too bad they'd been interrupted…

He realised the staff were watching him expectantly, waiting for his breakdown of the latest sales figures.

As Rhys turned back to the screen and explained the three-colour pie chart, Alastair listened and nodded and took dutiful notes. But his thoughts were elsewhere.

Hannah would be livid when she found out he'd recommended Jago for redundancy, even temporarily.

But he wanted Jago Sullivan out of Hannah's orbit, at least for the summer. He'd deal with his daughter's wrath later. His attention returned to Gordon.

And as his eyes met Rhys's, Alastair suddenly realised that he knew someone else with those same intense blue eyes, someone who, like Rhys, hailed from Edinburgh.

Fiona Walsh.

Alastair frowned. There was no denying the physical resemblance she and Rhys shared – both tall, with dark blond hair, and those striking blue eyes. Could Rhys possibly be Fiona's son? Of course his last name was different, but his former secretary had undoubtedly married since then, and taken her husband's name.

It certainly explained why she'd left Dashwood and James so suddenly. Fiona had been a bit free with her favours; it was one of the reasons she and Alastair had parted. She'd been involved with a couple of other store employees. Alastair wondered idly if she'd been pregnant, and if so, which of the poor sods was Rhys's father.

"Alastair?" Rhys flipped on the lights, signalling the end of the meeting. "Come to my office, and we'll discuss the particulars of your suggestion to cut the stockroom staff."

"Of course." Alastair stood as well, gathered up his notes, and followed Rhys out of the conference room.

When she returned to her office, Natalie called Phillip Pryce to postpone their meeting.

She left a message and hung up. One thing sorted, only two million more to go. Now, all she needed to do was put the money Dom had given her back into the cash box, and no one would be the wiser...

"Oh, Nat, there you are," Gemma said as she strode up to her desk. "There was barely enough money in petty cash to pay for the breakfast delivery for Sir Richard's meeting this morning."

Natalie's heart accelerated.

"Rhys was *not* pleased," Gemma added, and crossed her arms against her chest. "Did you pay for something and forget to deduct it from the tracking spreadsheet?"

Nat pretended to consider the question. "Oh, yes – I just remembered! I paid for a – a delivery, the other day."

"A delivery? A fifty-*quid* delivery? What was it?"

Yes, Miss Dashwood, what was it? Natalie thought wildly. "I don't remember, exactly. It was large. A crate. And it was cash on delivery."

Gemma narrowed her eyes. "Who was this large crate for?"

Her mobile rang. *Thank God.* "Sorry," she told Gemma, "I'm expecting an important call." She turned away and said, "Natalie Dashwood here—"

"You shouldn't have called last night," Ian bit off. "You don't dictate the terms of this arrangement."

"Oh, hello!" she said brightly as she stood and left her desk – and Gemma – behind. "How *are* you?"

"Don't ever phone me at home again. Do you understand?"

She slipped into the bathroom and locked herself in a stall. "I want proof from you before this goes any further."

"You'll have your proof, the next time we meet. And then I'll have what I want. And we both know what that is. A partnership with Dashwood and James... and with you."

She gripped the phone as fear washed over her. "It'll never happen, you know that! Why are you doing this?"

"I needn't justify myself to you." He paused. "I didn't appreciate being raked over the coals by your hot-tempered boss this morning, by the way. You haven't told him about me, have you?"

"No! What are you talking about?"

"Rhys lectured me on sexual harassment in the workplace, of all things, then warned me to stay away from you."

"I've never said a word to Rhys—"

"Yes, well, perhaps you did and perhaps you didn't. For your sake, I hope you didn't. If you did—" He stopped. "Well, let's just say you'll read all about your father very soon, along with the rest of England. Oh, and sorry to say, I can't make our lunch date today. Rhys has moved our meeting up to one o'clock, the prick."

"Ian, please don't drag my father's name through the mud. You'll cause no end of pain for my mother, and for me. I'm begging you, if you have even a shred of decency—"

He laughed. "That's just it, Natalie. I don't."

And the line went dead.

The stockroom was crowded with pallets of merchandise. New shipments would arrive on Tuesday; everything had to be inventoried and moved to the floor by then.

"Want to get lunch?" Hannah asked Jago at eleven. He usually brought a sandwich or a Pot Noodle and ate in his van.

"Sure. Let's go."

At Dim Sum Palace, they ate in companionable silence, exchanging amused glances as the chef screamed in Mandarin at someone in the kitchen.

"What are you doing on Sunday?" Hannah asked.

Jago took a bite of his spring roll. "I'm busy," he answered after a moment. "I got stuff to do."

"What stuff? I thought you said Sunday's your day off."

"It is," he said evasively. "But I… promised a mate I'd help him move. Probably take most of the day."

"Oh, well, OK. No big deal."

Although Hannah was silent as they stood and gathered up the emptied cartons of ginger beef and Mu Shu Pork, she knew – just *knew* – that Jago was lying.

"So what are you doing on Sunday, really?" she asked as they walked back to work.

He looked at her in annoyance. "I told you, I'm helping a mate move—"

"That's bollocks, and you know it."

Jago stopped and faced her. "Look, I can't hang out Sunday. I'm sorry. We can do something next Sunday, yeah?"

"Forget it," she said coolly. "I'm busy then."

He snorted. "Busy? Doing what, spending your dad's money? You're full of shit, Hannah. Sometimes you don't get what you want. Get over it."

Hannah stared at him, taken aback. Before she could form a reply, he shook his head in disgust, turned on his heel, and walked away.

It was done. Jago and Frank would be sacked at the end of the week. Alastair stood to leave Rhys's office. "Mr. Gordon, are you free for lunch? I'd like a word."

Rhys took a sip of his coffee and grimaced. "Bloody hell, this stuff gets worse every day." He set the cup aside.

"I've a meeting with Clarkson at one, so I need to be back by then."

They went to a gastro pub nearby and found a table in the bar. After placing their orders – a cheddar burger and stout for Rhys, white wine and a salad for Alastair – Rhys leaned forward. "What did you want to discuss?"

Alastair paused as the waiter put a cocktail napkin down in front of each of them. "Trimming the stockroom staff should save a fair bit of money over the summer, don't you agree?"

"Yes. It's a workable solution, so long as Duffy has enough employees to do the job." Rhys leaned back. "Now, tell me – what's the real reason we're here?"

The waiter returned to deposit their drinks and departed. Alastair took a sip of his wine. "You're direct, Mr. Gordon. I shall be direct as well. You don't like me," he said bluntly. "Why is that, I wonder?"

Rhys leaned forward. "I'm frustrated with the way you and Sir Richard have managed things. Together you own this wonderful, landmark department store, yet you've both let it slide for far too long."

Their food arrived. Alastair was silent as the plate of salad was set before him. There was little he could say in his defence. Rhys was right.

Rhys picked up his burger. "You've so much potential with Dashwood and James, so much history, yet you don't seem to care. You haven't kept up with the times, either of you.

"And yes," he added, "before you say it, I know you hired me to fix things. But at the end of the day, Alastair, it's your company, and Sir Richard's. Not mine." He shrugged. "Perhaps you both deserve to lose the stores."

"Perhaps we do," Alastair agreed, and picked up his fork. "My marriage is in trouble at the moment. My daughter, Hannah… she's a teenager, with all the drama and stress that entails. I'm not making excuses, mind; but it's difficult for my wife to manage things alone just now."

Rhys lifted his glass. "I'm sure it isn't easy, raising a family." There was an edge to his voice. "Requires a great deal of sacrifice, I should think."

"It's a constant balancing act," Alastair agreed. "What about you? Have you family in London?" he asked.

"No. I was born in Edinburgh and left my mam and half-brother behind to come here when I was seventeen. It's nothing you can't Google," he added dryly. "No need to ply me with overpriced burgers and stout."

Alastair smiled slightly. "No, I suppose not. I'm only curious. Is your mother still in Edinburgh?"

"Yes." He offered no additional information.

Rhys pushed aside his plate and glanced at his watch. "Time I went. Check, please," he called out to the bartender.

Alastair took out his wallet. "I've got it. Thank you for joining me."

"Thanks for lunch." Rhys stood and clapped a hand briefly on Alastair's shoulder.

Just then, Rhys saw Alastair's wife Cherie come in, accompanied by a handsome, sandy-haired man. His hand rested on Cherie's back. A waiter led them into the restaurant area and seated them by a corner window.

She was attractive, Rhys noted, her dark hair short and stylishly cut, her smile warm and wide. He'd never guess her youngest daughter was about to go off to university.

Curious, he glanced at Alastair to gauge his reaction.

Alastair stared at the two of them, a muscle working in his jaw. Rhys felt a stab of sympathy. It couldn't be easy for Alastair to see his wife and her lover, flaunting their affair – if that's what it was – in the middle of a restaurant crowded with his coworkers…

Ah well, Rhys mused as he followed Alastair out of the restaurant, extramarital affairs almost always ended badly – as he well knew. But as the French said, *tant pis*.

Tough luck, that.

Halfway through lunch at her desk, Gemma's phone rang. She held the receiver away from her ear as an angry flood of words assaulted her. "No need to shout!" she snapped. "Wait – Dominic wants *what*?" She lifted her finger to get Natalie's attention and pressed the speakerphone on.

Over the squawk of guitars and ear-wrenching microphone feedback, the director yelled, "The little tit showed up on set with an attitude, and now he's refusing to perform unless Miss Dashwood shows up."

"But Natalie can't come to the studio just because Dominic is having a meltdown—"

"She'd bloody well better," the director said grimly, "or this'll go down as the most expensive television commercial ever NOT made!" And he slammed down the phone.

Gemma rang off and looked at Natalie. "Sorry, but it sounds like you're going out to the studio today."

Natalie clutched her head in her hands. "I don't have time for Dominic and his drama today!"

"I've an idea." Gemma tapped a pencil against her lips. "Rhys is gone for the day, and I'm caught up. I'll go with you. I wouldn't mind seeing Dominic in action."

Natalie gave a derisive snort as she stood and grabbed her bag. "Just imagine a two-year-old having a tantrum on the floor, and you've seen Dominic in action."

They piled into Gemma's Skoda and headed for Soho. They found the studio twenty minutes later, on a side street at the end of an alley.

"Thank God!" the director exclaimed as they arrived. He indicated the brightly lit soundstage set up with drums, amplifiers, guitar stands and microphones with a jerk of his head. "It's the second day of shooting, and we haven't nearly enough usable footage yet. I hope you can make the little sod see reason, because I can't."

Dominic strummed a loud, discordant chord on his guitar. "There's more reverb in this place than my bloody bathroom!" he snarled, and kicked an amp cabinet. "How can we be expected to make music, much less film a commercial—"

He broke off as he saw Natalie and Gemma. "Nat! You're here."

"Yeah, I'm here," she said crossly. "You're costing us a fortune. What's wrong?"

"What's wrong? We could record in a garbage skip or inside a loo and sound better than we do in this echoing shithole, that's what's wrong." He scowled. "I'm not putting out a crap commercial. It's got to *sound* good, or what's the point?"

Gemma raised one perfectly groomed brow. "What do you suggest?"

"How should I know!" he snapped. "Probably sound better in the alley than it does in here." He regarded her through narrowed eyes. "Who are you, anyway?"

"Gemma Astley." She crossed her arms against her chest and glared back at him. "Not that it's your business, but I'm Rhys Gordon's personal assistant."

"Why aren't you assisting him, then?" he snapped. "I didn't know this was an open set, now they're letting any random bird just walk in off the bloody street."

"And I didn't know you were such a noxious little twat."

Before the conversation could deteriorate further, Natalie stepped between them and pulled Dominic aside. "I'll speak to the director, see if we can sort out the permits and move you and the boys outside. OK?"

He nodded, his expression still surly as he glared at Gemma. "Bitch," he muttered.

Gemma smirked. "Bit of advice, Dominic. Unless you fancy looking like a second-rate Alice Cooper in your video, you'd best get your eyeliner fixed while they're moving your gear."

He bridled. Natalie pulled him away before he could respond, and cast Gemma a quelling glare. "Come on, Dominic, let's talk to the director about moving your kit, then we'll get your eyeliner fixed."

"Stroppy cow!" he muttered, still scowling at Gemma. "She's toxic, just like that Gordon bloke."

Natalie threaded her way through the cameras and lights, dragging Dominic in her wake. "Come on, let's get this commercial made."

"Nat, wait." He stopped and ran a hand through his hair. "It's not just the sound that's got me crazy… it's you." He scowled down at his Converse trainers. "I miss you."

"Dominic," Nat said impatiently, "we've been through this! We don't work together, we never have—"

"I dumped Victoria," he interrupted. "That ought to count for something. It shouldn't have happened, but after half a bottle of Chivas, the next thing I knew we were in the broom closet, shagging for England—"

"If this is meant to make me feel better, it's not working," Natalie snapped. She took a deep breath. "Listen, your ad for *Dissolute* is all anyone's talking about. And your new single's at number three." She paused. "You need to focus on your career and forget about me."

She almost told him about Rhys. Natalie couldn't stop thinking about him, or the amazing kiss they'd so recently shared. Her thoughts drifted to Rhys Gordon at the oddest times... in a meeting, doing a downward dog in her yoga class...

...or filling out a petty cash tracking spreadsheet.

"I'll never forget you, Nat." Dominic gave her a sulky glance. "But I'll do the bloody commercial – if you promise to stay on and watch."

"We had to beg Maison Laroche to be allowed to use you in our advert, so yes, I'm staying. And so are you. Now quit being a pain in the arse and make this commercial."

With barricades erected at the entrance to the alley, the gear and equipment was moved outside. Sound technicians worked to minimise background noise as lights and camera tripods were adjusted. Dominic and the band picked up their instruments and rehearsed the new song. Everyone agreed the sound was much improved, and even Dominic was satisfied.

"He's good," Gemma shouted to Natalie as she watched Dominic slashing out guitar chords and singing into the microphone. "Too bad he's such an arschole."

The music had attracted a crowd, small at first, but growing in size by the moment. Dominic and his band fed off the energy from the crowd, and their performance was electric. In the end the police arrived to disperse the crowds, and a handful of tabloid photographers showed up to snap photos.

"I'd say," Natalie said as she and Gemma drove back to Knightsbridge late that afternoon, "it was a successful shoot."

"The rough cut looked great," Gemma agreed. "Dominic was amazing." She shifted gears. "Shame he's such a fuck-all."

Natalie glanced at her. "He's dumped Victoria, you know."

Gemma gave her a withering glance. "And why, exactly, would I care?"

"Oh, I don't know. I just thought I'd mention it."

"Well, I don't give a toss. I've no interest in Dominic bloody Heath."

Natalie said nothing more, but she saw a tiny glimmer of a smile on Gemma's lips.

CHAPTER 31

Dinner was finished and the dishes put away when Alastair came home that evening. Cherie folded the dishtowel atop the Aga and went into the foyer.

"Hello, darling, your dinner's in the warmer. I'll get it—"

"Don't bother. I've eaten." His words were clipped. "Where's Hannah?"

"She went with Jo to a movie."

"Good," he said, as he laid his briefcase and keys on the hallway table. "Tell me – what did you do today?"

Something in his tone alerted Cherie that this was more than just an idle question. "Nothing much… Neil returned a shirt to Harrod's. He asked me along. It was a bit spur of the moment, you know how these things are."

"Does the man never work?"

"He's a consultant for an engineering firm. He works from home two days a week."

"I had lunch today at Thomas Cubitt." He saw the quick, wary glance she cast his way. "I was with Rhys. I saw you come in with Neil."

"Alastair—"

"Don't bother to tell me it was nothing," he warned her. "I'm not an idiot. Have the two of you slept together yet?"

"No!" she cried. Guilt at how close she'd come to doing just that – and, more tellingly, how much she'd *wanted* to do it – made her defensive. "Do you think we'd be brazen enough to go round the corner from Dashwood and James for lunch, where anyone might see us, if we were really having an affair?"

"I don't know. Would you? Perhaps it's like that Edgar Allen Poe story, where the letter's hidden in plain view, yet no one sees it." He looked at her. "I never saw it, until today."

"Alastair," she said, her voice trembling, "this is ridiculous! If I'm to be accused of sleeping with Neil, no matter that I haven't, then perhaps I *should* sleep with him."

"Perhaps you should." He turned away and walked to the staircase.

Panic crossed her face. "Where are you going?"

He paused on the bottom step. "I'm going upstairs to change. Then I'm pouring myself a double scotch. After that, I'm moving my things into the guest bedroom."

"Alastair, for God's sake—"

"I'm not leaving, Cherie, if that's what's worrying you, or if that's what you're hoping. I've done nothing wrong. If anyone's to leave, it'll be you."

"You've done nothing wrong?" she echoed, suddenly furious. "All you do is work, cancel dinners, miss important family events, and turn me down for sex time and again, because you're always too bloody *tired*—"

"Because I'm too fucking busy trying to save the stores from bankruptcy!" he shouted. "Too busy trying to pay for this house, and the house in the country, and the school fees for Hannah's education!"

There was a shocked silence.

"My God, Cherie, have you any idea of the stress I've been under? Every day I deal with endless demands from Rhys, losses and overheads and falling profits; my daughter barely speaks to me, and my wife jumps into bed with the first man who comes along, because I'm too busy killing myself working to keep her properly entertained!"

Neither of them heard Hannah come in the front door.

"Mum? Dad?" she said, her eyes wide with uncertainty, one hand on the doorknob. "What's going on? Why are you shouting?"

Cherie cast Alastair a look of pure fury. "It's nothing, darling, just an argument." She forced a smile. "Go upstairs. I'll be up in a few minutes."

"So you can make me cocoa and tuck me up and read me a story about Jemima Puddle-Duck?" Hannah snapped. "I'm not a kid any more! Something's wrong. I heard you shouting! Why won't you just tell me the truth?"

"Hannah—"

But Hannah brushed past them both and stormed up the stairs to her room.

The television commercial featuring Dominic Heath aired four weeks later.

"Thanks to all of you," Rhys Gordon told the store employees assembled in the conference room. "And thanks to Natalie and Gemma for coping with Dominic's meltdown during the shoot. Good job, everyone."

As the others left, Rhys asked Natalie to remain behind. "Are Phillip's new designs ready for the re-launch? We haven't much time, less than a month now. We can't afford any delays."

"Yes. The clothes are gorgeous, better than his original designs. He's bringing samples today. Production starts soon."

"Good. What about promotional materials?"

"Dominic's record company's giving access to download his new single – free, of course. We're including store coupons and cosmetic samples in the swag bag as well."

"What about invitations, publicity?"

"We've ads in the papers and social media. The after-party's on a first-come, first-served basis. Oh, and there's a big, splashy ad on our website."

"Speaking of which, the site's vastly improved," Rhys observed as he gathered up his things. "Ian's team really turned it around."

Natalie's smile faded. "Good. If there's nothing else—"

"Actually, there is... Natalie, has Ian bothered you lately?" Rhys asked abruptly.

She looked at him, surprised. "No." Almost a month had passed since she'd heard from Ian. Every day she lived in fear that he'd make good on his threat, and she'd see her father's name splashed across every tabloid in London. But there'd been no phone calls, no press... nothing.

"Good. I've kept him busy." He fixed his dark blue eyes on hers. "Gemma told me he's harassed you at work. I had a word with him."

She bristled. "She had no right to tell you that."

"I'm glad she did," he said sharply. "*You* should have told me. You can still file a complaint, you know."

"I don't want any trouble. He's left me alone."

"All right, I'll drop it – for now." He glanced at her. "What are you doing on Sunday? Fancy spending the day with me?"

"Doing what, exactly? Buying more furniture? You don't have nearly enough, you know."

He lifted his brow. "What else does a man need but a sofa, a table, and a bed?"

"Beer, I suppose, and a flat-screen TV?"

"Too right," he agreed with a grin. "So? What do you say?"

"Well," she said doubtfully, "I normally do laundry, but I suppose it could wait. What did you have in mind?"

"We could both do with a break, we've worked really hard on the re-launch. I thought we'd do a bit of rural sightseeing. And that's all I intend to say on the matter."

"Can't you at least tell me where we're going? How should I dress for this mysterious outing?"

"Wear long sleeves and jeans, and proper shoes – no stripper heels, please. Save those for later."

Natalie blinked. "Rhys—!"

He came closer. "Don't look so shocked, Miss Dashwood. I know you want to finish what we started just as much as I do."

She blushed.

He grinned and turned away to pick up his things. "I'll pick you up at nine."

"Long sleeves and jeans—? But it's nearly June!" she protested. "Can't you tell me a bit more?"

"You'll see on Sunday." He smiled briefly and turned to go. "Now get back to work."

"The *Dissolute* campaign has great buzz," Simon Templeton, advertising director of the Templeton advertising agency, informed Klaus on Friday afternoon. "Everyone loves Dominic. Feedback's been positive, despite the Wedding-gate fiasco."

"Sometimes, notoriety is good."

An assistant brought Klaus an espresso. So far, the only information Dominic had produced concerning Phillip Pryce's line of clothing for Dashwood and James was a couple of sketches and a photo of a dress from last season's Rochas collection.

Von Richter scowled. Did Dominic Heath really believe him to be such a fool?

Since the rock star had produced nothing useful on Phillip, he'd have to find another way to sabotage Dashwood and James.

"Is the espresso not to your liking, Herr von Richter?" Simon Templeton enquired as displeasure flickered on the German designer's face. "I can assure you, it's made from the finest Sumatran fair trade beans."

"Fair trade," Klaus said derisively. "That's just an excuse to charge more money, *nein*?"

"Well, no. It ensures fair wages and treatment of the workers—"

Klaus snorted. "Workers should be glad to have any job and take what wages they get. It's preferable to starving in the streets, no?"

Simon kept his expression neutral. "Surely you don't advocate the use of sweatshops, Herr von Richter?"

"No, of course not. Bad for business, you know."

"The media would tear you apart," Simon agreed. "There's no tolerance for that sort of thing these days."

"No," Klaus agreed thoughtfully. "No tolerance at all."

"Well, if there's nothing else–?" Simon began.

Klaus stood up abruptly. "No, there is nothing else. I'll be in touch." He turned away to retrieve his mobile and called down to his driver. "I have an interview with *BritTEEN* magazine at two. And stop at the newsagents on the way."

The minute the staff meeting ended, Holly James left the *BritTEEN* offices and dashed downstairs to the corner newsagents. Every day she bought a pack of Polos and a Diet Coke from Rajid, the owner's son. Even on a completely crap day – today being no exception – he was always good for a laugh.

She waved to Rajid and went to the newsstand. As she flipped through the latest issue of *Vogue*, Klaus von Richter strode in, grabbed a newspaper, and flung it on the counter.

He wore the imperious air of an Important Person like an accessory.

Holly joined the queue and fished out her mobile. No messages. Out of boredom – the queue was longish – she decided to video Klaus for her sister. Klaus tossed a package of Mentos atop the *Telegraph* and handed his Amex Black to Rajid.

"May I see a photo ID, sir?" Rajid inquired politely.

Klaus gave him a withering stare. "You are joking."

Rajid shook his head. "It is store policy, sir."

"I'm buying two pounds' worth of items."

"I am sorry." Rajid was sympathetic but implacable. "Store policy."

"Listen to me, you idiot," Klaus snapped, "I'm Klaus von Richter, the creative director of Maison Laroche."

"A thousand apologies, sir," Rajid said firmly, "but I must see your identification. That is the rule."

By now, the queue had grown to half a dozen people, all in a hurry to purchase their newspapers and cough drops and Galaxy bars. "I don't care about rules, you stupid boy!" Klaus hissed, and leaned over to grab a fistful of Rajid's shirt. "Rules do not apply to me. Run my card now, or there'll be trouble."

"Release my son." Rajid's father, an older but far more implacable Sikh, joined his son. "Release him, or I promise I will have you charged with assault."

Klaus thrust Rajid away with a curse and a shocking string of racial epithets. "Keep your newspaper and your Mentos," he spat. He swept everything off the counter to the floor, then stormed out of the newsagents...

...unaware that Holly James had captured the entire ugly exchange on video.

CHAPTER 32

Promptly at nine on Sunday morning, Natalie heard the roar of an engine outside her flat.

"What in the world—?" She ran to the window and peered down. A gleaming silver Triumph motorcycle waited at the curb, a man in a helmet and a black leather jacket sitting astride. He rested one booted foot on the street, revved the engine, and lifted the visor of his helmet.

Dark blond hair, dark blue eyes…

"Rhys," Natalie murmured. She threw the sash up. "You can't be serious! You brought your motorbike?" she called out.

"Get your arse down here! Time's wasting."

"I think I prefer the Jag," Natalie said five minutes later as she regarded the Triumph doubtfully.

"Just put the helmet on. You loved it last time."

"I was drunk last time."

Once she was helmeted and straddled behind him, she wrapped her arms tightly around his waist.

"Hang on," he warned over the rumble of the engine. "I don't drive like your granny."

With a roar, they were off. Natalie clung to Rhys as they manoeuvreed their way out of London and onto the A3, headed west. Streets and buildings passed by in a blur, giving way gradually to rolling green countryside.

Exhilaration overtook her as they roared past hedgerows and fields dotted with cows and black-faced sheep. There was only the Triumph, the road, and Rhys's broad, muscled back. Her nose was assaulted by the smells of leather, petrol, and occasionally, the scent of wildflowers.

Just past noon, they stopped for lunch. Natalie was ravenous. Over fish and chips and pints of beer, Rhys told her about his Thunderbird and his love affair with motorcycles.

"It's my only escape," he said, and thrust a pickled onion in his mouth. "No mobile, no laptop, no demands – just me and the road and plenty of horsepower."

"I didn't think I'd like it," Natalie admitted, "but it's brilliant. Except for the seat... my bum's a bit sore."

Rhys nodded. "It will be, the first couple of times out. You'll feel it in your legs tomorrow."

"I already do."

Rhys paid the bill and they returned to the bike. "Ready?"

"Let's walk first," Nat suggested impulsively as she eyed the row of shops lining the main street.

"OK." He shoved his wallet in his back pocket. "But only if you promise not to buy anything."

"I'm very restrained in my spending these days." She stopped and pointed. "But there's a sweet shop, so I'm afraid—" she smiled triumphantly "—all bets are off."

Rhys took her hand, and they made their way to the confectioners. Outside the door he paused. "I'll probably regret this, but get whatever you like. I'll buy."

"Oh, you'll definitely regret it," Natalie agreed. "We'll get something for your mum. Jamie says she likes sweets."

"Jamie?"

"Yes, you know, your brother? We had a pint together the night you threw him out of your flat."

Rhys frowned. "I didn't throw him out."

"You did! When I left, we went to the pub around the corner."

"As I recall," Rhys murmured, "you left just as things got interesting. I had a very different idea of how the evening would end. And talking to Jamie wasn't it."

Natalie blushed. "Do you fancy shortbread?" she asked him. The woman at the till was avidly listening to every word.

Rhys leaned forward to kiss her. "I don't fancy shortbread," he said against her lips, "or chocolate, or gumdrops. I fancy you. I want to make you dinner. And I've dessert of another kind altogether in mind."

"You've forgotten Lesson Number One," she murmured. "'Behave with decorum at all times'."

"I'm the instructor, so I'm allowed to break the rules."

The woman behind the till rang everything up and handed the bag of sweets to Natalie. She leaned forward. "That's Rhys Gordon, that is," she whispered. "And you're Natalie Dashwood. I've read all about you in the tabloids."

"Oh, no," Natalie said hastily, "you're mistaken."

"No, I'm not." The woman looked past her and eyed Rhys appreciatively. "You want my advice? Run along and have some of that dessert on offer. I would!" She winked.

Scarlet-faced, Natalie took the bag and fled the shop.

Rhys tossed the candy into the Triumph's saddlebag and swung his leg over the seat. "Are you ready, Miss Dashwood?"

She settled herself in behind him and slid her arms tightly around his waist. "I'm ready, Mr. Gordon."

With a throaty rumble, they roared off into the drowsy late afternoon countryside, back to London.

"What should I do?" Holly fumed as she slid into a booth at the pub on Sunday afternoon.

"Do about what?" Hannah asked without looking up from her mobile. She was used to her sister's dramatics.

Holly brandished her mobile. "I've got a video of Klaus von Richter throwing a major tantrum at the newsagents on Friday," she confided in a low voice. "Rajid asked for ID, and Klaus went mental! Here, look."

As Hannah watched the video, her eyes grew wide. "Did you post this?"

"No! Are you crazy? If Klaus – or Sasha! – found out, I'd lose my job. Klaus is very important in the fashion world."

"But he treated Rajid horribly… and he's a racist git." Hannah leaned forward. "Hols, you have to post this. Offer the story to the tabloids, make yourself a bit of money—"

"No! If I go to the tabs, everyone including Klaus will know I took that video, and I'll be sacked."

"No, you wouldn't. Just say you want to be a – what do you call it? – an unnamed source," Hannah said.

Holly shook her head firmly. "I can't take the chance. My job means too much to me."

"Send me the video," Hannah offered. "I'll post it, and no one need know you had anything to do with it. Come on! What's the worst that could happen?"

"Losing my job, that's what. I'm not at home any more. I have to pay rent, not to mention buy groceries—"

Hannah snorted. "You eat nothing but salad and veg… a head of lettuce can't cost that much. And even if you lost your job, you could always come back home."

"No thanks!" Holly said, and shuddered. "I like being on my own. And I like my career as well, thank you very much."

"So you won't do it? You won't expose this guy's racist behaviour to the world?"

"No. I'm staying well out of it. Now let's order, I'm starving. Split some chips with me?"

Hannah nodded, distracted. The minute Holly went to the loo, she'd grab her mobile and forward the video to her own phone. And tonight, she'd upload it straight onto YouTube.

After all, Hannah reasoned, she was doing the right thing for Rajid and his father. Holly would thank her. Eventually.

"You never said you could cook like this," Natalie told Rhys that evening, as she squeezed lemon juice on her scallops.

Rhys dished out a generous portion of asparagus risotto onto her plate. "You never asked."

The scallops melted in her mouth, buttery and sweet. She closed her eyes. "This is really, really good."

He poured her a glass of Sancerre and sat down across from her. "I thought white was safer than red, in the event you decided to toss your glass at me."

"You'll never let me forget that, will you?" she demanded, indignant.

"Certainly not. I lost a perfectly good shirt to you that night. Not to mention a shoe."

"That's it – I'm buying you a shirt and a new pair of shoes. I should have done, anyway."

"You're on a budget. You can't afford it." He lifted his brow. "Besides, I have twelve other shirts just like it. I hardly need another. And I didn't like those shoes, anyway."

"You're impossible to please, you know that."

"I may be impossible," he conceded as he set aside his glass and leaned forward to take her hand in his, "but I'm not impossible to please." He turned her palm up and pressed his lips to the inside of her wrist.

A shiver of desire shot through her at the touch of his lips on her skin. Suddenly any clever remarks – or any remarks at all, for that matter – went straight out of her head.

Rhys glanced at her. Spending the day in the sun and wind on the motorbike had put a bloom of colour on Natalie's cheeks and left her hair tousled and messy.

"Riding on the back of a motorbike suits you," he said, his lips moving against her skin. "We should do it more often."

"Rhys," Natalie murmured as his lips moved slowly along the inside of her forearm, inch by delicious inch, "I wasn't quite finished with my risotto…"

He stood and pulled Natalie to her feet as he wrapped his arms around her. "You are now." His mouth came down on hers.

She gave herself over to the taste and feel and sheer physicality of him – the muscled length of his arms, the heat of his body against hers, the thick softness of his hair beneath her fingers. He smelled of a heady mix of soap and the outdoors, fresh and very, very masculine.

As his lips moved down the column of her neck to her throat, leaving a wet trail of heat, Natalie groaned.

"I want you," she breathed, "*now*…"

He undid the top buttons of her shirt with agonising slowness, until her lacy black bra was revealed. "I want to make love to you properly, on sheets with an indecently high thread count, and I intend to take my time doing it."

Natalie's hands slid over his shoulders and down the muscled length of his torso. "I can't wait," she said huskily against his mouth, and reached down to unclasp his belt.

He stayed her hand. "I don't want our first time to be on the kitchen floor."

"I don't care where it is." She put her hands on either side of his face and crushed her mouth against his.

He picked her up and carried her into his bedroom. "You're very impatient, Miss Dashwood," he said, his blue eyes fixed on hers as he lowered her onto his bed. "I had no idea you were so demanding."

"I hope you're worth the wait, Mr. Gordon."

"Oh, I am," he promised, and hooked his fingers on either side of her jeans and slid them slowly, teasingly, down the length of her legs.

Natalie kicked them off and reached behind her to unclasp her bra. Rhys's mouth collided with hers, demanding and receiving and giving all at once. When he lifted his lips from hers and devoured his way down her neck to her breasts, she let out a low whimper.

Her fingers tangled themselves in his hair as his tongue laved first one nipple with wet heat, then the other.

"I've wanted this since the night of that bloody party," he growled. "I don't know how I resisted you."

"Lots of very long, very cold showers," Natalie murmured, her skin tingling as his mouth began to move lower, down her stomach. "You... told me so yourself."

"Do shut up, darling."

Natalie clutched at the sheets as his lips and tongue moved slowly, oh so slowly, along the sensitive skin of her inner thighs, closer and closer to her most sensitive centre...

"If you want me to shut up," Natalie breathed, desperate with desire for him, "then you'd better make it good..."

And he proceeded, very skilfully, to do exactly that.

"Well… was I worth the wait?" Rhys asked afterwards, raising himself up on one elbow to look at her

"Umm," Natalie sighed. "Worth every minute. You were brilliant." Her eyes drifted closed.

He kissed her shoulder. "Sleep, darling."

She smiled and murmured something unintelligible.

Rhys pulled the blankets up and covered her, then kissed her tenderly on the side of her mouth. He studied her, loving the sight of her in his bed, then flung his arm over her and fell into a deep and satisfied sleep.

CHAPTER 33

The sound of the newsreader's voice on the clock radio woke Rhys and Natalie the next morning.

"—shocking video of the fashion designer verbally and physically abusing an Indian store clerk in Knightsbridge has gone viral—"

Rhys lifted his head from the pillow and squinted at the clock. "Shit!" He sat up abruptly and slapped the alarm off, then flung back the covers. He had a meeting with Sir Richard at nine, less than forty minutes from now.

"What time is it?" Natalie murmured, and rolled over sleepily.

"Eight-fifteen. We overslept." He pulled on a shirt and buttoned it up quickly. "I've a meeting with the board at nine to update them on the re-launch. Hurry and get dressed."

"But... we can't go in together!" she exclaimed as she got up.

"Why not?"

"Because then everyone will know we slept together."

He grabbed a tie from the tie rack. "Natalie, the entire UK already thinks we've slept together."

"That's different! I don't want Gemma, or Alastair, or, God forbid, grandfather to know about us just yet." *And especially not Ian*, she almost added. "I want to keep our relationship private. At least for now," she amended.

"Fine. Take a taxi, then," Rhys said shortly. "I haven't time to argue, I've got to go." He leaned forward as he knotted his tie and kissed her briefly. "I'll see you later."

Traffic through Knightsbridge on Monday morning was as thick and slow as treacle. Alastair moved to switch off the radio just as the presenter said, "Klaus von Richter, head of design for Maison Laroche couture, is in a bit of hot water this morning— "

Hannah stayed his hand. "Wait, dad, I want to hear this."

"Why, in heaven's name?" Alastair demanded irritably.

Hannah shushed him and leaned forward to listen to the newscaster. "A video of von Richter's verbal assault of 19-year-old store clerk Rajid Singh was posted to YouTube late yesterday and already has over three million hits. Singh's father has filed assault charges against the designer. Executives at Maison Laroche are demanding von Richter's resignation—"

Hannah switched off the radio and leaned back, stunned. Her mobile began to vibrate. Holly.

"Oh my God!" Holly wailed. "Klaus might lose his job because of me! Why did you post that bloody video? I told you not to! If anyone finds out—"

"Don't worry, they won't," Hannah assured her, aware of her father's curious glance. "I just got to work, talk later." She thrust her mobile in her handbag. "Holly," she said with a roll of her eyes. "She's such a drama queen."

Alastair negotiated a turn, his thoughts elsewhere. "Hannah, there's been a change in your work schedule."

She glanced at him warily. "What sort of change?"

He parked the Mercedes in his designated spot in front of the department store. "You'll be in the ladies' sportswear department for the rest of the week." Human resources assured him that Jago Sullivan would be sacked on Friday afternoon.

"But I only just started in the stockroom!" she protested.

"You've been there nearly a month. There's much more to Dashwood and James than the stockroom."

"It's because of Jago, isn't it?"

Alastair's hands tightened on the steering wheel. "No. I told you when you started that you'd be moving departments."

"You don't like him, so you're moving me out." When he said nothing, Hannah snapped, "You're judging Jago because he's working class. You're wrong about him, dad. He's ambitious. He's going to school at night to learn to be a chef—"

"We'll talk later." Alastair shut off the engine. "For now," he added as he cast his daughter a quelling glance, "report to the third floor. And I'll hear no more about it."

Natalie made it through the doors of Dashwood and James with only a couple of minutes to spare. The day passed in a blur of last-minute preparations for the re-launch – meetings with Phillip, Rhys and Sir Richard, calls to confirm delivery of the Portaloos, re-launch posters to review and approve… There was barely time for a salad at her desk.

It was six o'clock when Natalie finally slung her handbag over her shoulder and headed, exhausted, out the door.

Not only hadn't she done her laundry yesterday – too busy rolling in the sheets with Rhys, she reflected guiltily – but she had nothing in her fridge for dinner… unless you counted a month-old stalk of asparagus and a half-bottle of Krug.

God, what she'd give for a nice, juicy takeaway burger right now…

A shadow fell across her, and she looked up to see Ian standing before her. Natalie came to an abrupt stop.

"Keep walking." He took her elbow and propelled her forward; in his free hand he held a folder. "The park's just ahead. Let's find a bench and chat, shall we?"

Wordlessly Natalie walked with him, across the street and into Hyde Park, to an empty bench shaded by a lime tree. No one was about; only a young woman, walking her dog and talking on a mobile further along the path.

When they were seated, Ian handed her the folder. "Have a look. This should allay any doubts you might have about your father's guilt."

With trembling fingers, Natalie took the folder. She opened it and paged slowly through the photocopied ledger account entries. The method was clever. Small amounts of money – a hundred pounds here, fifty quid there – were paid out to various vendors.

"The vendors with tick marks—" Ian pointed to several entries "—billed the store and were paid, some in cash. But the vendors didn't exist, and the cash went straight into your father's pockets."

"I don't understand," she said, her expression confused. "Why would he risk everything for such small amounts of money?"

"It added up over time – two years, and almost £100,000 before he was found out. As to why—" he paused "—the money went to support his mistress." He leaned back against the bench and rested his arm along the back. "I do hope she was worth it."

Natalie stared at him in dismay. Everyone, including her mother, must have known that Roger Dashwood was having an affair.

Natalie clutched the folder. "I can't do this." She looked at Ian, her expression troubled. "I'll get you money, a car, whatever you want. But I can't do this to Alexa."

"You don't have a choice, Natalie. I thought you understood that." His expression hardened. "I'm divorcing my wife just as soon as she has the baby. After a decent interval, we can announce our engagement. You might want to talk to Sir Richard and mention that I be considered for a partnership."

"Grandfather will never make you a partner, Ian! You're mad if you think he will."

"Convince him. It shouldn't be difficult. He adores you, after all."

"There's Alastair to consider, and the board will have to vote on it—"

"I've reserved a room at the Savoy on the night of the re-launch." Ian went on as if she hadn't spoken. "That's two weeks from now. We can celebrate, you and I. Alexa will be in hospital having the baby. The doctors have scheduled her for a Caesarean." He smiled. "Isn't modern medicine wonderful?"

"Ian, you can't really mean to do this—"

"Sorry, but it's already done." He leaned forward and brushed his lips against hers; she was too numb to react. "I'll see you at eight-thirty. Go to the desk and ask for Mr. Gordon's room." He smirked. "You have to appreciate the irony, surely?"

She glared at him. "I promise you, Ian, Rhys has nothing to worry about on your account."

His laugh was low and ugly. "Got there first, did he? Well, Gordon might be first, but I'll be the last." Just before he stood, he added, "By the way – wear something sexy on the night. I like black heels and a short skirt, something a bit – tarty." With another smirk, he turned and walked away.

Natalie shouldered her handbag and stood, her legs trembling and her thoughts racing.

What to do? She had to tell Rhys, she couldn't let Ian do this. Being forced to sleep with him was bad enough; but she knew it wouldn't end there. He'd force her to play out his twisted little game until he tired of her.

Ian Clarkson had to be stopped. But how? *How?*

CHAPTER 34

The next morning, Alexa Clarkson left the obstetrician's office after her appointment and went to the newsagents. She rang Ian's mobile and got his voicemail.

"It's me. I just got back from Dr. Assam's office. Everything's fine; I'm still on for the Caesarean next Saturday. Call me."

Alexa put away her mobile. She had a sudden craving for a Cadbury Flake. She sighed. No wonder she was bigger than a Range Rover.

"Good morning," she said as she entered the shop. She picked up a Flake bar, shrugged and added a Dairy Milk, and set them on the counter. "I'll be right back."

The Indian woman behind the till nodded but didn't look up from her well-thumbed copy of *Hello!*.

Alexa studied the racks of publications. Klaus von Richter, the German designer, had assaulted a store clerk. The *Sun* caught her eye. 'Natalie's New Mystery Man?' the headline read. Curious, she picked it up.

The grainy photo showed Natalie sitting on a park bench next to a tallish man in sunglasses. Although his back faced the camera, he definitely wasn't Rhys. And they were kissing.

"Oho," Alexa murmured, surprised. "Rhys isn't enough for you, then, Nat?"

She tucked the *Sun* under her arm and scanned the other tabloids. When she saw the *Daily Mirror*, time ground to a halt. She picked it up with an unsteady hand. The photo showed Natalie sitting on the same park bench, her head bent forward in conversation with the same tall, brown-haired man. This photograph, however, was much sharper than the others.

The newsprint slipped from her nerveless fingers. She felt the baby move in her abdomen, and she let out a short, startled gasp. It couldn't be. Yet there was no mistake.

The man in the photo with Natalie was her husband. Ian.

"Are you all right, miss?" the clerk asked, clucking with concern as she put aside her magazine and hurried over.

"I'm fine. I had a… contraction. It was probably one of those Braxton-Hicks things." Alexa took the tabloid the clerk handed her. Methodically, she grabbed every tabloid with a photo of Natalie and Ian and carried them to the till.

The woman rang everything up. "Will this be all?"

"Yes," Alexa said grimly. "This will be quite enough."

Just before noon, Natalie arrived at Phillip Pryce's atelier on Great Portland Street and went up to his workroom. Phillip was marking a bias-cut skirt with tailor's chalk as the Scissor Sisters played at full volume.

He looked up as Natalie entered. "Well, hello, chickpea! I see our friend Klaus is in the news this morning." He set aside his tailor's chalk and lowered the stereo volume.

"Yes, he's in a bit of hot water, isn't he?"

"More like a vat, and it couldn't happen to a nicer prick," Phillip agreed. "But he's not the only one who's all over the tabs this morning. You are, too."

Dismayed, Natalie set her handbag down atop a teetering pile of bolts of fabric. "I am? Why, what have I done now?"

"You've been a naughty girl. You were caught snogging a man on a park bench... not Rhys, either." He raised his brow. "Tall, dark haired chap, looks quite dishy from what I saw. Do spill the details, please."

Her heart sank. "Do you have a copy?"

"Look on the cutting table, that's where I saw it last."

She picked up the latest issue of the *Sun*, and on the cover was a photo of her with Ian, his back to the camera, just as he'd pressed his lips to hers. How on earth had anyone got a picture of them? There'd been no one around...

...no one, that is, except for the woman walking her dog and talking on her mobile. She'd used her phone's camera to snap a picture, of course.

Natalie remembered Rhys's remark, the first time they'd had lunch together.

You never know when a photographer might be around, or someone with a camera phone.

"So?" Phillip prodded as she stared at the tabloid. "Who is he?"

"A friend," Natalie said, hoping her voice sounded sufficiently casual, and tossed the *Sun* aside. "His wife's pregnant, they've been trying for a baby for a long time. He was so happy that he got a bit carried away and kissed me. That's all."

"Hmm." Phillip didn't look particularly convinced. "Well, if that's your story... What can I do for you today?"

"It's about the clutch you're making for the dress I'm wearing in the fashion show. I wondered... can you make an opening, in the lining? So I can slip something in behind it?"

"I could," he said doubtfully, "but why? Planning on hiding your vial of ecstasy in there? I didn't think you were an 'E' sort of girl."

"I'm not! I just thought it might be a handy way to stash some extra cash. Or to hide one's credit card if one's in a dodgy neighbourhood."

Phillip raised a brow skeptically. "And does one often frequent dodgy neighbourhoods?"

"One never knows," Natalie said evasively.

"I'll do it for the sample," he agreed, "but not for the production line. If I do, costs will triple, and Rhys Gordon will have my arse." He smirked. "Ooh, now there's a visual…"

"You're an angel – tarnished, but an angel." She threw her arms around his neck. "Thanks. I love you, Phillip."

"Careful," Jacques called out from the adjoining room, "I might get jealous."

"What size for the opening?" Phillip asked.

She held up her mobile. "About this size, actually."

He nodded, a straight pin in his mouth as he readied a side seam for stitching. He removed the pin and thrust it in place. "You're not telling me what this is really about, are you?"

"No, Phillip. I'm not. I can't."

"You're not a spy, are you? Not concealing a Luger or a Walther PPK in there, perhaps?"

"I'm not Lara bloody Croft. You have an overactive imagination."

"It keeps our dull lives interesting," Jacques remarked.

"Come in here, please," Phillip called out to him. "I want you to alter the sample clutch for Nat's cocktail dress." Briefly he explained to Jacques what Natalie wanted.

"So much for the House of Holland party tonight, then," Jacques groused. "Instead, I'll be up to my elbows in grape leather."

"Don't be ridiculous. You can do it tomorrow. We're not missing Henry's party tonight." Phillip winked at Natalie. "Not even for you, chickpea."

At seven that evening, the door buzzer echoed through Natalie's flat. She got up from her laptop – damn Rhys and his damned budgeting spreadsheet – and went into the front hallway to press the button. "Yes?" she enquired.

"It's Alexa."

Nat gazed at the intercom in dismay. "Oh! Come on up."

As she pressed the button to let Ian's wife in downstairs, Natalie wondered uneasily if she'd seen the photographs of Ian and her in the tabloids. Of course she had. You couldn't walk past the newsagents without seeing the lurid headlines.

Natalie swung the door open a few minutes later. "Hello, Alexa. It's great to see you! Due soon, aren't you?"

Alexa regarded her as one might regard a poisonous insect.

"Please... come in." Nat's heart quickened as she led the way into the lounge. "Can I get you a cup of tea? Won't you sit down—?"

"No, I won't." Alexa brandished a copy of the *Mirror*. "And I don't want a cup of bloody *tea*. I want you to tell me what the hell's going on. That's what I want."

Natalie took the tabloid Alexa thrust at her and stared at the cover photo for the second time that day. It showed her walking with Ian in the park, their heads close together in conversation.

"Oh, yes... that," she managed to stammer eventually. Her thoughts raced. "It was nothing. Really—"

"Nothing?" Alexa asked softly. "In the *Mirror*, you're having a cosy chat with my husband; in the *Sun*, you're sitting on a park bench snogging, and it was *nothing*?"

"It isn't what you think."

"Oh, it is, there's no question of that. You called Ian not long ago, late on Sunday night." Her eyes narrowed. "Don't deny it. I saw your name listed in his mobile."

"I had a question about work." Natalie's throat tightened. This was awful. How to explain without telling Alexa the truth – that her husband planned to divorce her and cast her aside like an empty sweet wrapper?

"A question about work, so late on a Sunday night? Right. You must think I'm not only pregnant, but stupid." Alexa eyed her with contempt. "You're screwing my husband, aren't you?"

"No!" Shock sharpened her voice. "I'm seeing Rhys, and I have been for weeks. I have no interest in Ian, Alexa! You know how the tabloids are, how they distort the truth—"

"It's hard to argue with a photo, though, isn't it?" She slapped her hand hard against the picture. "The two of you are kissing, Natalie. Right here in black and white. You slag. You cheap, lying slag."

Natalie's eyes widened. "Alexa, please, if you'd just let me explain—"

"I don't need you to explain that you're fucking my husband," Alexa said succinctly. "It's plain enough, even to a stupid, trusting cow like me."

"Listen to me." Natalie reached out to touch her, to try and reason with her. "We've been friends for a long time—"

Alexa knocked her hand aside. "No longer. You're welcome to Ian, because he and I are through. I don't need him, and this baby doesn't need him. And I most certainly don't need *friends—*" the word was laced with rancour "—like you."

So saying, she flung the tabloids at Natalie in a wild flutter of newsprint, and left.

CHAPTER 35

After a tense and silent ride home with her father after work, Hannah stormed up the stairs and slammed her door.

"What's happened?" Cherie asked Alastair sharply as she sat across from him at dinner. "Why has Hannah gone upstairs?"

"I moved her out of the stockroom, away from that Sullivan boy. She's furious." He speared a roasted potato. "She'll get over it."

"Don't be so sure," Cherie retorted. The phone rang, and she got up to answer it. "Hello, James residence." There was no immediate response. "Who's calling, please?"

"It's Jago. Jago Sullivan. For Hannah," he added.

"One moment." Cherie glared at Alastair and went upstairs to knock on Hannah's door. "You've a call."

Hannah edged the door open. "Who is it?"

"It's Jago. I didn't tell your father. When you've finished," Cherie added, "come straight down to dinner."

"I will," Hannah promised. She hesitated. "Thanks, mum."

"They moved you," Jago said when Hannah picked up the phone.

"Yeah, to ladies' sportswear. I hate it."

"I'm sorry. Sorry about what I said, too." He paused. "We can meet up for lunch tomorrow, if you like."

"Dim Sum Palace?" Hannah asked tentatively.

"Twelve o'clock," Jago agreed. "Sharpish, mind."

Just before noon the next day, Rhys called Natalie into his office and asked her to shut the door.

He threw a copy of the previous day's *Sun* on his desk. "What's going on?" he demanded without preamble. "Are you having an affair with Ian Clarkson?"

"What? How can you even *ask* me that?" Natalie exclaimed angrily. "Of course I'm not!"

"It's right there in black and white." He looked at her, his blue eyes hard. "What else am I to think?"

"Think what you want. It sounds like you've already made up your mind, at any rate." Fury propelled her to the door. "Now if you'll excuse me, I have work to do."

"Tell me I'm wrong, Natalie," he demanded. He came round his desk and slapped his palm on the door, blocking her exit. "Tell me you're not screwing Ian."

"No, I'm not! Isn't my word enough?"

"You met him for drinks at the Connaught. I saw you myself! Now you've been photographed kissing him on a park bench, and it wasn't just a peck on the bloody cheek!"

"You've got the wrong idea—"

He dropped his hand. "It's obvious you don't trust me enough to tell me the truth. Go on, then," he snapped, "go."

His eyes were dark with anger. "With pleasure." She flung the door open and left his office.

"I have to leave right now, or I'll bloody well kill him," Natalie seethed as she stalked over to Gemma's desk.

"Well," Gemma remarked dryly, "I certainly don't have to ask who you're talking about. Come on, let's get some lunch."

They found seats in Pizza Express ten minutes later. Gemma looked over at Natalie expectantly. "What's

Rhys done now? I know you two had a closed-door this morning." She lifted a brow. "I heard shouting... mostly his."

Natalie bit her lip. In a low voice she said, "God, Gemma, I have to tell someone, or I'll go mad. I'm being blackmailed."

"You're not serious." Gemma's dark eyes searched her face. "You *are* serious! Who, Nat? What on earth have you done?"

"It's not what I've done. It's what my father did. He embezzled money from the store, a long time ago. Someone—" she tamped down the slow rise of panic "—someone has proof."

"But your dad died years ago!" Gemma exclaimed. "What difference does any of that make now?"

"This... person... has promised to go to the media. My father's name will be ruined." Natalie looked at Gemma in anguish. "He had a mistress."

"What?!"

"It was in all the papers when I was at school. I didn't understand it then, of course, but I remember the newsmen hanging round outside our front gate, snapping pictures, and I remember the fights he and mum had. He must've stolen money from the store to keep this woman – whoever she was – from talking to the press. God – this'll kill mum if it comes out. Dredging up all that muck again... not to mention grandfather. My father's suicide gutted him. And his health is already so frail... "

"Oh, Nat," Gemma murmured in concern, and reached out to cover her hand. "You've got to go to the police with this."

"I can't. He'll know, and he'll smear my father's name, and stir up bad publicity for the store. We're just about to reopen. He'll destroy everything we've worked so hard for."

"Who's doing this?" Gemma asked, her voice hard. "Who is it?" Her eyes widened as realisation hit her. "It's Ian, isn't it?"

Natalie hesitated, then nodded. "Yes. His stepfather was the head accountant at Dashwood and James when this all happened. Geoffrey Graham. He realised what was going on and blackmailed my father. It's why he committed suicide."

"So... let me get my head round this. Ian – the stepson of the man who was blackmailing your father – is blackmailing you, now... for the same exact reason."

Wordlessly, Natalie nodded.

"That's so twisted! And what does he want?"

"He wants me to get him a partnership in the store. And... he's arranged for a hotel room on Saturday night. The night of the re-launch," Natalie said dully. "So we can 'celebrate'."

Gemma leaned forward, her face stamped with outrage. "Nat, you have to tell someone! Tell Rhys. He'll know what to do. You can't let Ian menace you with this for the rest of your life."

"I'm afraid, Gemma. If I tell Rhys, and Ian finds out—" she stopped. "He'll ruin everything – my father's name, the re-launch, all of it. He's clever. I can't risk it."

"Screw your father's name!"

Natalie stared at her in shock. "How can you say that?"

"He didn't give much thought to you and your mum, did he, screwing around and stealing money to keep his bit on the side quiet? He sounded like a selfish prick, if you ask me."

Tears seeped from the corners of Natalie's eyes. "He may have been, Gemma – but he was still my father! I can't bear to see his name dragged through the mud. And we've all worked so bloody hard on the re-launch, Rhys most of all. Ian knows that."

"But you can't let him get away with this, either!" She reached out and took Natalie's hands in hers. "You know this is only the beginning, don't you? Natalie, you have to stop it. And you have to stop it *now.*"

The next morning, Natalie finalised the arrangements for the re-launch – confirmations, cancellations, updates to the after-party guest list, a try-on of Phillip's clothes for the fashion show. One of the models hired for the show called to say she'd turned her ankle.

Natalie rang off and glanced at Gemma. "I need a huge favour. Will you model in the show next Saturday? We're down one and I need a replacement."

"Me?" Gemma eyed her in shock. "I'm no bloody model."

"You're tall and gorgeous and a size eight. You're perfect," Natalie implored.

"Well, if you put it like that, how can I refuse?" She added in a low voice, "Have you told Rhys yet?"

"No." Natalie looked up to see her mother standing in Rhys's doorway. "But I will do, today. Excuse me."

She stood. "Mum! What are you doing here?"

Celia Dashwood turned and, with a guilty expression, came forward to kiss her daughter. "I came to see you. I thought we might have lunch in the tearoom today."

"Sorry, I can't," Natalie said. "I have a million things to do—"

"Gemma will see to them," Rhys called out from his office. "Go and have lunch with your mum. You're no good to anyone if you're stressed."

"I'm not stressed," she said shortly. "I'm busy. There's a difference."

"Go," Rhys said as he stood in the doorway. He fixed her with a steely blue glare. "That's a bloody order."

Natalie scowled and turned to her mother. "Very well. I'll meet you upstairs in ten minutes."

"What a gracious acceptance," Lady Dashwood harrumphed.

Nat finished her calls and went to freshen up before lunch. She eyed herself in the bathroom mirror. She looked awful, with dark circles from sleepless nights spent worrying about Ian's threats, and now the misunderstanding with Alexa... not to mention her doubts about the night she'd spent with Rhys.

The sex had been spectacular, no question. And she loved spending time with Rhys Gordon.

Had their night together meant anything to him? Or was this another dead-end relationship, destined, like her time with Dominic, to end badly?

Natalie didn't know. She did know, however, that Rhys would most likely leave after the re-launch. His work here was nearly done; he had no reason to stay.

And the thought of never seeing him again was almost more than she could bear.

CHAPTER 36

"What will you have?" Celia Dashwood asked Natalie as she studied the tearoom's menu.

She shrugged. "Prawn cocktail, I suppose."

"Surely you want something more substantial…?"

"No." Natalie laid the menu aside. "Just the prawns."

"Darling," her mother prodded, "is something wrong?"

"Yes, something's wrong," Nat snapped. "I'm sick and bloody tired of you asking me if something's wrong!"

Her mother subsided into frosty silence as the waiter arrived and took their orders, retrieved their menus, and left.

"I'm sorry." Natalie spoke quietly. "I shouldn't have snapped at you. I'm under enormous pressure at the moment."

"I know you are, darling." Her mother and laid a comforting hand atop Natalie's. "Is it too much? Working at the store with Rhys, I mean?"

"No, of course not. I love it. I just have so much to do right now, with the re-launch only a week away."

"I'll be glad when it's over," Lady Dashwood said, and frowned. "I just hope it's worth the time and expense. Rhys is convinced that this re-launch will make a huge difference."

"It will. We've got Dominic to perform, and there'll be a fashion show with Phillip Pryce's new clothing line, and a DJ, and all sorts of lovely swag—"

Natalie's voice trailed away. A trolley bearing an enormous cake was wheeled out to their table. Lit sparklers were stuck in the top. "What in the world—?"

Suddenly everyone surrounded their table and began singing 'Happy Birthday'. Natalie heard her grandfather's quavery voice, and Gemma's off-key one; only Rhys wasn't singing. *Typical.*

Her throat tightened. God, she adored them all. They were her family, the ones who loved her and always had her back. She'd completely forgotten today was her birthday.

"… happy birthday to you," they finished with a flourish.

Amidst the clapping and cheers, Natalie thrust her chair back and stood. Her eyes stung with unshed tears as everyone waited for her to make a short speech.

"I don't know what to say," she managed to choke out. Her throat closed. "Thank you all, so, so much…"

But she couldn't go on. Overcome with emotion, sick with worry, exhausted from her preparations for the re-launch and night after night of poor sleep, Natalie began to cry. She pushed blindly past them and ran from the room, leaving a sea of bewildered faces behind.

With a muttered curse Rhys went after her.

"I knew something was wrong!" Lady Dashwood exclaimed.

The office hallway was empty; everyone was gathered in the tearoom. Rhys strode towards the conference room at the end of the hallway, where he heard the muted sound of crying.

He pushed the door open. Natalie was slumped at the table, her head in her arms, her face swollen with tears. She lifted her head and saw him; wordlessly she stood and flung herself into his arms.

"Oh, Rhys," she sobbed, "I'm afraid… I don't know what to do… should've told you at the start—"

"It's all right, darling," he murmured, and stroked her hair. A surge of protectiveness overtook him, fierce and strong. "Tell me what's happened to upset you." His face hardened. "It's Ian, isn't it?"

Natalie nodded. Haltingly, the story of Ian's blackmail came out. "He wants me to persuade grandfather to make him a partner."

Rhys let out a short, disbelieving laugh. "A partner? He's mad."

"I'm to meet him at the Savoy next Saturday night," she added, and lifted her tear-stained face to his. "He's got a room for us, Rhys. And he said it'll be under the name 'Mr. Gordon'."

"I wish you'd told me about this sooner," he said grimly.

"I know. I'm sorry." She took a shuddering breath. "But if Ian finds out I've talked to you—"

"He won't, he's not here. I sent him to the Croydon store, he'll be there all day." He held her at arm's length and studied her face. "The question is – what'll we do about this?"

"We can't go to the police," Natalie said firmly. "I can't risk it."

"We have to tell Sir Richard." Rhys released her and frowned. "This concerns his son. It's his call as to what we should do next."

"What would you do," Natalie asked, "if it were up to you?"

"I'd go to the press," Rhys said without hesitation. "I'd tell them the whole story, and take away Ian's power over you."

"But the scandal—"

"Let's leave it for the moment," Rhys said firmly. "Come back, have some cake. Let everyone see you're OK, then we'll ask to meet with Sir Richard privately."

When they returned to the tearoom, everyone came up to Natalie and clustered around her in concern.

"Are you all right, darling?" her mother asked as she enveloped Natalie in a perfume-scented embrace.

"I'm fine." Natalie hugged her tightly, then stepped away and smiled apologetically at everyone. "Sorry. I had a bit too much on my plate and I had a meltdown... rather like Dominic." Over the scattered laughter, she added, "I'm fine now, and hungry. So... where's my cake?"

Rhys handed her a plate. When they sat down, Natalie turned to him. "Why is Ian at the Croydon store?"

"I wanted him out of the way for your birthday celebration. He's working on their website." Grimly he pushed his plate aside. "A good thing, too, or I'd have killed him already."

Natalie eyed him in panic. "He can't know I've told you about this—"

"Don't worry, he won't. I can't stand him on a normal day as it is, and the feeling is mutual."

Sir Richard appeared next to Natalie. "Happy birthday, dear girl." He leaned down and kissed her cheek.

Natalie reached up and clasped his hand tightly. "Thank you, grandfather. Have you had cake?"

"Only a taste; I have to watch my sugar, you know." He lowered himself into the seat beside her.

Rhys leaned forward. "Sir Richard, Natalie and I need to speak privately with you. It's a matter of some urgency."

He nodded. "Come by this evening. I'll be waiting."

At half-past seven, Rhys and Natalie arrived at Sir Richard's townhouse in Belsize Park.

"I hope this isn't too much of a shock for him," Natalie worried as Lyons showed them in.

Rhys rested one hand on her shoulder. "Sir Richard is stronger than you think. He might surprise you."

"It wouldn't be the first time," Natalie agreed. She followed the butler to her grandfather's study.

Lyons knocked discreetly and opened the door. "Sir Richard? Miss Natalie and Mr. Gordon are here."

"Come in," he called out from the sofa. He indicated a crystal decanter on the coffee table. "Whiskey?"

Rhys nodded. "Thank you."

"I'll have one as well," Natalie said. "It's been a trying day." She sat down and took the glass he handed her. "We have something – well, I have something – to tell you."

"Ran up another outrageous bill? Smashed up your car?"

"No, nothing like that." She hesitated. "The truth is, I'm... I'm being blackmailed."

There. She'd said it. The words fell into the silence like stones to the bottom of a well. The sound of the carriage clock on the mantel filled the room, its measured ticking far outpaced by Natalie's racing heart.

Sir Richard leaned forward. "Blackmailed! By whom?"

"Ian Clarkson," Rhys said.

He drew his silvery brows together. "Ian's on the board, isn't he?"

Natalie nodded, silent.

Sir Richard's frown deepened. "What in God's name have you done, Natalie?"

"Nothing, honestly! It's what dad did. He embezzled from the store, for two years. He needed the money to support his mistress."

With a muttered imprecation, Sir Richard set his glass down with a crack on the table. "How the devil did Clarkson find out about that? It was a private family matter. It happened so long ago... I thought we'd buried it all, along with your father."

CHAPTER 37

Stunned, Natalie stared at Sir Richard. "You *knew* about the blackmail?"

"Of course I knew." He scowled. "Where do you think your father got the money to pay off Geoffrey Graham?"

Natalie sagged back against the sofa. "All this time, I worried the shock would prove too much for you, and you've known all along."

"It's just as well Roger committed suicide," Sir Richard said, his face set. "Otherwise, I'd have killed him myself."

"Grandfather!" Natalie exclaimed, and sat bolt upright. "How can you say such a thing?"

He regarded her, his expression hard. "Your father put us through hell, Natalie, your mother in particular. It cost me half a million pounds in payouts before it ended – and that was only because Graham died. That money was meant for improvements to the store. Without it, Dashwood and James began its decline... all because my son couldn't keep his trousers zipped."

"Did Lady Dashwood know about the affair?" Rhys asked.

"Oh, I daresay she did, although she never spoke of it. How could she not? There were stories in the papers, photographs of Roger ducking out of restaurants and hotels with another woman. He was shockingly indiscreet."

"Poor mum." Natalie frowned. "I thought she never married again because she loved dad so much."

Sir Richard snorted. "I can't speak for your mother, of course, but in view of Roger's affairs, I doubt she wanted to marry again. Nor did she want to bring someone into your lives who mightn't stay. She wanted you and your sister to have stability."

"But that's so unfair on mum!" Natalie objected, crushed. "She spent all these years alone because of me and Caro?"

"Oh, don't feel too sorry for her," Sir Richard told her, and sipped his whiskey. "Celia loves her fêtes and church rotas almost as much as she loves her independence, and she adores you girls. I'd say she's quite happy as things are."

Rhys leaned forward. "What do you recommend we do, Sir Richard?"

"Go to the press," the elderly man said without preamble, echoing Rhys's own words. "Tell them exactly what you've told me. Then we'll have control, not Clarkson."

"But the scandal," Natalie said as she clasped her hands tightly together, "coming just at the re-launch—"

"The timing is regrettable," Sir Richard agreed. He made a dismissive gesture. "But this is old news, after all. It will cause a brief media flurry, but I don't think it'll hurt the store to any measurable degree." His expression was steely. "Even if it does, I don't care. Your safety is more important."

"I agree," Rhys said. He reached out and took Natalie's hand in his. "That's why I think we should notify the police."

"Yes," Sir Richard said. "Talk to them and see what they recommend. No doubt they'll want proof. If Clarkson is

clever enough to unearth a decades-old scandal and use it
to blackmail my granddaughter—" Sir Richard paused, his
face set in implacable lines "—then he's capable of God
knows what else. I want Natalie protected."

"But... suppose Ian finds out?" Natalie asked, and bit
her lip.

"He won't," Rhys said decisively, and stood. "The CID
handle blackmail cases every day. Sir Richard's right,
they'll need proof in order to arrest him. They'll likely
want you to meet Clarkson on Saturday as planned."

"This is all so cloak and dagger!" Natalie exclaimed as
she stood up, her eyes wide. "I'm really scared."

"Don't be." Rhys took her hand and gave it a reassuring
squeeze. "You'll be in good hands, darling. We've got to
put Ian behind bars. And right now, you're the only way we
can do it."

Early Friday evening, the Vauxhall Astra juddered to a
stop in front of Hannah's house on Cavendish Avenue. Jago
let the engine run; if he turned it off, he knew it wouldn't
start again.

He glanced at the house. The curtains twitched at one of
the upstairs windows. He hoped it was Hannah peering out,
not her mum or – God forbid – her father.

"They've been in that van for twenty minutes," Alastair
fumed as he glared out the guest room window.

"They're talking, that's all." Cherie came to stand next to
him. "It's nothing to worry about."

"I don't want Hannah seeing him." He flicked the
curtains closed and brushed past her to the stairs. "He was
sacked today. He's got a bloody cheek, coming here."

Cherie followed him. "Alastair, I hope you didn't have
anything to do with getting that poor boy sacked—?"

He didn't answer; he was already charging down the stairs and striding out the front door.

"I can't stay long," Hannah told Jago as she climbed into the van. "I'm helping mum tag stuff for the church fête."

He leaned over to kiss her. "I can't either. Hannah," he said without preamble, "bad news. I've been sacked."

"What? When?" Shock and dismay clouded her face.

"Today, when my shift ended. Cutbacks," he added bitterly.

"Oh, Jago – no! What'll you do?"

"I'll work at the chippy until I find something else."

"But how will you pay rent on your flat?"

He shifted uncomfortably in his seat. "Well, as to that," he said, "the flat isn't actually mine."

"Oh. So you have a flat mate?" she asked, puzzled.

"Yeah." Before he could elaborate, Hannah's father came striding down the front path, and the words he'd been about to say died in his throat.

"I want you to leave," Alastair told Jago as he rounded the van. "You're not welcome here."

Hannah jumped down and came around to face him. "What are you doing? How dare you talk to Jago like that—"

"It's OK, Hannah," Jago cut in, wanting only to leave. "He's right, I should go." He cast Alastair a hostile glare. "I'll call you later." He let out the clutch and pulled away with a jerk and a puff of blue smoke.

"Couldn't get away fast enough, could he?" Alastair observed with satisfaction. "That should tell you something."

She rounded on him, fists bunched at her sides. "Jago lost his job today! His mum's on the dole, she needs his pay! You'd know that if you'd ever given him a chance."

"He'll find another job. If business picks up, he'll likely be re-hired in the autumn."

Hannah's eyes widened. "It was you, wasn't it? *You* had something to do with getting him sacked! Because you don't like him, and you don't want me seeing him—"

He didn't confirm or deny it. "You're not to see Jago Sullivan again, Hannah. I forbid it."

"You know, dad," Hannah said evenly, "I hate you right now. But worse than that, I don't even *like* you." She turned on her heel and stalked back up the path to the front door.

Natalie parked in front of her flat that evening, then picked up her mobile and scrolled to her sister's number.

"Caro? Where are you? You didn't show up at my birthday 'do'."

"I'm at the fitter's. I found a wedding gown at John Lewis and I've been here all afternoon."

"Oh, good. Grandfather and mum were worried when you didn't show. You might have called."

"I know, sorry. I'll call now, and grovel."

"You'd better do a lot of grovelling." Natalie glanced at her watch. "I've got groceries. I'll talk to you later."

"Wait! How's the re-launch going? And how's Rhys? Are you two an item?"

Were they? Natalie still wasn't sure. Since the night they'd spent together, they'd not discussed their relationship, if that's what it even was; nor had they exchanged more than a few hurried kisses. There simply wasn't time.

"The marquees arrive next week, the Portaloos are coming on Friday, and a thousand things have gone wrong. In other words," she finished, "it's business as usual."

"What about you and Rhys?" her sister prodded.

Nat bit her lip. "Hello? Caro? Sorry, you're breaking up..." she said, and pressed 'End Call'.

It rang almost immediately. Resigned, Natalie answered it.

"Breaking up, my arse," Caroline snapped. "Spill, Nat. Have you slept with him, then?"

"That's none of your business!" Natalie said, indignant.

"So you *have* slept with him." She radiated smugness. "I knew it! I'm glad, Nat. If he makes you happy, and he's not Dominic, that's two points in his favour, and I'm all for it."

"Thanks for your approval," Natalie retorted, although she was secretly pleased. "Bye, Caro." She shut off her mobile and tossed it in one of the carrier bags.

As she let herself in, she smelled the acrid stench of a cigarette. She wrinkled her nose.

"Dominic," she called out irritably as she groped for the light switch, "that's it, I'm changing the locks. You had an extra key made, didn't you? I told you, I don't want you popping round unannounced like this any more—"

"Hello, Natalie."

Ian Clarkson was sprawled on her sofa, a cigarette in hand. A rucksack was on the floor. A half-drunk cup of tea and an ashtray littered with butts sat on the coffee table in front of him. It was the ashtray she kept for Dominic... the one tucked on the top shelf of her kitchen cupboard.

"How did you get in?" she demanded, her voice unsteady.

He leaned forward to crush out his cigarette. "Your landlord let me in. I told him I was your brother, down from Oxford for the weekend. Very obliging of him, don't you think?" He smiled. "You see how easy it is."

"Get out."

"I hope you don't treat all your guests so rudely, Nat." He paused. "Alexa's thrown me out, alas. I've nowhere to go." He sat back and rested his arm out along the top of the sofa. "Fancy a flatmate?"

"You can't stay here!" Natalie exclaimed, panicked. "If you don't leave at once, I'll call the police. I'll file a harassment complaint at work, and you'll lose your job. Is that what you want?"

He laughed. "Calm down, Nat. Keep your knickers on... at least for now. I'm not staying."

"How long have you been here?"

He shrugged. "Not long. I see you went shopping." He indicated the carrier bags she'd dropped by the door. "I do hope you haven't said anything to anyone about me." His eyes met hers as he stood.

"Of course I haven't." She turned away, her pulse racing, to retrieve the bags and put them in the kitchen.

"I did some digging on your boy Rhys," he remarked as he followed her into the kitchen. "Quite a career he's had."

Natalie withdrew tins of tomatoes from one bag with shaking hands and thrust them onto a shelf. "What do you mean?"

Ian stood behind her. "He leveraged several buyouts and headed a couple of hostile takeovers, early on. Nothing illegal, mind, but he's come close. If I were you, I'd ask myself what his intentions for the stores really are."

"Rhys's improved our bottom line. We're turning a profit again, and he's done it in a remarkably short time."

"But what happens when he leaves? Did you ever ask yourself that? And he will leave, once the re-launch is over."

"What do you mean?" she asked shortly as she put milk in the fridge. "We'll go on as we are."

He shook his head. "Without Rhys, everything will go back to shit. Sir Richard will die eventually, the old bastard, and who'll take over then?" He smirked. "Alastair can't run things alone, he hasn't the balls. That's why I need to take the helm, and soon. Otherwise, Rhys will come back and offer to buy you out, Natalie, and at a rock-bottom price. By then things will be so bad you'll be desperate to sell. If it's occurred to me," he finished, "you can be sure it's occurred to Rhys."

Natalie slammed the fridge door. "I won't listen to any more of this. Please leave."

"Do you honestly think Rhys cares about you? You're just a means to an end, a convenient way to work himself into your grandfather's company... while he works his way into your knickers."

"You're disgusting. Get out, Ian."

He returned to the sitting room and picked up his rucksack. "I'll see you on Saturday night at the Savoy." He took a sip of his tea and made a face. "Ugh, it's gone cold. By the way – you're low on sugar. I hope you bought more. It wouldn't do to run out, as I'll want something sweet with my tea, next time."

With a low laugh, he brushed his lips against her cheek, shouldered his bag, and left.

CHAPTER 38

Ian had barely left when the buzzer went downstairs.

Bloody hell, what now? "Yes?" Nat snapped as she pressed the intercom button.

"S'me, Nat," Dominic Heath mumbled into the intercom in a slurred voice, "and I'm screwed. Really, massively—" he belched "—fucked. My secret's out, it's all over the tabs."

Natalie leaned her forehead against the speaker and closed her eyes. Dominic was drunk – what a perfect way to top off an absolutely crap day. "Come up," she said resignedly, and pressed the button to let him in.

A few minutes later he was slumped against her doorjamb. He was in desperate need of a shower and a cup of coffee.

She did not invite him in. "What's happened?"

"The whole world knows who I am, that's what's happened." He hiccupped. "I'm the top story in all the tabs. Fucking Klaus, it's all that bald-headed German bastard's fault."

Holding the door wider, she sighed. "Come in. I'll make coffee. Crikey, but you're pissed."

He staggered inside. "Didn't interrupt anything, did I? You're not with that arsehole Gordon, are you?" He peered around her shoulder, as if she'd hidden Rhys in a closet, or stashed him underneath the coffee table.

"No." Natalie glared at him. "You can't stay here, Dominic. I have work in the morning, and lots to do. It's the last week before the re-launch. And you've got rehearsals tomorrow. You can't be drunk. I'll put on a pot of coffee—"

"Nat." He swayed unsteadily on his feet. "I don't want any bloody coffee, I want—" he winked "—you."

Natalie pushed him away. "Dominic, you're drunk, and you reek. In the shower," she ordered, and took his arm. "Now."

His face lit up. "Best offer I've had all night."

"Alone," she added grimly.

"You know what, Nat?" he confided, and slung his arm around her shoulder. "So many girls want me, sometimes I can't keep up. And Vicks… she was insatiable. Had to pop a Viagra just to keep her happy, you know?"

"No, I don't. And I don't *want* to know." She led him to the bathroom and handed him soap, a towel, and a spare toothbrush. "Scrub up. In the meantime, I'll make that coffee." She closed the door on his protests and went into the kitchen.

Honestly, would Dom's dramas never end? As kids growing up in Warwickshire, they'd been in each other's pockets; then they fell in love, or a close approximation, and spent two years sharing a tour bus and the crazy, exhilarating, unpredictable life of a rock star.

But that was over, and they'd moved on. Yet here Dom was again, drunk and despondent because his life was in a mess.

Oh, well, Natalie thought grudgingly, *you don't turn your back on a friend. And Dominic is still my oldest friend.*

When the coffee was ready, she poured a cup and added two sugars and plenty of milk, just the way he liked it. She paused to listen. The shower had stopped.

Natalie knocked. "Coffee's ready."

He opened the door. A towel was wrapped around his hips, and his hair stood up in a wet quiff, like a punk rooster.

"Are you hungry?" she asked him as she handed him the cup. "I'll make an omelette if you like."

He shook his head and wrapped his hands round the cup. "Just coffee, thanks." He scowled. "And don't go telling anyone about the Viagra thing. That's just between us."

In the kitchen, she put biscuits on a plate and set them on the table. "Now tell me what's happened. We agreed that you'd give Klaus Phillip's discarded sketches, and those photos we took of last season's dresses in my closet."

"I did! But he threw them back and said he wasn't a fool, that he knew the difference between Rochas and Pryce. Whatever that means. Sound like a pair of solicitors to me." He picked up a biscuit and dunked it disconsolately in his coffee.

"It means," Nat said grimly, "that Klaus is too clever to be fooled so easily. He *is* the fashion director for Maison Laroche, after all. Or he *was*." Guilt stabbed her. "Oh, Dominic… I'm sorry. This is partly my fault."

"My fans are saying I'm a fake, a hypocrite…"

"Not all of them think so, surely—"

He snorted. "Then tell me why 'I Got Mine' slipped from three to thirty-nine on the charts practically overnight? The band's pissed at me for not telling them the truth, and Mick's threatening to quit."

"He won't," Natalie reassured him.

"Well, whether he does or not, it doesn't matter," Dominic said glumly. "Either way, my career's over. It can't get any worse than this. Right, I take that back. It'll get much worse once my father gets wind of all this."

"Your father," Natalie agreed, "will be livid."

"I promised I'd never drag the family name into my music career. Now look." He put his head in his hands.

"It'll work out," Natalie promised, with more conviction than she felt. "In the meantime," she said, "you can stay the night. You're in no shape to drive... or to walk, for that matter," she added as she went to the airing cupboard.

Dominic raised his head hopefully. "You mean you and me—?"

"No," Nat said firmly, "I mean you and the sofa." She withdrew a blanket and sheet and thrust them at him. "It's only for tonight, mind."

"But I can't stay at the hotel any longer. The paparazzi found me out. I need a new place to hide."

"Sorry, but you can't hide here. Here's a waste bin," she added, and set it by the sofa. "I don't want your sick on my carpet. Good night."

"'Night," he echoed, his expression contrite. "Thanks, Nat, you're a star—"

"Just go to sleep, Dominic. We'll figure out what to do tomorrow." Natalie went in her bedroom and shut the door, and made a point of turning the lock.

Despite her irritation at Dominic and her worries about Ian and the re-launch, she fell almost instantly into an immediate and exhausted sleep.

Dominic sat cross-legged on Nat's sofa and sipped his coffee. He made a face. Nasty stuff... it needed a double shot of whiskey.

He picked up the TV remote and listlessly surfed the channels. His brain was still reeling, but at least he was alert, thanks to the caffeine.

Hold up – what was that? He paused to watch a breaking BBC news story, something about Phillip Pryce, the designer that Klaus was so interested in. Dominic turned up the sound.

"—clothing for the Dashwood and James line is manufactured in Nepal by workers making less than two pounds a day," the female BBC correspondent stated. "As you can see, working conditions here in the factory are appalling." The camera panned to show a filthy workroom crowded with sewing machines manned by thin, exhausted-looking workers.

"Shit," Dominic breathed.

The correspondent held up a striped top. "Under Phillip Pryce's label, this item sells in Dashwood and James department stores for £35. Yet the women who sew this garment make 20 pence apiece. According to statistics from the International Labour Organization, the shift of work to Asia and the resultant proliferation of sweatshops is a growing global phenomenon—"

Dazed, Dominic switched off the TV. As he debated whether to wake Nat to tell her, the buzzer sounded. Who the hell was that, wanting to be let up at – he squinted at the clock in the kitchen – eleven o'clock on a Wednesday night?

A towel wrapped tightly around his hips, Dominic pressed the intercom button. "Yeah?"

There was a pause. "Dominic?" Rhys Gordon said.

"Yeah, that's me. What do you want, Gordon?"

"Where's Natalie?"

"In bed, I reckon," he replied. "Guess you could say I wore her out." God, he loved yanking that smug arsehole's chain. "I'll tell her you came by. In the morning," he added pointedly.

But there was no reply. Gordon was gone.

A few minutes later the buzzer went again. "Bloody hell," Dominic snarled as he stalked back to the intercom, "what now, Gordon?"

There was a pause. "Dominic? What are *you* doing there?" Gemma demanded.

"What's it to you?"

"I came to check on Nat," she retorted, "not that's it's any of your concern. I wanted to see if she'd heard about your latest disaster... *Rupert*. Let me up."

"Bloody hell," he muttered as he pressed the button. He threw the towel aside and changed back into his jeans. A few minutes later, as he tugged his shirt on, Gemma knocked and he went to get the door.

"Why are you staying at Nat's, then?" she demanded as she came inside.

"Bit of paparazzi trouble."

"Fancy that," Gemma said, her words rife with sarcasm. "Everyone knows you're Lord Locksley's son and heir, and you lied to your fans about it. The only person in Britain less popular than you right now is Klaus von Richter."

Dominic looked at her blankly. "Why? What's he done?"

"Don't you ever read the papers? Someone videotaped him verbally abusing a Sikh shop assistant and posted it online, and now he's lost his job. Where's Nat?"

"She went to bed already. She's got a lot on tomorrow; it's the last week before the re-launch. And it's nearly midnight," he pointed out.

Gemma glanced at her wristwatch. "Oh, so it is. Listen, Dominic," she added as she preceded him to the sofa, "Nat's been through a lot. She doesn't need any more trouble." She tilted her head back and studied him through narrowed eyes. "Where are you sleeping, then? On the sofa?"

"Yeah, but only for tonight. I dunno what I'll do tomorrow," he said glumly. "I can't go back to the hotel."

Gemma perched on the arm of the sofa and crossed one designer denim-clad leg over the other. "The tabs say you're from a posh family. Are you? Why'd you lie about it?"

"Because I promised my father I wouldn't use the family name. He doesn't exactly approve of my career."

"But you make masses of money, and you're famous. You even met the Queen last year, at one of those benefit balls. How can your father possibly object to that?"

"Because in my family, the heir isn't meant to wear eyeliner and sing in a punk band," he said, and scowled. "I'm expected to marry and pursue finance, or law, or adjudicate for the high court – not sing 'Up the Monarchy's Arse' at Glasto." He sighed. "The truth is, it's exhausting, always acting laddish and surly. I get tired of it."

"Why'd you go and bollocks things up with Keeley, then?"

"Lots of reasons," Dominic said, and sat on the sofa. "Number one being, she's a right bitch. We only got back together for the publicity. And demanding... she expected me to tidy up, and cook."

"The nerve," Gemma said witheringly. "Well, I don't expect you'd want to stay at mine, then."

He eyed her with a mixture of suspicion and hope. "What do you mean, stay at yours?"

"I mean," she said, as if she were addressing a child – which, let's face it, he almost was – "I'll let you have the spare room... *if* you tidy up during the day when I'm gone. And *if* you cook the occasional meal when I'm home. You *can* cook, can't you?"

Dominic shrugged. "Macaroni cheese, pot noodles, and omelettes. That's what me and the boys lived on when we started out."

"Impressive," she said dryly. "We can share the lav, and you'll share a room with Nikki."

He perked up. "Who's Nikki? One of your mates?" He pictured a blonde with pillowy lips and pert breasts.

"My French bulldog."

"Oh, hell, no," Dominic said, disgusted. "I'm not sharing my bed with a dog!"

Gemma sat down next to him. She reached out to trace her fingernail deliberately down along his chest. "Where you sleep," she murmured, "depends entirely on you."

Dominic stared at her. The words were barely out of her mouth when he pulled her down on his lap and ground his mouth against hers. With a moan, Gemma wound her arms around his neck. "Umm," she breathed, "you taste like mint. And whiskey."

"I just brushed my teeth," he muttered against her lips.

"Shh," she breathed as his mouth moved down her neck to her collarbone. "Don't want to… wake Nat."

"No," he agreed as he returned his mouth to hers. It was his turn to groan as she parted her lips and touched her tongue to his. He reached down for the waistband of her jeans.

She slapped his hand away and sat up, outraged. "Hold up – what kind of girl do you think I am? We just met! I'm not one of your cheap backstage slappers."

"No," he said again, and fell back against the sofa, his hopes for a quickie dashed. "Course you're not." He sighed and picked up the remote, and flicked the TV back on.

"What are you doing?" Gemma demanded.

He shrugged. "Watching TV."

She grabbed the remote and flicked it back off. "Oh, no, you're not." She laced her arms around his neck.

"But you just said—"

"I'm just establishing the boundaries," she informed him. "So you don't overstep yours. Now – where were we?"

Dominic grinned and kissed the side of her mouth. "Right here, I think." His tongue traced the seam of her lips as his hand fanned out over her breast. "Or was it here?"

"Blimey," he breathed as he tore his mouth from hers a few minutes later, "I never spent this much time kissing. Most girls just drop their knickers for me and boom! Sex on a plate, with all the options."

"Is that right?" Her eyes narrowed. "Well, I'm not 'most girls'."

"No, you're not, and I'm glad you're not," he murmured as he nibbled on her luscious bottom lip. He hated to admit it, but the novelty of being with a girl who wouldn't let him bend her over and shag her senseless straight away was… well, it was refreshing. Romantic, even.

He worked his way slowly down her neck and throat, kissing and licking and tasting her skin until she moaned and wriggled against him.

"Shit, Gemma," he groaned, "you're driving me crazy, you are." He reached up and began to unbutton her shirt. "Come on, let's get naked."

Again, she slapped his hand away. "Boundaries," she warned, slightly out of breath, and pushed herself to her feet. "It's late. I should go."

"You can't leave, not yet."

"I'm not having sex with you on Natalie Dashwood's *sofa*," she said, piqued. "I told you, I'm—"

"—not that kind of girl," he finished, and scowled. "All right then, go. Can I see you again?" He looked around until he found a pen and a takeaway menu, scribbled a number on it, and held it out. "That's my private mobile number. No one has it but my agent, my ex-wife, and Natalie."

"I thought you and Nat broke up," Gemma said, her green eyes darkening with suspicion.

"We did. I dumped her. Stupidest thing I ever did," he added morosely.

"So you still have feelings for her."

"No! Yes! I mean, I still care about Nat – we practically grew up together, after all. We've been mates a long time."

"Then you're friends? That's all?"

"Yeah, that's all." His expression darkened. "Nat's seeing that Gordon arsehole now, anyway." He snorted. "God knows why."

Gemma retrieved her handbag and rummaged through it until she found a tube of Violet Vixen lip tint and slicked it on. "Sounds to me like you're still hung up on her." She dropped the tube back in her bag and strode down the hall to the door.

"I'm not!" Dominic protested as he hurried after her. He reached out to turn her around. "I'm hung up on *you*." He pulled her, resisting slightly, into his arms. "I like you, Gemma. You're different. And you taste really good." He began trailing kisses along her jawline to the corner of her mouth.

She felt her resolve – to run from Dominic Heath and his complicated life just as fast and far as her stiletto-heeled booties would take her – waver. "Well—" he was nibbling once again at her lower lip "—I suppose… I suppose we could give it a try."

He covered Gemma's mouth with his and kissed her senseless, using every tool in his considerable pop-star arsenal, until she finally wrenched herself away, murmured a breathless goodbye, and flung herself, smiling, out the door.

CHAPTER 39

When Natalie woke on Friday, Dominic was gone. His blanket and sheet were folded on the back of the sofa; the waste bin was back in its place in the kitchen. Everything was tidy, but the sofa cushions were askew.

And a tube of Violet Vixen lip tint lay on the hallway floor.

Natalie bent down to retrieve it, her eyebrows drawn together in a frown. It was a cheap brand, not the MAC that she favoured; besides, she hadn't worn lip tint since she was fifteen. *What on earth had Dominic got up to last night?* she wondered. And to think that he'd got up to it – whatever 'it' was – right in her own flat. Probably better that she didn't know…

With no time to dwell on Dominic's debaucheries, Natalie tossed the tube in the bin and got dressed. She'd be run off her feet today, might as well wear trousers and flats. With only a few days left before the re-launch, it was her last chance to make sure everything was ready.

She grabbed her mobile and handbag. Everything hinged on the re-launch – the store's future, her reputation as an events planner, and most importantly of all – Rhys Gordon's approval.

No pressure there…

"Good morning, Nat," Gemma chirped as Natalie passed by her desk. "Gorgeous day, isn't it?"

Natalie stopped and stared at Gemma. "You're smiling," she accused, "and it's early, and you don't have your coffee yet. Who are you, and what have you done with Gemma?"

She lifted her brow. "It's a lovely day, that's all." A vase filled with freesias and irises sat on her desk.

"They're gorgeous!" Nat exclaimed, leaning forward to breathe in the scent. "Who're they from?" she exclaimed, and smiled impishly. "Did you meet a new man?"

Gemma looked uncomfortable. "Well, about that..."

"Here's the card. May I?" Natalie asked, and grabbed it.

"Nat, wait—"

"'Gemma,'" Natalie read out loud, "'you rocked my world last night!!!'" She raised a brow. "Ooh, three exclamations, it must've been really good."

Gemma reached out to grab the card, her expression panicked. "Nat," she hissed, "give that back, right now—"

But Natalie held the card out of reach and read the rest out loud. "'Hope I rocked your world too. See you tonight at yours. Your omelette will be ready. And so will I.'" Natalie waggled her brows and laughed.

"Natalie, honestly—"

"'All my best,'" Natalie said, dodging Gemma's attempts to grab the card, "'and I do mean all...'" her words trailed off. She lowered the card and looked incredulously at Gemma. "'Dominic?'" she squeaked.

"I can explain," Gemma said quickly. "It just sort of... happened. I stopped by last night to check that you were all right, and Dominic was there, and one thing led to another."

"So... it was *your* Violet Vixen lip tint I found on the hallway floor?" Natalie said, incredulous.

Gemma blushed. "Oh, hell... I wondered what happened to it."

"So you and Dominic hooked up on my sofa last night—?"

"We didn't hook up," Gemma hastened to correct her, "not exactly."

"What do you mean, 'not exactly'?"

Gemma bristled. "I mean, I'm *not* that kind of girl. I made sure Dominic knew that, too." She flushed. "We... snogged a bit. That's all."

"Oh, crikey," Natalie said faintly as she turned away, "I can't take this in."

"Nat," Gemma assured her, feeling nine kinds of horrible, "I'm desperately sorry. Kissing your mate's ex-boyfriend is skeevy. I hope you don't hate me, I know you and he were together for two years—"

She broke off in dismay as she saw Natalie's shoulders begin to shake. "God, please don't cry, Nat! I won't see him again if it bothers you—"

Natalie turned back to face her. "I'm not crying, you berk," she said with a grin, "I'm laughing! You and Dominic – it's perfect! You're exactly what he needs – someone who won't put up with his crap."

Confused, Gemma said uncertainly, "So... you're not mad? You don't mind?"

"No, why should I?" Natalie turned the card over slowly. "We broke up. And I'm seeing Rhys, anyway." She frowned. "At least I think I am." She lowered her voice and leaned forward. "It's just that we're both always so bloody busy—"

"Natalie," Rhys said grimly as he arrived and strode past them, briefcase in hand, "I want you in my office. Now."

Gemma met Natalie's eyes. "Someone's in a right temper this morning," she murmured. "Would you like to borrow my Violet Vixen? I have an extra tube. It works a treat."

Natalie sighed. "I'm sure it does, but until the re-launch is over, we'll both be too tired to even think about sex—"

"Miss Dashwood?" Rhys snapped from inside the office. "I'll not ask again. Kindly stop wittering and get in here now."

"Uh-oh, he called you 'Miss Dashwood'," Gemma whispered. "You're in serious trouble, you are."

Natalie threw her handbag on her desk and hurried into Rhys's office. "Yes?" she asked warily from the doorway.

He turned from his position in front of the window and fixed her with a hard blue stare. "Have you followed the news lately?"

"Well, if you mean the Dominic thing," Natalie said, "yes. It's nothing we can't deal with—"

"No, the 'Dominic thing', as you call it, is the least of our problems right now."

"What do you mean?"

"It's all over the news that Phillip Pryce's clothing line for Dashwood and James is manufactured in Nepal… in a sweatshop." His face was a thundercloud.

"A sweatshop?" Natalie gasped, shocked. "Phillip would never allow it! He won't drink anything but fair trade coffee, and he insists that all his veg be locally sourced. He's very hands-on in all aspects of the business—"

"Not hands-on enough, it seems," Rhys bit off.

"But… he toured the factory himself! He told me so. He said everything was fine – the facility was clean, wages were fair, the bathrooms were modern—"

"Tell, me, Natalie – was Phillip's visit to the factory in Nepal a surprise?" Rhys asked evenly. "Or was it planned?"

"Planned, of course," Natalie said with a frown. "He arranged it beforehand with the factory manager."

"Then I've no doubt he was given a nice dog-and-pony show. Management had time enough to pretty everything up before Phillip's arrival."

"But that's sneaky and dishonest and... reprehensible."

"Phillip was tricked, yes. But he should've been more careful. According to the tabloids, he's surpassed Klaus von Richter *and* Dominic as the most hated man in Britain."

Natalie sank down in the nearest chair. "Poor Phillip."

"Poor Phillip?" he bit off. "Poor us, more like. The conditions in the factory are substandard. The workers are given one bathroom break in ten hours, and they work six days a week. And for every skirt we sell for £50, the workers make less than 20 pence."

"Crikey," Natalie said in a small voice.

"'Crikey'," Rhys said savagely, "doesn't begin to describe it. This is a fucking public relations nightmare." He glared at her. "And we have only one week before the re-launch to somehow make things right."

Natalie's mobile rang. "Jacques! How's Phillip?" She listened, nodded somberly, and lowered the phone. "He's gutted. This completely blindsided him."

"Tell him to get his arse in here straight away." Rhys reached across his desk for the phone. "We need to work out a strategy, and fast. And tell Gemma to get me the best PR firm in London on the phone. It'll take nothing short of a miracle to repair Dashwood and James's tarnished image now."

"Well, Hannah," Cherie pronounced on Friday morning as she held up the thermometer, "you've got a slight fever." She touched her daughter's cheek. "I'll tell your father you're not going in to work with him today."

"Thanks, mum," Hannah murmured. Guilt swamped her for lying to her mother. But the thought of sharing the ride in to work with her father today was more than she could bear.

She'd never forgive him for getting Jago sacked.

With the store's re-launch scheduled just a week from tomorrow, her father would be crazy busy all day; and it was mum's day to do the weekly grocery shop, so she'd be gone all morning. But most importantly, Jago was home today. It was his birthday, and his uncle had given him the day off.

Hannah listened to her father getting ready in the guest bedroom across the hall. She heard the hiss of the shower, the hum of his electric shaver, then his footsteps – pausing briefly outside her closed door – before he moved on down the hall and descended the stairs. The smell of coffee drifted upstairs, as well as the sound of the BBC morning news presenter on the TV; but there was little conversation.

Her parents barely spoke to one another these days.

Hannah's fingers tightened on the edge of her blanket. Even before their row, they'd acted like strangers. She knew her father was sleeping in the guest bedroom.

She wondered if her parents, like Duncan's, would divorce. Where would she live if that happened? Not with her father, Hannah thought determinedly, no way. She heard the whine of the garage door as he drove off to work.

She pushed back the covers and crept to the door to listen. Her mother's footsteps, light and quick, came up the stairs. She dived back under the covers just as Cherie tapped on the door and edged it open.

"Hannah? Bad news for your father, I'm afraid. That designer the store hired, Phillip Pryce, is in serious trouble.

The BBC says his clothing line is manufactured in a sweatshop. It's all over the media."

Hannah sat up. "A sweatshop… oh, that's awful! Poor dad." Despite herself, she felt a stab of sympathy for him.

"Yes, it's a nightmare. Good thing you're home today, there's already a half a dozen news vans outside."

Shit. Hannah bit her lip. How was she to leave the house and get past a bunch of nosy reporters without being seen?

"I'm off. I'll be back in a couple of hours. Will you be all right?"

Hannah nodded. "I'll just sleep for a while longer."

"Yes, get some rest, darling. Don't answer the door. You have my mobile number; call if you need anything."

"I will," Hannah promised. She waited impatiently as her mother gathered up her keys and purse, and went back downstairs and out the front door.

The second that Cherie's red Fiat roared off past the reporters and their news vans, Hannah leapt out of bed and dragged her duffel bag down from the closet shelf. She'd packed a few things, and now she tossed in some toiletries. She pulled on capris and a Tshirt and hastily slicked on lip tint.

After ensuring she had money for the bus fare to Holborn, Hannah eased her window open. Luckily, her room faced the back garden. She dropped her duffel bag to the ground, wincing at the loud thunk it made, and climbed onto the nearest branch of the ash tree outside her window. In a couple of minutes she dropped to the grass, retrieved her duffel, and hurried out through the back garden gate.

CHAPTER 40

Alastair James called a press conference on Friday afternoon, to meet the sweatshop issue head-on.

"Why haven't you shut down the factory in Nepal?" one of the reporters demanded.

"Closing the factory would eliminate jobs. We want to keep the workers employed and ensure they receive fair and humane working conditions going forward."

"How could Dashwood and James be unaware of the working conditions at the factory?" a BBC reporter called out.

Rhys took the microphone. "Phillip Pryce was given a false impression of working conditions when he toured the factory. The managers cleaned up the premises; when the inspectors and visitors left, they returned to business as usual. Unfortunately, it's a common occurrence."

"How do you know it won't happen again?"

"We've hired an independent monitor," Rhys replied, "to conduct random inspections of the facilities of all of our manufacturers." His expression was steely. "We stand behind Phillip Pryce. He's learnt a hard lesson, one that I daresay he'll never forget. None of us will. But the problem has been corrected. Thank you all."

As the press dispersed, Rhys shook Alastair's hand. "Well done." He glanced at Phillip – white-faced and silent – and Natalie. "All of you."

"Thank you for standing behind me," Phillip said quietly.

"You couldn't have known." Rhys shrugged. "You made a mistake. Just don't make the same mistake twice."

Alastair, standing alongside Rhys, looked at him sharply. *Don't make the same mistake twice.* The words jogged a long-forgotten memory in his mind.

"So that's it, then?" Fiona demanded, *her face swollen from crying. "You're engaged now, to someone else. Out with the old, in with the new, isn't that what they say?"*

"I'm sorry, Fi, but you knew this couldn't last." He *glanced uneasily around the office. Thank God everyone had left for the day. "You knew I was seeing Cherie—"*

"While you kept right on seeing me," *she hissed. "You dated her, pleasing your father no end, I'm sure, while you carried on screwing me."* She *pummelled his chest, weeping. "You bastard! And now..."* Her words trailed away.

"Now, what?" he *prodded as he caught her by the wrists.*

A look – secretive, fleeting – passed over her face. "Nothing," *she answered, and pushed him away. "It's over between us. I shan't bother you again. I won't make the same mistake twice."*

And suddenly, he knew. Alastair knew why Rhys Gordon looked vaguely familiar.

Natalie's mobile buzzed. "Dominic's just texted me. He wants to do a duet with Keeley at the re-launch, for the encore. They wrote a song together before they split up."

"Is he mad?" Rhys demanded, incredulous. "The two of them haven't spoken except through solicitors since Wedding-gate."

"But that's just it. They'll be together publicly for the first time at the re-launch. And they've never performed together before. People will flock to the re-launch just to see them. It'll be a huge draw."

Rhys didn't look convinced.

"There's only one problem," Natalie added. "Keeley hasn't agreed yet. But Dominic is sure he can convince her."

Rhys closed his eyes briefly. He felt a headache coming on. "I see. Is everything else on schedule, with no other surprises waiting to jump out and bite me on the arse?"

"Only the usual things," Nat assured him. "Dominic is rehearsing with the band this afternoon. He's worried about performing now that his identity as Rupert Locksley is out."

Rhys snorted. "He should be. I only hope his aristocratic notoriety works in our favour. Either way, we have no choice but to put up with the manky little sod."

"I know you don't like him," Natalie said sharply, "but he's done all of this – the adverts, the concert, the song download – for free. We owe him a lot."

"Perhaps. But he's still a manky little sod."

She smirked. "You're not jealous, are you?"

"I understand he stayed with you last night."

Natalie blinked. "Yes. No!" she added hastily. "He slept on the sofa. How did you know about that?"

"I stopped by to talk to you after the sweatshop story broke, and Dominic answered the buzzer. He said he'd 'worn you out' and you'd gone to bed."

Natalie gasped in outrage. "The little shit! He showed up drunk, so I let him sleep on the sofa. That's all."

"I knew he was taking the piss." Rhys ran a hand over his face. "But we've more serious matters to deal with. I spoke to the central London police this morning. They want you to meet with Ian tomorrow night as planned."

Natalie suddenly knew how a balloon must feel when all the air is let out. "Oh. I see."

"Sorry, but I told you they'd want proof." He took hold of her arm. "You're upset. Here, sit down."

Dazed, she complied, and lowered herself into a chair. "What... what else did the police say?"

"You're to wear a wire. You'll meet Ian at the Savoy at eight-thirty; a couple of plainclothes detectives will be in an unmarked vehicle outside, monitoring your conversation. Another will be inside the hotel, in the next room."

"A wire?" Natalie looked at Rhys with real fear in her eyes. "What if Ian finds it? He'll be furious! He'll know I've lied to him—"

"The police will be listening in. They'll show up the minute, the *second* something goes wrong. At least—" his expression was grim "—that's the plan."

"He was in my flat yesterday," Natalie said.

Stunned, Rhys stared at her. "What? How did he get in? Why didn't you tell me? Did he hurt you—?"

"No," Natalie said, "he only wanted to show me how easy it was. He told the landlord he was my brother. When I came in he was on the sofa, smoking a cigarette."

"I fucking hate this." Rhys paced the conference room like a restless tiger, fury stamped on his face. "I'd kill him right now if I could."

"Well, you can't. I'll just go through with it and hope that nothing goes wrong."

"Nothing will." Rhys reached out and pulled her up into his arms. "You'll stay with me tonight, until this is sorted. I won't let anything happen to you, Natalie," he said fiercely into her hair. "I promise you that."

As she nestled against him, steadied by his arms around her, Natalie hoped – really hoped – that Rhys was right.

Cherie's mobile rang as she pulled into a parking space on the Kilburn High Road. She glanced at the screen and sighed. *Neil*. She'd avoided him since the night they'd kissed, torn between wanting to see him and equally determined to stay away.

"Why won't you see me?" he asked in a low, measured voice.

"I'm married, Neil!" She grabbed her handbag and unlocked the car door. "I have a great deal more to lose than you."

"You have a right to be happy, Cherie. If we're to have any chance together—"

"We don't," Cherie said firmly. "I *am* happy. I love Alastair." She got out of the car.

"You're lying. You're not happy, I know it. You told me yourself that he's moved into the spare room—"

"He saw us, Neil. He suspects there's something between us, something more than friendship. It can't continue. It's too risky." Resolutely she locked the car and put her keys away. Her hand was shaking.

"Please, Cherie," Neil implored her, "I need to see you again. There *is* something between us. You know I'm right."

The thing was, much as she hated to admit it, she wanted to see him again, too. Once more wouldn't hurt, surely? Cherie waited for a van to pass by and walked quickly across the road. "I'm not at home," she said finally. "I'll be back by noon. Perhaps I'll see you then."

She pressed 'end call' with a trembling finger and went into the grocery store, ashamed at how quickly her resolve had crumbled.

Jago's building was halfway down Little Russell Street. Hannah went inside and trudged up the stairs to the second floor. She found flat 2B at the end of the hall and stood in front of the door uncertainly. The strap of her duffel bag cut into her shoulder. Suppose Jago wasn't here?

Well, she'd sit in the hall and wait.

After a moment's hesitation she lifted her hand and knocked. A minute passed, then another. She knocked again. 'Coronation Street' was blaring into the silence from behind the neighbour's door, and the smell of bacon hung in the air. She was about to turn away when the door opened.

A tall, leggy girl with black hair and kohl-rimmed eyes regarded Hannah coolly. "Yes?"

Disconcerted, Hannah blinked. "Um – I'm looking for Jago. Jago Sullivan. This is his flat, isn't it?"

For some reason, Miss Kohl-Eyes found this amusing. "*His* flat, is it?" She continued to stare at Hannah. "He might be here. And who are you?"

"Hannah James. We – we work together, he and I. Or we did," she amended.

She regarded Hannah a moment longer, then turned and bellowed, "Jago! Get your arse up! You've a visitor."

She disappeared back inside, leaving Hannah in the hallway. After a moment Jago appeared, pulling a T-shirt over his rumpled hair and skinning it down over his chest. He looked like he'd just got out of bed.

Surprise chased by confusion crossed his face. "Hannah! What are you doing here?" he asked, and pulled the door to behind him as he stepped into the hallway.

"I… I need a place to stay." She fiddled with the duffel bag strap, wondering if she'd been wrong to come here. "I had a row with dad, and I wondered if… I might stay here for a bit."

Jago shifted on his feet – they were bare – and tugged at his ear. He looked decidedly uncomfortable. "Sorry, but it's not a good idea, Hannah, really—"

"I won't be a bother," she said quickly, "I promise. I can sleep on the sofa." She added, "I'll pay my share of the rent—"

"The thing is—" he hesitated, and glanced back over his shoulder at the closed door "—your dad wouldn't like you being here. And Belle wouldn't, either."

She stared at him. "Belle? Is she your girlfriend? You never said. Why didn't you tell me?"

"I told you we were just mates, you and I," he pointed out. "I did tell you that."

"I know. But you... but I thought—" Her throat constricted and closed, and she couldn't speak. *You kissed me*, she wanted to accuse him, *in the chip shop, you kissed me in front of everyone, like I really* meant *something to you...*

"I'm sorry," he said, his expression miserable. "I didn't mean to give you the wrong idea. I like you, Han. You're a good kid. But you can't stay. It's Belle's flat, not mine."

"You *like* me? I'm a good *kid*?" she echoed. "I thought I meant a bit more to you than that, Jago."

"What's going on?" Belle called out as she came to stand beside Jago. She glared at Hannah. "What is it you want?"

"Nothing," Hannah mumbled. "I don't want anything."

Belle rounded on Jago. "Have you been seeing her, then?"

"No! For God's sake, leave us, Belle," Jago snapped. "We'll talk later, you and I. Just let me take care of this."

Hannah clutched the duffle bag strap. Jago lived with Belle. He'd neglected to mention this crucial bit of information, and it changed everything.

At any rate, he was right. She couldn't stay here.

Numbly, she turned to go. "Sorry I bothered you." She wouldn't cry in front of him, or even worse, in front of Belle, she bloody well wouldn't...

"Hannah, wait." Jago stepped out into the hall and touched her arm. "I can take you home, if you need a ride—"

"No, I don't need a *ride*." She glared at him and shook his hand off. "I have to go." *I need someone I can depend on,* she thought, *someone who won't lie to me, or let me down when I need them most.*

She suddenly, desperately wanted to be home. Mum would make her a mug of hot cocoa with real chocolate, not one of those powdery mixes, and cinnamon toast, and she'd kiss the top of Hannah's head and tell her it was all going to work out, and they'd watch old episodes of *Dr. Who* or *Midsomer Murders* with their legs tucked up under them on the sofa.

That, more than anything, was what Hannah wanted.

CHAPTER 41

At noon, Sir Richard summoned Rhys to his office. Rhys nodded to Mabel, the elderly man's secretary, and knocked on the door. "You wanted to see me?"

"Yes, come in, please. Close the door."

He complied and approached Sir Richard's desk. "I've a lot to do today, I haven't much time—"

"This won't take long. Sit down."

Tamping down his irritation, Rhys sat on the edge of one of the leather wingchairs angled before his desk and waited.

Sir Richard's eyebrows were knitted in a scowl. "I'll come straight out with it. What are your intentions towards my granddaughter?"

"Natalie?" *Bloody hell.* "That's something I intend to discuss with her, when the time is right."

"I see." Sir Richard leaned back in his chair. "Another question, then. What are your intentions towards this company?"

"I have no 'intentions,'" Rhys said. "My job here is nearly done. I'm leaving after the re-launch."

"I know that's what we agreed to when you took on this task. But things have changed. I'm unwilling – and frankly, unable – to continue the day-to-day management of Dashwood and James any longer. Alastair and I hoped you might be persuaded to stay on." He paused. "Permanently."

Rhys's expression was neutral. "I see. What are the terms?"

"A full partnership, of course. You'll have a seat on the board, as well as the last word on all business decisions, provisional on my final approval. Alastair's in complete agreement. And of course you'll have a share in the profits."

"What percentage?"

"Twenty."

"Thirty."

"Twenty-five," Sir Richard said shortly, "and that's as high as I'm willing to go. That's a very generous offer, Mr. Gordon. And it won't be on the table for long."

"Yes, it's quite generous," Rhys's expression was hard. "Which begs the question, Sir Richard... what's the catch? What is it you expect in return?"

"I expect you to do right by my granddaughter."

"There's never been a question of that," Rhys said abruptly, and stood up. "I don't like the suggestion of *quid pro quo*. It's unnecessary. And frankly, it's beneath you."

"Sit down!" Sir Richard barked. He leaned forward as Rhys glared at him, and his own eyes flashed ire. "You misread me."

Rhys resumed his seat. "Then please enlighten me. Because if you're suggesting I need to be persuaded to marry Natalie, with a partnership thrown in to sweeten the deal, you insult me. And you insult Natalie."

"I'd like nothing better than for you to marry Natalie and take over my half of this company, Mr. Gordon. But your partnership is not contingent on marriage to my granddaughter."

"Indeed?" Rhys remained unconvinced. "You're willing to give over a quarter of your company to me, an outsider, in return for... what?" He leaned back in the chair. "You're not a fool, Sir Richard, nor am I. Tell me what's really going on."

The elderly man sighed. "Very well, Mr. Gordon, I shall speak plainly. You've taken Dashwood and James and turned it back into profitability. You and I both know that if you leave, the store will slide into the red again. Alastair hasn't the backbone or the tenacity to run the business on his own. But with Roger gone, I've no one else to take over.

"Put simply, Gordon, I need you. Dashwood and James need you. And most of all, Natalie needs you. You make her happy. And you give her the ballast she so desperately requires."

"I'm honoured, Sir Richard," Rhys said after a moment. "I care very deeply for Natalie. But staying on? It's impossible. I've already agreed to take on another project."

"Well, cancel it."

"That's impossible—"

"As far as I'm concerned," Sir Richard said firmly, "the matter's settled. I'll have my lawyers draw up the paperwork."

Rhys eyed him with grudging respect. "You're a very stubborn man. You won't take no for an answer, will you?"

"No." He looked at Rhys thoughtfully. "Do you know what it was that changed my initial opinion of you, Mr. Gordon?"

"I've no doubt it was the profit margin."

Sir Richard smiled briefly. "No, my opinion changed when Natalie told me about the night you took her home, after Alastair's anniversary party. She behaved deplorably that night – getting inebriated, flinging her wine on you, flinging *herself* at you—!" His expression registered disapproval. "You could have taken advantage of the situation. But you didn't. That showed character, Rhys. And ethics... something lacking in most young men these days."

"I was attracted to Natalie from that very first night," Rhys admitted. "She was unlike anyone I'd ever met."

Sir Richard looked at him with a distinct twinkle in his eye. "Perhaps Natalie should be your next project."

"That's one project I'd have no success with, I'm afraid."

Sir Richard chuckled. "I fear you're right. But who knows? If you stay here at Dashwood and James, you'll have a lifetime to work on it." He pushed back his chair and stood.

Rhys stood as well. "Thank you, Sir Richard." He gripped the man's hand firmly in his own. "Draw up the papers and we'll talk again. Now, I really must go."

"Are we ready for the re-launch?" Sir Richard questioned.

Rhys paused in the doorway. "Yes," he said. "If Dominic Heath isn't booed off the stage by his fans, if there aren't hordes of human rights protesters, and if Natalie hasn't left anything to chance, tomorrow should turn things around for Dashwood and James in a big way."

As least, Rhys reflected as he returned to his office, he bloody well hoped so.

It was twelve-fifteen when Cherie finished putting the groceries away. The reporters were gone, off to chase a bigger story, no doubt. She glimpsed Neil's Range Rover turning into the driveway. She paused, a bag of pasta in hand, and watched him come up the walk. He really was a handsome man. She could so easily have fallen in love with him.

After all, she nearly had.

But she'd realised, when Alastair called her out of the blue to say he missed her, that Neil could never be what Alastair was – father to her children, her champion, her lover, her best friend. She wouldn't jeopardise thirty years of marriage or risk her family for a couple of hours of pleasure with Neil Hadley.

Her marriage deserved more than that.

If circumstances were different, she might have married Neil. But she'd married Alastair. He was a good and true man, who worked hard to provide for his family, and who'd always loved her unconditionally. He wasn't to blame for the current state of affairs at Dashwood and James; she saw that now. And she was an idiot for not appreciating the true depth of his love for her, and his family.

Cherie felt remarkably clear-eyed as she met Neil at the door. She'd been lonely, and Neil had eased the emptiness she'd felt with his charm and attention. And she'd needed that. But despite the problems in her marriage, she loved Alastair. She always had, always would. It was as simple as that.

Neil would just have to understand.

The bus ride home was endless. Hannah, her forehead pressed to the window, stared out dully at the passing cars and the houses and rows of shops as tears tracked silently down her face. She couldn't seem to stop crying.

How stupid was she? How could she have thought that someone like Jago could care anything for her? He must've had a laugh with Belle. They must think her a complete knob.

By the time she got off the bus and walked back to Cavendish Avenue, Hannah's feet dragged. All she wanted was to go upstairs, burrow under the covers, and stay there forever.

She went through the front gate and trudged up the walk. The news vans were gone. Her mum's Fiat was in the driveway, and a dark green Range Rover was parked behind it. She frowned. What was Mr. Hadley's car doing here? She hoped Duncan wasn't here; he was the last person she wanted to see. Hannah scrubbed at her teary eyes with one fist.

Get yourself together, she told herself fiercely.

She decided to slip in through the kitchen. With any luck, her mother was in the sitting room with Duncan's dad, and she could sneak upstairs and avoid them altogether. Hopefully mum hadn't realised that Hannah wasn't still upstairs in bed.

She dug out her key and inserted it carefully in the lock. The kitchen door swung open and she slipped inside. As she came round the corner, she froze, and the duffel bag strap slipped down her shoulder. "Mum—?"

Duncan's father stood in the kitchen with his arms wrapped around her mother. They broke apart and turned to face her with twin expressions of guilt and shock.

"Hannah!" Cherie exclaimed. Her hand rose to her throat. "My God, you gave me a fright! What are you doing there? I thought you were upstairs sleeping!"

"Mum... how could you?" Hannah demanded, her face distorted with mingled shock and rage. The duffel bag slid from her shoulder to the floor. "It's bad enough, you cheating on dad... but with Duncan's *father*?"

"Hannah, there's nothing going on," Neil Hadley said, and stepped forward. "There never was. You've got it wrong. Listen to me—"

"I won't listen to you. And I haven't got it wrong, have I? You're having it off with my mother!"

Blinded by tears, she whirled around, fumbled with the doorknob, and ran back out of the kitchen. Blood pounded in her ears. She heard her mother call after her, but she didn't stop.

"It's not what you think!" Cherie cried, pushing past Neil as she rushed after her daughter. "Hannah, for heaven's sake – stop being so bloody dramatic! Please, wait—"

It's not what you think. No, nothing was, Hannah thought disjointedly, that was the problem. Duncan, Jago, even mum – they'd all let her down, disappointed her, lied to her, in one way or another. How ironic that her father – whom she'd been so furious with – had been right about so many things… about Jago, in particular. Why hadn't she listened?

Lost in her misery, desperate to get away from her mother and Duncan's father and their lies and excuses and treachery, Hannah stepped off the kerb and ran behind the Number 113 bus to Edgware, re-emerging straight into the path of an oncoming motorcycle.

There was a shriek of brakes and the acrid smell of burning rubber as the motorcycle skewed sideways, skidding the last hundred yards on the tarmac before it hit Hannah, sending her hurtling up and onto the grass embankment.

CHAPTER 42

Late Friday afternoon, Ian turned the Audi A8 onto the gated drive of their house – oh, who was he kidding, it was *Alexa's* bloody house – and drove up to the front door. At least she'd had the foresight to leave the gates open.

The front door was unlocked. "Alexa?" he called out from the foyer.

Footsteps sounded at the top of the stairs. "Ian?"

"Yes. I've come to collect my stuff. I left a message."

She appeared on the top step. "I know. I left the gates open and the door unlocked."

"Thanks," he said shortly, and moved past her up the stairs. "I shan't be long."

"I go to hospital tomorrow."

He paused on the step below her. "Yes, I know. I didn't think you'd want me there."

"I don't. But—" she took a breath "—if you want to come, I won't object. It's your child too, after all."

"Yes, well, with the re-launch tomorrow, I don't know when – or if – I can get away."

She bristled. "Surely you can 'get away' for the birth of your child! You can't bear to leave *her*, can you?"

Ian regarded her coldly. "This is so unnecessary, Alexa. Natalie and I aren't having an affair. I can't believe you'd take a tabloid photo at face value. There's nothing wrong in talking to someone on a park bench—"

"But there's something wrong with *kissing* someone on a park bench – especially when that 'someone' isn't your wife!" Alexa snapped. "Or should I not have taken *that* particular photo at face value?"

"Oh, for fuck's sake," Ian bit off, "I haven't time for this," and he stormed past her up the remaining steps and strode down the hallway. "I'll get my stuff and go."

"Yes, do." Alexa, arms crossed, waited on the stairs as he went into their bedroom and rummaged through his dresser.

In a moment he appeared at the top of the stairs with a rucksack and a few suits slung over his shoulder. "I've got what I need. I'll call tomorrow to check you're all right."

Alexa pressed herself against the wall as he went back down. "Don't bother. I don't want you to put yourself out."

He paused. "Look, you threw me out, Alexa. If you need me, call. I've got my mobile." He descended the stairs and left, slamming the front door behind him.

As she heard the Audi drive off, Alexa took a deep shaky breath and went back upstairs. *She wouldn't cry. She wouldn't.* She needed a clean nightgown for her hospital stay; might as well pack now, while she still had a bit of energy left—

Halfway down the hall, she paused. Something black lay on the carpet. She lowered herself into an awkward squat and picked it up.

It was Ian's mobile phone.

He sometimes clipped it to his belt; he must've dropped it when he was fetching his clothes. He'd soon realise it was gone. She'd have to hurry.

Without hesitation, Alexa scanned his text messages, looking for anything to or from Natalie Dashwood. There was nothing. Next, she checked his photos to see if he had pictures of Nat on his mobile. Again, there was nothing.

She frowned. Ian was clever, of course he wouldn't leave evidence of his affair on his mobile for her to find. Still, she'd check his phone messages too, just in case.

The messages were all recent, all mundane – an appointment reminder from Dr. Martin, his GP; a call from Rhys about a cancelled meeting; scheduled maintenance for the Audi. Alexa was about to switch off the mobile when she noticed a single, saved message.

It was dated two weeks ago – Sunday, the night Natalie had called Ian so late. Alexa played it back.

"Ian, it's Natalie." Her voice was low but determined. "I want proof before this goes any further. Prove that what you say is true, or I promise you, I'll call the police." There was a click as she abruptly rang off.

Alexa lowered the phone and stared at it in confusion. What was Natalie on about? Proof of what, exactly?

The phone on the hall table jangled, startling her. She grabbed it. "Hello?"

"I've lost my mobile," Ian said shortly. "I'm calling from the petrol station. Can you see if I left it?"

"I'll go and check." She made a point of putting the phone down, and picked it up a moment later. "Sorry. It's not here."

"You're certain? It's got to be there."

"It's not. Sorry." She hung up and put Ian's mobile in her hospital bag, under a pile of knickers.

Whatever was going on, she'd find out. And the only place to start, Alexa decided as she fetched her handbag and car keys, was London… Ladbroke Grove, to be exact.

She had to talk to Natalie.

Tomorrow would be too late. Between the re-launch and her scheduled C-section, there'd be no chance to get to the bottom of this. Alexa returned to the bedroom and dug Ian's mobile back out, then tucked it in her handbag and went downstairs.

Should she call Natalie? Alexa wondered as she got in the car and started the engine.

No. This visit definitely needed to be made in person.

There was a knock on the conference room door, and Alastair's secretary came in. "Mr. James, sorry to disturb, but you have a call. It's urgent."

Alastair rose and excused himself from the meeting. Rhys scowled but made no comment. There were still several last-minute details to go over before the re-launch the next day – the distinct possibility of sweatshop protesters at Phillip's fashion show being only one of them — and time, like Rhys's temper, was running dangerously short.

"It's Mrs. James," Corinne said as she led Alastair back to his office. "Hannah's been injured."

"Injured?" Confusion clouded his expression. "How on earth could she be injured? She stayed home today, she wasn't feeling well…" He strode into his office and stabbed at the blinking line. "Cherie, what's happened?"

"Alastair? Oh, God, please get here as soon as you can! I'm at St. George's, Hannah may need surgery—"

Between her sobs and disjointed attempts to explain, Alastair determined that his daughter had been struck by a motorcycle and had suffered a concussion and possible internal injuries. Exactly how this sequence of events had happened was not clear.

"I'm on my way," he said tersely, and went back to the conference room to inform Rhys he was leaving.

"Leaving?" Rhys threw down his pen. "For God's sake, man, we've a dozen details yet to discuss—"

"My daughter's in hospital," Alastair snapped. "Sorry, Gordon, but my family comes first."

There was a shocked silence. "Of course. Carry on," Rhys told the others as he thrust his chair back and stood up. "Keep me informed of your decisions. I'll have my mobile with me. I'm going with Alastair."

He followed Alastair out. "You're upset, you shouldn't drive," he said. "I'll take you to the hospital."

Twenty minutes later, a ward sister at St. George's General Critical Care Unit directed Alastair to a curtained cubicle. Only family were allowed into the surgery area; Rhys remained behind in the waiting room.

Cherie saw Alastair and went, sobbing, into his arms. "This is my fault," she told him brokenly, "my fault."

"Of course it's not, darling," he murmured, perplexed, as he stroked her hair. "It was an accident."

"But it *is* my fault!" She looked up at him, her expression bleak. "Hannah snuck out of the house while I was at Waitrose. I didn't know she was gone. At noon she came in the kitchen door. Neil was there – I'd just told him we couldn't see one other. I told him I love *you*, and only you—"

Alastair stepped back and dropped his hands from her. "I don't care what you told him. Tell me what happened to Hannah. What did she see? Whatever it was, it obviously upset her."

"She saw us together, and jumped to the wrong conclusion."

"And why would she do that?" he asked softly.

Cherie sobbed. "It was... we were hugging, Neil and I. I'd just told him we shouldn't see one another; that it would only lead to trouble. Hannah saw us and completely misread the situation, and she ran out, and I went after her, but she ran into the street behind a bus, straight in the path of a motorcycle." Sobs shook her shoulders. "It knocked her into the air, Alastair, like a... a rag doll."

There was a long, terrible silence before Alastair spoke. "If anything happens to Hannah, Cherie," he informed his wife with quiet conviction, "I'll hold you and Neil personally responsible. And I'll never forgive either one of you."

CHAPTER 43

Midway through the Destroyers' rehearsal on Friday afternoon, Dominic's mobile rang. "Dom," his agent, Max Moore, said in a rush, "thank God I reached you!"

"What is it, Max?" Dominic said as he towelled his face off. Things weren't going well. The boys in the band were throwing major attitude, and Mick kept giving Dominic mock bows and calling him 'yer lordship'.

"I've got someone on the line, wants to speak with you." Max paused. He added in an awed whisper, "It's your father, Lord Locksley."

Dominic swore. He hadn't spoken to his father in almost eleven years. "I don't want to talk to him," he snapped, but Max had already transferred the call.

There was a pause. "Rather too late for that, Rupert," his father said.

Shit. "Rather too late all round, isn't it?" Dominic retorted. "Sorry about the media flap, but someone found out my identity and leaked it to the press. It wasn't me."

"Well, in the end, it doesn't matter who it was, does it? The damage is done. Your mother and I have been besieged by reporters ever since the story came out."

Dominic's hand tightened on the phone. "Yeah, well, at least I spared you from embarrassment for ten years."

"I wouldn't say that," his lordship returned, his words chilly. "Your behaviour is a continued source of embarrassment, particularly to me."

"Right," Dominic agreed, and tightened his jaw. "Never mind the fact that I make shedloads of money and donate to charity and sell millions of records." He felt the same old mingled anger and hurt welling up. "I met the Queen last year, did you know? But none of that matters, because I'm not doing what *you* want. I've never measured up to your impossible standards, have I, dad? And I never will."

"I won't deny that I'm profoundly disappointed in you, Rupert. And while I agree that you've done well for yourself, materially at least, I don't consider the scandal-plagued life you lead as something to be proud of." He paused. "But I didn't call to revisit old ground."

"Why did you call, then?" Dominic asked. "Enlighten me."

"I wished to inform you that as far as I'm concerned—" his words were coldly polite "—you're no longer my son."

Dominic felt as if he'd been punched in the stomach. Although he'd known this day would come, hearing the words spoken left him momentarily stunned, scarcely able to breathe.

"I'm seeing the family solicitor early next week. It's against your mother's wishes, I might add, but nonetheless—" Lord Locksley cleared his throat "—I'm disowning you. Upon my death, the title and property will pass to your brother, Liam. I'm sorry it's come to this. Goodbye, Rupert."

And with that, he disconnected.

"What's wrong?" Gemma asked, her face creased with concern as she sat next to him and slipped her arm through his. "I took the afternoon off to come and watch you rehearse, but you look like you just lost your best mate *and* the EuroMillions, all in one go."

"It's my father. He's about to disown me. The old sod," he added with a scowl.

"Oh, Dom – I'm sorry. That's rough. Is there anything I can do?"

He smiled wanly and gave her thigh a squeeze. "You're doing it. You're here, and that's all that matters."

She leaned over and brushed her lips against his. "I don't like to see you sad," she murmured, and stroked his cheek.

He reached up and took her face in his hands. "Thanks, babes. You're an angel." He kissed her, tenderly at first, then with increasing ardour. A moment later, out of breath, he dragged his mouth away and groaned. "God... I want you so bad."

"Me, too. Let's go," Gemma whispered, her forehead pressed against Dominic's. "Let's get out of here."

He grinned. "Come on. I know just the place."

"You've got on too many bloody clothes!" Dominic complained five minutes later.

"Careful, these jeans cost £150," Gemma scolded as he yanked them over her hips and down her legs.

"I don't care what they cost, I just want 'em off," he said testily, and paused. They were hiding out in the band's cramped storage room, twined together behind a ragtag collection of half-stacks, guitar stands, and towering amp cabinets. "I don't have a condom."

"I do." Gemma smiled as he tugged impatiently at the buttons of her shirt. "Good thing I always carry one in my handbag." She reached over and retrieved it.

"I thought you weren't that kind of girl," Dominic muttered as he pushed her shirt off.

"I'm not! I keep it just in case."

"Just in case what? You shag a random rock star?"

She laid her hand lightly on the bulge in his jeans, and her eyes widened. "Oh, Dominic," she murmured, and blushed. "No wonder Nat stayed with you for two years."

"I never had no complaints," he said smugly.

"Show me," Gemma breathed, and planted her mouth firmly on his.

And with a grin, he did.

"Hannah has a mild concussion, and trauma to the spleen," Dr. Tran informed Alastair and Cherie outside Hannah's hospital room. "We'll need to remove it straight away."

"But if you remove it, what then?" Cherie asked anxiously. "Will she be all right?"

"Her liver will assume the spleen's functions, such as filtering her blood; but she'll be more susceptible to infection. The liver can't compensate for that." He smiled. "But she's young and in excellent health, so her prognosis is very good."

"Is there someone in the family who can donate O-negative blood?" a nurse asked Alastair and Cherie.

They shook their heads. "Neither of us is O-negative," Alastair said.

"Unfortunately, O-neg is the most common blood type, so we've a short supply at the moment. Hannah will need a transfusion during her surgery."

"Let me see what I can do," Alastair said, and strode away to the waiting room.

"What's happening?" Rhys asked, his face creased with concern. He stood and threw away the Styrofoam cup of coffee he held. "How's Hannah?"

"She needs surgery. Her spleen needs to come out. She'll need O-negative blood, but supplies are low. I've got to find a donor, as quickly as possible." Alastair's hand shook as he withdrew his mobile phone and began to press buttons.

"Put your phone away. Take me back to the surgery," Rhys told him.

Alastair looked at him in puzzlement. "You? But you're not a family member—"

"I'm O-negative," Rhys said, his words impatient. "And yes, I'm a family member. This probably isn't the best time or place to tell you—"

"Tell me what?" Alastair asked, and lowered his mobile phone in confusion.

Rhys took his arm. "I can't go into it at the moment, but right now all you need to know, Alastair, is that..." He paused. "I'm your son."

CHAPTER 44

On Friday evening, Natalie went to her flat to pack a few clothes. Her mobile rang as she got out of her car. "Rhys! Where are you? Are you still at work?"

"No, I'm at St. George's. They're prepping Hannah James for surgery. She was hit by a motorcycle this afternoon."

"Oh, my God!" Natalie exclaimed. "What happened? Poor girl… is she all right?"

"I don't know the details. She'll need blood, and I match her type, so I'm donating. I'm not sure when I'll get home."

"Don't worry, take your time. I'm just packing my things up. I'll be waiting for you at yours."

"Hmm," he murmured, "I like the sound of that. Wear that T-shirt I like, why don't you? And nothing else."

Natalie smiled. "So you prefer me in a faded T-shirt instead of, say, sexy, lace-trimmed lingerie?"

"Either would do very nicely," he said. He sighed. "It's been a really long day."

"I'm glad you're there," Natalie told him. "Alastair and Cherie must be wrecked."

"They are. And they're having problems of their own as well. They've barely spoken to one another."

Natalie frowned. "That's odd – they always get on so well. I expect they're just worried about Hannah. Give them my love." She paused as Alexa Clarkson pulled up behind her and parked. "Oh, crikey… Alexa's here, I've got to go."

"Ian's wife? That can't be good."

Nat sighed. "She probably wants to have another go at me."

"I hope not. I'll keep you updated on Hannah. Talk to you later, darling." Rhys ended the call and scowled. If anything should happen to Natalie tomorrow night…

Ian Clarkson would be a dead man. He'd see to it himself.

As Natalie unlocked the door to let them in a few minutes later, Alexa came straight to the point. "Nat, tell me what's going on."

"I've told you, nothing's going on." Natalie tossed her handbag on a chair. "I'm only here to pack a few things. I'm moving in with Rhys tonight."

Alexa reached in her handbag and withdrew a mobile phone. "Ian dropped this upstairs when he came by to pick up his things. I threw him out," she added matter-of-factly. "I want you to listen to something."

Natalie was silent as Alexa replayed the message.

"'Ian, it's Natalie. I want proof before this goes any further. Prove that what you say is true, or I promise you, I'll call the police.'"

Alexa met Nat's eyes as she put the mobile away. "What's going on, Nat? I want the truth. Is Ian threatening you?"

"I'm sorry, but I can't really talk about it," Natalie said, and turned away, distraught. "It's a police matter now."

"A police matter?" Alexa grabbed Nat's arm. "Right, you've *got* to tell me what he's done. This involves my husband, Nat! I have a right to know."

Natalie sighed. "Of course you do. Come and sit down." She led the way into the sitting room and helped Alexa lower herself awkwardly onto the sofa. "You should be at home, resting," Natalie scolded her. "This can't be good for the baby."

"I'm fine. I need to know what Ian's done. And not knowing is far more upsetting. Please, Nat."

"Ian's blackmailing me," she admitted. "He found proof that my father was embezzling from Dashwood and James. He's threatened to go to the media with the story if I don't cooperate. He'll ruin my father's name, and stir up damaging publicity just as we're trying to re-launch the store."

Alexa's eyes widened. "My God! Why didn't you tell me any of this before?"

"I didn't want to upset you. And I couldn't risk Ian finding out that I told anyone. He's far too clever, and I'm a crap liar. Besides," she added reprovingly, "you didn't exactly give me a chance to explain."

Alexa had the grace to look uncomfortable. "No, I didn't. I'm sorry. I was so bloody angry—"

"You thought I was having an affair with Ian." Natalie leaned forward. "If I saw photos of you and Rhys in the tabloids kissing, I'd jump to the same conclusion."

"Well," Alexa said ruefully as she rubbed the enormous mound of her stomach, "I'm far too big around – and far too tired – to get up to anything like that now."

"You're gorgeous," Natalie said staunchly, and took Alexa's hands in hers. "Ian's a fool if he can't see that."

"He's been indifferent through my entire pregnancy," Alexa said slowly. "He's had a couple of other affairs. I told myself it didn't matter, that it was me he loved. But I have to face facts. I don't think he ever really loved me."

Natalie hesitated. "Ian's hit on me so many times I've lost count. Gemma, too. Once he found evidence of my father's guilt, he couldn't wait to use it against me."

"How did he find out?" Alexa asked.

"He found copies of the account books in a box of his stepfather's things in your attic. His stepfather was the head accountant for Dashwood and James. He noticed the books had been tampered with, and blackmailed my father. And so Ian decided to blackmail me."

"It's all so crazy!" Alexa exclaimed, "Why would anyone even care what your father did all those years ago?"

"Ian knew I wouldn't want to see my father's name dragged through the mud. Dad had a mistress, Alexa. He embezzled money to support her, and probably to keep her quiet."

"And what does Ian want in return, exactly?" Alexa asked. "It can't be money."

Alexa's family money was old, and plentiful. Something to do with the manufacture of Scottish woollens, Natalie knew, and a tea plantation in Kenya…

"No, it isn't money." Natalie's voice was a thread. "He wants a partnership in the stores. And he's reserved a room at the Savoy tomorrow night, after the re-launch. I'm to meet him there, to… celebrate."

Alexa paled. "I know he's gone off me since my pregnancy," she murmured. "But to think that he'd go to such lengths, just to get you in bed…! And he's mad if he thinks Alastair or Sir Richard would ever give him a partnership. I just can't get my head around this. It's like some kind of sick... game."

"You can see why I couldn't tell you the truth."

Alexa nodded slowly. "I'm sorry he put you through this."

"I'm to meet him tomorrow night as planned, so the police will have proof against him in court. Then they'll arrest him." She looked up, her eyes wide. "I'm scared, Alexa. I don't want to go through with this."

"You don't actually think he'd hurt you—?"

"No, but if he finds out I've gone to the police he'll be furious. He calls me on my mobile, he's cornered me by the copier and in the kitchen at work... he even let himself into my flat. He told the landlord he was my brother." She paused. "Rhys insisted I stay at his until this is over."

"Yes, he's quite right," Alexa agreed, still numb with shock. "I can't believe this. What a bloody nightmare."

As they returned to their cars, Natalie told Alexa, "You shouldn't drive. I can take you home."

"I'm fine." Alexa leaned forward and kissed her cheek. "Don't worry about me, just please... be careful."

"I will. Call me as soon as the baby's born."

Alexa promised she would. "I'm sorry, Nat, for everything. I hate that Ian's doing this. And I hate that I doubted you."

"It's OK, really." Natalie frowned. "What'll you do if Ian's arrested? You and the baby can come and stay with us—"

"No need," Alexa reassured her. "Mum's coming down tomorrow, and my sisters are already arguing over names for the baby. And money's not a problem, so we'll be fine."

"If you're sure… you know I'm always here for you. Drive safely." Natalie hugged Alexa tightly and waved as she pulled away.

Later, as she put her duffel bag into the Peugeot's boot, her mobile rang. "Rhys! How's Hannah?"

"I'm on my way home," he said. "Hannah came through the surgery with flying colours. She'll be home by Tuesday."

"Oh, I'm so glad! I'm just leaving."

"What did Alexa want? She didn't have another go at you—?"

"No, she apologised." Briefly Natalie related the details of Alexa finding Ian's mobile phone.

"Good, now she can put the blame on Ian, where it belongs." Rhys paused. "I haven't had anything to eat but a couple of biscuits and watered-down juice after they took my blood."

"I'll make spag bol if you've got tomatoes and pasta and a bit of red wine—"

"No red wine," he said firmly. "I'd have to take off my shirt, in that case."

"I like the sound of that," Natalie mused as she slid behind the wheel. "I'm picturing you sitting shirtless across the table, spilling sauce down your chest…"

"I never spill sauce down my chest." He paused. "It usually lands a bit further south than that."

"I'll look forward to the cleanup, then."

Rhys's laugh was low and throaty. "Careful, Natalie, I'll wreck the Jag if you keep talking like that."

The news that Hannah's surgery had gone well left Cherie limp with relief. Alastair hadn't spoken to her since he'd arrived. As she got up and headed to reception to enquire about visiting hours, she heard someone call her name, and turned around. "Sarah! What are you doing here?"

Sarah Hadley gave her a quick hug. "I volunteer a couple of evenings a week. Never mind that – I heard Hannah was hurt! Is she all right?"

"Yes, she just got out of surgery. She was hit by a motorbike."

"Poor girl!" Sarah didn't press for details; she could see the shadows of exhaustion under Cherie's eyes. "Come and have a coffee, we can catch up."

"Hannah and Duncan broke up," Cherie said after they sat down. "She's been working at the store for the summer. She met a stock clerk, and Alastair didn't approve. He moved her to another department, and she was furious."

"It's not easy, is it?" Sarah said in sympathy. "Those teenage hormones…"

"Yes, between Hannah's dramas and Alastair's long hours at work, it's been difficult."

"Neil said the two of you had dinner at that new French restaurant."

Cherie took a measured sip of her coffee. "Yes. Alastair cancelled at the last minute, and suggested I ask you, but you'd gone to Bath. I hope you don't mind–?"

"Mind?" she echoed. "We're divorced. Besides, you and Alastair are the gold standard of marital bliss."

"Not any longer." Cherie hesitated. "Alastair's always working. It's caused a… strain."

"Let me guess – Neil was always there, ready to comfort you, compliment you, make you laugh."

Cherie stared at her. "Well… yes. He's been a rock. How did you know?"

"I was married to him for seventeen years! He used that self-deprecating charm to lure Duncan's English teacher, and a neighbour's wife, into bed." She set her coffee down. "I divorced Neil because he was a serial cheater."

Cherie pressed her lips together. To think she'd nearly become one of his conquests. Anger swept over her, not only at Neil, but at herself, for being so bloody stupid. She'd risked almost thirty years of marriage to a good man for no good reason other than her own selfishness and vanity.

And unless she could convince Alastair otherwise, it might already be too late to salvage what was left of their marriage.

CHAPTER 45

Dominic threw his mobile down in frustration. His calls to Keeley's private number went straight to voicemail. He'd tried all afternoon to reach her, without success. The news of his upcoming duet with Keeley at the re-launch had been posted on the D&J website and all over the social media networks.

Never mind that she hadn't agreed to do it yet…

Dominic had to convince her before tomorrow's re-launch. But how could he do that if she wouldn't bloody *talk* to him?

There was only one thing to do, he decided, and grabbed the keys to his Maserati.

He'd drive to Notting Hill and ask her in person.

"Miss Pennington's not home. Especially," the bodyguard added as he blocked Keeley's front door, "not to you."

"Then I hope you like music, mate." Dominic jerked his head in the direction of the Maserati. "'Cause I brought my amp and guitar, and I'll plug up and play 'Up the Monarchy's Arse' at full whack until Keeley opens that fucking door."

The front door swung open. "What's going on?" Keeley demanded. "Dominic? What are you doing here? You've got a nerve—"

"Never mind that, I need to talk to you," he interrupted her. "It's important. I've got a business proposal."

The bodyguard shoved him. "I said bugger off, mate."

Dominic shoved him back. "Listen, you stupid twat—"

"Let him in," Keeley told the bodyguard. She glared at Dominic. "You have exactly—" she looked at her wristwatch "—five minutes. Starting now."

"Keels," he said as she shut the door and turned to face him, "I'm sorry about the wedding thing, OK? But you know as well as me that we would've been divorced in ten minutes anyway."

"You humiliated me in front of the entire world!" she snapped. "That's a bit hard to forgive." She glanced pointedly at her watch. "Four minutes, thirty seconds."

"Yeah, well, you told the *Mirror* my willy was so small you needed sat nav to find it," he retorted. "So we're even. Besides, that bloke you're seeing, the reporter who got the exclusive – you wouldn't have met him if it wasn't for me."

"Jonathan's the best thing that's ever happened to me." She sniffed, only partly mollified. "Three minutes."

"Remember that song we wrote together?"

"Of course I do." Her expression softened. "You wrote it for me."

"Yeah, it was good, wasn't it? The thing is," he added carefully, "I want to… change the lyrics round a bit."

Keeley narrowed her eyes. "Change the lyrics how, exactly?"

"Well, there's this girl—"

"There's always a girl," Keeley snapped. "Two minutes."

"This is different." Dominic raked a hand through his hair. "Her name's Gemma," he added in a rush, "and I really like her, maybe even love her, so I want to change the words a bit. And I want you to sing it with me at the

Dashwood and James re-launch tomorrow… for the encore." He looked at her expectantly. "Well… what do you think?"

"I think this is about saving your arse, that's what I think. Your fans are pissed. You're afraid they'll pelt you with rubbish, so you want me to be a target for the lobbed tomatoes as well!" She scowled. "You have a bloody nerve—"

"It's not only for me. Think of the publicity… for both of us! We'll be together in public for the first time since—" He stopped. "Since I fucked things up," he admitted. "Everyone will be there just to see how we get on."

Despite herself, Keeley was tempted. Dominic was right; they'd make the cover of every tabloid in London. "We'll split the royalties from the single 50/50," she announced. "And I get a songwriting credit… the melody's mine, after all."

"Yeah, of course," Dominic agreed.

A frown clouded her brow. "What about your father? He must be furious now that everyone knows who you really are."

"You could say that. He's disowning me."

"Oh, Dominic," Keeley said in dismay, "that's so unfair! I'm sorry."

He shrugged. "I'm not. I'm not cut out for that aristo crap."

She reached out and squeezed his hand. "Guess I'll never be Lady Locksley now, will I?"

"No," Dominic agreed. "I hope you're not too disappointed. Come on, then," he urged, "let's have a go at re-writing this song, shall we?"

"Rhys," Natalie asked as she stood in the middle of his kitchen a half hour later, "where's your basil?"

"My basil?" He glanced down. "Well, I hadn't named him yet, but Basil should do. Would you like an introduction? He's very friendly, if a bit headstrong."

"We've met," Natalie said, nudging him aside as she rummaged through the cabinets. "I thought he was quite pushy."

"You ought to give him another go," Rhys said as he came to stand behind her and wrapped his arms around her waist. "Basil only wants to please."

Natalie closed her eyes as Rhys nuzzled the curve of her neck. "What about the passata sauce?"

"I'll make you forget all about the passata, darling."

And he proceeded, in a breathtakingly inventive fashion, to do just that.

Afterwards, Rhys kissed her and said, "I want to go to bed with you every night, and wake up with you every morning. I want to see your knickers hanging from the shower rod. I want to argue about whose turn it is to change the loo roll." He kissed her shoulder. "And Basil's in complete agreement."

"If that's a proposal," Natalie said indignantly, "it's the most crap proposal I've ever heard."

"And how many have you had, exactly?" Rhys inquired.

"None," Nat admitted, "but every girl imagines it. Will he ask for her hand in the middle of a crowded restaurant, or on a beach in Goa, or atop a double-decker bus—"

"Atop a bus?" Rhys echoed. "The exhaust would give the poor sod a headache."

"Well, at least he'd get points for trying. Your proposal, on the other hand, is completely unromantic."

Rhys rolled over on one elbow and regarded her steadily. "Well, I'll have to do better, won't I?"

"You should whisk me off to Paris for the weekend, then surprise me with a diamond ring in my chateaubriand—" she paused and wrinkled her nose "—no, bit of a mess, make it a glass of champagne instead – then take me on a long, moonlit ride on a bateau down the Seine. That's romantic."

"It's not very original," he countered. "Bit touristy, too. I have a better idea. I'll whisk you away to a chip shop on my motorbike. It's cheaper, and much more practical. I'll put the ring in the mushy peas."

She smiled sleepily and snuggled her head against his shoulder. "I love mushy peas," she murmured. "And I love you."

And before Rhys could find the words to respond, Natalie was asleep.

The telephone woke Natalie early Saturday morning. She rolled over and reached for Rhys, but he was gone. Abruptly, she sat up. She glanced at the alarm clock as she reached out to answer the shrilling phone. It was barely six a.m.

Who on earth was calling so early?

She lifted the handset to answer the phone just as Rhys picked up the kitchen extension. "Yes?" she heard him say.

"Rhys, it's Sir Richard. Hope I didn't disturb, I know it's early, but I wanted to catch you before you left. I know you'll be terribly busy at the re-launch today."

"It's OK, I'm making coffee. What can I do for you?"

"The lawyers have drawn up the paperwork. All I need is your signature to move ahead. With the board's approval, you'll become a full partner in Dashwood and James, effective Monday."

Natalie blinked, surprised. Grandfather hadn't said a word about making Rhys a partner. Nor had Rhys.

She bit her lip. She only hoped Ian didn't know…

"I can't read it today," Rhys said, "but leave it with Gemma, and I'll take a look on Sunday."

Natalie was about to hang up when Rhys added, "You'll be happy to know that I've asked Natalie to marry me. I know it's what you wanted."

"It's what I've wanted since you first came to work here. And has she agreed?"

"She didn't exactly approve of my proposal," Rhys said dryly, "but yes, she agreed."

"Good. I know the stores will be in capable hands going forward, and Natalie will, as well."

Natalie lowered the handset, stunned. So grandfather was making Rhys a partner. All Rhys had to do in exchange, apparently, was marry her. No marriage, no partnership. Two birds, one stone, wasn't that the saying?

Numb, she pushed the covers aside and stood up. Must get dressed, busy day ahead…

"I brought you coffee." Rhys came in and placed a mug on the nightstand. He leaned forward and kissed the top of her head. "You'd best get a move on, today's the big day."

Natalie said nothing. She was far too shocked – and far too upset – to formulate words just yet.

"When the re-launch is over," he added as he slid his arms into a shirt, "we can start planning the wedding."

"Planning, yes," Natalie said tightly, and stood up. "I'll leave that to you, since you're so good at it." If he noticed the edge in her voice, he gave no sign.

He chose a tie and slid it around his neck. "Do you fancy a big wedding, or something smaller? Jamie can cater the food—"

"I have a better idea," Natalie said, and stepped into a navy blue dress. "Let's forget the whole thing."

Rhys adjusted his tie. "Just bunk off and elope to a nice, sandy beach somewhere?" he asked, and grinned. "I like the sound of that."

"No." Natalie turned suddenly to face him, her expression hard. "No eloping. No sandy beach. No wedding." She thrust her feet into a pair of kitten-heeled shoes. "Congratulations, Rhys, you're off the hook."

His hands stilled on the knot of his tie. "What?"

"I'm not marrying you." She stood before the mirror and stabbed a diamond stud into first one ear, then the other.

"What the hell are you talking about?"

She met his eyes in the mirror. "I picked up the phone earlier, and I overheard your conversation with grandfather. You're to become a partner in the store. Congratulations."

"It isn't final yet," Rhys said, irritated. "And what has that to do with our wedding?"

"Everything, apparently. One can't happen without the other. No marriage, no partnership. Isn't that the deal you and grandfather struck?"

His hands dropped to his sides. "There is no 'deal'," he said, his voice hard. "The partnership was Sir Richard's idea. He's asked me to stay on permanently. I haven't agreed yet."

"Well, now that I've agreed to marry you, and you've convinced grandfather to make you a partner, there's no need to leave. You got everything you wanted."

"Natalie—"

"—and you used me to do it."

"*Used* you?" Rhys demanded, incredulous. "I asked you to marry me! How is that using you, exactly? Please explain."

She rounded on him. "You're only marrying me because it's what grandfather wants. If you don't, you won't become a partner. That's what you've wanted all along, isn't it? A partnership?"

"You know, Natalie," he said finally, his voice dangerously calm, "when you get it wrong, you really get it wrong. Marrying you isn't a condition of my becoming a partner."

"Isn't it?"

"No!" He reined in his anger. "I admit that I intended to acquire Dashwood and James eventually, yes. I knew the store would go back in the crapper when I left. I planned to return and buy Sir Richard and Alastair out."

Natalie stared at him, gutted by his admission. Ian, much as she despised him, had been absolutely right about Rhys.

"Nothing would have changed," he continued, "only the ownership. Sir Richard and Alastair would've made a tidy sum on the sale and been divested of the headaches of running the stores as well."

"I can't believe this! You calculating bastard—"

"Oh for God's sake, grow up, Natalie," Rhys cut in, his words savage. "I'm a businessman. It's what I do. Turn companies round. Make a profit. You knew that from the start."

"Of course I did! But I thought Dashwood and James meant more to you than profits and bottom lines. I thought—" her voice wobbled, damn it all "—I thought you cared."

"I do care! But you're naïve as hell if you think I'm not in business to make a profit."

"Yes, I suppose I am," Natalie said, stung. "Naïve... stupid, too, because I thought you were invested in Sir Richard, and me. Not just in the store."

He came and stood before her and gripped her shoulders, his blue eyes glittering. "I love you, Natalie. I fell for you somewhere along the way. And when I did… it changed everything." He dropped his hands. "But don't worry. When I leave, I won't return. Dashwood and James can stand or fall on its own. I won't profit from it either way."

"You might as well stay. Take the partnership. But if you do," she added as she leaned down and snatched up her handbag, "just know that I'm not part of the package."

"Oh, sod this." Rhys turned angrily away. "I've better things to do than try and reason with you and your convoluted feminine logic. I'm leaving. We'll talk about this later."

"Reason with me?" she echoed, outraged. "I apologise for trying your patience with my 'convoluted feminine logic'. I'm sorry, Rhys, but I'm done. We're done."

He reached out and grabbed her arm. "Listen to me, Natalie. I'm a businessman. I grew up hard, and fast, and it's made me who I am. I'm sorry if I've fallen short of your vision of the perfect man. I didn't row for Oxford or inherit a title. I won't be someone I'm not… not even for you."

She jerked free. "Don't worry, no one would ever mistake you for a man of breeding," she said, her words chosen expressly to wound him. "Oh, you dress impeccably, with your bespoke suits and your John Lobb shoes, and you drive an expensive car, but at the end of the day you're still just a rough bloke with rough manners from a council estate."

There was a horrible, charged silence.

"You're right," Rhys said, and finished knotting his tie with jerky motions. "I hope you get the man you deserve," he added as he grabbed his suit jacket, "one with a title and a silver spoon stuck up his arse. But I'm not that man."

She was swamped with remorse. "Rhys—"

"Sir Richard's partnership offer has nothing to do with my decision to marry you. I asked you because I love you. But if you doubt that," Rhys continued in cold, clipped tones, "then I'm wasting my time here." He brushed past her and strode to the door. "I'm leaving after the re-launch. And I'm turning down Sir Richard's offer."

Suddenly horribly ashamed of her behaviour, and longing to take back the hurtful words she'd said, Natalie bit her lip and turned round. "Rhys, please, wait. I'm sorry—"

But he was already gone, leaving her standing alone in the middle of the bedroom.

CHAPTER 46

Saturday dawned clear and warm, a perfect English summer day for Dashwood and James's re-launch. Sporting her headset and a clipboard, Natalie was headed for the Portaloos.

"We need more wheelie bins by the back entrance," she said into the mouthpiece. She glanced at the rows of portable toilets tucked away behind the furthest marquee. "And make sure there's plenty of loo rolls, please. What? Yes, you need to check *every* loo."

Natalie turned back towards the store. Everything looked amazing – from the marquees draped in yards of billowing white silk, to the giant photos of Dominic hung in the store windows, leaping in mid-air with his guitar in hand, dressed entirely in clothing from Dashwood and James's racks.

She should have been thrilled. She *was* thrilled. But her argument with Rhys that morning had left her rudderless and miserable.

And tonight Ian Clarkson would be waiting for her at the Savoy hotel.

The thought paralysed her with fear. So much could go wrong... but she shoved her fears aside. There wasn't time to dwell on Ian now; instead, she focused on the immediate problems facing her with the re-launch. Of which, she reflected grimly, there were plenty.

"Have you seen Dominic?" one of the roadies asked Natalie.

"No." She glanced at her watch. "It's early; he's probably not here yet. Is there a problem?"

"You could say that. Mick's completely rat-arsed. He can't even stand upright. I've never seen him this bad before."

Dominic's bass player, as notorious for his blue Mohawk as he was for his capacity for drink, had proven unreliable before.

"There's coffee in the refreshments marquee," Natalie told him. "Fill a Thermos and pour it down his throat. Or his pants," she added grimly. "Whichever wakes him up first."

"OK," he muttered, "right," and backed away.

Her mobile rang and she glanced at the number. "Alexa!" she exclaimed. "How are you? Have you had the baby?"

"No, they're about to prep me for surgery." She paused. "I just wanted to say sorry, and wish you luck. I know you and Rhys worked hard on the re-launch. Give him my best wishes."

"I can't."

"Why not?"

"He's not speaking to me," Natalie replied, and bit her lip. "He told me he's leaving when the re-launch is over."

"Oh, Nat, no," Alexa exclaimed in dismay. "But things were going so well! What happened?"

Natalie saw the roadie coming back, with Mick's arm slung around his neck as he dragged the comatose bass player towards her. "Can't talk now," she sighed, "but it's my fault."

"So you'll grovel, and make things right."

But Natalie was certain an apology couldn't begin to repair the damage she'd done to their relationship.

"What do you think you're doing?" Rhys Gordon demanded.

Dominic, a bottle of Chivas Regal tipped up to his lips, took a long, deliberate swallow and wiped his mouth with the back of his hand. "I'm having a slug before the show, like always." He eyed Rhys insolently. "What's it to you, anyway?"

"We've no licence for alcohol, that's what. This isn't Glastonbury. No drinking."

Dominic threw him a mock salute. "Clean and sober, that's me, mate."

"See that you stay that way." Rhys regarded him with distaste. "I don't want anything spoiling Natalie's hard work today. And that includes you. *Mate*." He pushed past Dominic to find the sound engineer.

"Yeah, well, if it weren't for you," Dominic called after him, spoiling for a fight, "I'd still be with Nat."

Gemma, who'd just arrived with a bag of bacon sandwiches to share with Dominic, came to a halt behind him.

Rhys turned back. "Excuse me, but *you* dumped her, Dominic." He cocked one eyebrow up. "Thanks, by the way. Your loss, my gain, isn't that what they say? At any rate," he added, "she planned to give you the boot after the party anyway. You just got there first."

"That's bullshit," Dominic said dismissively. "No one's ever dumped me."

One of the sound engineers called to him from the edge of the stage. "Where's Mick? He needs to do his sound check."

"How should I know?" Dominic snapped. He turned back to Rhys, unaware that Gemma stood, grease-spotted bag in hand, behind him. "You're right about one thing – I messed up with Nat. I tried to get her back. But it's you she wants, God knows why. Just don't fuck it up like I did." And with another glare at Rhys, he stalked off to find Mick.

"Dominic? Dominic, wait." Gemma strode after him, still clutching the greasy paper bag.

He stopped and turned around, and his face lit up. "Babes! I didn't know you were here." He leaned forward. "You were incredible yesterday, by the way. Give us a kiss."

"I'll give you something, all right," Gemma retorted, and hurled the bag of bacon butties at him as hard as she could. Bacon, grease, and soggy toast exploded on his chest. "Enjoy your breakfast. Arsehole!" She turned and stormed away.

Dominic plucked a piece of streaky bacon from his chin and stared after her in outrage. "Why the fuck did you do that?" he bellowed. "This bacon's hot!"

She whirled back around. "Ask Natalie to put some salve on you. I'm sure she'll be happy to oblige." Her eyes glittered with angry unshed tears. "I hope you have grease burns… third degree… all over your miserable, lying, manky little body!"

Dominic skinned his shirt off and ran after her. "Gemma, hold up!" He caught up to her and grabbed her by the elbow. "What are you on about?"

"I heard what you said to Rhys." She shook his hand off. "What a shame you couldn't patch it up with Natalie." Gemma crossed her arms against her chest and glowered at him. "So what am I – the bloody consolation prize?"

"Nat and I are over, Gemma. You know that!"

"Yeah, well, guess what? So are we, Dominic. Over, that is. So don't bother coming back to mine tonight. You're not welcome." And with that, she turned and left him standing alone, with nothing but bits of bacon, soggy toast, and grease to keep him company.

Backstage at Phillip Pryce's fashion show, controlled chaos reigned. Outfits hung on rails, each pinned with a photo of the ensemble and accessories – shoes, jewellery, handbag, etc. A white board displayed photos of each outfit in order of appearance in the show. Tables for makeup and hair, covered with brushes, cosmetics, hair grips, and hair products, crowded the tiny perimeter.

"Where's the sticky tape?" someone demanded. "I need it for these Manolos!"

Natalie, dazed by the frantic activity, looked inquiringly at Jacques as he flitted past. "Why are they putting sticky tape on the shoes?"

"To keep the straps from slipping," Jacques said impatiently, as if it were obvious to anyone but an idiot. "What's the order for the models?" he asked.

Natalie consulted her list. "Gemma, Bryony, Elspeth, then once again each. Then me."

"OK, be back here in—" he consulted his watch with a frown "—two hours for hair and makeup. Don't be late." He flounced away and shouted, "Has anyone seen Phillip?"

Natalie brushed past a photographer, snapping photos backstage, and wondered where Dominic was. He was scheduled to perform in less than an hour.

She'd seen Rhys only once; he glanced at her without expression and turned away. She threaded her way out of the tent, past clusters of photographers and PR people, and guilt washed over her. She'd find him once the re-launch was over and apologise for the horrible things she'd said.

Her mobile vibrated. *Alexa.* "Have you had the baby? Was it a girl?" Natalie said in a rush. "Is everything all right?"

"Yes, yes, and yes," Alexa said groggily. "I have a girl, a perfect little girl."

"Congratulations! Are your family there?"

"Yes, and they're driving me mad. I'll be here until tomorrow, so come and say hello to Emily Kate."

"I will," Natalie promised. "Have you heard from Ian?"

"No. I'm filing for a divorce next week. Nat—" Alexa hesitated "—be careful, tonight. Ian isn't what he seems – we've been married for eight years and I'm just realising that. I hope everything goes according to plan."

"So do I," Natalie said grimly, and rang off.

Halfway through rehearsal, the bass amp emitted a ragged, humming sound. The volume dropped, and died out completely.

Mick stopped playing. "Fucking hell, a tube blew again."

"Come on," one of the sound crew said. "Move it out and bring in the backup."

Dominic, who'd shed his grease-splotched clothing for an Armani jacket worn over a Kaiser Chiefs T-shirt, jeans, and red Louboutin trainers, snarled, "Hurry your arses up, you lot, we're on in forty-five minutes." His fight with Gemma earlier had done nothing to improve his black mood. He slung his guitar strap over his head and struck a chord

There was a flurry of activity backstage as Keeley arrived. "Sorry I'm late," she breathed as she joined him on the curtained-off stage, "but traffic's completely arsed! Everyone in London must be here today."

"Right, well, at least you made it." Dominic made room for her at the microphone. "Let's run through the first verse and chorus, like we rehearsed it—"

"What's *she* doing here?" Gemma, her hands on her hips, stormed backstage and stopped in front of them. She glared at Keeley, then at Dominic, with equal outrage. "I turn my back for one bloody minute to get ready for the fashion show, and she swans in like she owns you!"

Keeley, heavily made up for the show, gave Gemma a pitying glance. "I'm here to perform," she said condescendingly, as if Gemma were an idiot. "I'm singing tonight. Dominic and I—"

Gemma stepped forward and gave Keeley a shove. "There is no 'Dominic and you'," she snapped. "It's over, you tarted-up cow, and he's mine now. Keep your bloody mitts off."

"Piss off!" Keeley hissed, and shoved Gemma back as she regained her footing. "I have no interest in Dominic. Besides, I'm seeing someone else now—"

"I'm sure you are," Gemma retorted. "According to the tabloids, you've shagged every footballer in Britain."

"How dare you!" Keeley screeched, and reached out to grab a hank of Gemma's hair.

"Stop it, both of you!" Dominic shouted. He stood between them and held Keeley at arm's length to keep her away from Gemma. "I don't have time for this. Shut the hell up right now!"

"If anyone's interested," Mick called out as he took a drag on his cigarette, "my amp's working. Could we get on with the rehearsal, please?"

"That's it," Keeley said, and turned away from the microphone. "I'm done. I don't need this. Sorry, Dominic."

"Keeley, wait!" He grabbed her arm. "You can't go – we're doing the encore together."

Gemma looked at Dominic, and then at Keeley. "Encore?" she echoed.

"Yeah." Dominic glowered. "Keeley and I wrote a song together, as a surprise... for you."

"I tried to tell her," Keeley said to Dominic as she eyed Gemma with disdain. "It's true. He wrote a song for you, you silly twat. We were doing it after the Destroyers' last song."

Gemma's heavily kohled eyes widened as she looked back at Dominic. "You wrote a song… for me?"

"Yeah." His expression was murderous. "Don't know why I bothered, though. I might as well change the name of the song from 'Gemma' to 'Stroppy Cow'. Shit! First you throw bacon butties at me and ruin my clothes, and now this. Fuck it all," he decided, "that's it. I've had enough."

Dominic yanked his guitar over his head and thrust it unceremoniously at a passing roadie, then stormed off the stage and disappeared.

CHAPTER 47

The crowd was restive. Natalie frowned and said into her headset, "What time does the show start?"

"Ten minutes ago," came the reply. "Dominic and Gemma had a row during rehearsal and he's walked out."

"What do you mean, he's walked out? As in, he *left*?"

"Yeah. Don't know where he went."

"Well, find him!" she snapped. Panic overtook her as she began to search frantically inside the crowded marquees. Blimey, if Dominic was gone, there'd be no show. And if there was no show, there'd be a lot of very angry, disappointed people.

And Rhys Gordon would be the absolute angriest.

Dominic couldn't do this to her. He bloody well couldn't!

Someone started to chant, "We want Dominic," and soon the chant grew louder. Rhys made his way through the crowd and stopped in front of Natalie.

"Where's Dominic?" he hissed. "It's past time he went on stage. People are getting restless."

"He and Gemma had a row and he's refused to go on." Natalie met his furious blue gaze. "We're looking for him now."

"He can't pull this crap, not today," Rhys snapped. "If you don't find him—" He stopped and glared at her, and the threat hung unspoken between them. "The whole re-launch is fucked," he finished ominously. "And so is Dashwood and James."

"I'll find him." Natalie's words were grim as she pushed past him and marched off after Dominic. "He'll be on that stage in five minutes, I promise."

"See that he is. We can't afford a cock-up now."

Up ahead, she saw a red Vespa. She knew Dominic liked to ride his motor scooter when he was angry – which, let's face it, was most of the time – and hurried towards it. She just hoped she could reach him before he roared away.

Natalie wove her way through the stagehands and roadies, past the roped-off VIP section where Keeley and Phillip and an assortment of models mingled, until she spotted the recalcitrant rock singer just swinging his leg over his Vespa.

"Dom!" she shouted as he kick-started the engine. "Wait!"

He regarded her sullenly through his sunglasses as he waited for her to approach him. "I'm not doing it, Nat."

"You signed a contract, Dominic."

"I'll pay for breach, I don't fucking care. I've got enough dosh to afford it. Now piss off."

She blocked his way. "No. You're doing this concert, Dominic," she told him calmly. "Because if you don't, I'll get on the PA system right now, and I'll tell everyone—" her arm swept out to encompass the swelling, restless crowds "—that you need Viagra to perform. And I'll make it clear I don't mean performing as in singing, either."

For once, Dominic was speechless. "You wouldn't."

"Oh, yes, I would. You're not spoiling this day for me, or Alastair, or grandfather. I've worked too bloody hard! Get your arse up on that stage right now, or I'll make you a laughingstock in front of everyone here, including the press. Because every reporter in Britain's here today, just waiting for a nice, juicy story… and I'll make sure your willy's the headline on every single one."

He saw from the hard glint in Natalie's eyes that she meant business. He panicked. Where had the sweet, malleable girl he'd known such a short time ago gone?

"OK," he grumbled, and got off the Vespa. "I'm going. Fellow Destroyers, here I come. Fucking hell."

Dominic and the band exploded on stage ten minutes later, and despite a handful of hecklers at the onset, the crowd went wild. They put on a memorable set of not just five, but eight songs, plus the encore with Keeley.

"This last one's for my girlfriend, Gemma," Dominic announced, sweat glistening on his skin. He paused and looked out over the crowd. "Wherever you are, babes, this is for you."

He launched into an edgy ballad, and Keeley joined him onstage for the chorus. The crowd loved it.

"You did it." Rhys appeared next to Natalie as the concert ended. "You pulled it off, despite everything." He looked at the throngs of people, and turned to her. "I'm amazed. Well done." He turned to go.

"Rhys, wait." Natalie caught at his sleeve and searched his eyes. His expression was unreadable. "I'm sorry for the things I said this morning. I wish I could un-say them. I didn't mean it. Any of it…"

"It's all right. Forget it."

"No, it's not all right. When I overheard you talking to grandfather, I thought you only wanted to marry me to get the partnership."

"You should know me better than that." His jaw tightened. "I never meant to stay; I'm already committed to another project. But Sir Richard was very persuasive. He's thrilled we're getting married." His eyes met hers. "We *are* still getting married, aren't we?"

"If you still want to, after I said you had no breeding," Natalie said in a small voice.

"Us rough blokes from council estates don't, as a rule," Rhys remarked. "Have breeding, that is. But we're great in a bar fight." His eye gleamed. "And bloody good in bed, too."

Natalie blushed. "I've dated men with breeding," she said, "and you're nothing like them. And I'm glad you're not."

"I love you, Natalie, and that's all that matters." He bent his head down to kiss her, long and lingeringly.

And of course her mobile chose that precise moment to ring.

"Nat," Phillip said, "we're ready to start the fashion show. You're on in ten minutes, chickpea."

"I'll be right there." She put her phone away. "I have to go. It's nearly time for my catwalk debut."

"You'll be great, darling, like you were at the photo shoot." He took her face tenderly in his hands. "I've never been prouder of anyone than I am of you right now. You're amazing, Natalie Dashwood."

"I'm glad you've finally realised that. It took you long enough." She kissed him and reluctantly broke away. "Phillip's waiting." Her smile faded. "I'm going to the Savoy once the fashion show's done and we've put in an appearance at the after-party. I'll be wearing Phillip's black cocktail dress. Rhys—" she clutched his hand "—I'm really scared."

"Don't be." He pulled her back into his arms. "I'll be in the incident van with the police. They'll arrest the bastard at the first opportunity."

She kissed him again, and pulled away. As she hurried off to join the backstage chaos, Natalie was glad she hadn't told Rhys her plan to conceal her smart phone behind the lining of Phillip's clutch. He wouldn't approve. And it *was* dangerous; if Ian found the phone, God knows what he'd do. But the risk was worth it. With the satellite navigation system enabled, the police could track her exact location.

Her mobile rang. Ian Clarkson.

"Natalie, hello. I'm looking forward to our rendezvous tonight." His voice was low and intimate.

"I'm busy," she said shortly as she took a seat backstage in Tamara's makeup chair. "What do you want?"

"Improve your attitude, for a start. We'll work on that tonight." He paused and added, "Eight-thirty, the Savoy. Don't be late."

With trembling fingers, Natalie pressed 'Call End' and turned off all sounds on the mobile. It wouldn't do to have a ring tone shrilling out in the hotel room at the wrong moment.

She closed her eyes as Tamara applied eye shadow and mascara. *Focus*, Nat told herself. Just get through the next five minutes… ten minutes… half-hour. Don't think about Ian, or the wire, or all the things that might go wrong tonight.

But she couldn't shake her unease. Ian was clever, and determined. And that made her very, very nervous.

"All right, girls, let's go!" Phillip called out just before the show. "The mood's upbeat, enthusiastic. Think happy, sexy thoughts."

"Happy, sexy thoughts," Gemma muttered, and scowled. She wore a giraffe-print jersey dress with an asymmetrical hem and black Jimmy Choo booties.

"Ready?" Jacques asked her as he eyed her critically. "You're first out."

"Yes," she answered grimly. "I'm happy. I'm sexy."

He regarded her with a raised brow. "You look like you just swallowed a boot. You should be over the moon. Didn't you hear Keeley and Dominic singing the encore? He wrote that song especially *pour vous*!"

She nodded. "I know, and I feel awful because I was a shit to him this morning. I even threw a bag of bacon butties at him."

"Not nice," he agreed. "Sounds like something *he'd* do."

"I want to say sorry, but I haven't had a chance."

"Give me your mobile," he commanded, and held out his hand.

"What?" She stared at him blankly.

"Give me your mobile. I'll text him, get the ball rolling. Hurry, it's almost time for you to go out."

Gemma lunged for her handbag and took out her mobile. She scrolled to Dominic's number and handed Jacques the phone. "Tell him I'm sorry. Tell him the song was incredible. And tell him—" she hesitated "—I love him. Thanks."

"Done. Never let it be said I stood in the way of true love. Now, go! And smile, damn it!"

To the sound of dozens of shutters clicking and flashbulbs popping, Gemma took a shaky breath and strode out on the catwalk. She had a vague impression of fashionably-dressed men and women seated alongside the walkway, brandishing pens and mobile phones, their faces turned up expectantly as she walked past.

A sea of people crowded the grass and the walkways beyond the stage. She smiled and paused briefly at the end of the catwalk, one hand on her hip as she'd been instructed. Then she swivelled and retraced her steps, returning to backstage chaos.

The rip of double-sided fashion tape, the click of Manolos, Choos, and Louboutins as one model came in to change and the next sashayed out, the relentless shutter-click and flash of the cameras... these were the sounds that filled Natalie's ears as she waited to go out on the catwalk.

Clothes, shoes, and jewellery were changed quickly. As the models dressed, stylists fluffed their hair, assistants taped shoe straps securely into place on ankles, makeup artists flicked brushes over upturned faces – like race cars being serviced at a pit stop, Natalie reflected.

Reporters' and editors' pens flew, bloggers texted and Tweeted, and photos were uploaded. Photographers from every publication in Britain crowded together at the end of the catwalk. Those in the centre got the best pictures – photographers from *Elle*, *Vogue*, *Marie Claire*, television crews, the *Telegraph* and the *Guardian* – while the rest jammed in along the sides, elbows jabbing ruthlessly as they vied for the best shots.

"You're next, Nat," Phillip called out. "Go out and wow them, chickpea!"

As Jacques and his assistant made sure her rope-heeled espadrilles were tied securely around her ankles, Natalie put all thoughts of Ian and the Savoy out of her mind. She wore a yellow striped Breton shirt under a bright blue denim pinafore, with a leather schoolgirl's satchel slung over her shoulder.

I'm sexy and happy, Nat told herself as Elspeth returned. With a deep breath, she launched herself onto the catwalk.

In ten minutes the show was almost over. The time passed in a blur of clothing changes, rapid-fire instructions, popping flashbulbs, and the stares of the reporters and fashion editors who studied every outfit with single-minded concentration.

"OK," Jacques told Natalie as she returned for her final clothing change, "you're wearing the sheath dress and the silver Louboutins, correct?"

She nodded. Her mobile rang and she glanced at the screen. "Poppy! What a surprise. When did you get back from Sri Lanka?"

"Just now. I'll be there in five minutes. Not too late for your show, am I?"

"No! That's fantastic, see you soon." Natalie thanked her and rang off, then let out a whoop. "Poppy Simone is on her way!" she told Phillip.

He nearly swooned. "Poppy? I thought you said she couldn't make it. Will she model an outfit? What'll she wear?" he wondered, and grabbed a long, sexy halter dress with silkscreened peacock feathers. "What about this?"

Nat laughed. "Phillip, calm down! Poppy's lovely. She'll be here in five minutes."

"Shit! What an amazing finale this'll be for the show!" Phillip said fervently. "Not that you're not amazing, too," he told Natalie hastily.

"But I'm not Poppy Simone," she pointed out as she slipped into the sheath dress.

"No," Jacques agreed, "but we love you anyway, sweetie. You're still Britain's 'It' Girl. Now, out you go!"

Natalie smoothed her hands over her hips. The sheath was black, with a sweetheart neckline, and it fitted her body snugly. Paired with gunmetal grey Louboutin heels and Phillip's purple leather clutch, the outfit was extremely sexy.

"I like black heels and a short skirt, something just a bit – tarty."

Ian's words echoed in her head, and fear threatened to swamp her. But there wasn't time to be afraid. With a plastered-on smile, Natalie strode out for the last time onto the catwalk, determined to think happy, sexy thoughts.

When Poppy Simone arrived, wearing a short denim skirt, a T-shirt, and Uggs, Phillip embraced her.

"Poppy, welcome! I'm Phillip. I'm thrilled you're here."

"I love your clothes," Poppy told him. She fingered a navy-blue bouclé jacket hanging on the rack.

"It's yours, after the show," he promised her. He took the peacock-print gown from Jacques and handed it to her. "You're wearing the last outfit. When Natalie comes back, you're on."

"It's gorgeous." Poppy eyed the dress, vivid with shades of turquoise, blue, and green, then stepped out of her skirt and T-shirt and slid the slinky gown over her head. Tamara and Gavin worked quickly together to touch up her hair and makeup.

"Shoes!" Phillip said to Jacques. "Where are the shoes for Poppy's dress?"

A pair of Miu Miu gold and black leopard-print platforms was produced, and Poppy thrust her feet inside.

Jacques frowned and pressed one finger against his lip. "Should we announce her?"

"No," Phillip decided. "Poppy Simone doesn't need an introduction. Send her out. Everyone'll recognise her, and go wild."

Natalie returned, breathless, from her final turn down the catwalk. "Poppy!" she squealed as they hugged one another. "Thanks for this, it means everything to Phillip. And to me."

"It's no problem." Poppy slid the armload of silver bangles that Jacques held out over her wrist. "Wish me luck."

"Luck!" they chorused as Poppy strode out onto the catwalk.

As the crowds and flashbulbs went wild, one of the event staff rushed up to Natalie and blurted, "Miss Dashwood? You've just had a call from Dr. Findlay's office."

Natalie paled. Dr. Findlay was Sir Richard's physician. "Is it grandfather? Is he all right?"

"I'm sorry," the young woman apologised, "I only know that he's been admitted to hospital, St. George's. They think he's had a heart attack."

Groping blindly behind her, Natalie found a folding chair and sat down. "Oh, God, no…"

"They said a ward sister will meet you at the General Critical Care Unit and give you more details."

"St. George's, the GCCU. Right, I'm on my way." Natalie stood up unsteadily and hurried out to her car, all thoughts of Ian and their meeting at the Savoy hotel completely forgotten.

CHAPTER 48

At the GCCU entrance, Natalie parked the Peugeot with a squeal of tyres. She grabbed Phillip's purple clutch and walked as quickly as she dared in her Louboutin heels towards the building. Although her catwalk outfit attracted plenty of curious glances, she didn't care.

All that mattered was seeing grandfather and ensuring he was all right.

"Natalie?"

She stopped and turned around as a familiar voice behind her called her name. "Ian! What are you doing here?"

He came up and took her elbow in a firm grip as he said pleasantly, "Hello, Natalie. What a surprise." In a low voice he added, "Get in the car." He thrust something hard and cold and cylindrical against her ribs. A gun, she realised. "Don't be tiresome and make a scene."

She resisted as he propelled her towards a black Audi idling at the curb. "I can't go with you! Grandfather's here."

"No, he's not. He's at home," Ian said briefly. "He's fine. Now get in the car."

He opened the passenger door, still pressing the gun in her side, and thrust her inside. Natalie teetered on her heels and half-stumbled onto the seat. Ian shut the door and quickly got in and slid behind the wheel.

"I like your outfit." He glanced in approval at the long expanse of her legs as he pulled away. "Is that what the typical model's wearing on the catwalk these days? I ought to go to fashion shows more often. That was more Alexa's thing."

"There's nothing wrong with grandfather," Natalie murmured. "He's all right." Relief overwhelmed her.

"As far as I know, the old bastard's fine, more's the pity. Using the heart attack ploy worked a treat to get you away from the re-launch, though."

Natalie stared at him, stunned by his lack of remorse. "It's all a joke to you, isn't it? A game."

"Not at all." He turned south on Queen's Gate Terrace. "I take it very seriously. Because the prize at the end of the game—" he smiled "—is you, Natalie."

She cursed herself for her stupidity, blindly rushing off to St. George's without telling anyone, without checking that grandfather really was in hospital. She'd placed herself in serious danger. Now, the plans the police had in place – the surveillance van, the wire, the plainclothes detectives – meant nothing. Ian had seen to that.

"Where are we going?" she demanded, swallowing down the sudden rise of panic.

"Not the Savoy." He turned left onto the A4. "Sorry, I hope you're not too disappointed."

"You never meant to go there, did you?"

"No. Pity, it's a very nice hotel. But it was a red herring, in the event you told anyone about our rendezvous." He looked at her, his face unreadable. "I don't fancy the police interrupting us."

"Why should they? I haven't told them anything."

"I drove by the Savoy earlier. I saw a van outside, no doubt rigged to the teeth with surveillance equipment. You're disappointingly predictable, Natalie."

"And you're paranoid."

"If you're wearing a wire," he went on, as if she hadn't spoken, "I'll find it soon enough." His glance raked over her.

Natalie said nothing, her thoughts racing. She'd tucked her mobile behind the lining of her clutch before the show began. The police could locate her using sat nav – as long as Ian didn't find the phone first. She hadn't told anyone she was leaving; she'd been far too upset to think straight.

Play along, she told herself. *Stall for time*. Give Rhys and the police the time they needed to find her...

"Give me that." Ian, his eyes focused on the road, held out his hand for the clutch.

"There's only a tube of lipstick and a couple of quid in there," she protested. "It's a Phillip Pryce original—"

"Give it here." He snatched it from her. As he glanced inside, the car in front of them suddenly slammed on its brakes. Ian cursed and tossed the clutch aside.

"Fucking idiot!" he muttered. "These London drivers get worse every bloody day."

The clutch slid off the seat onto the floor near her feet. Natalie was dismayed to see that the mobile had slid loose when Ian tossed it, and was partly visible.

He hadn't noticed it yet. "Can't you at least tell me where we're going?"

"You'll see soon enough." He kept his eyes on the road as he negotiated a traffic circle. "You know, I like you, Natalie. I always have done."

"Well, you've an odd way of showing it. Blackmail, trickery, scaring me half to death—"

He smiled briefly. "You've forced me to be creative."

Ten minutes later, they were headed along the Victoria Embankment, following the Thames River. In the sweep of the Audi's headlights, for it was fully dark now, Natalie glimpsed boatyards, quays, and warehouses. Her unease grew as the car slowed and stopped at the end of a quay. Yachts, narrowboats, and sailboats were tied securely to pilings and bobbed gently on the tide.

She looked around uneasily. "I don't see a hotel."

"That's because there isn't one." Ian shut off the engine and pocketed the keys. He held up another key, this one dangling from a floatation ring. "We'll be spending tonight aboard the *Alexa*."

He indicated a Ferretti yacht, perhaps 16 metres long, tied up at one end of the quay. Natalie let out a short breath. The *Alexa* was beautiful, no question, with sleek lines that spoke of fine – and expensive – Italian craftsmanship.

"She holds twelve. Of course, tonight—" Ian's gaze lingered on her face "—it'll just be two."

Natalie fought down the panic that threatened to overset her. How in the world would the police rescue her from a bloody *boat*? "I hope you're not planning to take us out on the river. I get seasick. That might put a damper on things."

"There's no need to leave the dock. The galley's stocked with enough provisions to last a week." He reached across her and opened the door. "I do hope you're worth all this trouble. Remember, don't try anything, I still have the gun. Let's go."

"I'm too bloody tired to try anything," Natalie snapped.

"You do like to whinge, don't you?" Amused, he got out and shut the door.

As he walked round the car, Natalie retrieved the clutch. Quickly, she thrust the mobile behind the lining once again, just before Ian opened her door. She slid her legs out and reluctantly took his hand. There really was no graceful way to exit a car wearing such a short, form-fitting dress, and the heels made running impossible...

Ian slid his arm around her. "It's time to pay up, Natalie," he murmured. "It's only fair you show me some appreciation for keeping your father's secret all this time."

"I'd like to kick you square in the balls." She fell silent as they passed another couple coming down the quay. "And I will," she added in a low voice, "at the first opportunity."

"Good. I like a challenge." With a low laugh, Ian placed his hand on her lower back and thrust her forward, down the quay and up the ramp to board the *Alexa*.

"Phillip Pryce's exclusive line of clothing for Dashwood and James further distinguishes the department store as an innovative purveyor of style and value. This is fashion for real women, fun and on-trend, wearable and affordable. Pryce is unquestionably a new star in the London designer firmament."

Jacques finished reading the *Telegraph's* online article and closed the laptop. "Hear that? You're a star, Phillip!"

"We're all stars," Phillip corrected him, and grinned at the motley collection of models, stylists, PR people, and assistants still milling about backstage. "Great show, everyone. My sincere thanks go out to all of you. Don't forget to head up to the fourth floor for the after-party!"

"Where's Natalie?" he asked as he glanced around him. "I haven't seen her in a while."

"She left," Bryony said. "Said her grandfather took ill. He's in hospital, a heart attack, or something."

"Oh, poor Nat," Jacques exclaimed. "She loves Sir Richard to bits. I hope he'll be all right."

Rhys came backstage. "Is Natalie ready? I told her I'd meet her here for the after-party."

"She's gone," Phillip told him. "Sir Richard was taken to hospital."

"What?" Rhys asked sharply. "When?"

"About half an hour ago," Bryony told him.

"I spoke to Sir Richard not five minutes ago," Rhys said grimly. "He's at home, getting ready to come to the party. He's not in hospital. He's fine."

"What?" Phillip met Rhys's gaze, his expression concerned. "Then someone's fed Natalie a big load of crap. But who would do something like that?"

Ian Clarkson. "Who gave her the message?" Rhys demanded.

"One of the events staff," Bryony said. "Sir Richard's doctor called, said Nat was to go to the GCCU at St. George's—"

Rhys was already turning away to leave. Ian had tricked Natalie, the clever bastard, and God only knew where he'd taken her. He cursed himself for a fool for thinking they could outsmart the sociopathic little prick. *What was the saying? We make our plans, and God laughs...*

"Wait!" Phillip called after him. "I just remembered... Natalie made an odd request recently. She asked me to put an opening in the lining of her clutch, the one she carried on her last trip down the catwalk. She said it needed to be big enough to accommodate a credit card." He paused. "Or a mobile phone."

Rhys met his eyes. "Let's hope she has it with her. That mobile might be the only way we can find her, now."

"Good luck." Phillip and Jacques followed him out, their faces etched with concern. "Call us the minute you find her."

Rhys grabbed his helmet and swung one leg over the Triumph. "Call the police," he told them, and gave them the name and number of the detective staked out outside the Savoy. "Tell him what's happened, and tell him she's got her mobile. They can track her with sat nav."

With that, he started the engine and roared off to St. George's to find Natalie.

CHAPTER 49

The *Alexa*'s stateroom offered a panoramic view of the river Thames and a stylish interior. Under normal circumstances, Natalie might have appreciated the expanse of blonde wood with wraparound seating, and the small but elegant galley.

But as it was, she was far too jumpy to give a toss about anything but getting out of this nightmare unscathed. How long, she wondered, before Rhys and the police found her? *And they will find me*, Natalie told herself fiercely. *They will.*

"Would you like a drink?" Ian asked as he opened one of the galley cabinets. "You seem a bit on edge."

She turned away from the view of the darkened river to glare at him. "And why is that, I wonder? I've only been blackmailed, abducted at gunpoint, and forced onto a boat in the middle of bloody Wapping, with no one knowing where I've gone, after a long, exhausting day. Why should I be on edge?"

He poured two glasses of Pinot and handed one to her. "Please, sit down," he said, and indicated the table set for two. "I'm truly sorry if I frightened you, Natalie. I never meant to do that." His expression was contrite.

And the crazy thing was, Natalie realised as she sat down on the banquette, he was completely sincere. "You let me think that my grandfather had a heart attack. I was sick with worry." Her fingers tightened on the stem of her wineglass. "If not for you, I'd be at the after-party with Rhys right now."

Ian smiled, unperturbed. "Ah yes, Gordon... by now, he's realised you've gone, followed your trail to St. George's, and found your abandoned Peugeot." He took a leisurely sip of his wine. "I imagine he's frantic right about now. Poor chap."

Natalie's throat tightened. Rhys. She was glad they'd patched things up before she left. She should never have doubted him. "He'll find me." Her words were low but fierce.

"I wish I shared your conviction, but I doubt it." He placed his glass with deliberate care onto the table. "At any rate, it's down to you and me. Let's make the most of our time, shall we?"

Time. It was the only weapon Natalie had. The police needed time to find them; and if the only way to buy time was to play along with Ian's perverse game, then that's what she'd do.

Ian retrieved a box of matches and lit the candles. "I've made asparagus quiche and salad. I hope you like it. I'm quite a good cook, you know."

"Among your many other talents?" she snapped.

"Temper, Natalie," he chided her, and smiled. "You'll feel better after you have something to eat."

She took a tiny sip of the Pinot. The table setting was lovely – china, crystal glasses, linen napkins. "I'm not hungry." She was far too keyed up to think of food.

"You'll change your mind." Ian stood and went into the galley.

Her glance flickered to her purple clutch, tossed at one end of the banquette. Thank God she'd brought her mobile. She only hoped that Ian didn't find it...

As he returned with the quiche and two plated frisée salads, Natalie attempted a smile. "It looks lovely."

"I learned to cook from my stepfather." He placed a slice of quiche on her plate and sat down. "Go on, try it."

"How do I know you haven't laced it with something? A sedative, perhaps?"

He laughed, cut himself a piece, and took a large bite. "There. No sedatives. No poison, either."

Natalie picked up her fork and had a taste. "It's good," she admitted. *Stall for time, keep him talking...* "You've mentioned your stepfather. What about your mother?"

"She abandoned me when I was five. Ran off one night and left me in the flat, alone." He held up the bottle. "More wine?"

"No, thank you... What did you do?"

Ian shrugged and wiped his mouth. "I went into care. I went through twenty-five foster homes by the time I was nine. I wasn't wanted in any of them. But that's the way the council handled things back then – don't let a child in care get too attached, because they'd leave soon enough, shunted on to the next place."

Pity for that little boy, alone and unwanted, softened Natalie's words. "That must've been incredibly hard. I can't imagine."

"No, you can't." He laid his fork aside. "You grew up with dogs and horses and weekend gymkhanas, living the sort of life that I could only dream of, then."

"Still, you made something of yourself, Ian," she pointed out. "You're on the board of Dashwood and James, you've got an excellent job and a beautiful home—"

"The house belongs to Alexa," he cut in. "Like every other place I've ever lived, it isn't mine. Until you help me get that partnership, I won't have achieved nearly enough." His eyes, dark and gleaming in the candlelight, met hers. "But enough of me… let's talk about you, Natalie. You're far more interesting."

"No, I'm not." She pushed a bit of frisée around on her plate, echoing the circular, panicked thoughts in her head.

"On the contrary," Ian murmured as he reached out to touch her face, "I think you're fascinating. And very beautiful." He leaned forward to kiss her.

"I think," Natalie said hastily, dropping her fork to her plate as she drew back, "we need music. To set the proper mood."

Ian looked at her, his expression unreadable. "You're not stalling, are you, Natalie?"

"Of course not. I just… need a bit more wine, and some music, to help me relax. This isn't easy for me, you know."

"Very well." He tossed his napkin down and went aft to turn on the stereo. The muted sounds of a jazz quartet filled the air.

"Better?" he inquired as he topped up her drink and resumed his seat next to her.

She managed a nod and a tiny sip of wine. "Yes, much."

"Good." He rested his arm along the back of the banquette behind her and leaned closer. "I've waited a long time for this moment, Natalie." He began, hungrily, to nuzzle her neck.

She pushed him away. "I need the lav. I want to freshen up a bit, first—"

"You don't need the lav. And you don't need to freshen up." His jaw tightened. "You're stalling, Natalie, and you're trying my patience. No more games."

And before she could react, his mouth descended hard on hers, and he forced her back against the banquette. Panicked, she twisted her head away. "Ian, please, wait—"

"I'm done waiting," he said, and dragged her legs roughly up onto the banquette. "I've waited far too long as it is."

She reached up to rake her nails across his cheek. But Ian anticipated the move and gripped her by the wrist. "Natalie," he breathed, "I'm disappointed in you. You're not showing the proper enthusiasm. You'll have to do better."

As he gripped her wrist and forced his mouth once again on hers, Natalie twisted away and tried desperately to kick him, but the weight of his body pressed atop hers limited her mobility. Unfortunately, all she managed to do was kick the bloody clutch to the floor with her foot…

…where her mobile phone flew out and skidded to a stop, landing smack in the middle of the stateroom floor.

Rhys turned the Triumph into the entrance to St. George's General Critical Care Unit and skidded to a stop. He scanned the car park and immediately saw Natalie's yellow Peugeot. It was empty, and locked. A quick word with the ward sister at the front desk established that no one recalled seeing a young woman wearing a short black cocktail dress and silver high heels.

"I most definitely," the ward sister informed him primly, "would have remembered that."

Rhys turned away with a muttered curse and strode back to his motorbike. His mobile rang just as he swung his leg over. He grabbed it. "Yes?"

"Sergeant Bixby, Central London Police. We've pinpointed Miss Dashwood's location. She's in Wapping, just a couple of miles from Tower Bridge."

"Wapping," Rhys repeated grimly. "What the hell are they doing there? Never mind, I'm on my way."

"This is a police matter, sir. We already have an all ports warning out for Ian Clarkson's vehicle. I'd ask you to stay well out of it and let our men handle the matter—"

"Sod you," Rhys snapped, and rang off. No way in hell he'd let the police handle this, they'd only bollocks things up.

Ian was far too unpredictable, and Natalie far too precious, to trust her safe return via the bloody police.

As he started the engine, his mobile rang again. "Yes?" he snapped. "What is it now?"

There was a pause. "Mr. Gordon? Alexa Clarkson."

"Oh. Sorry. You know Natalie's missing, I presume?"

"Yes. How awful… and I'm certain Ian's to blame. The police were just here, asking if I'd seen or spoken to him today. I haven't." She paused. "In fact, I'm calling because I know where he's taken Nat."

"The police just told me sat nav shows her in Wapping."

"Then I'm right. While the police were here at the hospital, my housekeeper called. She noticed a set of keys missing from the hook in the kitchen. At some point in the last day or two, Ian took the keys to the *Alexa*, our yacht. It's docked in Wapping. I'm certain that's where he's taken Nat."

Rhys listened intently as she relayed the quay number, a description of the Ferretti yacht, and directions to the marina. "I've got it, thanks."

"Good luck, Mr. Gordon. I hope you find her."

"I'll find her. Thanks." He promised to inform Alexa the minute he had anything to tell and rang off, then immediately dialled the Wapping police station. Rhys relayed the information Alexa had given him to the dispatcher. "Send someone out there at once."

"I'll notify the Marine Support Unit. A Fast Response Boat will be launched immediately."

"Just tell them to hurry." He rang off, revved the engine, and headed at top speed for Wapping.

CHAPTER 50

"What's this?" Ian snarled.

He thrust Natalie aside and lunged down to retrieve the mobile. "It's a fucking mobile… with the sat nav enabled." He turned on her, enraged. "You clever little bitch! No wonder you kept stalling for time."

Trembling, Natalie skittered away down the banquette. "You can get away if you leave me behind. I'll only slow you down—"

"Oh, no." He reached out and grabbed her roughly by the arm and dragged her off the banquette. "No more of your bullshit. You're coming with me."

Grimly Ian considered and discarded the idea of untying the boat and making his getaway on the river. The *Alexa* would never outrun a police boat; she was made for cruising, not speed. His only hope of escape was the Audi.

And it might even be too late for that, thanks to Natalie and her bloody mobile.

"Don't try anything," he hissed as he propelled Natalie forward. He brandished his gun. "I've had enough of your stunts. One more, and I'll use this."

Natalie knew Ian meant what he said. Numb with fear, she stumbled as he thrust her across the stateroom and down several steps onto the aft deck. Waves washed against the hull and a warm breeze carried the smell of the river. *Keep calm*, she told herself. *Don't panic*.

Sod that. She'd never been so frightened in her life.

Ian stepped off the boat and pulled her roughly down onto the quay. "Hurry," he snapped as she stumbled.

"I'm going as fast as I can!" she retorted. "Why don't you go on without me? I can't walk fast in these bloody heels, or I'll turn my ankle."

"Shut up." He continued to drag her along behind him down the wooden quay, intent on getting them both the hell out of there.

Natalie knew she had to stall; her life might depend on it. Every step they took down the quay was one step closer to his car, and Ian's escape. Once they were in the Audi, he could take her anywhere. And without her mobile, the police – and Rhys – would never find her.

She couldn't let that happen. But how was she to stop him?

Suddenly, she had an idea. Not the most brilliant idea, perhaps, but with no weapon and no one to help her, it was the best she could manage…

The quay was constructed of wooden boards nailed crosswise, with a narrow space between each board. Sending up a silent prayer that her ploy would work and that Phillip Pryce would forgive her, Natalie thrust one of her spindly Louboutin heels firmly into the space between one of the boards.

It worked a treat. It also, unfortunately, very nearly dislocated her ankle as Ian continued to drag her forward. She let out a cry of pain. "Ian, stop! I've caught my heel."

He let go of her hand and reached for his gun. "Take the fucking shoe off!" he snarled.

"I can't, the straps are tiny, and there's so many of them! And I can't see a thing—"

With a curse Ian bent down to inspect the shoe. "Bloody fucking shoe! If I had a penknife I'd cut the straps off. But I don't." He met her frightened eyes. "And I haven't any time to waste."

"What… what happens now?" she whispered, her eyes wide.

"I can't take you with me," he snapped, "so I'll have to leave you behind." He straightened, keeping his gun trained on her. "I value my own skin more than yours. And I've no desire to add murder to my sins. Sorry, Natalie, but even *you're* not worth all this trouble."

And with that, he turned and sprinted down the quay, jumped into the Audi, and roared away.

Within minutes, Natalie heard the rumble of a motorbike in the distance, growing louder. She massaged her throbbing ankle and waited. Abruptly the motorbike's engine cut off and someone pounded down the quay.

"Natalie!" Rhys said hoarsely. He took in her bent leg, and knelt beside her and held her tightly. "My God, are you OK?" he asked, drawing back. "Has he hurt you?"

"No, I'm fine, except for a turned ankle."

"What happened?" Grimly he worked the straps free and tossed the shoe aside.

"Ian found my mobile, and dragged me off the boat to his car. I panicked. I knew you'd never find me if we got in the car. I couldn't think what else to do, so I caught my heel in the one of the dock boards. Ian was furious." She looked up at Rhys, her eyes wide. "Phillip will be, too. These Louboutins cost a fortune, and I've ruined them." Belatedly, shock set in, and she began to shiver.

"Sod the shoes. I'm just glad you're all right." He removed the other shoe. "Can you put any weight on your foot?"

Natalie nodded. "I think so… oh!" Pain shot through her ankle as she attempted to stand. "Well… perhaps not."

Rhys swung her up into his arms. "Poor girl," he said tenderly. "Those damned shoes will be the death of you yet."

"Those damned shoes saved my life," she retorted.

"Well, if nothing else, at least you proved you can think on your feet."

"Ha bloody ha," Natalie murmured. Despite the twist to her ankle and the fact that she couldn't stop shivering, she wanted, more than anything else, to wrap herself up in a blanket with Rhys, and sleep… for days.

The sound of a motorboat launch rapidly approaching the quay cut through the darkness. "That'll be the marine police," Rhys observed. "They took their bloody time getting here."

"I don't care." Natalie nestled her head against his chest. "You're here, and Ian's gone, and that's all that matters."

He kissed the top of her head. "Glad we agree on that."

The police disembarked from the launch and pounded down the quay, guns drawn. "Has the suspect gone?" a heavyset sergeant asked them.

"Yes, ten minutes ago, no thanks to you lot," Rhys said shortly. Briefly he related the details of Ian's escape and added, "But it doesn't matter. The police issued an APW before I left Knightsbridge."

"Mr. Clarkson won't get far," the sergeant assured them. "We'll just need a statement from you, miss."

But Natalie, overcome from the trauma and the exhausting events of a long, trying day, had fallen asleep in Rhys's arms.

It was late when Alastair returned from the hospital. Cherie looked up as he paused in the doorway. "How's Hannah?" she asked, and set aside her tea. "The nurse insisted I go home, but I can't stop replaying everything in my head."

"She's sleeping." He seemed about to say more, then thought the better of it. "I'm tired, I'm going to bed."

"Alastair, wait." She leaned forward on the sofa. "We need to talk. I won't let you throw our marriage away."

"You did that when you slept with Neil."

"I never *slept* with Neil," Cherie said sharply. "I'll admit I was tempted, yes – only because he was there, and you weren't. I'm not proud of that, mind. But nothing happened."

"It doesn't matter. I don't trust you any longer."

"I hardly think my almost-affair with Neil compares to your secret love child with Fiona Walsh," she snapped.

"Good God, Cherie, you sound like one of those bloody tabloids!" Alastair said irritably. "I didn't know Rhys was my son until today."

"No. But you knew what you were doing when you slept with Fiona, *after* your engagement to me." Her eyes met his. "I did the maths, Alastair."

Suddenly all the fight went out of him, and he came and sat down heavily beside her. His face was haggard with exhaustion.

"It was stupid," he murmured, and shook his head at the memory. "A mistake. It happened the night I told Fiona that you and I were engaged. She was beside herself, unable to accept it was over. I'd had a couple of drinks beforehand, for Dutch courage."

Cherie was silent.

"Fiona wept, she threw her arms around me and begged me to stay, and… God forgive me, I did. I slept with her." He looked at his wife. "That must've been the night Rhys was conceived. It never happened again."

"You cheated on me." Cherie was calm. "After all, I only thought about cheating on you, with Neil. I didn't. But I daresay I would have, given the proper chance." She sighed. "I'd say that makes us even, doesn't it? Neither of us is blameless."

"No. No, I suppose not."

"Do you think Fiona planned it?" Cherie asked after a moment. "She couldn't have you, so she had your child instead?"

Alastair looked at her, startled. "I hadn't thought about it, but perhaps she did."

"Well," Cherie ventured, "at least one good thing came out of this – Rhys. He's your son. You must be terribly proud of him. He's quite a remarkable man."

"Sir Richard certainly thinks so. He's offered Rhys a partnership. I still can't believe he's my son." He looked at her, and smiled. "You know what this means, don't you?"

"No. What?"

"I'll have a son to carry on at the store when I'm gone. And it means," he added as he reached out to take her hands in his, "I can work more reasonable hours. We might even manage to have dinner together now and then."

"Imagine that," Cherie said dryly, and leaned forward to kiss him.

CHAPTER 51

The next morning, as Rhys lay in bed watching Natalie sleep, her lashes drifted open. "Good morning," she murmured, and stretched.

"Good morning." He smiled. "Have I told you how proud I am of you, darling? Or how much I love you?"

"You might have mentioned it, yes."

"Well, it's true. You're amazing."

"I thought I was spoilt and terrible with money and a not-very-good cook."

He kissed the corner of her mouth. "You're all of those... but don't forget that I'm impatient, demanding, and short-tempered," he pointed out. "Not to mention offensive and ill bred." He raised a brow. "Did I miss anything?"

"I don't think so. But I wouldn't change a thing." She snuggled next to him. "Except, perhaps, your habit of ordering for me at dinner – crikey, but that's annoying!"

"Old habits die hard, darling. But I'll try. Good thing the city has plenty of restaurants. At least we won't starve."

"No. But we'll need to keep extravagance to a minimum. So I expect we'll be eating lots of spag bol at home."

Rhys ran his hand leisurely along the curve of her hip. "I love spaghetti Bolognese as much as the next man, but we can afford to dine out at least once a week, surely?"

"We'll have to budget for it," Natalie said primly.

"Good thinking," he murmured, and leaned forward to nuzzle her neck. "Are you awake now?"

Distracted by the warmth of his hand sliding down her hip, Natalie managed a nod.

"Then let's stay in bed for the rest of the day," he said as he caressed the inside of her thigh. "I have some ideas for what we might do."

"Rhys," she protested, torn between desire to do just that yet knowing that remaining in bed was impossible, "we can't! Mum's invited everyone for Sunday dinner, and I'm the guest of honour! We can't not go – it'd be selfish, not to mention inexcusably rude—"

"Lesson number four, darling," he murmured in her ear, unperturbed by her protestations. "You have to take your opportunities when – and where – you find them."

And they did.

EPILOGUE

Thank goodness for the new, improved sound system, Natalie reflected as she set aside a tray of rings to answer the phone. 'The Holly and the Ivy' had never sounded better.

"Good afternoon, Dashwood and James jewellery department, how may I help you?" Natalie enquired.

"Nat, hi, it's Alexa. Rhys told me I'd find you here."

"Well, you know what it's like at Christmas," Natalie replied. "I'm helping out. Business has tripled since the re-launch. How's Emily Kate?"

"She's a lamb, aside from her aversion to sleep."

Natalie hesitated. "What about Ian? Has he seen her yet?"

Ian, apprehended two days after his escape, was serving time in Broadmoor, a high-security psychiatric hospital.

"No. I can't bear the thought of taking Emily Kate to that place." Alexa paused. "Not that Ian has asked to see her."

"Perhaps it's better that way."

Alexa's laugh was bitter. "Better, not knowing her daddy's a criminal sociopath? Yes. I'd say so."

"Excuse me."

Natalie looked up to see a tall blond man with penetrating blue eyes standing before her at the counter.

"Sorry, I have a customer," she told Alexa. "I'm here if you need me... for anything." She rang off and enquired politely, "May I help you, sir?"

"I certainly hope so." He leaned back to survey the jewels arranged in velvet-lined trays inside the display case. "I'm looking for something for a special lady."

"Well, we have necklaces, bracelets, earrings, watches—"

His eyes met hers. "I'd like to see the engagement rings, please."

"Of course." With a quickening heartbeat, Natalie bent down to retrieve two velvet-lined trays fitted with an assortment of rings. "Did you have a price range in mind?"

"No. The cost is immaterial. The only thing that matters is finding the perfect ring."

Despite the staccato beating of her heart, Natalie calmly indicated the tray to the left. "These are the men's rings, and these are the women's." She eyed him reprovingly. "You know, your fiancée really ought to be here to help choose her wedding ring. I'm sure she'll have an opinion."

"Oh, I've no doubt she will," he agreed dryly. "She always does." He studied her with a frown. "You know, now that I think of it, you're very like her. And your hand—" he took her fingers in his "—is about the same size."

"Really? Imagine that," she murmured.

"Do you think she'd like any of these? After all," he added with a gleam in his eye, "a substantial store discount would be applied to the purchase."

"How romantic," Natalie retorted, and pulled her hand free. "We've some discontinued styles if saving money is your object—"

And then he did the most extraordinary thing. He reached into his overcoat pocket (Burberry Prorsum) and withdrew a small, pale blue box (well – Tiffany, obviously).

"I know she hates me to make decisions for her," he said quietly, "but I took the liberty of choosing this, with the understanding that it could be returned if she didn't fancy it."

With trembling fingers Natalie opened the box and withdrew a small, black velvet case. She let out a gasp as she lifted the lid. "Oh, Rhys," she breathed, "it's beautiful."

An open, curved diamond band with a diamond solitaire nestled in the centre glittered against the velvet. There was a matching diamond wedding band.

"If you don't like it—"

"Of course I like it!" she cried, and came around the counter to fling her arms around his neck. "I love it!" Tears glistened in her eyes as she looked at him. "But not nearly as much as I love you, Mr. Gordon."

He kissed her. "You have to admit," he said when he finally lifted his mouth from hers, "that I have exceedingly good taste for a man with no breeding."

"You do," Natalie agreed, her eyes shining. She smiled. "After all, you chose me, didn't you?"

Also from
CARINA

Did you enjoy reading this book?
If so, why not leave a review…we'd love to hear your thoughts!

WWW.CARINAUK.COM
Facebook.com/UKCarina
@UKCarina

Also from
CARINA